# ONE NIGHT, TWIN CONSEQUENCES

BY
ANNIE O'NEIL

# TWIN SURPRISE FOR THE SINGLE DOC

BY
SUSANNE HAMPTON

# *The Monticello Baby Miracles*

*Double bundles of joy!*

Twin sisters, spontaneous Claudia and reserved Harriet
might be chalk and cheese, but no matter the distance
between them they are each other's best friend.
And then they both get news which
will change their lives for ever!

For the Monticello sisters it seems miracles
will always come in twos…

Read Harriet's story in
*One Night, Twin Consequences*
by Annie O'Neil

An invitation from the delectable Dr Matteo Torres to
work with orphans in Argentina is a dream come true
for Harriet. It's also right out of her comfort zone! And
then one night of seduction leads to a *very* unexpected
consequence and double the trouble!

and

Read Claudia's story in
*Twin Surprise for the Single Doc*
by Susanne Hampton

Claudia Monticello must accept former obstetrician
Patrick Spencer's help when she goes into labour in
a broken lift! But after seeing her sons in gorgeous
Patrick's arms Claudia finds herself hoping this
handsome stranger might just be the daddy
her little family needs!

# ONE NIGHT, TWIN CONSEQUENCES

BY
ANNIE O'NEIL

Published in Great Britain 2016
By Mills & Boon, an imprint of HarperCollins*Publishers*
1 London Bridge Street, London, SE1 9GF

© 2016 Annie O'Neil

ISBN: 978-0-263-91492-4

Our policy is to use papers that are natural, renewable and recyclable
products and made from wood grown in sustainable forests.
The logging and manufacturing processes conform to the legal
environmental regulations of the country of origin.

Printed and bound in Spain
by CPI, Barcelona

Dear Reader,

Welcome to *One Night, Twin Consequences*. This is the first time I've written a duet with someone—and let me tell you Susanne Hampton is *fabulous* to work with! Kind, thoughtful and, lucky for me, riding exactly the same train of thought. She was the ying to my yang, and I hope you enjoy the intertwined lives and love stories these two sisters share.

I absolutely fell in love with writing about Harriet and Matteo. Matteo because he's totally gorgeous and I'm a sucker for an accent. Harriet because she has about as much grace and elegance as I do—read: very little!

So strap on your seatbelts—and I hope you enjoy the ride!

*Annie O* xo

PS Don't be shy. Be sure to get in touch! You can reach me at my website, annieoneilbooks.com, or on Twitter @AnnieONeilBooks.

I absolutely loved writing this book—
in large part because it was about a big sister…
even if she *is* older only by a minute! Always competitive,
me! Whilst completely different, Harriet and Claudia share the
unbreakable bond of sisterhood—and for that reason I dedicate
this book with unfathomable love to my sister, Michelle. Xxx

**Annie O'Neil** spent most of her childhood with her leg draped
over the family rocking chair and a book in her hand. Novels,
baking and writing too much teenage angst poetry ate up most
of her youth. Now Annie splits her time between corralling
her husband into helping her with their cows, baking, reading,
barrel racing (not really!) and spending some very happy hours
at her computer, writing.

### Books by Annie O'Neil

### Mills & Boon Medical Romance

*The Surgeon's Christmas Wish*
*The Firefighter to Heal Her Heart*
*Doctor…to Duchess?*
*One Night…with Her Boss*
*London's Most Eligible Doctor*

Visit the Author Profile page at
millsandboon.co.uk for more titles.

### Praise for
### Annie O'Neil

'This is a beautifully written story that will pull you in from
page one and keep you up late and turning the pages.'
—*Goodreads* on
*Doctor…to Duchess?*

'A poignant and enjoyable romance that held me spellbound
from start to finish. Annie O'Neil writes with plenty of humour,
sensitivity and heart, and she has penned a compelling tale that
will touch your heart and make you smile as well as shed a tear
or two.'

—*CataRomance* on
*The Surgeon's Christmas Wish*

# CHAPTER ONE

"YOU WANT ME to do *what* tonight?" Harriet all but choked on her freshly dunked ginger biscuit. How did her boss know the perfect way to throw her off balance? Besides, didn't he know nice cup of tea and ginger biscuit o'clock was sacrosanct?

"Give the lecture tonight. You never take enough credit for your work and this would be the perfect way to showcase your research." Dr. Bailey handed her a serviette with a smile. "Crumbs."

"Ack! Oops!"

More mortification. Disintegrated biscuit was now decorating the front of her navy uniform. Typical graceful behavior. Not! Normally the fitted dress flattered Harriet's slim build—created the illusion she was more woman than tomboy. But with a mushy bit of biscuit on her front resembling something more akin to…well…. You saw everything in a children's hospital. She accepted the serviette with an embarrassed laugh. She'd had all sorts on her uniform through the years, so this was hardly a disaster. Not that scrubbing her bosom in front of her boss was the epitome of a comfortable moment.

"I don't know…." She opted for the old reliable, "My sister needs me—"

"Your sister lives in Los Angeles. Nice try, Harriet."

"Actually, she's coming over?"

*Hmm.* That wasn't meant to come out like a question.

"When?" Dr. Bailey was no stranger to Harriet's advanced conversational duck-and-dive technique. This was their drill every time he wanted her behind a podium. Although this time she really did have a legitimate excuse. Maybe.

"She rang last night to say she was coming over."

*That much was true.*

"It's a long flight from Los Angeles and in my experience they tend to arrive the next day. Which means you're free to give your lecture tonight."

"Yes, but she's having twins!" Harriet explained, knowing, as the words came out that her very, very pregnant sister hadn't strictly said she was arriving that night and was incredibly unlikely to be appearing until well after the twins were born. A good three months away. Flying weeks before you're due with twins? Not a good idea. Probably not even allowed. Although when her sister set her mind to something, it happened. So that little problem about turning their childhood home into a baby friendly zone over the next few weeks was a nut that needed cracking. Not to mention it being the first time in years her independent sister had well and truly needed her. Enough to add a little kick to her step. Harriet the Reliable was back in action!

Harriet chanced a glance up at Dr. Bailey. Yes. He was still patiently waiting for her to answer.

"You know public speaking isn't really my forte." And that was putting it mildly.

"Since when have you backed away from a challenge?" her boss riposted.

"Since *always* if it involves public speaking!"

"Most people would kill to be the opening act for Dr. Torres."

Harriet kept her lips tightly clenched to hold in a spontaneous sigh. *Swoon!* Dr. Matteo Torres—the unwitting man of her dreams.

"Harriet..." Dr. Bailey narrowed his eyes. "Has Dr. Torres done something to offend you during his stay here?"

"Uh....no?" Apart from being drop-dead gorgeous, intelligent, a leader in his field and so far out of her league she couldn't see straight. Not that she'd talked to him or anything. Tactical avoidance had been her approach and it had worked just fine during his fortnight of "observation" at St. Nick's. His presence hadn't just made her feel jittery. It made her... Oh, blimey...it made her *lusty.*

Along with ever other red-blooded female in a mile or so's range of the man.

*Smokin' hot. Burn the tips of your fingers hot with extra hotness.*

And she never said that about anyone. She wasn't trendy enough. By a long shot.

Just catching a glimpse of the man made her feel giddy!

No!

Distracting. Off-putting. Non-essential. Which was why she'd been playing her very own, proactive game of hide-and-*don't*-seek whenever he was within a ward's reach. If she didn't see or speak to Dr. Torres, she wouldn't go all rubber-kneed and act like an idiot. That was her plan anyway and she was sticking with it.

"Matteo is particularly interested in hearing your talk."

"You mean *your* talk." She grabbed hold of the counter edge and feigned a little finger drumming along the worn Formica. *Nope! No rubber knees here!*

"Harriet…there's no need to be modest. It's a chance to shine for our guest!"

"If he's into muttering and stuttering, sure. No problem," she grumbled. Fat chance she'd be able to form a sentence, let alone an entire speech in front of the Latin Lothario, as he was now referenced in the tearoom. Not terribly original, but everyone knew who they were talking about. It wasn't like the corridors of St. Nick's were overridden with gorgeous, swarthy obstetricians.

"Harriet." Dr. Bailey put on his stentorian tone. The "dad voice" as she liked to think of it. "This is a chance for you to present your work to the world's largest collection of pediatric elite. People who work with orphaned children all the time. What you've proved here at St. Nick's, and elsewhere, is groundbreaking and could change how wards of the state are treated around the world. Don't you want that for yourself?"

"No!"

Dr. Bailey's expression crumpled to one of pure dismay.

*Oops. Wrong answer.*

"But I do want it for St. Nick's." A smile lit up her face when an idea hit her. "Hey! What if we have my sister do it by remote video link? She's a gifted speaker and no one would know the difference!"

"Harriet Monticello." Dr. Bailey lost his battle with hiding his exasperation. "You're not an identical twin. What I recall from her odd visit here is that the only thing you two have in common is a surname."

Just because she was a homebody and her sister was exotically thrilling didn't make them all that different!

"Love, you've got this." He gave her arm a reassuring pat. "There is nothing to be intimidated by. I know you prefer being 'the girl behind the screen' but it's time to get you out there. Put yourself in the limelight."

"Dr. Bailey, you're really the public speaker for the department. I'm not sure the Child Care Symposium is really the place—"

"Tush and nonsense!" Her boss cut in. "You're more than capable of delivering the lecture. Apart from which, my wife won't hear of my doing it as it's our anniversary tonight and… I may have accidentally forgotten last year's so you'd be doing me quite a favor. I'm officially in the doghouse until she has a glass of champagne in one hand and a bouquet of roses in the other." His voice shifted back to the confident tone that had won him the trust of countless colleagues and patients. "You're every bit as qualified as I am to give the lecture, Harriet. It was your research that got us the invitation to speak for the CCS in the first place. You should take the credit…" He leaned in for added emphasis. "For once."

Harriet waved away his kind words. "You're the one who gave me the time to do the research."

"And you're the one who connected the dots about the impact of staffing rotas on the children. Take some credit where credit is due! Don't you think it's time to stop hiding behind your sister's shadow?"

"My sister has a very nice shadow, thank you very much," Harriet replied primly, slightly abashed he'd seen through her. Again.

"It's a fascinating topic and many orphanages could benefit. One I know a lot of health professionals will be keen to hear. Including…" Harriet watched the older doctor's eyes scan the ward as if he'd misplaced something. Or, rather, someone.

Their eyes simultaneously lit on the man who'd just set the swinging double doors at the end of the ward in motion as if cued to make a dramatic entrance.

He was tall, ebony-haired and had an easygoing grace about him. Not movie-star-ish. More…cowboy…or fighter pilot. Not a drop of vanity about him. But, sweet cherry pies, did that man ever exude confidence. Hair long enough to see it had a sexy wavy thing going on. Was that a bit of a five o'clock shadow? And…mmm… he didn't just wear clothes, he showed them off. Or did they show him off? Either way, the effect…oh, the effect! Trousers just skimming along his trim hipline. Long legs you could take a zip line ride on if you were into that sort of thing. Shoulders filling out his open-at-the-neck shirt. Not too much. But enough to know that if he lifted a child in his arms there would be some biceps action. Not that she'd imagined him doing that or anything.

*Maybe once or twice?*

The first time she had seen him—ensuring, of course, she'd been safely tucked behind the curtained confines of a patient's cubicle—her eyes had nearly popped out of her head. Pretty much each time she'd seen him after that? No change.

Raw, unadulterated lust.

There was no other description for it. She had the hots for this man and hiding each time she saw him coming had been her only salvation. Not that she was five or anything. She was just acutely tuned into the child within. It helped with her work. Besides, behaving like a grown-up was highly overrated. Particularly if survival was a factor.

For her entire life, Harriet had been "the sensible twin", the "shy twin", the "wallflower twin" and for about as long as she could remember she'd always happily agreed. Her twin sister, Claudia—pronounced like a beautiful, fluffy cloud versus a gray, dull clod—was about as vivacious, gorgeous, gutsy and go-get-'em as a girl could get… And Harriet? Polar opposites was a pretty good starting place.

As the doors *phwapped* shut, a surge of energy shot through her so powerfully there was no doubt she would always remember this instant in time. Another daydream to tuck away for the years ahead when Dr. Torres was safely back in his homeland.

The dozen or so patients between them faded into soft focus, their chatter and laughter muted by the thump of her heartbeat ascending to her ears. Everything slowed down, sensations quadrupled and her very breath caught in her throat then released in a sigh as her gaze linked with his incredibly green eyes.

Was that *heat* she felt flickering away below her waist? *Heat?*

How inopportune. And… *What were those?*

Tingles?

Harriet Monticello didn't get *tingles*, for goodness' sake! And now she was being tickled with *flickering tingles* of *heat*? What was going on?

The closer he got to them, the more she felt everything inside her shift and twist and lift… Good grief!

It wasn't like she was a complete novice in the world of romance. There'd been a handful of boyfriends over the years. Sort of. All of whom she'd parted from amicably. No point in letting them know they hadn't really baked her cake. But responding to a virtual stranger on such a primal level? Brand spanking new.

Was this what *blossoming* was? At a few months shy of thirty, she was a bit late for that, wasn't she? Love at first sight? Or just pure, undiluted desire?

Each microscopic change in her body was wholly in response to him. And utterly involuntary.

He was taller than her, which wasn't difficult—her being the "petite" one to her sister's "statuesque beauty". As he neared, Harriet's chin tipped upwards, opening up the length of her throat in a way that almost felt suggestive. Her shoulder blades shimmied down her back as her shoulders gave a little wiggle to better present themselves. As if such a thing were possible in a staff dress. Sure, it had a clingy cheongsam cut, but it was, at the end of the day, a uniform.

She felt her breasts pressing against the well-worn cotton of the snap-fronted dress, and for the tiniest of moments wondered what it would feel like if Matteo were to trace a finger along the diamond shaped neckline then begin, one by one, to pop open each of the snaps. Would his fingers be rough or smooth? How would it feel if he were to draw one of his hands across her belly and begin to explore elsewhere? Would she touch him back? Or, for the very first time, luxuriate in letting herself be caressed before seeing to her lover's needs? Would his unruly black hair feel as silky as it looked? Would he moan if she scratched his back in an untamed moment of desire? Or call out *mi corazon*! Or whatever hot Latin doctors called out in a moment of passion.

The roar of blood in her ears shot up a few decibels.

When he arrived in front of them—a smile play-

ing across his full lips—a heated flush flashed across
her cheeks. Could he read minds as well? Anyone with
eyes so lusciously green surely had access to the deeper
reaches of a woman's soul.

Er... Get a grip!

Harriet silently tsked at herself. Too many romance
novels during the overnight shift. Nevertheless, she did
a quick check to see if he really did have thick, dark
eyelashes. The final dab of icing on a very tasty-look-
ing cake.

Yup! *Of course he did.*

"Matteo! You found us. I'm so pleased." Dr. Bailey
reached out to shake his hand.

She watched as Matteo—*Matteo!*—extended his long,
lovely fingers with sun-bleached hairs, not too thick, running along the length of his forearm, and shook hands
with her boss. They turned to her, an expectant look in
Matteo's eyes, which was when Harriet realized the entire time he'd been walking towards them in slow motion
she'd been wiping her disintegrated biscuit into the fabric
of her dress right...over...her breast. Classy.

Cheeks properly on fire now, she stuffed her hands
into the front patch pockets of her dress, squeezing her
eyes tightly shut in a lame attempt to regroup.

"And if I'm not mistaken," she heard Dr. Bailey continue, either oblivious to or trying to cover for her gaffe,
"this young woman here is the reason you've come along
to see us!"

Harriet's eyes popped open to take an involuntary
glance over each of her shoulders. Had one of their colleagues arrived without her knowing? She thought she'd
left the rest of the nurses deep in discussion over how to
rearrange the supplies cupboard.

Nope. Still just her. All alone with… *Matteo*…and, of course, Dr. Bailey, who was now looking at her with a particularly bemused expression. Maybe she should shut her mouth. Gape-jawed wasn't really her look.

"This is Sister Monticello?"

*Oh, sweet wonders of the universe.* He had a scrummy accent to boot. Of course he did! The man was Argentinian. What did she expect? Cut-glass British? Even so… It was all sexy and smoky. Yum.

She was pretty sure they didn't make men this—this *male* over here on the sceptered isle. Or if they did, they were already taken and hidden away by their lucky wives and girlfriends. Too bad she'd all but shelved dreams of having a family of her own… *Stop dreaming!* She adjusted her gaze, eyes narrowing just a bit. Maybe she could dream just a little bit?

Matteo made her want to howl. He probably ate steak. Lots of it, searing it nightly over a naked flame. Without wearing a shirt. Just buckskins and a deep caramel tan illuminated by the flickering fire and a splash of starlight. At which point Matteo turned to her with a smile so warm she hardly knew what to do with herself.

"I was expecting…" Matteo stopped to give a self-effacing laugh. "I am such an idiot. *Sister* Monticello! I've heard so much about you and I'm still not used to calling the nurses 'Sister.' I was expecting a nun!"

"Aha-ha-ha!" Harriet could hear herself giving a weird, cackly, laugh-along laugh. The oh-ho-ho wasn't that funny variety, but if there was anyone in the world who could bewitch the knickers off a nun she would bet her entire sensibly accrued pension Matteo could. Not that her knickers had fallen off or anything. Yet.

He reached out and took her hand, his cheek moving

towards hers faster than she could react. As their cheeks met, she inhaled a delicious waft of peppery gingerbread and heard a kissing noise, but didn't feel the touch of his lips. Pity.

*"Encantada."*

Oh, blimey. Had he just whispered a sweet nothing into her ear?

"It's nice to smell—I mean meet you!" she all but shouted.

What was that? She didn't even know this guy and she was falling to bits right in front of him. Sure, she'd been watching him from afar for the past fortnight. But afar was safe. And right here was….really, really close. He smelled distinctly delicious. So much so, she mused, he really should be a cologne. Eau de Argentine Doc. Man Scent by Matteo. The ad campaign would be a cinch.

Why did her sister have to be eight blinking thousand miles away in Los Angeles just when she'd be *incredibly* handy? Claudia could dig her out of this socially awkward moment without breaking a sweat. Then again, Claudia was drop-dead gorgeous and if she met Matteo before Harriet did, it wouldn't be very good, would it? Even heavily pregnant with twins, her sister was a knockout. She had the pictures to prove it. Harriet felt an unexpected attack of let-him-be mine come over her.

She'd never really cared when the hot man in the room took a shine to her sister in lieu of her. That was how things had always been. But this time…

*Calm, calm, calm yourself, Harriet.*

It wasn't like she stood even the slightest of chances in the universe of having a man like this one desiring, let alone falling completely and madly in love with her. Like she already virtually was with him. Just a few more minutes and she'd have their china pattern and curtains all picked out.

She ran a hand through her blonde pixie cut, jutting out her lower lip as she did so to blow some air up into the fringe. Another sexy move she'd crafted in how-to-look-like-an-idiot class.

"Nice to meet you, Sister." Matteo held out his hand, which she took and pumped up and down too hard because she was already picturing her cobweb-laced spinsterhood spreading out before her now that she'd ruined any chance of marrying the man of her dreams.

"Harriet's fine—uh…" She made her, *yeesh, I don't know what to call you* face.

"Matteo works—or Dr. Torres if you prefer. I know how formal you Brits are."

"Yes, well…yes."

*Was it too soon to dive into the nearest broom cupboard?*

"Harriet," Dr. Bailey interjected. "Perhaps you'd like to show Dr. Torres around the hospital? Give him your perspective on how St. Nick's works. He's been trying to track you down for the past fortnight and for some peculiar reason has found it near impossible to find you."

"Excuse me?" Harriet tried her best to wipe the horrified expression off of her face, realizing in an instant she hadn't been successful.

"Seeing that you could be working together in the longer term, it's probably a good idea to get to know each other."

Harriet's jaw dropped again. *Who'd stolen Dr. Bailey and replaced him with this man who was yanking away all her safety blankets?*

Matteo grinned, a glint in his eye betraying something akin to frustration. "Dr. Bailey didn't tell you?"

"Tell me what?" Her voice was so strangled she was pretty sure the dogs of London would be howling in unison if she continued.

"This trip—my 'visit' here…" He left a small silence to see if she could fill in the air quotes, but there was nothing jostling away the question marks careening round her mind.

Dr. Bailey jumped in. "Harriet, I was going to tell you all about this in good time, but—"

"It looks like—in the hope of some funding—you might be coming to Buenos Aires," Matteo finished for him, an appraising eyebrow arching upwards as he spoke. "To assess me."

His expression shifted into something strangely neutral. It was difficult to tell if he was pleased by the scenario or resentful. Something told her it was the latter. *Great.* Five seconds with Mr. Perfect and already he hated her.

How did one respond to *that*? Her head swung from Dr. Bailey's consternated face to Matteo's unreadable smile. Funding was very dependent on conditions. Lots of i-dotting and t-crossing—

*Uh-oh.* Wait a minute. She forced her brain to play catch-up.

Was he saying *she* was the condition? She sought each of their faces for answers, feeling a bit like she was watching a tennis match at close range minus the tennis bits.

"Buenos Aires?"

She had been hoping to sound casually interested. Noncommittal. What came out instead was a high-pitched, dog whistle screechy thing. Not really what she'd been going for. Particularly since a trip to Buenos Aires would be about the scariest, most exciting, incredibly interesting, totally top of the list of things she'd never be brave enough to ever consider doing sort of trip. Which was why she had barely ever left the hallowed borders of London town.

"Don't worry." Matteo waved away her response. "I know what it's like to be handed something unwelcome when you least expect it."

"I didn't even know I had been invited anywhere and now I'm unwelcome?" She didn't mean to sound churlish, but c'mon! Every single speck of this was news to her.

"No, no. It wasn't meant like that—but don't worry. It might not even happen. Nothing's set in stone."

"What if I wanted to see the stone? Part of the stone even?" Harriet pinched her fingers into her best little-bit visual aid. Could you miss something you hadn't even known was going to happen?

Matteo considered Harriet a moment before answering. Apart from looking entirely different from what he'd anticipated, she struck him as a woman who preferred facts over spin. Action over coddling. Someone he could, potentially, work with. Which made a change from most of the research-based medical personnel he came in contact with.

"It's all to do with a possible expansion. More of a new build, actually," Matteo corrected himself. "A clinic. A proper one. And one that's dependent, I am afraid, on charitable donations. Strangely, homes for pregnant teens and orphaned babies aren't big money spinners."

Matteo enjoyed seeing the light enter Harriet's blue

eyes at his words. The click of recognition. The spark of interest.

"If they did, I bet Casita Verde Para Niños would rake it in!"

"You know it?" *Impressive.* Most people couldn't name an orphanage in their hometown, let alone one on the other side of the world.

"Of course I know it!" She gave an embarrassed giggle. "Even if I can't pronounce it properly."

All tension dropped from her face and was replaced by utter engagement. Work talk, it seemed, put her at ease. *Interesting.* Maybe the stories floating round St. Nick's were true. All work and no play made Harriet Monticello a delightful woman—because work was her play. The pretty blonde was a far cry from the dried-up nun he'd been picturing.

"Didn't you single-handedly drag children's homes in Argentina into the twenty-first century?"

"Well…" Matteo felt an unfamiliar wash of modesty come over him. "People don't usually see what I do that way." Particularly his socialite parents, whose business dealings saw more money change hands in a single day than he had as annual budget. "Black hole with no economic return" was the more frequently used description. "Of course, you'll know it's quite specialized. It's a place pregnant teens can receive the support they might not be getting at home or are afraid—" He caught himself on the brink of speech-making and held back. "It's nice to hear someone thinks highly of the Casitas."

She gave him a flustered smile and looked away, side-tracking Dr. Bailey with a question about rosters. Matteo examined Harriet again. Given she didn't look a thing like the mental image he'd conjured up, it was little wonder he hadn't singled her out over the past couple of weeks. Particularly given the role her bosses seemed keen for her to play: The Woman Who Would Deign Him Worthy of Funding.

And now she didn't know a thing about it? If the joint clinic meant that little to the board of St. Nicholas Hospital, he may as well turn around and go home. He'd enjoyed the two-week secondment to the high-tech hospital's obstetrics unit, but his main aim was a clinic for his own. Then again… Harriet knew Casita Verde and the work he did without so much as a prompt. *Best not to be too hasty...*

He'd been prepared to go into his usual charm offensive routine. It worked a treat in Argentina's moneyed circles. The elite of Buenos Aires rarely if ever went for earnest, over-keen do-gooders. Appearing as though he could live with or without their money always seemed the best tack. That, and a lavishing of compliments. He had yet to meet an ego that didn't like to be fed. Something told him cocktail-party chatter and superficial compliments wouldn't work with this woman.

She was pretty, in a completely natural way. Gamine, honey-blonde hair, a single swish of mascara on lashes overhanging a doey pair of bright blue eyes. A sweet splash of pink grew on her cheeks when she realized he was looking at her. She seemed…kind. A far cry from the dolled-up heiresses his parents wished he spent more time courting.

"You can't expect your grandfather's trust fund to keep Casita Verde's doors open forever!" they warned on a regular basis—making it more than clear which way their wills wouldn't be bent. Which was fine. He'd done all right so far. And they were family. Definitely not perfect, but they were all the family he had left.

"Great!" Dr. Bailey clapped his hands together and gave them a quick rub as if they'd all just agreed on a ground-breaking deal. "I'll leave you two to it, shall I?"

"No!"

Matteo couldn't help but laugh. It seemed Harriet disliked the position of the "chooser" as much as he hated being the beggar.

"I'm pretty good at being invisible, if you need to get work done." Matteo gave her an out. The last thing a busy nurse needed was a hanger-on weighing her down.

"Sorry, Dr. Torres, I didn't mean you. I just…" The pleading look she sent in Dr. Bailey's direction brought another smile to his face. Harriet Monticello didn't just wear her heart on her sleeve—what she felt was written all over her face. From the looks of things? The idea of spending time with him was pretty low on her list.

Perfect! That made two of them, then. She didn't want someone tagging along after her and he didn't really want a research nurse being posted in the heart of Casita Verde to see whether she deigned him worthy of funding.

But unless teenaged pregnancy became a thing of the past, there would never be a day when the center didn't need more money. Not to mention the fact that money wasn't printed on tears and there would be plenty of those if he didn't get the go-ahead. Their resources were limited, and he was having to toughen his already thick exterior with each girl they were forced to turn away because of a lack of resources.

"Could you tell me just a bit more about this Argentina thing before you disappear off to your candlelit dinner?"

Harriet had a hand on her boss's arm now, her blue eyes virtually begging him not to leave.

Dr. Bailey looked like a deer caught in headlights. Matteo leaned against the nurses' counter, trying to look casually interested instead of downright humored. If his own fate hadn't been dangling from the threads of their conversation he would have laughed out loud.

"The board of directors thinks you need some field-work. After speaking with Matteo about how things stand at the casitas—the board suggested seeing how you go tonight. How you present yourself."

"So you've known all along I needed to give the speech tonight?" Harriet's eyes opened so wide she almost looked like a child.

"If—*when*—everything goes well…" Her boss stopped to clear his throat and throw an apologetic look Matteo's way. "The board would like you to go out to Buenos Aires for a few weeks—maybe months—to see whether your research could be implemented at Casita Verde. If so, St. Nick's would open a clinical outpost—in cooperation with Matteo, of course. A partnership."

*Interesting.*

Matteo hid his surprise. She was the one being played. Not him. Unusual.

"You're *bartering* me?"

And it sat with her as well as it sat with him. He was genuinely starting to warm to this woman. Again— unusual.

"One good turn does deserve another, Harriet," Dr. Bailey continued with a patient smile. "You hardly ever leave the hospital, let alone Britain. I thought putting your research into practice in a different—"

"Apologies, Dr. Bailey." Matteo stepped forward, his

expression quite sober as he nodded in Harriet's direction. "I probably shouldn't interfere, particularly with the board's decision pending. But I must be clear. Sister Monticello's nursing skills would be valued at Casita Verde, but as far as her research goes? She is welcome to come, to observe and to offer suggestions. Lend a hand where necessary. But changes are down to me. In my experience, academic studies are often just that."

"I beg your pardon?" Harriet's hackles went straight up. "I think you'll find my study comprehensive enough to see the changes we've implemented in *numerous* children's homes here in the UK, including St. Nicks, are making a very, *very* big impact on the children's well-being. My methods *work*." She ground out the word with an imperiously arched eyebrow for emphasis.

Matteo rocked back on his heels and smiled broadly. He liked this woman. She was passionate and about as into playing politics as he was. Not at all.

But if Harriet were to come to Buenos Aires, she would need to toughen up to deal with his "every day". St. Nick's had amenities. Lots of them. He watched as the set of her jaw tightened enough for a muscle twitch. Then again…maybe a stint on his patch would be good for her. And him.

"Shall I leave you two to the ward tour, then? It's Harriet's showcase!" Dr. Bailey had already turned to go, not leaving them much of a choice. Harriet nodded curtly, just the tiniest hint of "don't leave me" left in her eyes as he and Dr. Bailey shook hands.

"Sister?"

Matteo couldn't help grinning as she unclenched her lips and forced on a "guess we're stuck with each other" smile.

His amusement increased as Harriet excused herself for a moment to fiddle round with some charts in faux preparation for his tour. She obviously wasn't happy about the avalanche of information she'd just been handed. Not to say he was ready to click his heels up in the air in a fit of glee, but none of this was of her making. An unfamiliar urge to make sure Harriet came out of this unscathed niggled away at his conscience. If anything, she was the biggest pawn in the scenario. No point in dumping all of his reservations onto her plate. She tugged her form-fitting uniform down a notch, accenting the perfect swoosh of waist to hip ratio.

*Hmm...* Perhaps this whole palaver would be easier if she had been a nun.

Nuns? He could deal with nuns. Unlike most of his childhood friends, he'd enjoyed Catholic boarding school—the structure had suited him. A nice contrast to his parent's whirlwind, round-the-globe lifestyle. He'd take a nun over a Buenos Aires socialite any day of the week. Not literally, of course. He shuddered away the thought. Nuns and socialites. Ugh. He stopped another shudder. He'd rather a night of romance with Harriet than—

Uh… *Que paso?* One second he was keeping Harriet at arm's length, the next he…?

No. He didn't. Casita Verde kept him busy. Incredibly busy. Not to mention his "no children" policy that sent most Argentinian women flying out the door. "What kind of man doesn't want children of his own?" they all asked.

One whose sister had died in childbirth. That's who. One who worked with scores of orphans no one wanted to adopt every day. One who'd vowed to be a doctor and nothing more to said orphans, the teens who gave birth to them and anyone else who crossed the threshold into the *casita*. That's who. Not that he had issues. He had facts. And perspective. Children of his own? Not an option.

He looked across at Harriet, still engaged in her chart-juggling. From what he heard, she spent as many hours at St. Nick's as he did at the *casita*. Birds of a feather? He watched her face break into a smile as a sock puppet fell out of one of the record folders.

He doubted it.

She was a wisp of a thing, slight. Complete with flushed cheeks, an untidy swish of honey-blonde hair and clear blue eyes that didn't seem able to lie. *Real.* He liked her. And, coming from him, that was saying a lot. He didn't "do" personal. Couldn't broach "real". Cool, calm reserve. It served him well. And yet…

"Should I go out then come in again?" Matteo offered, pointing to the swing doors.

"Why would you do that?"

"So we could start over. Or—at the very least—it would buy you some time to pretend being forced to have a puppy dog follow you round all day wasn't the worst thing to ever happen."

"Unfortunately, we don't allow dogs in the hospital," Harriet blurted, covering her mouth with both hands in horror after the words flew out.

Matteo laughed and put what was meant to be a re-assuring hand on her shoulder. Her shoulders instantly shot up to her ears, briefly trapping his fingers between them. He only just managed to stop himself from running a finger along her jawline as he withdrew his hand, taking a mental note as he did so: Argentine ways were too tactile. This woman needed her space. And he found himself wanting to respect that.

Winning Harriet Monticello's confidence seemed like something of genuine value. He totted up a notch in the pro-Harriet camp and another in the watch-it category to check himself. Being emotional about things—about *people*—didn't get you very far.

"Let's say we get this tour underway."

# CHAPTER TWO

"AND NOW FOR one of my favorite places...."

Harriet smiled broadly but widened the gap between them as they made their way to a glass-fronted ward. She definitely liked to keep him at arm's length. He dipped for a surreptitious sniff of his shirt. He was certain he'd showered this morning...

He covered the move with a smile and an earnest nod. "It's nice to see changes implemented that don't necessarily require huge injections of cash.

"The whole world is slashing budgets and we're no different. But it's the staffing changes that make the biggest impact and those are completely free. Makes work seem less like...work."

"It seems to me you do a lot more than work here." And that was putting it mildly. There were staffers and then there were people whose work was their passion—their calling. Harriet knew every patient, staffer, nook and cranny of St. Nick's. Not many people were like that. He felt that way. From the day his sister had died he'd known where to pour his energies. His rage. But Harriet seemed fueled by other fires. She was pure compassion.

"Ta-da!" She twirled around, swirling her hands into a presentation pose as his heart sank. A row of little cots filled with pink and blue bundles spread out before him. The infants' ward. He'd been so busy focusing on Harriet's take on pediatric staffing he hadn't even noticed where they were heading.

"Want to go in for a snuggle? I always come here when I'm feeling a bit down. Baby therapy!" Her eyes sparkled in anticipation of his affirmative answer. 'You know, a whole new world…little tiny fingers, little tiny toes. Endless possibilities!"

Wrong customer. Wrong question. He flicked his eyes towards the large wall clock.

"I think we should probably press on." He knew his smile was tight, but at least he'd managed one of those. "How about we work our way back to your office and I can get out of your hair."

She threw him a questioning look, but didn't press him.

He didn't do cuddling, cooing or coddling. He helped young women through often complicated births, took care of the casita's orphans if they required medical attention—but getting attached to any of them? Not his bag. Caring only led to heartbreak and he'd had more than his fair share of that nonsense.

"Not everyone has the stomach for this kind of work." He tried to cover the awkward silence settling between them. "And yet you choose to be with children most people prefer to ignore. A ward full of dying orphans—"

"*Children,*" she firmly corrected.

"*Orphaned* children," he couldn't stop himself from riposting. "I'm surprised you, of all people, would wrap everything up in politically correct language to make things softer and fluffier for them. Life is tough and will continue to be so—especially for children like these. Orphans."

From the flash of ire in her eyes it looked like he'd hit a nerve.

"They're *children* first and foremost, Dr. Torres— and that's how I see them. How *we* see them. Not a single one of them is harboring an illusion that the world is solely made up of happy families and that they're on a little spa break, thank you very much. The children in my ward have all most likely come here to die, and they know that. So having things a bit 'fluffy bunny' is *exactly* what we're after."

Harriet only just stopped herself from harrumphing. She prided herself on choosing her language at St. Nick's very carefully and patronizing her about it didn't go down well, no matter how nice a package it came in.

"'Fluffy bunny'?" He arched an eyebrow.

*Hmm...that may not have had the gravitas she had been aiming for.*

"It's interesting you should ask, *Dr. Torres*. Terminology is one of the things I was going to talk about tonight in my speech. Something that can make a real difference for the *children* here. And very possibly at Casita Verde. I wouldn't like to judge before I set foot in the place."

*Ha! Take that, you—you aspersion-caster, you!*

"So you *will* be giving the speech tonight, then?"

Another amused eyebrow shifted upwards.

Oh. *Wait a minute.*

"I…" She scanned the ward for an invisible Dr. Bailey. "I think my esteemed boss hasn't really given me much of a choice."

"There is a rather nice carrot dangling at the end of the stick if it goes well, no?"

Her eyes caught his. A ridiculous image of Matteo beckoning to her with a single crooked finger as he lay bare chested on a satin-sheeted bed blinded her for a moment. He wasn't talking about himself, was he?

*Was he?*

She sought answers in his eyes—almost verdant they were so green. So dreamy green… This wouldn't do. She turned course abruptly in an attempt to swish away down the corridor, only narrowly avoiding tripping over a six-year-old playing airplane. Grace, it seemed, was continuing to elude her.

"Don't you want to show me around your part of St Nicholas's?" Matteo appeared at her side in a couple of long-legged strides. He, apparently, had children dodging down to a fine art.

She didn't answer. There were a whole host of things she'd like to do with him, but show him the place that mattered to her most? Open herself up to more disparaging comments? Not particularly.

"I bet you could have done anything you set your mind to," Matteo pressed, enjoying watching Harriet veer across the corridor to give herself more distance from him. Was she shy, or just repulsed? Not the usual effect he had on a woman, but he was open to firsts. "Were you ever tempted to become a doctor?"

"Ha! Good one. Not for a second. Nursing is exactly where I belong. It suits me perfectly."

Her words sounded positive, but from the expression on her face Matteo could see Harriet's laugh-it-off demeanor was a defense mechanism.

"What's wrong with aiming higher?"

"What's wrong with life in the trenches?" Her expression dared him to come up with an answer.

"Good point." And he meant it. He fixed his gaze to

hers—clear and blue, imbued with a healthy dose of trust. Innocent—but not naive. It wouldn't surprise him in the least to discover that what you saw was what you got with Harriet Monticello. What did surprise him was that he wanted to know more. Another first. He switched course.

"Would I be correct in presuming your father was Italian with a surname like Monticello?"

"I thought we weren't going to talk about me." She waved off his question.

"I never said any such thing. You did."

"Was." She nodded, her mood taking a visible dip. "He and my mother—who was Irish…" she pointed at her blonde hair "…died quite a few years back. Gosh… ten years ago. When I was just starting my nursing training here."

"I'm sorry to hear that." And he meant it. Family was precious. He wished he was better at fostering what little relationship he had with his parents. After the fog had cleared in the wake of his sister's death they had all but gone their separate ways. Acknowledging the work he did meant remembering their daughter. He'd already accepted that might never happen.

"It happens to everyone, eventually." Her lips arced into a sad smile as she turned to look out a window towards a flourishing garden courtyard. Not as lush as in Argentina—but it was nice. Another Harriet touch?

He turned and saw her fighting a glaze of tears forming, her blue eyes fastidiously taking a swing round the leafy courtyard. He understood instantly. St. Nick's was filling an emptiness in her. The space her family had filled. The same way his work stood in for what he could never replace. The dreams he would never realize. Would there ever come a day when he'd done enough? A day when he felt at peace?

Something deep within him said no. Something deeper prayed he was wrong.

He pressed his hands onto his thighs before giving them a conclusive clap. This was all getting a bit too deep and heavy and he needed to be on his top game tonight. There weren't just peers in the audience. There were donors. Ones with deep pockets. Including a very pretty research nurse who could be the key to a new clinic.

"Well, I, for one, am looking forward to seeing you ace that speech tonight."

"From your lips—" Harriet began as she turned from the window then stopped, her eyes snagged on Matteo's full mouth. One lip resting atop the other, parting to speak…

"And then you'll come to Buenos Aires and show me your dazzling research in action?" His smile was leading. He was aware she'd been staring—and that she liked what she saw.

"When you put it that way, how could I resist?" She looked away from his inquisitive gaze. To push boundaries? Change things further afield? Tickles of possibility teased at Harriet's utilitarian shoes and practical hairdo. To live twenty-four seven with a man who turned her into the equivalent of a weeping Beatles fan? Emotional yo-yo? Oh, yeah. She was riding that thing like it was going out of style.

*No. No way.*

Her sister did wild and wonderful. *She* did sensible and sane. It's why her sister needed her. Why she stayed put, holding onto the family home…just in case. If she wasn't needed, then… *Best not go there.*

"So, I guess I'd better offer you some tips on life in my country," Matteo commented, as if the trip was a done deal. "Lesson number one? In Argentina, there is a lot of kissing. Anything and everything—especially an agreement—comes with a kiss. You'll have to get used to it if—*when*—you come."

He didn't seem like the flirting type, but… Was he *flirting*?

She nodded dumbly.

Wait. Were his lips getting closer? Had her eyelashes just fluttered? She didn't flutter—oh, he was coming closer. Was he aiming for her cheek? Which way was she meant to turn? Right? Left? Was this like the cheek-rub thing earlier with the kissing noise but no contact? Blimey, she wished she'd traveled more.

His hands touched each of her shoulders. Her brain did a little short-circuit before reconnecting with her ability to see straight. Undecided, Harriet changed direction at the precise moment Matteo's very obviously intended cheek kiss landed squarely on her lightly parted lips.

Everything inside her responded to his touch.

Her entire bloodstream surged and performed a ready-for-Vegas dance routine. Had he stayed there…his lips tasting hers…just a little longer than one would for an accidental snog? Or had she made that up? Fact and fiction were blurring at a rate of knots.

She pulled back and instantly wanted more. Matteo was giving his chin a scrub, a curious expression playing across his features. Had she just grown antlers? Insecurity began to unfurl its fingers through her. If this was how things worked in Argentina, she was definitely going to stay right in England where a handshake was a handshake and cheek kisses were precisely what they said on the label.

She tugged her hand from his, took an unnecessary glance at her watch and backed into her office. Keeping her eye on the prey. Enemy? *Something like that.*

"I think I've taken up enough of your time." Matteo stepped back, wondering what the hell had possessed him to give a spontaneous kissing lesson. No one got under his skin and yet…

Harriet gave a nervous laugh and ducked farther into the confines of her office.

No bets on that one. Matteo knew himself enough to know he'd wanted to be close to Harriet, had wanted to touch her. Just a couple of hours wandering around the hospital together and he'd felt a connection he rarely felt. Something genuine. Something real. Not the confident, rule-setting guy who flew to conferences to show his wares in exchange for shiny new clinics. The Matteo whose heart was every bit as much a part of the *Casitas* as Harriet's was with St. Nick's. The part that was searching for…*enough* and having no idea where to find it.

"I guess I'll see you at the hall?" She shifted from foot to foot, not unlike a skittish colt.

"Yes, perfect." He dug into his jacket pocket and pulled out a wodge of papers he'd folded and refolded into ever-decreasing squares. "I've got all of the details here. What do you call it? The bumph?"

Harriet smiled, a little dimple he hadn't noticed before appearing in her cheek. It made her appear pretty and vulnerable all at once, bringing out a protectiveness in him he hadn't felt for a woman in a long, long time.

"Yes. The bumph. Well done. You're going to have to teach me Argentinian lingo—"

"Spanish? No problem. Dinner afterwards?"

"Uh… I don't know about that."

"Of course you do. Come to dinner with me after the lectures and we can toast your public speaking success."

"I'm not so sure—"

"Sister, can you come?" A nurse knocked and stuck her head in the door, her face looking strained with worry. "It's Cora."

"Is she seizing?" Harriet scooted round him and was in the corridor in an instant.

"SFS. She says she tastes pickles and has the seasick feeling. She won't move until you come."

Matteo didn't even stop to think. He followed Harriet to the play area the nurse indicated. A simple focal seizure could quickly lead to another much more dramatic attack. Grand mal seizures weren't uncommon.

"Does she usually have a stage two?"

"Yes." Harriet kept up the quick pace. "Childhood absence. Unresponsive to voice, automatisms. Eyelid flickering and some lip smacking," she explained.

"So nothing violent?" Matteo matched her stride for stride.

"No." She shook away her own answer. "She's had one tonic-clonic, but overall she's been responding well to meds."

"Sodium valproate?"

"In combination with lamotrigine. It seems to work well for her. We wanted to steer clear of phenobarbital and phenytoin."

"Adverse affects on cognitive development?"

Harriet nodded. They'd both clearly read the same studies.

Harriet headed towards a skinny little redhead standing in the center of the play area.

"Hey there, Cora." Harriet's tone was soft as she gently lowered herself to the girl's eye level. Matteo nodded approvingly at how Harriet moved—careful not to give the girl any rapid movements to take in. If she was already feeling unwell, too much commotion could make her feel worse. "What do you say we get you to your bed?"

"I don't feel well." Cora's gaze remained static on the wall.

"I know, sweetheart. That's why I'm here. Shall we get you to your bed?"

"I'm too dizzy."

"How about I put my hands on your eyes for a bit and you think of your bed?"

"Mmm-hmm."

Harriet shifted behind Cora. "I'm going to do it now, Cora. All right?"

"Okay." The girl's voice was tiny and frightened. The more stressed she became, the more likely another seizure was.

"Matteo." Harriet's voice was a near whisper. "Could you grab that chair, please?" She nodded towards a well-worn wing chair with high sides and a deep seat.

"Absolutely."

Harriet moved to the side, fingers still covering Cora's eyes, as Matteo brought the chair round—aiming it at a portion of the wall that contained a single horizontal line. When Cora felt well enough to focus her eyes on something, that line could help. Another one of Harriet's touches? He wouldn't be surprised.

"All right, sweetheart. Ready to sit down? We've got Christopher here."

Matteo shot her a questioning look. Christopher?

Harriet nodded at the chair. Apparently it was called Christopher.

His instinct was to laugh but common sense caught up with him as they each took hold of one of Cora's arms and guided her into the chair. The girl was feeling panicked, needed her eyes closed, and required reassurance all at once. If she knew she was going to settle back into Christopher, it would be reassuring. Simple. Clever. He was pretty certain he knew who had thought up the idea and couldn't stop a big 'Aha!" smile from forming as they tucked Cora into the chair along with a couple of throw pillows so she'd feel extra cozy and safe.

A few minutes later, Cora was feeling much better and asked Harriet to take her to her room for a rest.

After she'd been tucked into her bed, they each took a side of the door frame to lean on and watch her for a bit, with Harriet making a few notes in Cora's chart. When she'd finished, Harriet looked across at Matteo, their eyes meeting with a look of mutual understanding. She was much more than an academic. He'd been quick off the mark to slot her into a "books and flowcharts only" file and, while the incident hadn't been an extreme one, she'd shown swift and effective responses to the girl's plight.

He'd need to be a bit more generous in the Doctor Knows Best department. Be open to her input.

A little zip of anticipation surged through him at the idea of Harriet at Casita Verde. There could be more advantages to her visit than he'd thought. A clinic at the *casita*—a proper one—so that they wouldn't have to send the children away to hospital would be a godsend. It near enough gave him physical pain each time they had to sign a child over to the state but their resources were stretched beyond reason. Perhaps with Harriet on their side…

Would she wear that form-hugging nurse's uniform? he wondered. Then stopped himself. Re-dressing Harriet Monticello was not the route to getting funding. Not the way to stay focused.

He shook his head to clear it as Harriet slipped the chart onto a hook just inside Cora's door. "I'm off to see a couple more of the kids. Did you want to come?"

It didn't sound like an invitation and he needed to get his head straight.

"I think I'll leave you to it. Make sure I'm at my best tonight." He was about to give her a wink and a smile, but thought better of it. He was no Casanova, and this was a business trip…

He cleared his throat a bit too pointedly. *¡Qué quilombo!* Wasn't he the one who liked keeping things professional?

He tipped his head towards Cora's room as they walked away. "Has she been here long? She seems to rely on you."

"Only a couple of months. She'd been in foster-care, but the parents… The parents weren't up to it." Her lips tightened before she quickly shook off any judgment she'd been going to make.

*More kudos to her.* He was judgmental as hell when it came to backing out on a commitment like that. Better not to make one at all. That's what he did. The only commitments he made were professional. It made life much easier.

Harriet pointed to a large, colorful chart with names and times on it. "The children know the shifts and have one person of their choice to call on when they're feeling anxious. She hasn't chosen yet, so I'm the interim 'go to' girl."

"Is this part of your staffing thing?" *How about sounding a bit more patronizing?* He could've kicked himself.

"It's part of being consistent with the children. Something, as you well know, most of these kids haven't had." She swept away a lock of blonde hair before continuing. "Cora, like a lot of the residents here, had been in a foster home. Well, several foster homes, and she also has minor ADHD that kicks up a notch with each change. The more anxious it makes her, the worse her epilepsy becomes, and the worse her epilepsy becomes—"

"The harder it is to place her," Matteo finished for her. It was the same drill where he came from. The worse the medical condition, the less likely it was they'd find adoptive parents, let alone foster parents. Who wanted to open their wallets, let alone their hearts, to a child with so many hurdles to leap?

"Got it in one!" She smiled up at him, another one of those hits of connection pinging him straight in the chest. Practical, emotional and as committed as they got. This woman was a medical triple threat.

"It looks like we might have more in common than I thought." Matteo gave her a rueful smile. "Professionally speaking, of course."

Her smiled disappeared in an instant.

*Why had he said that?*

He knew exactly why he'd said it. To keep his emotions where he liked them. All tucked up in his very own…er… Christopher. But taking away that smile of hers? A bad move.

"Of course. Well, then…" Harriet's voice became clipped. "If you don't mind, I'd like to finish seeing the pa—the *children* and then get home to work on my lecture. I don't want to be letting you down tonight. Professionally speaking, of course."

*Touché.*

# CHAPTER THREE

"You stood me up."

Harriet screamed and flew out of her office chair at the sound of Matteo's voice.

"What are you doing here?"

"Trying to find my dinner date."

"What?"

"You said you'd have dinner with me."

"But that was…" *Before I made such a hash of things.*

"That was what you agreed to do after the speeches. So…" He looked around what he could see of the ward from Harriet's doorway. Low lights, a couple of nurses huddled at a station farther down the corridor, some classical music coming from one of the children's rooms… exactly the type of mellow atmosphere she'd needed after Speech-gate. Being at St. Nick's always centered her.

Well, it had always centered her before a certain Argentinian doctor had started creeping round corners, insisting on people going out to dinner with him.

"C'mon. Your shift ended hours ago. Get your coat."

*See? There was no telling the man.*

"I'm not really hungry."

*That should shush him.*

"Keep me company, then?"

*Um… Waver, waver, waver.*

His voice was gentle. It was obvious he was trying to make her feel better and she was grateful to him for that. She tangled a couple of fingers into a loose twirl of hair just to up her maturity factor a notch.

"It's my last night in London. You can show me the sights!"

Harriet laughed. "I think I'd be about the worst tour guide ever."

"Why? This is your home, isn't it?" He spread his arms wide as if to encompass the whole of London.

"This is my home is more like it." Harriet indicated the ward.

"Well, then, you're all dressed up. It would be a shame not to go out and explore together—at least a little."

Harriet shot him a noncommittal look. She didn't *do* spontaneous! Didn't he get that? Then again… Another image of herself draped in cobwebs, an aged version of her "public speaking dress" layered with dust flitted past her mind's eye. Not particularly appealing…

"C'mon. I have a few more hours left. Shall we explore together?" He jigged his shoulders up and down in anticipation, then held out a hand. A lovely hand. All five fingers gave a little open-close gesture indicating she should take it. Her temperature went up a degree. Or seven.

He looked so…sweet! Like a young man arriving to pick up his first date. A few nerves, a bit of bravura.

He had come back *all this way* to find her. How had he known to—? Okay. Okay. She was predictable and it had taken him less than a day to work it out.

She felt a grin forming. It was the first time she'd seen him look…not vulnerable… Equal? On the same level.

That was it. Two colleagues. One night. And a handful of hours.

She didn't do spontaneous. She didn't do flirty. But Matteo was flying back to Argentina before she began her next shift. What could go wrong in just a few hours? Or…what could go right?

She pressed her nails into her palm as if it would give her more courage.

*Claudia would say yes.* She would've already been out the door.

"Why not?" Harriet grabbed her discarded pashmina from the back of her chair and twirled it round her shoulders à la Claudia. If her sister was brave enough to have twins on her own then she could surely manage having dinner with a man she'd never see again. It wasn't like she'd make a complete idiot out of herself. She'd already cracked that nut at the lecture hall.

She looked at her hand in his, felt a shiver of anticipation run up her arm then made herself give him a smile. *In for a penny…*


"Well, thanks for showing me what I won't be having."

Harriet tried to tack a fun, spirited laugh onto the end of her last bite of Argentinian steak but Matteo could see the words were forced.

"It's just a glimpse." He pointed his knife at the nearly empty plate. "This is passable. Not as good as at home but passable." Matteo took a final bite of his steak, speckled with the piquant chimichurri sauce. "But the *asado*?" He made a *mmm…yummy* sound and licked his lips. "The *asado* is to die for. You can come here and have *asado*. I give you permission to think it is just like home." He smiled, then clarified. "My home."

Harriet stared at him, her forehead crinkling in a growing picture of dismay.

"I can't believe I was so awful tonight!" She groaned, pushing her plate away and letting her head collapse into her hands. When she peeked through her fingers at Matteo she looked so adorable he had to resist reaching across and ruffling his fingers through her hair. And not in an aren't-you-a-cute-kid kind of way. She'd lost her nervy edge over the hours, replaced by excitement at their shared passion for the work they did. He could've talked to her all night long. He hadn't met someone who had kindled that sort of response in him in... *Dios*, was it *ever*? He felt something grow within him he hadn't felt in a while.

Regret.

Regret that he wouldn't have more time with her. There were so many dimensions to Harriet Monticello he had yet to discover and yet part of him felt he knew her already. A kindred spirit. He would've genuinely enjoyed taking his time getting to know her.

He leaned back in the booth seat and drummed his fingertips along the table's edge. "Maybe it's not all terrible. Look on the bright side. At least you got your message through to the person who counts most."

She raised her blue eyes a fraction above her fingers. "Yeah, that'd be about right. And who exactly do you think I impressed?"

"Me!" He reached across and stole a forkful of leftover chimichurri sauce. "Don't look at me like that! How often do you think I sit through four-hour dinners with uninteresting people? Particularly when I have a flight in..." he glanced at his watch "...about six hours from now."

"Uh...not very often?"

"*Sí, correcto.* In fact, I think it'd be a safe bet to say never." He looked her square in the eye. "Life's too short. Too precious to waste time not doing what you believe in."

Their eyes met for a moment and he felt a genuine hit of attraction for her. Not just the superficial one he'd enjoyed when they'd first met but a genuine tug of desire hitting him in the solar plexus. He looked away.

"I believe in what I said," Harriet answered miserably. "I just couldn't communicate it effectively."

"You've been pretty coherent the last few hours." He pressed his back into the booth seat and shifted his position. *Mind over matter.*

"That's different." She shook her head as if trying to get the facts straight.

"Why? Because you think you could show me a thing or two?"

"Yes." Her eyes popped wide open. "I mean no! Oh, blimey. Do you see what I mean? If there's a chance to stick my foot straight in it, I do it."

"Stick your foot in what?"

"It," Harriet answered. Then giggled. "Language barrier! Oh…let's see."

"Harriet." Matteo's voice went down a notch, latching onto droll. The English weren't the only ones with a dry sense of humor. "I knew what you were talking about, I was just trying to see if you knew why you found addressing a crowd so difficult."

"Oh. Right." Her lips twitched, her eyes solidly on the plate.

"*Cara*, you've missed my meaning. I think what you have to say is wonderful. I'd be lucky to have you come to Casita Verde, even if…"

"Even if what? I tanked it in front of the people who were going to let me go?"

"You would've come if they'd said yes?"

She drew a smiley face in the remains of her sauce before the weary waiter scooped up their plates. He grinned at her and she smiled back, apologizing for keeping him so late. That was who Harriet was. A woman who did countless little kindnesses, expecting nothing in return.

"I would like to think I would have. If I would've been of any use," she added quickly, popping her finger into her mouth where he could just see her tongue circling away, retrieving the remains of the sauce.

He shifted in his seat again and cleared his throat. Staying...*neutral* was becoming more difficult.

"I'm fairly certain you would have been nothing but an asset." And he meant it.

"Well, that's just grand, then, isn't it?" She gave him a sad smile before trying to scrub away the frustration. "Too bad the board is no doubt busily shredding my name into oblivion and looking for another suitable candidate." Harriet dropped her hands from her face and began to twist her serviette this way and that. "Hey! Maybe we could form a mutual admiration society across the seas!" She shimmied her serviette across the table to him, having folded it into the shape of a little swan, and grinned.

"It's a shame." Matteo picked up the bird and admired her handiwork. He was actually going to miss her, this woman he hardly knew. "I would've liked to work with you."

"Me, too." She raised her gaze from the table and met his eyes. "But I guess some people just aren't meant to stray from their path."

"What do you mean by that?"

"Oh, nothing really. It's just…" she reached across the table and took back the swan, untwisting it as she spoke "…sticking to what I know has always been a good idea."

She smiled up at him, something clouding the azure clarity of her eyes. Disappointment? Sorrow?

"And what would happen, exactly, if you did something new?" He bridled on her behalf. "Are you going to sit there and just let them decide your future for you?" As the words came out, he was surprised to hear the heat behind them. He actually wanted her to come to Casita Verde. See what he'd done. Offer a new perspective. Just a few hours with Harriet wasn't near enough. He wanted more.

"That's more my sister's terrain!" Harriet tried to laugh away his suggestion. "She's the real star in the family," she finished quietly. It sounded practiced. Something she was far too used to saying.

"And is that something you tell yourself or something someone else is telling you? If they are, they need their eyes and minds tested," Matteo protested.

"I'm not sure I follow."

"Well, let's see." He held up a finger for each point. "You're beautiful. Intelligent. You've turned the lives of countless children into something they can bear. Your sister must be pretty amazing to overshadow all that."

"She is," Harriet replied without hesitation, their eyes locking as she spoke. "She really is."

There was no jealousy in her words, just admiration. The same way he'd felt about his sister. Just love. No expectations.

"I'm getting hot." Harriet started fanning herself with the hem of her pashmina, her eyes suddenly keen to alight anywhere but on him. "Are you hot? I think maybe I could do with a walk."

Harriet shot out of her chair without a second glance at Matteo. Their conversation was getting a bit overwhelming. Out on the street she gulped in a lungful of cool air as if she'd been suffocating.

Maybe she had been. Not from Matteo. Not by a long shot. But from the things he was saying. The cages he was unwittingly rattling? He was rapidly unzipping the safe, cozy cocoon she'd built for herself and had been terribly happy in, thank you very much. Her sister needed her to be the stable one, the one who didn't change. That was her role. Wasn't it?

Then again…what exactly would happen if she took some chances of her own?

She blew out a slow breath, trying to regain some perspective. But all she could see was herself through Matteo's eyes: a woman too frightened to change.

"Harriet! *Chuchera!*" Matteo ran to catch up with her. "Are you all right?"

"Yes, fine." *No. Not even remotely.*

"Sorry, I was just paying the bill, and then you were—" He stopped, his hands taking ahold of her shoulders and turning her towards him. "Are you all right, *chuchera?*"

Harriet nodded dumbly. He was…divine. Exactly the type of man she'd never imagined being with and now he was hunting her down after failed speeches, paying supper bills she'd scarpered on and running after her to make sure she was all right?

*One ticket for Matteo the Dreamboat Ride, please!*

Her eyes widened. Not exactly a hostess with the mostest moment.

"You shouldn't have paid the bill!" She started digging in her handbag for her purse and felt his hand slip down her shoulder to her wrist, stopping her frantic movements. If there was such a thing as sexy lava it was pouring through her everywhere Matteo's fingers had touched and doing a swirly, pooling thing in her belly. She didn't dare look at him. She was superimposing far too much on him. It was easy to make someone into perfection when you only had eight hours together. Eight amazing hours. The knowledge that they would quickly come to an end all but brought a cry of despair to her throat. She curled her lips in past her teeth, dragging them back out, no doubt pale with the absence of blood in them. Feeling the sting of pain at what she'd never have.

"How do you fancy a walk along the river?" She used her best tour-guide voice. "It's really lovely at night. I'm sure you'll just love the Houses of Parliament!"

It wasn't much of a surprise to Matteo that their riverside walk was both bereft of conversation and came to an end at St. Nick's. Something had passed between them after dinner and Harriet hadn't looked him in the eye once since then.

He watched, smiling, as she peeked into each of the children's rooms, pulling up a bit of duvet here or there, tucking in a wayward teddy bear or two. It was obvious to see the place was Harriet's go-to comfort zone.

He couldn't really judge. He actually *lived* at the original Casita Verde. The fact that it had been a monastery in its former life appealed to him. Solidified his future. Not that his life was entirely monk-like…he saw women. Occasionally. Women who wanted nothing more than a fling—because he never promised more. The likelihood of a woman agreeing to live at Casita Verde and never have children of her own? Pretty slim. So monk's quarters suited him just fine.

"Now we have to be very, very quiet." Harriet held a slim finger to her lips as they made their way across the open common area. "This bit of flooring is super-creaky and I promised the other nurses I wouldn't come back."

"Why?" Matteo grinned down at her, all hunched shoulders and poised on tiptoe. "Are you the big bad boss?"

"The research nurse with no life is more like it." Harriet's mouth shot into an apologetic *oops* position. A perfect red moue.

This time he laid a finger on her lips. She had a life, she just didn't have confidence, and Harriet was a woman who should have confidence in herself.

In the instant their eyes met the atmosphere went taut with something he knew he didn't want to fight again. Something that had been fizzing and crackling away between them from the moment they'd met.

Beneath the pad of his finger he felt the accelerated rhythm of her pulse beating in sync with her heart. Her pupils were dilated in the dim light of the corridor, nearly eclipsing the luminous blue irises. Her breath was held so tightly in her chest he could feel the release against his own when she let finally let herself breathe again. She blinked a couple of times, lips still pressed to his finger. It took him a moment to appreciate she hadn't pulled back. She was responding to his touch.

Before he could stop himself he was kissing her with an urgency he hadn't thought himself capable of. His hands slid up and along her back, straight up the center of her spine, enjoying the feeling of her body responding to the movement of his hands as he did so. Holding her slender frame against his own felt entirely natural. And unbelievably satisfying.

He was surprised at the surge of desire eclipsing his ever-present pragmatism. After tonight, the chances they'd see each other again were slim to nil. More likely nil. But meeting Harriet, he was shocked to realize, had meant something to him. The fact he'd come to find her to see if she was all right after the speech, insisting they go to dinner, talking and walking for hours were absolutely out of the ordinary. He didn't hunt down complications. He never sought love. And now here he was, kissing her as if his life depended on it.

"We shouldn't be doing this."

Harriet's lips moved against his as he teased kiss after kiss out of her.

"Why not?"

"The children?"

"Are you asking me or telling me?" Matteo murmured as his thumb gently pressed and moved along her jawline, exposing the creamy expanse of neck he was itching to kiss and explore with his tongue.

A low gasp of pleasure vibrated along Harriet's throat as he nibbled and tasted his way towards the nook between her neck and the extra-sensitive spot just below her earlobe. When his teeth gave her earlobe a little tug, the resonance of her response deepened to a groan of unmistakable pleasure.

"Let's go to your office."

He felt her entire body tense then, as she made a swift decision, turn electric with intent.

It was all Harriet could do to stop herself from jumping up, wrapping her legs round Matteo's sexy waist and begging him to take her right there and then. She settled for exercising the most self-control she'd ever had to use for the thirty-second race-walk to her office.

This was a carpe diem moment if ever there was one. The chances of a man like Matteo igniting her intellect and her body coming around again? Non-existent to…ooooh, never again in her lifetime! Especially with months—years—of diapers, laundry, feedings and who knew what else that would consume her time once her sister arrived with the twins. She'd be back to being Harriet the Reliable. Tonight she wanted to be Harriet the Wild One. Harriet the Brave.

Kissing and touching and being held by a man who had made her believe in herself for a few ridiculously perfect hours? It was an emotional risk she was going to take.

Just once.

She owed herself that. To see what it felt like to *live*.

The door to her office had barely clicked shut before Matteo had her pressed up against the wall, the fingers of one hand teasing along the décolletage of her wraparound dress. Her breasts were instinctively pressing up against the suggestion of a touch, practically begging him to caress them as his other hand held both of hers above her head in a surprisingly sexy clinch. Fully clothed, aching for more and wholly aware of the growing urgency of desire between them had her feeling saucy and emboldened.

She had never, not once, ever, in her deeply practical life had naughty sex. And right now it was all she wanted. If there had been a pair of pink feathery cuffs in her desk drawer she would be pleading with him to use them. She wished she'd worn her sexy-girl boots her sister had given her, but she'd never felt scrumptious enough to dare. Until now. Matteo was bringing her body alive in a way she hadn't dreamed possible.

"Are you sure you want to do this?" She was surprised at the husky sound of her voice. *Where had that come from?*

"Shouldn't I be asking you that?" Matteo replied smoothly with a tropically heated wink.

*How did he even do that?*

The look that passed between them as he lazily traced a finger across her collarbones said they both knew what was happening here. They were two consenting adults who would never see each other again. After tonight they could go back to being strangers who occasionally saw one another's names in medical journals.

Would it have been amazing to go to Argentina and dazzle him with her research? Absolutely. Would she trade that for the kisses and touches bringing her body to heightened levels of response? Not that she really had a choice in the matter, but, *Oh, yes*! Again and again and again.

Unexpectedly, Matteo's hand slipped beneath the fabric of her dress and cupped her breast. Harriet had to stop herself from crying out as he swept the fabric aside, unclipped the front clasp of her bra and took her breast in his mouth. Her nails dug into his hand, still holding hers tight against the wall. The last thing she felt like was a captor. She wanted to be taken. She wanted to be his.

Her breath quickened as his tongue took its lazy time exploring first one breast, then the other, her nipples instantly peaking at each touch of his tongue. If her hands had been freed she would have dragged him up to receive countless hungry, insatiable kisses. Held against the wall, she understood, for the first time, the luxury of only being able to respond, reveling in the generosity of the layers of pleasure he was unwrapping within her.

Matteo's free hand shifted away the fabric belt and then the skirt section of her dress, his fingers moving along her stomach, her hipbone, her— *Oh!* His mouth covered hers the instant her cry of response became a moan of sheer, undiluted longing. His fingers slipped and slid, explored and discovered, as her brain short-circuited with need. All her body could do was respond to his touch. She flicked off her heels and went on tiptoe as her legs parted to receive the strokes and cupping of his hand, the shift of fingers, until she couldn't bear it any longer and was forced to give in to heated wave after wave of release.

"Please," she whispered. "I want you."

"Are you sure you want to do this?"

A twist of panic caught up with her longing. Protection. Her nurse's brain kicked into turbo gear. She'd given a few classes on safe sex to the older residents. Did she have anything in her office? She definitely didn't in her handbag. Had never even *presumed* to have something in her handbag.

"I'm not sure I have protection."

"We have to use something." Matteo's voice was thick with emotion. "Practice what we preach."

"Of course. Absolutely!" A nervous giggle leapt past her lips. "The voice of reason speaks!" She was grateful to see a smile playing upon his lips as well. Wouldn't that be rich? A nurse working with orphans getting pregnant from unprotected sex with a man she would most likely never see again. The tabloids would love a naughty nurse scandal. For about thirty seconds. And then she'd have to deal with everything on her own. Just like her sister—

*Stop!*

She had to stop thinking. Thinking too much was what had made her The Sensible One. The one who didn't take risks.

Tonight? She wanted to be the one who finally, at long last, came out of her cocoon. *Sensibility be damned*!

At least for tonight.

She wiggled out of his hold, her dress shifting along her sides, the cool evening air sending a tickle of goose pimples across her belly. Unbelievably she didn't feel like a class-A idiot.

She felt sexy.

All barefoot and tiptoeing across her office to scrabble in the back reaches of her desk for a condom? This was better than a soap opera! She pulled the wide, central desk drawer open. The one with the dull-from-use pencils, the pen caps without an owner, the mishmash of medical brochures she'd not read yet, or might not ever have a chance to read.

As she stretched and reached into the farther reaches of the drawer she felt Matteo's hands glide over her hips and across her buttocks. Her body swayed along with the exploratory cadence his hands made along her body, bringing out a great desire *to find the blinkin' protection* as soon as humanly possible. Urgency overtook the need to be tidy. Office supplies were flying out of her hands any which way. *Where were the condoms?*

The more intimately Matteo's hands explored, the faster she expelled items from the drawer until, after what felt like forever, she felt a foil-lined packet with a familiar shape. She grabbed it triumphantly and turned around, holding it between them like a trophy.

Matteo tugged his fingers through the twisted tendrils of her hair, the pins plinking to the floor as he pressed himself against Harriet's body. The red-blooded Latin side of him surged to the fore. He wouldn't be able to leave without having her. Feeling her skin against his as she responded to his caresses forced a decision.

*"Me quiero que seas mío."* His voice was gruff with desire. He wanted her and he wanted her to know how much.

Harriet pressed herself against his erection, her teeth taking hold of one of the buttons of his shirt in an untethered, primal attempt to get closer. He almost laughed at the wonderfulness of it. Had he seen the tigress in her when they'd first met? The kitten maybe. Now she was ready to roar.

He ripped his shirt up and over his head. Another two seconds and Matteo had dispensed with both of their sets of clothes. He turned Harriet round to face the wall, hands shifting along the shivers that accompanied his touch. He was moved by her response to him. Again it struck him how real, how true a person she was. Harriet could only be herself. A part of him regretted that they would never know each other beyond this night. The thought doubled the intensity of his desire. He wanted to know he could tap the part of his mind busy memorizing the feel of her skin, her scent, her gasps and soft cries of pleasure at his touch. He'd take his time, give them each plenty to remember.

Restraint was harder to exercise in practice. The tigress was well and truly alive in Harriet. Having already brought her to one peak of desire, Matteo was soon clear she had more than enough energy to burn. As he pressed against her, luxuriously enjoying the sensation of her bum shifting and wiggling against his erection, she trapped two of his fingers in her mouth and began to suck them in an achingly slow foreshadowing of what he would be feeling when he was finally inside her.

Wicked thoughts of Harriet in a nun's habit flashed past his mind's eye, sending long pulses of heat straight through to his very marrow. If she'd been all prim-and-proper nursey this morning, she was anything but to-night.

He whipped her round to face him, cupped her buttocks and pulled her up until her legs encircled his waist. When he went to kiss her, he saw she held the wrapped condom between her teeth, eyes glinting with anticipation. One swift move and he cleared her desk of the debris she'd covered it in. Being tidy was the last thing on his mind.

From the luxuriously slow cadence with which Harriet was unwrapping the packet, Matteo could see she was savoring each moment they had together. Yes, it was to be a one-off—but, by God, it would be memorable.

She touched and tasted the length of his erection, before beginning the excruciatingly sexy act of sheathing him. He marveled that he'd ever thought her shy at all. Now wearing only a single strand of necklace gently weighted with a tiny locket, Harriet Monticello was a first-class seductress.

Unable to hold back any longer, Matteo lifted her in his arms, slowly lowering her until they were together, exchanging heat, sharing a heartbeat. He backed her against the wall, moving slowly at first then swiftly, deeply, until his only option was to join her in an intense, full-bodied release. He felt her teeth dig into his shoulder, her breasts pressed into his chest as he came inside her again and again. When their breathing had steadied, he stayed inside her, unwilling to break the spell. Once they said goodbye, he would never see her again.

Just thinking it hurt. Going through it would hurt more. But he didn't do relationships. And he didn't do love. All it led to was heartbreak.

Work. It was the only way he was ever going to heal the hole his sister's death had left in his soul. The only way he could try to make things right.

He tipped his head back, enjoying the sensation of Harriet's fingers tracing the muscles of his back, his sides. She asked for nothing. She seemed to be completely at one with the intimacy they had just shared and he found himself fighting the feeling of completion it elicited in his heart.

How could he do it? Expose himself to the pain loving someone inevitably brought? He tugged her a bit more tightly into his chest and enjoyed her body's response. A little shimmy and nestling into the angle of his neck and shoulder as he lowered them both to the floor, her legs still wrapped tightly round his waist as if she would never let him go. Perhaps she was coming to terms with saying goodbye as well.

He closed his eyes and breathed Harriet in, painfully aware he was in danger of losing the battle of wills with himself. If anyone was able to handle the extremes of his life, he believed it would be Harriet. The incredible highs. The lows haunting him to this day.

Would she understand that was who he was? Both light and shade? Someone very likely in need of a good woman to help ground him? Someone at risk of drowning in his own vain efforts to make his sister's death be of some value? Someone who would never bring another child into this world?

No. She deserved more. She deserved everything her heart desired and, blinkered as he was, he couldn't see a way to give her a world of happiness.

*"Amorcito."* Matteo gently unlocked her feet, still twisted at the base of his spine, and slowly began the inevitable separation, finishing with a soft kiss on her forehead so he could avoid the questions in her eyes. "I must go."

## CHAPTER FOUR

"HARRIET!"

*Thunk.*

"Oops! Are you all right there? I didn't mean to make you bang your head."

Harriet reversed out from beneath her desk. Funny the things that had turned up there this morning.

"Are you all right?"

Dr. Bailey's voice was a bit too bright for first thing in the morning. She looked up at him and attempted a smile.

"You're looking well!"

Check that. *Far* too bright.

Harriet wasn't nursing a hangover—she'd steered clear of drowning her sorrows. What she was nursing? Something much more debilitating. A what? A sex-over? It wasn't like she was used to having wanton sex in her office. Or, more accurately, it wasn't like she was used to having wanton sex, full stop.

Or was everything she was feeling post Matteo's abrupt departure a twenty-four-hour version of a broken heart? When he'd left, it had felt as if her personal wattage had been lowered to dim. She hadn't even bothered going home. A sneaky shower in the surgical ward, a pair of scrubs and one of the sofas had seen her through until dawn. Opening her eyes to a new day hadn't been the rose-colored wonder she'd been banking on.

It had felt, for the first time since her sister had left years ago, lonely.

She had been missing something. No, that wasn't it. She'd been missing *someone*.

She looked beyond Dr. Bailey's feet, a bit surprised to see the stapler had been flung to the opposite side of her office—but at this stage in the game anything could have been anywhere. Last night had been… Last night had been just about the most scrumptious, unreal thing she thought she'd ever lived through.

"Bit late for a spring clean, isn't it, Harriet?"

"What? Sorry?" Harriet scrambled up from the floor, her mind shifting into work mode after a decidedly X-rated journey elsewhere. "Sorry, Dr. Bailey?"

"I said it's a bit late for a spring clean."

She looked at him blankly.

"It being July and all."

"Ah. Yes!" She put on her bright, efficient voice, realizing her office was still looking a bit more post-cyclone than uber-organized. Her normal mode. As if she had a normal any more now that she'd had such a wickedly wonderful night with… *Matteo*. She couldn't even think his name without her belly launching into a heated pole dance.

"Well, it's a good thing you're setting your office to rights as your replacement will be needing everything clearly laid out."

If eyes could actually boing out of their sockets Harriet was certain hers would've chosen this moment to do so. Was she being fired?

"I beg your pardon?" *There weren't cameras in the offices, were there?*

"You'll be off soon."

"Off?" She felt as dumb as she was certain she sounded. A spinster and jobless? She should've stayed under the desk.

"Yes. To Buenos Aires."

Her breath caught in her throat. *Wow. Tongues really did go dry when shocking news was received.*

"Do you fancy a cup of tea?" she croaked.

"Don't you mean yerba mate?" Dr. Bailey chortled. "You'll be wanting to hone your Spanish skills, my dear." Dr. Bailey gave her a warm smile before nodding towards her wall calendar. "The board would like you to head out to Buenos Aires to work at Casita Verde in a fortnight or so—at end of the month at the latest. Time enough for a handover and a quick Spanish course."

"But I was terrible!"

"Well…" Dr. Bailey coughed away some embarrassment. "I did hear things might have gone a bit better. But we received an email this morning from Dr. Torres saying the two of you had had an in-depth talk afterwards and his impressions were all very favorable."

*Too right!*

Harriet made a nondescript noise, hoping it said, *Yes— we spoke academically all night long. Nothing naked happened here. No nakedness at all.*

"It's your work, not your public speaking the board is really interested in. So—if you're up for a risk, a bit of excitement, you're heading to new climes."

"Great!" she said in her fake happy voice, taking a slurp of day-old tea that had survived the night's cyclonic lovemaking.

"You did get along with Dr. Torres, didn't you, Harriet?"

"I'm sorry?" Harriet all but spat out her tea before realizing he'd not said "get it on." *Ooh, subconscious! Quit your trickery!*

"So you wouldn't mind working with him?"

It was, of course, in that moment that Harriet eagle-eyed one of Matteo's socks, which was hanging from the filing-cabinet drawer. She sidled over to block it and put on her best casually delighted face.

"No! Absolutely not. Fine. Just fine."

"Well, that's just fantastic! I was hoping you'd be pleased. The two of you have so much in common."

*Like the smokin' hot passion we gave in to all because we thought we'd never see each other ever again!*

"Now, Harriet. Don't look so worried. We'll look after everyone and everything here as if you were doing it yourself."

Harriet was feeling the foundations of who she believed herself to be crumbling away. When her parents had died and her sister had left town, St. Nick's had filled her need to be needed, and now Dr. Bailey was saying everything would run smoothly without her? Oh, no, no, no! Wait. The twins! Her sister was coming back. She couldn't go. No. She wouldn't leave.

"What about my sister? She needs me!"

"When is she coming?"

Honesty forced an answer. "Ten…maybe twelve weeks from now? But I have to change so much in the house. Child-proofing…washing sheets…" Even she knew she was waffling now.

Dr. Bailey slung a fatherly arm across her shoulders as she snatched Matteo's sock from her filing cabinet and stuffed it in her pocket. "Plenty of time to go to Buenos

Aires and come back again. We'll miss you, of course—but change does a person the world of good sometimes."

"I can't wait!" she squeaked through a frozen smile. Nothing like a bit of change.

Harriet was feeling an awful lot like Maria von Trapp.

Casita Verde's flagship center was big. Grand, actually. And here she was, standing outside, suitcase in hand, with an endless stream of questions yet to be answered and absolutely no ability to play the guitar or make dresses out of drapery. So perhaps a bit less like Maria von Trapp than she'd originally thought.

At this juncture? She was willing to try… Or to run after the taxi driver and beg him to take her back to the airport.

She tilted her head back and looked up. She wasn't quite sure what she'd expected, but an enormous stone edifice with beautiful tile mosaics of trees, flowers and other happy-making shapes hadn't exactly been what had popped into her mind. The huge front door was a deep green. Like Matteo's eyes.

Her stomach churned.

If she'd had any confidence in her singing she might've burst into some sort of plucky song in a vain attempt to give herself courage or confidence or whatever it was she needed in order to reach out and press the brass buzzer.

*Why, why why had she agreed to this?*

She was supposed to be at home, finishing up baby-proofing the house for her sister. Only six tiny little weeks to go before she would officially be an aunt, and she was here in the land of tango and voracious carnivores? And Matteo.

She gave herself a little shake.

She'd be home in four weeks so she would still have time for the finishing touches but... She took in a deep breath. *How does* air *smell different?* She shook her head in disbelief. Being here was something she'd never, ever in a million squillion years imagined herself doing.

Then again, quite a few things had been falling into that category lately. Having naughty sex in her office with just about the most amazing man she'd ever met was pretty close to topping the charts at this juncture. Her body responded with a shivery reminder of just how nice it had been. Not that she'd heard so much as a whisper from Matteo since he'd disappeared That Night. *What a confidence builder!*

Not that she'd expected daily contact. They'd made no promises to one another and certainly she'd never expected to see him again. It was probably one of the reasons she'd been so brazen That Night. Who was fooling who here? It was all the brazen she had! And using it all up in one go when she wouldn't need it anymore? Not the sharpest of moves.

When she'd received Matteo's invitation, via Dr. Bailey, to work at Casita Verde, it had been as if all the oxygen had been sucked out of her body and replaced with helium. She hadn't even been able to answer. She had just nodded. A lot. Matteo wanted to see her again.

And then...nothing.

Unless you counted a politely worded informational PDF sent via "Administrator" with no personal add-ons other than a reminder that it was winter in Buenos Aires so she'd best pack a warm coat and summer clothes as the weather was variable. She'd harrumphed at the computer.

At least "Administrator" had cared if she got frostbite.

And she'd said as much to the non-English-speaking taxi driver on her way into Buenos Aires after thanking the heavens she'd printed out the address of Casita Verde in large print on a huge piece of paper. Preparedness was key when you had no idea what was coming. Two weeks of intensive Spanish classes weren't all they were cracked up to be.

"I doubt he even knows I'm arriving today." Harriet had begun, her voice not particularly audible above the blare of a tango song filling the cab. At least it had made talking to herself less embarrassing.

"Dr. Bailey probably made the entire thing up to see if I was brave enough to leave St. Nick's for the first time in, well, forever. It was almost like he didn't want me there! He practically booted me out the door!" She'd given her best astonished face in the direction of the rear-view mirror and continued, the taxi driver taking no notice of her whatsoever.

"I mean, honestly! I really needed at least—*at least*—a month, maybe two, to hand over everything to the staff nurses, and what did he give me?" She'd looked into the rearview mirror again, half expecting to see an eyebrow lifting with curiosity.

Nothing.

The driver had been too engrossed in his radio singalong. *Typical.* Sign number two she shouldn't have boarded the plane. Not beyond passport control more than half an hour and already she was invisible.

She carried on.

"Three weeks! Can you believe it? Three weeks to hand over a decade's worth of diligence. Or…well…a lot of years. And diligence. And having no life, even though that part might be my fault. But seriously? What does he think I am? A pair of castanets on overdrive?" She gave the rearview mirror another indignant look. She was on a roll now.

The car lurched and Harriet's hands flew to her stomach. She'd been sick on the plane and had put it down to nerves—but as the car zigzagged through the thick morning traffic she was beginning to wonder if she didn't suffer a bit from motion sickness. She blew her breath into her hand and sniffed. Thank goodness for that little toothbrush and toothpaste they give you on the plane. The driver unleashed a flurry of what she expected were ruby-colored unpleasantries as a lorry all but took the front of the taxi off. *Sign number three?*

"You want to take a guess at what Dr. Bailey said when I protested?" Harriet didn't bother pausing. This was obviously a soliloquy and she was going to make the most of it.

"Go on! Get out of here and go buy yourself something *Argentinian* to wear! Whatever that might be. It's not like the streets of London are flooded with…with whatever Argentinians wear."

Her voice petered out with her confidence so she pressed her nose against the window finally taking in all the sights and sounds she hadn't even begun to imagine. Including floods of sleek-looking ebony-haired Argentinian women looking all sexy and chic while she just felt rumpled and jet-lagged.

A sting of tears threatened as the newness of it all hit her.

When Dr. Bailey had all but shooed her out of the office she hadn't known whether to laugh or cry. He'd practically chased her out of the ward as if she'd been a bad smell. So what if she was a homebody? Or, more accurately, a St. Nick's body. She loved it there. It was her life! And, from the looks of things, her "all" hadn't been enough for her boss and mentor.

"There's more to life than St. Nick's has to offer!"

Those were Dr. Bailey's words that had felt the stabbiest. Akin to betrayal.

When her parents had died ten years ago she'd shifted from useful daughter to useful sister. Claudia had taken their parents' death as a cue to grab life voraciously by the collar and shake as much fun, passion, and drama out of it as she could. "If I go down? I want to be in a plane flying across the savannah of Africa, too! I am going to go down sucking the very marrow out of life!"

In fact, when she'd rung Claudia to tell her about her ignominious booting out, her twin had all but offered to trade places. Her voice had lowered and gone all *are-you-freakin'-kidding-me?* on her. "A month with a sexy Latin doctor in Buenos Aires? You'd be mad not to go!"

"But what about the house? About my job? About your twins?"

"What about them?" Claudia had asked, as if jumping on the plane was a done deal. "I'm not due for weeks yet and won't be flying with them straight out of the womb. Chill!"

Too much California or just plain nutter?

Then again, what else was it her sister had said? She ran a finger over the door's buzzer as if it were a magic eight ball. "Finally!" Her sister's voice reverberated through her memory. "Acting from your heart and not that overactive head of yours!"

Little tingles of delight shimmied through her tummy as if to back up her sister's words. It was true that when she'd been with Matteo it had felt incredibly...liberating.

Tears swooped into her eyes as she stared at the brass doorbell some more.

*No-o-o-o!*

This was not how she wanted Matteo to see her. It would be, she imagined, exactly the scenario he had anticipated. Why he'd put "Administrator" in charge of her welcome. She was a nerdy, change-resistant, too-fragile-to-take-it-on-the-chin research nurse.

She turned away from the epically huge wooden door and shook her head, willing the emotions squeezing at her chest, her throat, her eyes to leave her be. Give her a moment's respite to be brave. She stamped her feet and gave her shoulders a shake.

*C'mon, Harriet.* Channel your sister if you have to, but you did not just spend twenty hours having a four-year-old kick the back of your seat only to go running back home with your tail between your legs. It is time for you to stand on your own two feet!

*"¡Cuidado!"*

Harriet's head whipped to the left just in time to see a swarm of children careening towards her at high speed. Her Spanish might not be up to much but she was pretty sure she was being told to get out of the way—and fast.

She took a step back and immediately regretted it. Her foot hit a slick of wet leaves with no intention of staying stationary. Her arms windmilled to gain balance as her knees buckled against the bulk of her suitcase. As she somersaulted over the back of it she felt a microsecond's regret she hadn't brought the one with wheels.

"Whoa!"

Harriet's battle with gravity was being lost in a slow-motion collapse towards the pavement. Her hands hit the ground with a skidding jolt. She was already feeling the abrasion's initial burn as one of her knees took a hit of gravel. Looked like her "good impression skirt" had been a bad idea, then.

There would be a need for tweezers in her immediate future.

What she hadn't expected was such an apocalyptically klutzy landing that she'd received a face full of dirt, more gravel and— Oh… Actually, those were some very nice tiles. What a beautiful blue!

Her eyes remained focused on the ground, but she could hear the children circle her, speaking in rapid-fire Spanish. Her brain was too addled by the fall to make much sense of what they were saying. After a moment's assessment that, no, she hadn't broken anything, she took a slow breath, regrouped and turned herself round to face her spectators.

Standing above her, backlit by a clear blue sky, was none other than… Matteo Torres.

"Harriet! I see you've met the children."

Who made him behave like a bemused Captain Von Trapp? *Had someone sent a memo?*

She pulled her hand away from her face. Could she really feel any more like an idiot?

Well.

She could be naked.

She yanked at the hem of her skirt to make sure she wasn't doing a fresh pair of underwear display to boot.

Her tummy did its own special gymnastics routine. The sexy kind. Who knew her insides were capable of feeling *torrid*? The fuzz of memory shifted into a connection between her eyes and brain. Matteo was offering her a hand up. He did not look amused.

*Awkward!*

"Thank you. *Gracias*," she mumbled, reaching out her scraped hand with not a little mortification.

"Good to see you have such a command of our native tongue."

Matteo's face was unreadable but she would've put money on his tone: Smug.

"*Bueno verte tambien*, Dr. Torres." Harriet tugged her hand out of his with a sniff.

She hadn't spent the entire flight watching the Spanish language films without subtitles for nothing. *Y Tu Mama Tambien* that!

She wiped her hand uselessly along her filthy skirt. Jaunty riposte or no, she got the message. Matteo didn't want her here.

Without a second glance at her, she watched as he briskly began dispensing children hither and yon. Some through the big green door, some down around the corner and a couple of youngsters who were… Oh! Picking up her suitcase and her carry-on bags, lugging them through the stone portico into…

*Oh*… The most beautiful courtyard she thought she'd ever seen in her life. It was…bewitching.

A fire lit in her chest. If she'd not left home, she never would have seen this magical place.

Red terracotta tiles bedecked a covered walkway encircling a large—huge!—central green, dotted here and there with what she guessed were fruit trees, each ringed with gorgeous mosaics made from a mishmash of broken ceramics.

Had the *children* done those? Amazing.

In fact, now that she'd given herself a few moments to take it all in, the entire courtyard was bedecked by one art project after the other. Tables and benches made of reclaimed wood. Were those old pallets made into a tree swing? Genius! Broken bits of mirror, pottery and pebbles bedecked the columns holding up a second-story walkway. It was brilliant. If this place was anything like St. Nick's, there were breakages aplenty. And to turn them into art? Inspired.

A little shiver worked its way along her spine despite the mild winter weather. What did they call the summery winter? *El veranito de San Juan?* The guidebook had warned of it and she'd scrambled to take off her sensible tights on the plane. She chanced a glance at her grubby legs. Who knew she'd need kneepads at the ripe age of twenty-nine?

Hiding her grimace, she continued to soak in the details of the courtyard. It wasn't opulent—wonderfully comforting was more like it. Exactly what she would have done in England if it were more like…right here. Green wooden doors nestled within the walkway, signs on the outside of each door delineating bedrooms, offices and—

"Like what you see?"

Matteo materialized in front of her. Uh. Why, yes, she did, thank you very much, indeed.

The fact she could only nod was probably a giveaway on that front. His dark hair, still a rumpled, silky swatch of perfection, was all but begging to be touched. So close she could see there were shadows beneath those green eyes of his. Her fingers itched to reach out and stroke his cheeks, feel the scratch of his five o'clock shadow making an appearance too early in the day. He turned to face the courtyard, reminding her she was meant to be commenting on the casita.

"Beautiful." That was all she managed.

"I think you might want to come with me." She felt Matteo's hand press against the small of her back, steering her towards a nearby door with a large red cross on the front of it. She fought the urge to crane her neck and see what his face was doing. Confirm he was as grumpy as he sounded.

Her back gave a little quiver as his fingers shifted a bit closer to her bum when she stepped up into the doorway. Talk about *verboten*! She'd have to have a talk with her body about that. Sexy, sexy, naughty nursey couldn't undo her hairpins here. In fact…sexy, sexy, naughty nursey was someone she thought she'd never see again. Curious. She just managed to catch sight of the door sign before she entered.

*Enfermería.*

The clinic.

*Perfecto!* Just the reunion she'd been hoping for! Scraped knees and a stone-faced Matteo in a clinic… about seven thousand miles from anything and everything that was familiar to her. Except medicine. Her tried and true friend.

"You want me to start right away?" she asked hopefully, pushing open the door and scanning the room. *Nice.* Simple, but nice. She was a bit tired, but if popping her into the clinic to keep her out of harm's way was how things were going to be, then she was ready to roll up her sleeves.

"No, you silly goose." Matteo's voice deepened, hinting at the warmth she knew it was capable of. Harriet spied the odd pair of dark eyes darting in and out of the doorway with an accompanying giggle. Children were just as curious here as they were at home. Matteo gave her a self-effacing smirk as he spread out a clean swatch of paper on the exam table. When he moved to ease her up onto the table via a children's footstool—how helpless did he think she was?—his scent flooded her nostrils anew. "I thought we'd see to your cuts and scrapes before you met the boss. He's very strict about welfare. And hygiene."

*Why did he have to smell so nice?*

"He doesn't seem all that welcoming either," Harriet chanced, presuming they were discussing Matteo in the third person. Which was weird. *He was being weird!* She might be klutzy, but this version of Matteo was not the relaxed, passionate man she'd met less than a month ago. Had it all been an act for funding? The thought didn't sit right. She knew she didn't excel at a lot of things but was certain about her skills at judging a man's character.

She narrowed her eyes and squinted at him. He was busily opening a cabinet and gathering an arsenal of bandages and cleaning agents. "What are you doing? It's only a scraped hand and a knee full of gravel!"

"I'm trying to be civil."

"Civil?" She couldn't help bridling. "How about friendly? Maybe *friendly* would be a nice way to treat someone who's just flown halfway around the world to lend a hand?"

Matteo said nothing. Harriet felt a bit shell-shocked herself. She never spoke out like this. She was mousy, quiet Harriet, not a lippy demander of pleasantries.

"I'm trying to…" he began, then stopped.

"Trying to what?" She was going to go with this demanding-answers vibe that had bubbled up from somewhere she'd never tapped before. It felt good to speak so openly. So freely. "Why not issue me with a whistle and a set of guidelines and just be done with it? Then you can get on with your life and I can get on with mine."

Matteo pressed his hands into the counter where he'd been laying out anesthetic wipes alongside some tweezers and froze.

So she'd hit the nail on the head. *Terrific!* She'd finally taken a chance—an absolutely bonkers chance that, admittedly, she'd actually been kind of forced to take, but never mind that—and had flown all this way to discover Matteo didn't even want her here. Absolutely brilliant.

She swiped at the tears falling from her eyes. Her feisty say-it-out-loud self was taking a nosedive back into Insecurityville. A fleeting case of false bravura. Nothing more.

She tilted her head up to heaven, grateful Matteo wasn't looking at her. Thankfully, it also helped stem the onset of tears. Every cloud had its silver lining. Right?

"I invited you in a spur-of-the-moment decision." Matteo's eyes were still glued to the counter. He was making a right and utter hash of this. This wasn't how he'd wanted to greet Harriet. Not by a long shot. Hell. Who was he kidding? Fifty percent of him had been hoping she wouldn't come. The other fifty percent?

He turned to face her. *Might as well know the truth.*

*Sí.* Still sucker-punched by her beauty. By the impact she'd had on him in such a short time. Even if she did have dirt smeared all over her face and grimy hands and knees, like one of the children. Unexpectedly, he started laughing.

"What?" Harriet's purse-lipped response preceded an erratic once-over of her injuries before she hobbled from the table to examine herself in the mirror.

"Why didn't you tell me?" She rounded on him.

Matteo was fully laughing now.

"What? That you look like one of the children who scavenge for garbage?"

"Yes!"

She was irate now—hands on hips, blue eyes wide, open demanding an explanation—and for some reason it fueled his laughter even more.

"Because, *amorcito*…" he stuffed a fist in front of his mouth, trying to fake-cough away his laughter "…you look like an angelic urchin with your blue eyes and blonde hair. The children will think you are from heaven."

His voice trailed off, leaving a silence humming with expectation. It would've been so easy to pull her into his arms. Cup her face in his hands and kiss her sweet rosebud of a mouth. Laughing children and the buzz of activity could be heard out in the courtyard as they stood there, eyes connected to each other's as if they could stay that way forever. But that's not how things worked here. How he worked. Even so…another moment wouldn't hurt.

Slowly, but very surely, he saw the puff of indignation in her deflate. A smile started to tease at her lips, gradually climbing into her eyes. Unexpectedly, she too began to laugh.

"It looks like I'll have a shiner by the end of the day. Whatever day it is. Is it Sunday or Monday?"

"It's Monday, *chuchura*. You must be exhausted. Come here." He patted the exam table. "Up you get."

He might have been using the same words he would with one of the children, but when she slipped up onto the table, and he pulled his wheelie stool over so that he was in prime position to pluck the grit out of her knee, image after image of their night in her office flooded his mind, making it virtually impossible to focus.

"Scraped knees aren't contagious, you know."

"I know. I am just thinking of the best approach."

"For a scraped knee?" Harriet wasn't convinced by his peculiar expression. "Do you want me to do it? Give me the tweezers."

"No! Not unless you want to do it. I've got things to do."

*What was he doing? Playing medical table tennis?*

"If I'm keeping you from something…" Her defenses flew up at the increasing level of testiness in his voice.

"No! No." He forced himself to level his tone. "You're good. I'm good. We're all good."

Harriet tipped her chin to the side and shot him a dubious look.

"Somehow I don't quite believe you."

What could he say to that? She was absolutely right. The fact that she was here had upended everything. And it wasn't exactly as if he could say that, could he? He'd been the one to invite her here and now he was giving her the cold shoulder?

He was going to have to face facts. Having Harriet here would challenge everything he'd set so solidly in stone after his sister had died. And he didn't want things challenged. Wasn't ready for change. And yet…it had been his invitation that had brought her here.

He barked out a hollow laugh into the tiled room. What was it his mother always said? If you ask, then you shall receive?

"Harriet, I—I need you to know I don't normally

have…" He opened his eyes a bit wider as if it was some sort of magical code for one-night stands.

"What? And you think I do?"

*Apparently it was.*

"No—not at all." He didn't. Not in the slightest. What had happened between them had been special. Singular. He knew it in his very core. He hoped she knew it. But saying as much could mean opening the doors to further possibility and that's not how he worked. How life worked.

"Because if that's what you think of me, then you can just think yourself right out of that thought." She gave him a prim nod and pressed her hands against the exam table as if to dismount then stopped herself, as he was directly blocking her exit route. "You know what?" She started over with a brusque shake of her head, blonde hair forming a halo round her face. "Don't worry. You don't have to say it."

"You don't even know—"

She held up a hand to stop him. "Yes, I do. I might not get the wording exactly right, but you want what happened between us to be…what *happened* between us. *Niente. Nada. Nul.* No more. I know. I get it."

She had more courage than he did. Saying out loud the words that coming from him would sound so…so arrogant! Dismissive, even.

A twist of self-loathing shot through him. She didn't deserve this.

"I can't offer you what you want."

"How do you even know what I want?"

Her expression was defiant. Defensively so. Had he meant something to her in so short a time? Stupid question. She wasn't someone who had casual sex. Neither was he. And she meant something to him. That's why he was doing this. Setting boundaries. To keep both of their lives in order.

*At least that's what he would keep telling himself.*

He clapped his hands in a let's-get-going way and took up the pair of tweezers. "Shall we get you cleaned up so you can meet the children?"

"Absolutely." He watched as she forced on a bright smile. "The children are why I'm here. Aren't they, Dr. Torres?"

# CHAPTER FIVE

HARRIET STABBED THE long number into her mobile, knowing her phone bill would be about a trillion pounds when she got home, but she didn't care. She needed a dose of Claudia. Strong-willed, deeply passionate, problem-conquering Claudia. She gave her freshly bandaged knee a rub. Staring at Matteo as he had plucked the bits of gravel out of her as if she were a rascally five-year-old had been a test. The first of many, she imagined.

As the click and whir of the number began to go through, she suddenly noticed the time. It was still morning in Buenos Aires and Argentina was well ahead of Los Angeles. Being overtired wasn't something she wanted to add to Claudia's list of pregnancy woes. She probably already had fatigue mastered without an insecure sister unleashing a stream of worries on her. No. Check that. Harriet wasn't insecure—she was just overwhelmed with "new."

"New" was Claudia's specialty. Same old, same old was Harriet's. They balanced one another. The yin to the other's yang. Or whichever way round that was meant to work. Claudia would be the exciting-as-they-come mother and she'd be the reliable auntie.

A shot of excitement at her impending auntie-hood

brought a smile to her lips as she pressed the hang-up symbol. Six weeks, two days and a handful of hours from now she would be Auntie to two little boys! Who would, no doubt, be gorgeous, like their mother.

Their mother, who was in stupid Los Angeles, not helping her out of this stupid mess with Mr. Stupid right here in the heart of Stupidville.

Not that she was a grown woman or anything who could sort out her own problems. Right?

A little moan of self-pity escaped her lips as she leant back on the wooden bench she'd found tucked away in this far corner of the courtyard. She traced a finger along a thick plank. It, like most of the furniture she'd seen, looked solid. Well crafted. Beautiful.

One of Matteo's resources?

No doubt. She imagined he had fingers in all sorts of fruitful pies.

An image of him lifting a forkful of glossy cherry pie in her direction sped across her brain.

That wasn't going to get her anywhere, was it?

She tried to cut the image into bits with each lazy swing of the overhead fan. Chop. Chop. Chop.

Not working! Picturing an imaginary Matteo being obliterated by the world's slowest ceiling fan was not a problem solver.

Frustration began to nibble away at her already frayed nerve endings. Why did Matteo have to be so…so…? So… *Matteo*?

She was going to have to regroup. Block That Night from her mind. It, after all, wasn't the reason she'd leapt onto a plane as if it were the beginning of a magical rainbow-laced journey.

The reason she'd come was because of Casita Verde's

children and the good that would come of a new clinic. Nothing to do with the dark-haired, golden-tanned, green-eyed hunk of gorgeousness who ran it. The one who'd run his hands just about everywhere over her naked body before—

*Stop it.*

Fantasizing about what had been didn't make right now any better.

A flash of irritation shot through her. One acknowledging that Matteo was right.

If they were busy having a delicious romance, all of their time, all of their *energy* wouldn't be going to the children. St. Nick's was making an investment in her. In her work. And if she came up trumps, Casita Verde would get a new clinic and she could go home to follow exactly the same routine she'd been following quite happily for her entire adult life. Back to the status quo in no time. Just what she wanted. So! Harriet shook her head and forced on a smile, Operation Crush the Crush was going to have to be put in motion.

An unexpected rush of children into the courtyard brought her to her feet. She saw a woman being ushered in and— Oh, no!

Harriet quickly wove her way through the children to reach the heavily pregnant woman's side. She was young. Teenager young. Fifteen, sixteen maybe? And letting out the most extraordinary howl of pain Harriet thought she had ever heard. Her arms, legs, face…everything about her looked unnaturally swollen.

Pre-eclampsia. It had to be. Common in teenaged pregnancies. The only way to prevent the swelling from causing this woman's death was to deliver the child immediately.

She took hold of the young woman's arm and steered her the handful of steps up into the clinic.

*"Cómo te llamas?"*

"Carlita," the young woman managed to gasp.

"Carlita. That's a lovely name. *Hablo Ingles?*" Harriet wasn't going to risk her limited Spanish on an emergency like this if she didn't have to. She scanned the courtyard, which suddenly felt as large as an aircraft hangar.

*Where was Matteo?* She asked a couple of young boys to find him.

*"Sí."* She began again after blowing a steadying breath through tightly pursed lips, "Yes, I studied it in school."

"I'm just bringing you to the clinic. How far along are you?"

"Maybe thirty-six weeks. I'm not sure."

Harriet winced. Carlita very likely hadn't been receiving check-ups. Thirty-six weeks was early but not too risky. Any earlier than that and the child could face severe medical issues.

"How long have you been having contractions?"

"Bring her in here." Matteo materialized in the doorway, the expression on his face completely devoid of light as his eyes hit Carlita. This was a side to him she hadn't seen. Her heart clenched tight. There was something personal in his response to the young woman.

He indicated they enter a room Harriet hadn't seen yet. When he swung the door open her eyes widened.

"Were you saving this as a surprise for later?"

"I was saving it," Matteo replied matter-of-factly, "for someone who was about to give birth."

The immaculately maintained obstetrics room might not have had every single bell and whistle but it was well equipped enough to handle, at the very least, straight-forward situations.

"Can you get a urine sample and then prep her on the table, please? I just need to make a quick call." Matteo had a phone tucked between his chin and shoulder as he scanned the medicine cabinet.

"Are you happy to give an intramuscular injection?"

"Of course." Harriet tried not to take offense at his tone. This was an emergency. Not the time to quarrel about how much she could and couldn't do.

"Magnesium sulfate?" she asked as he began speaking in rapid Spanish.

He nodded and handed over the syringe, mouthing, "Four grams in an IV," as he listened to the response before hanging up and going back to the medicine cupboard.

"Gloves are over there." Matteo pointed at well-stocked box in the corner.

She snapped on a pair and gave the teen a smile. "Carlita, do you know if you have HIV?"

"I'm okay."

"Excellent." At least that wouldn't be a problem the teen would have to deal with in addition to a newborn.

Matteo cut in, "One of my colleagues—friends—from a local hospital is coming to help. The more hands the better."

Harriet nodded, swabbing Carlita's hand after hanging the IV bag on a nearby stand. She gave the teen her best reassuring smile and said, "This won't hurt too much," before slipping the needle into her hand after injecting the magnesium sulfate into the IV bag. It wasn't a cure-all and would take five to ten minutes to be given via infusion pump, but it would help prevent convulsions. Essential if they were to hope for a positive outcome.

"Hydralazine?" Harriet asked when Matteo handed her another syringe.

"Yes. For the blood pressure. We'll start with ten milligrams and see how she's doing in ten minutes. Could be it needs to be injected intravenously."

"Fluid regimen?"

"What happened with the urine test?" Matteo's eyes scanned the room as if it could answer.

"I didn't test it."

Matteo shot her a dark look. *Calm. Calm. Be the calm in the storm.*

"She's only just arrived and I don't know where the dipsticks are."

His expression softened.

There was some understanding in there. Somewhere. Besides, an emergency birth wasn't the place for egos. Pure concentration was the only solution.

Matteo began asking Carlita questions in a slow, steady voice as he slipped the blood-pressure sleeve gently along her swollen arm.

Harriet was pleased to realize she was able understand a lot more Spanish than she could speak. At least she wouldn't be completely in the dark.

"Have you had any seizures?"

"One. That is why I came."

"You were already in labor?"

"I don't know." Her eyes widened with fear. "What is going to happen to my baby?"

"BP is one fifty over ninety-five." Matteo met Harriet's eyes with a modicum of relief as he took off the sleeve. If it had been higher—one-seventy over one hundred and ten?—Carlita's chances of a cerebral hemorrhage would have been increased. As would the likelihood of death for both mother and child.

"Headaches? Blurred vision? How long have your ankles been this swollen?"

Matteo rattled off the questions and Carlita stumbled through her answers as they worked in unison to prepare for delivery. They would need to lower her blood pressure—but not too rapidly, otherwise they risked an acute reduction in the flow of blood and oxygen to the placenta.

"Can you test her reflexes?" Matteo handed Harriet the small instrument as he continued the flow of questions. Abdominal pain? An absence of or reduced urine over the past few hours? Days? They were all clues that, had she been receiving regular prenatal check-ups, would have prevented the severity of her case. Matteo's face was grim.

"Can you cut off her clothes, please? We need to check the baby."

"Of course, Doctor."

Matteo shot her a look. One that was impossible to read. What did he expect? It was hardly the place to call him lover boy. Not that she'd ever, ever call him that.

A sharp rap sounded on the door and a middle-aged man wearing scrubs entered without waiting for a response.

"Matteo." He gave him a quick nod followed up by a questioning look when he saw Harriet.

"Harriet, this is Dr. Morales, an obstetrician from Hospital de los Porteños. He will help us with the delivery. Carlita? How are you feeling?" Matteo's attention returned to Carlita, whose eyes suddenly rolled up behind her lids.

"She's seizing." Harriet's words were lost in the flurry of action that followed.

After checking her airway, breathing and circulation, Harriet helped stabilize Carlita's head and upper body as Dr. Morales administered an additional magnesium sulfate bolus of two grams.

"Do you think we need to use a prophylactic?" Harriet asked. It had been a while since she'd been in a delivery room, but everything she knew was flooding back at a rate of knots.

"Let's hold off and see how she goes. It could be that her labor has progressed enough that we can deliver," Dr. Morales replied. "Matteo? How is it looking?"

"She's already dilated to eight centimeters. Want to wait until ten?"

"I'm not getting much of a read on the baby. Episiotomy?"

Harriet winced when she realized Carlita saw her flinch at the word. An episiotomy would speed things up and with proper anesthetics she wouldn't feel the cut at all. On top of which, the sooner she had the child, the better. The only way to stop pre-eclampsia from taking both of their lives was delivery of the child.

She took the young woman's hand in hers and held it tight. Where was Carlita's family? It must be so frightening to be alone like this.

She looked across at Matteo and Dr. Morales, who were working together like a well-oiled machine. Their exchanges were brief but explanatory. Harriet kept an eye on the obs as they prepped both themselves and Carlita for the delivery, talking her through each step of the journey. Any darkness Matteo's eyes had carried earlier had lifted, leaving behind the kind, confident doctor she had first met. This was the man she'd heard about for so many years, the one who offered girls a place of refuge, help in a time of critical need.

"It's okay." She spoke quietly into Carlita's ear as they prepared to make the incision. "You're in good hands."

"Here she is!" Matteo gave the infant a swift wipe to clear away any blood and mucus before expertly swaddling her in a light green blanket.

"Look!" He held the tiny infant outstretched in his arms. "We've had a baby."

He'd meant to look at Carlita when he said the words, gave the smile. It was his standard line, but he meant it every time he said it. Especially in cases like this when such a critical medical situation ended with both mother and baby in good shape. Alive. But as he spoke, his body betrayed him and his eyes solidly latched onto Harriet's.

*We've had a baby.*

Harriet's lips parted, her eyes widened then clamped tight shut for a moment as if to regroup. No wonder!

The words—usually just a warm welcome for an infant and a "well done" for an exhausted new mother—were suddenly weighted with meaning.

He'd vowed never to have children of his own. It was why this was always the first and last time he held a woman's child. His fingers suddenly ached to hand the child over. What they'd just been through was a vivid reminder of his vow. Matteo's sister and her child had died from pre-eclampsia, his sister too frightened by her own pregnancy to seek prenatal treatment. Carlita, he had little doubt, was the same. It was why Casita Verde existed. To try and allow other families' daughters not to become a statistic, the kind that ended with a funeral.

"Do you want to hold her?"

Harriet's eyes lit up as Matteo handed the baby across so that she could pass the infant to Carlita.

Something in him softened as he handed over the tiny, wriggling parcel, already complete with a head of thick, dark hair. He shifted his hands away from Harriet's arms as she took the weight of the baby and again became acutely aware of the connection between them. And not just on a physical level.

She'd more than impressed him today.

Without a thought for herself she had jumped straight in at the deep end, still exhausted from her journey and no doubt wondering where the hell the man who had made love to her with untethered desire had gone. The one who had *invited* her here and all but cast her aside in the first five minutes.

And here she was, nurturing and supporting someone with utter focus, as if Carlita was the very first new mother in the world. It took a generosity of spirit not everyone possessed. Yes, it was her job. But she did it well. Very well. That much was clear. He added another tick to her list of good qualities.

Harriet ran a finger along the infant's face, the instinct to nurture coming to the fore before she turned to Carlita.

"Meet your daughter."

"Do I have to?" Carlita's pained voice broke the spell.

Harriet looked across at Matteo, unsure what to do. The baby let out a small cry and they all turned to look. Harriet's arms automatically began an instinctive rocking motion. A lullaby, just audible above the whir of an outdoor generator, came in a low hum from her lips.

"Carlita, *mija*." Matteo moved to the opposite side of

the bed. "There is no 'have to' here. You know that. But I think it might be a good idea."

"Why?"

He could feel Harriet's eyes on him. She didn't really know his style yet and would be seeing first hand how he liked to handle things at Casita Verde.

"I think it is important to say hello," he began, drawing Carlita's hand between both of his and giving it a squeeze. "*Gracias* and *adios*." Something he'd never had a chance to say to his sister or her child. And the reason he never cuddled or cooed at an infant. Ten years on it was still too painful. Too raw.

"Thank you?"

"*Sí*. You are very, very lucky. You almost lost your life today. And your child might have too, but she was smart enough to know you needed to go into labor straight away." He gave a soft smile. "You haven't had any prenatal appointments, have you?"

"Not exactly." Her eyes began darting anxiously around the room.

"There's no one here to judge you, Carlita. We are here to help you. But what happens now is largely up to you."

"I know. But she is going to have a good home, so it's all right! I don't need to hold her."

"Which home?" Matteo's voice intensified. They'd not met Carlita before today and, as far as he knew, she'd not been to the other clinics.

"Here. That's what you do, right? You'll find her a nice home and my parents will never have to know." She began to push herself up, her body and mind still clearly under the light haze of anesthetics.

"No, you don't, darling." Harriet pressed a hand on Carlita's shoulder. "You need rest now. And plenty of it." She gave her a smile. "How are we going to monitor your blood pressure, your *health*, if you don't stay for a while?"

"You've got a few days here, *mija*. Not to mention," chipped in Dr. Morales, "we'll need to check your liver for enzymes, thrombocytopenia, hemolytic uremic—"

"Okay!" Carlita waved her hands in the air, desperate for him to stop. "Okay."

Matteo rose from the side of her bed. "We'll transfer you to a more comfortable room where you can rest over the next few days and we can keep an eye on you. We will take care of your baby—but as far as your baby is concerned there is no automatic home. No magic queue of parents waiting outside the door."

Carlita's eyes widened and instantly filled with tears.

"She won't go to someone today?"

"No." He nodded at Harriet, indicating she should hand the baby to Carlita.

"So you have time to say thank you, little one. Thank you for helping to save my life."

"I was the one who came here!" Carlita protested.

"Because you were in labor. If you hadn't been…?" Matteo left the question hanging in the air.

Carlita looked at the baby again, lifted her arms then lowered them, nerves getting the better of her.

"What will holding her do?" Carlita sent Matteo a plaintive look.

"*Aiie—guapita*. Hold her. Just say thank you to *la chiquita*. If you are old enough to make a baby, you are old enough to say thank you to her for saving your life," Matteo rebuked the young woman, but with a smile playing on his lips. She was seventeen. Too young and too worldly in equal parts.

He found this moment in the process difficult. He saw it as helping with the parenting he wished his sister had received. And it was so personal. There was no universally accepted way to deal with each and every teen birth. And how to find that perfect balance? Stern, loving, with a healthy dose of arm's-length understanding?

Carlita looked at her daughter, still being rocked in Harriet's arms, her wary expression shifting to one of awe. The one that made it worth it. The one that helped them *learn*.

"Then we will talk about when to call your parents."

*"Que?"* There was no mistaking the dismay on Carlita's face.

"Sí. That's right. Adoption can't get underway without approval from a judge and you are going to need their help. I will help, too, but family is important. Now, let's deal with first things first," he continued briskly, before she could get too caught up in all the information she'd just received. "What do you think of this little beauty, eh? She has a nice head of hair, no?"

*"Sí,* Doctor." Carlita gave him a bashful smile before turning to Harriet to receive the expertly wrapped bundle of baby.

"What will happen to them?" Harriet had to run a couple of steps to catch up with Matteo as he crossed the courtyard a couple of hours after the baby and Carlita had been settled and they'd said farewell to Dr. Morales.

The sunny, smiling doctor had all but disappeared when they'd left the delivery room. In his stead she saw a man wrestling with something. Balance in a world that would never make sense?

Her question remained unanswered.

"Is that pretty standard?" Harriet tried to match his long, swift strides.

"They're all different. This is one of the good ones, believe it or not. There will be a bit of a process with the courts to get the child made ready for adoption. Nothing we haven't dealt with before. It all takes time. Patience." He snapped the last word as if she'd been hounding him.

Charming! Especially considering all she was doing was trying to work out how things ran, see where she would best fit in for next few weeks.

Out of the way, from the look of things. Rendering this entire journey pointless.

"Shall I just leave you to it, then?" Harriet stopped walking, her voice sounding more confident than she felt. "Now that I've played my part in your good deed of the day?"

*Where had that come from?*

Her fingers automatically went to rub her locket. Pictures of her sister and her parents were in there—a never-ending source of courage. They would've been impressed to see her so full of gumption. As well she should be!

Matteo was being cagey. And he wasn't being fair. She crossed her arms in front of her chest, waiting, watching for Matteo to stop his purposeful striding and pay her the common courtesy she had paid him when he had come to visit St. Nick's.

A little flush crept onto her cheeks. If you didn't count spending the best part of two weeks hiding in the patients' rooms to avoid him. She giggled at her schoolgirl behavior.

"So you think this is all funny, do you?" Matteo wheeled round to face her, green eyes dark with emotion. The irritation in his voice startled her. She hadn't meant to offend and certainly didn't expect this sort of behavior from him. What was going on?

"Of course not." She stayed silent, arms slipping to her sides along with her courage.

He raked a hand through his hair and looked up at the blue sky above them before tipping his head down, eyes meeting hers. "I'm not really rolling out the proverbial welcome carpet as I had intended."

"Have I done something wrong?"

"No! Absolutely not. It's just…"

"Just…" she softly encouraged. She needed to know, otherwise there was little point in staying. And in that instant—just imagining picking up her suitcase to leave—she already knew she wanted to stay.

"These situations are complicated."

"I do work in an orphanage." She fought the urge to cross her arms. Protect herself. "One filled with dying children, so I'm pretty used to complicated."

"Of course you are. It's just… I have a particular way of dealing with the girls. You're going to see a lot of things that are done very differently."

"So? I thought the point of my being here was exactly that. To expand my horizons." She lobbed the words he'd used at her reluctance to leave London straight back at him. If they were going to have this talk? They were going to have this talk.

"What's so different about what you do anyhow? All I saw was a doctor who saved a teenage girl from dying after safely delivering her child. Then you asked her to acknowledge a few facts about the situation."

"*Sí.* Yes, I know what you saw." He gave her a look that practically screamed, *Isn't it obvious what you're missing?*

*Er...no!*

"I'm afraid you're going to have to spell it out for me, Matteo."

"I'm just not used to being scrutinized."

*"What?"* Harriet looked round the courtyard as if hoping to garner some support. "Is that what you feel I've been doing? *Scrutinizing* you? I thought I was just doing what you asked me to do."

"You did, you were. Are." The words piled on top of each other as if he was trying to find just the right one.

"Then what is it? What have I done?"

He crossed to her and placed a hand on her shoulder. She shrugged it off. He didn't get to play nicey-nicey in the throes of this type of conversation.

He took a step back, hands raised as if admitting to an error of judgment. "You've done nothing, *dulce*. It's me. As I said, I'm just not used to being judged."

He turned to go. Harriet was shaking her head. No. This wasn't right. He was speaking in riddles or covering up something deeper. Something that meant more. She couldn't just let this go.

"Is that what you think I'm doing?" she called after him. "That I've flown in from my fancy hospital in London to sanctimoniously *judge* you?"

"No, Harriet—you're getting the wrong idea."

"Then how about explaining to me the right idea? Because from where I'm standing it seems you're the one doing the bulk of the judging here."

Unexpectedly, a broad smile replaced the tight-lipped frown dominating Matteo's face. "Miss Monticello has called the spade a spade!" The light returned to his eyes—the spark of a challenge or the warm glow of acquiescence? It was difficult to tell and she wasn't entirely sure if she should trust it. He beckoned for her to follow him. "Come. Come with me."

Harriet had to force herself to pick up her feet and follow him. She didn't much feel like jumping back on the Dr. Torres Yo-Yo ride.

He'd already made it perfectly clear where she stood with him personally. Absolutely nowhere. And if he was just going to give her the runaround professionally, there wasn't much point in standing around calling spades much of anything.

Matteo was obviously King of the Mountain here. As he would and should be. Casita Verde was his dream child. He did the work, he secured the funding and he was more hands on than most administrators would ever dream of.

But she was hardly the first person to cross into the courtyard who wanted to know how it worked. Particularly when she was here to roll up her sleeves and help. She knew for a fact he'd had donors, visitors, people "inspecting" before. Surely there was a ream of government departments that had to come in with their clipboards, pens poised to pass judgment, ensure he was doing things to a certain standard. Had he never had anyone come along just to good old-fashioned *help*?

What had made him so touchy about a tiny little *giggle*? A self-deprecating one at that. Not that he had bothered to ask. She marched along behind him, staring at his back. An annoyingly nice back, his shoulders filling out a dark blue linen shirt as if it had been made for him. Her eyes shifted lower…then a little lower. She humphed under her breath.

He was lucky that staring at his backside was such a

pleasant affair, otherwise she had a good mind to high-tail it back to the airport. Maybe her sister would need her in Los Angeles…

Matteo kept checking behind him to ensure Harriet was following. Not that he would have blamed her if she'd turned on her heel and left. She was absolutely right. He was the one being difficult. Negative.

He'd had scores of people come to Casita Verde who'd wished to donate but had wanted to "see before they bought". It was completely natural. Fair, even. And normally he never gave a monkey's. If they gave, they gave. If they didn't, he'd carry on. His way. What was so different about Harriet's visit?

Well, that one was easy.

*Harriet.*

She was what was different.

He cared what she thought and it scared him. He had been moved when handing over the tiny infant and watching her hold it in her arms, the glow of happiness shifting from her to the child as fluidly as if it had been her own.

And seeing that pure, organic, joy…joy he would never know…brought back the endless stream of questions he tortured himself with about his sister. What if there had been somewhere she could go? What if she'd seen a doctor just once and had been warned of the dangers? It physically hurt each time he laid himself bare to the thoughts and now Harriet was seeing the side of himself he worked so hard to keep private. The side he had hoped to keep away from the people he cared about.

Maintaining a blinkered, passionate commitment to what he believed when no one else's opinion mattered was one thing, but now? He wanted Harriet to admire what he'd done. He wanted her to admire *him*. And when she'd laughed? He'd taken it the wrong way. He knew he had and he could *thunk* himself on the head for being so hypersensitive.

Carlita's story, ultimately, would very likely be a successful one. But it was one of thousands and, despite his desire to protect her, Harriet needed to see that many of the children born here, not to mention their young mothers, were not so lucky.

They reached the very back of the compound—not a word passing between them—and he stood for a moment in front of the door, wondering if he was being entirely fair. The turmoil he was feeling was of his own making, but any decisions Harriet made would also stem from what he did now. If she wanted to see what made him so intense, too earnest perhaps, she needed to see this.

He pushed opened the big wooden doors and watched as Harriet's eyes all but turned into saucers. One of the many *villas miserias* of Buenos Aires had crept and crawled, expanding with a speed that almost frightened him, up to the very doorstep of the historic monastery that was now Casita Verde. These were just some of Argentina's impoverished, scraping a living from the nation's capital in any way they could. They lived in huts, lean-tos, under the open sky—anywhere they were able to, doing anything they could to survive.

There was never a chance he'd be able to help a fraction of them, let alone fully open the doors to one and all. Which was why he stayed so focused on teenaged mothers. And why he had to maintain that cool, distanced focus. Letting Harriet into his heart wouldn't help.

He watched her take it in. The children wearing scraps

of T-shirts, torn skirts, too-short trousers. The mothers kneading the day's empanada dough in front of fires made of bits of wood scavenged from who knew where. The sprawl—the expanse of it—was breathtaking, even to him, and he saw it every day.

"We solved one problem today," he said, "but out here lie countless more."

"Well, then." Harriet fixed him with her clear blue eyes, her gaze unwavering. "I guess we'd better get to work."

# CHAPTER SIX

HARRIET JUST MANAGED to dodge out of the way to avoid a high-speed game of tag weaving in and out of the court-yard's covered walkway. School was finished for the day and the casita's dozen or so school-aged children were burning off some excess energy. She laughed with sheer delight. Matteo might be all frowny and furrowed brow around them—all of them!—but the atmosphere he fostered was definitely child friendly. She had to give him that. She swerved again, her arm getting a silky whip-lash from a pair of plaits streaming behind a beautiful eight-year-old girl.

"Mind the—"

"Ow!"

Too late. Camila, in looking behind her, had done a first-class crash into one of the walkway's columns. Harriet was by her side in an instant. Stone columns weren't very forgiving.

"Let's have a look, love." Harriet swept away a thick swatch of black fringe from the little girl's face, only just stopping herself from wincing. One fat lip, a bloody nose and a good old-fashioned shiner coming up. "I think you and I are going to have something in common!" Harriet put on a smile.

"What?" sniffled Camila.

Harriet pointed at her own fading black eye. "You're going to get one of these!"

Camila stopped crying long enough to give Harriet a shy grin and sweep a hand across her mouth, only to discover it was covered in blood from her streaming nose. Her eyes widened in horror and the tears began anew.

"It's all right, Camila. No—no don't tip your head back. It makes you swallow the blood." Harriet made her best icky face and took one of the little girl's hands. "Can you pinch your nose or would you like me to?"

"I can do it," Camila whimpered.

"Good girl."

"Why don't you vagabonds go and see if Juanita needs some help peeling vegetables?" Matteo's voice came loud and clear from the clinic doorway. The children responded instantly. When Matteo spoke, everyone listened. Too bad he didn't seem keen on speaking with her. Harriet's lips pressed together as she steered Camila towards the clinic.

Matteo had been doing a most excellent job of keeping Harriet as far away as possible from him and the clinic for the past week. She'd unexpectedly been fighting some serious jet-lag and a bit of a tummy bug so didn't mind too much. Fighting fatigue was one thing, but wrestling with her insecurities was growing more challenging…in the kitchen, the laundry, the children's rooms, the public rooms. Anywhere but in the clinic with Matteo. "All to get you better acquainted with how things work," he'd said. She'd kept her expression neutral with each assignment before accepting it with a smile. He'd run out of ways to keep her out of the clinic soon enough, she'd reasoned. And it looked like patience was rewarding her today.

"Mind the step." Harriet led Camila up the wide stone slabs leading up and into the clinic.

"One bloody nose and a possible black eye coming up!"

Harriet realized she wasn't just speaking to Matteo but a young woman as well. Almost painfully thin, she was visibly pregnant—perhaps a few months —and sitting in the room's only chair with her arm by the blood-pressure cuff. Must've been a check-up.

"Oops." She turned back to Camila, whose blood was now pooling on the floor. "You've got to keep hold of that nose for a good ten minutes, love. Can—?"

"Shall I...?" Matteo's patient moved to get up, gasping with pain as her legs and hips took her standing weight. She pressed her hands to the arms of the chair for support.

"No, you don't," Matteo interjected, putting a hand on her shoulder. "You stay put." He turned and pulled a length of blue toweling off a rack and grabbed some antiseptic spray, making quick work of the pool of blood as Harriet went down on her knees to take over the nose-pinching job with a handful of tissues to catch any overflow.

"I want to lie down." Camila was crying again.

"No, love. You can't lie down yet. Not until we stop the bleeding and check everything's all right." Harriet gave the girl's cheek a soft brush with the backs of her fingers as she scanned the small room. The only other place to go was the delivery room and keeping that sterile was essential. The casita's need for a bigger clinic and more exam rooms, was pretty obvious right now. Something she would've understood straight away if Matteo had deigned her worthy to help him out over the past week!

"We'll go next door." Matteo made the decision for her. Surprise, surprise. "You all right to handle this?"

"I think I can just about handle a bloody nose," Harriet couldn't help retorting. She'd been doing a ridiculous amount of tongue biting over the past week, but Matteo was crossing a line now. He had no right to question her nursing skills. She'd worked too hard to let someone—let him—patronize her just because she wasn't on her home turf and he had issues about being judged. She was here to help, for heaven's sake, and he was ruddy well going to get the message if it killed her!

"Fine." Matteo's voice said the opposite—but she had a patient to see to, and so did he. No time for egos. Even someone as bull-headed as he was turning out to be should recognize that.

Harriet held Camila to the side as Matteo removed the blood-pressure cuff from the young woman's arm. Signs of pain shot across her eyes again as she pressed her hands to the chair to rise. Interesting. Unusual. When the woman—girl? —began to walk, Harriet thought it was more of a pronounced waddle than would normally be expected for someone who didn't look to be much past the five-month mark. Her mind whirred and reeled through a catalogue of symptoms and possible afflictions. Could it be osteomalacia? Harriet had never seen an actual case of the brittle-bone disease in a pregnant woman before. It was rare—but it happened. And if... Her eyes scanned from the woman's ashen face to her clenched hands and... No. She was probably just leaping to conclusions, too keen to prove to Matteo she was more useful in the clinic than out.

"Let's get you up on the exam table, shall we?" Harriet rose, finding herself playing out an awkward shifting of one person past the other as they tried to move to their new locations. The limited space found her brushing against first the young woman and then Matteo. The woman stopped for a moment to catch her breath just as Matteo was passing Harriet. Their eyes caught and for the first time since she had arrived Harriet felt that instant click of connection that made everything else fade away. Matteo appealed to her on so many levels and it shook her to realize emotion could have such depth. Such a physical impact. Did he feel the same? She searched his green eyes for answers, not even sure herself what the questions were. Her breath caught in her throat as an urge to touch him threatened to engulf her well-honed common sense.

"'Arriet!" Camila whimpered.

Harriet shook her head and returned her focus to her young charge. One thing she knew for sure. Matteo wouldn't rate anyone who put feelings over their work. Such an arm's-length approach for a man who was so devoted to his cause. She couldn't imagine doing her job without pouring her entire heart into it. How he stayed so reserved was beyond her. She turned just as the door to the delivery room clicked shut. He, it appeared, found it as easy as pie. She pictured throwing a huge cream pie right into his gorgeous, all-knowing face and smiled.

"Now, then, Camila. Let's take a look at your sweet little button nose!"

"Your blood pressure and other stats seem fine, but I'm concerned about the amount of pain you are feeling. It's mostly in your hips, you say?"

"*Sí*. But today I have started feeling tingles in my hands and feet. It's why I came along."

Matteo abstained from launching into his usual speech about how she should've come along the instant she'd learned she was pregnant. He would've been able to supply her with essential vitamin and mineral supplements, information about the pregnancy, started the wheels rolling on the adoption process if that's what she was hoping for. He wished the girls knew the door was open to them at any time. An imagine of Harriet standing in the doorway of the casita, a soft smile playing along her lips as she opened her arms wide in welcome eclipsed his thoughts. Her golden hair, lit by the sun. Those blue eyes of hers— *Mierda!* He shook the picture away.

*Focus, man!*

Having Harriet here was creating fault lines in a decade's worth of intense single-mindedness. Without it he wasn't sure he would be able to... *Enough!* He took the girl's hand in his, kneading, prodding, trying to see if there was anything obvious causing the tingles. Shingles, diabetes, a mini-stroke, all things that could dramatically affect both her health and her unborn child's. He mouthed a silent curse as he continued the examination. If she'd come earlier this could've been prevented but Theresa was here now. It would have to do.

A soft knock on the door caught his attention. Locks of Harriet's honey-blonde hair were just visible in the small opening.

"*Sí?* What is it?"

"Sorry...um...sorry, Dr. Torres. May I have a quick word?"

"Can't it wait?" His tone was sharp, one he didn't

like to hear coming from himself. Especially in front of a patient.

"No."

There wasn't even a glimmer of a waver in her tone. He pushed his irritation into his emotional garbage chute and forced himself to regroup. Harriet was a nurse who more than understood medical protocol. She wouldn't have interrupted unless she'd felt it was necessary. He excused himself to Theresa and walked into the other room where Camila was now lying, head elevated, on the exam table, holding an ice packet to her bruised eye and cuddling a small blanket Harriet had twisted into the shape of a poodle. How did she know how to do that sort of thing?

"Sorry to interrupt." Harriet kept her voice low. "You've probably already got your diagnosis for your patient, but I couldn't help but wondering if she wasn't showing signs of osteomalacia." Her eyes met his, nervous expectation playing across them as she waited for his response. He began to dismiss her suggestion but stopped himself. Tingling hands. A distinct waddle when she walked, often indicative of tiny cracks in her hip bones. Pale skin, making it very likely that the healthy percentage of Vitamin D a person should absorb through the skin wasn't present.

He gave her a curt nod. He should have connected the dots himself. "Good call. I'll make her an appointment at the hospital. We don't have the facilities to do all the mineral tests and X-rays she'll need."

"I'll go along with her, if you like."

Matteo pulled himself up to his full height. The alpha male in him bridled. He was capable of looking after his patients—as he had done for many years—without her help, thank you very much! The pragmatist in him countered that someone needed to be at the clinic. He still wasn't ready to figuratively or literally hand over control to anyone else. This was his baby. His effort to make peace with the past. No one but him could understand how the clinic needed to run to right the wrongs.

"That would be very helpful." He gave a grimace and a nod of assent, then tacked on, "Thank you," to take off the edge.

*Just a few more weeks.* For the love of all things beautiful! He'd made *love* to this woman not a handful of weeks ago! A moment of weakness when he'd let someone see a glimpse of the man he used to be. He glanced at Harriet again before returning to the delivery room. Confusion played across her features. He needed to stop being such a jerk. None of this was her fault. All his idiotic behavior was rooted deep within him, surfacing too often over the past week. Just a few more weeks. And then she'd be gone. Back in England where— *Dios...* He pressed his forehead briefly on the door before turning to face Theresa. He might like not having Harriet here, but he already knew that having her leave was going to be worse.

"Well?" Matteo looked up from his paperwork without so much as a greeting when Harriet finally returned to the clinic.

It had been a long afternoon at the hospital. Her Spanish was still very basic and communicating via a dictionary and her own limited vocabulary had taken it out of her. She was bushed. A smile and a nice cup of tea would've been incredibly welcoming about now.

"We won't know for at least a day. If not two."

"And Theresa?" Matteo craned his head as if Harriet had been hiding the pregnant girl behind her.

"She's gone back to her dormitory."

"Dormitory?"

"She's at university. Her parents don't know," she added before Matteo had a chance to question her. "I've got her mobile number and a promise that she'll meet me for the results when we get the call." She put up a hand when she saw Matteo was about to interrupt her. *Give a girl a chance, why don't you?* "Here. And, yes, I went back with her to her dormitory so I know how to find her if she doesn't show up. We also obtained permission from the doctor for the results of her tests to be phoned to us here at the casita. She said she'd prefer to come here than the hospital. Oh! And I bought her some prenatal multivitamins."

"Oh?" He pulled open a drawer and shifted things around until he unearthed a small yellow pad. "I can get you a reimbursement right away."

Harriet waved it away with a smile. "This one can be on me. I have a daily stipend from St. Nick's and since I haven't been out at all since I arrived it's not a problem."

"Were you planning on doing much sightseeing?" Matteo leaned back in his chair, an eyebrow quirked with curiosity.

Harriet stayed silent, fighting the urge to scream. Or cry. She'd fought that urge frequently over the past few days. She obviously knew him less well than she'd thought, but, goodness gracious, Matteo really knew how to bring out the heavily ignored ends of her emotional spectrum. The sting of tears threatened as her fingers crept up to give her locket a rub. *C'mon Harriet! You're the calm, rational, steady-tempered twin.* And yet she was already beginning to feel worn, careening from one emotional extreme to the other. This was all new terrain for her and if Matteo would just take a few moments to behave with a bit of much-needed *compassion*, it would be much easier to approach the next few weeks with Mr. Grumpy with a smile.

"No," Harriet amazed herself by replying in a bright voice. "As I said on the first day, I am here to work. So, if you'll excuse me…?" She didn't even wait for a reply, just turned on her heel and swiftly left the clinic.

She needed to get to her tiny little room, and fast. Its cozy interior had given her comfort in the past few days as she'd adjusted to the new surroundings, the new language, the new Matteo.

Miraculously, she managed to maintain the tiniest grip of emotional control until she reached her room. The last thing she was going to do was let Matteo see her cry. Let him know how much she longed to be with him. Because that was what was happening. She was fighting desire the way a musketeer fought baddies. With every ounce of energy she had.

Harriet shut the door to her room behind her, only just making it to her bed before the tears began to flow in earnest. It was all she could do to stop the sobs burning her chest from filling the room. She stuffed her head into her pillow and poured the tumult of emotions into the downy silencer. She cried until there were no more tears. Her emotions spent, she rolled onto her back and stared into the growing darkness of her room.

They worked well together, her ever rational side told her. And that's what she needed to focus on. All the emotional tension bouncing between them had stood in the way of her really putting her nose to the grindstone for the assessment she'd promised Dr. Bailey.

She pushed herself up in surprise.

She hadn't thought of Dr. Bailey or St. Nick's, not really, for...*days*. A whole week! The world she had thought completed her own had all but disappeared since she had been here. It didn't take much divining to know it was a "who" rather than a "what" that had opened her eyes to so much more in the world.

She lay back on to the quilt with a heightened sense of awareness of just how much she had seen and learned in such a short time.

Her mind drifted and wandered and she realized with a start she must've dozed off as her room was cloaked in darkness. The night was still warm and her small window was cracked open enough to smell the fresh scent of the late-night air. She'd have to be fully awake in a few hours, ready for a new day. A day where she and Matteo would behave with professional respect towards each other and nothing more. Just as the Queen herself might've behaved.

An ironic smile hit her lips in gratitude for her English stoicism. Her ability to behave as if everything was perfectly all right, even if everything inside her was devastated by a romance that could never be.

She stood to undo her blouse and skirt, uncharacteristically letting them drop to the floor. She lay back on the bed, focusing on the sensation of the well-worn cotton sheet against her skin. The softness of it. She shifted a leg, imagining the soft caress of the sheet was, in fact, Matteo's hands. His fingers skimming along the length of her thigh. A warmth began to grown within her. She knew she should fight it, but didn't. Just this once.

Her hands shifted across her belly. She was surprised to feel how soft it was. The tiniest of arcs upwards, instead of the gentle slope and swoop it normally made. She hadn't remembered eating more than she usually did. Sure, the food here was good but... She laid her hands on top of her belly as if it would help her divine if her body really had changed or if she was imagining things.

A thought came to her. A shocking thought.

She lifted her hands and moved them so that they hovered above her breasts. When she finally raised the courage to touch them, feeling the added plumpness, recalling the slight hint of blue veins she had noted but dismissed that morning, she knew instantly what she needed to do. Inching herself out of bed as if she were surrounded by a floor full of sleeping children, she moved with exaggerated stealth. After tugging on a T-shirt and her skirt, she decided to forego flip-flops and, as quietly as she could, made her way to the clinic.

By the time she arrived, her stomach was churning. She clicked the door shut as quietly as she could, hoping the light wouldn't disturb anyone in the courtyard. She checked the wall clock. Three a.m.

All being well, she would have the place to herself for a while.

Good. She would need the privacy for what she was about to do.

She went to the cupboard to get the nail-file-length stick, sheathed in its protective foil wrapping. They preferred to let teenage girls who needed the test to use these at first. It brought them some privacy. Some time to register what might or might not be happening in their bellies.

The door to the loo gave an eerie creak as she pulled it open and scanned the room, as if the noise would suddenly bring all of the children running. She waited a few moments, just to be safe, then closed herself in the small room to take the test.

It was nearly impossible to keep up with surge after surge of thoughts and images racing through her mind as the seconds ticked past at an interminably slow pace.

Sitting in the loo wasn't helping, so she pushed out of the door and back into the clinic just as the front door opened.

"*Que paso?* What's going on?"

It was Matteo. Green eyes dark as a forest, worry lines creasing his forehead.

Harriet's heart all but stopped beating, a shiver of goose pimples shuddering down her arms as she met his beautiful eyes again.

"Harriet?"

She looked at him, the test dangling from her fingers, completely tongue-tied. She knew and she didn't. All it would take was one look.

"Harriet?" Matteo asked again, the concern in his voice growing tighter. "Is everything all right?"

She lifted the test between them, holding it so that they could both see the little window where there either would or wouldn't be a brightly colored plus sign.

Both of them stayed stationary as the result of the test registered, first visually, then cognitively, and as her body began to tremble, Harriet returned her unblinking gaze to Matteo's wide-eyed expression and spoke the words they both already knew.

"I'm pregnant."

The words rang and rang in Matteo's ears.

Words he'd thought he'd never hear in his wildest dreams.

And not just hearing. Seeing the *proof*!

Everything he'd counseled the countless teens he'd seen in the same situation completely left him. For the very first time he knew exactly how they felt. Lost. Bewildered. Hopeful. Terrified. Microseconds away from panic gripping every one of his carefully controlled sensibilities.

He pressed his lips together to stop himself from asking the questions he already knew the answers to. They had used protection. She hadn't been with anyone else. So the "mistakes happen" adage was true. It was his child. The child growing in Harriet's belly was his.

His eyes fixed on her hands, protectively crossed over her tummy, the maternal instinct already alive and well within her.

A primal urge to erase the fear racing through her eyes took hold of him but his gut checked him. And in the instant he hesitated he could see resolve harden in her eyes.

"Don't worry, I've already figured out that you don't want children."

"How?"

"I'm not blind."

"What are you talking about?"

"You keep the children at arm's length. You are kind but you certainly aren't cuddly with them."

"What does any of that prove?"

"You don't like to get close to them. I mean, what kind of pediatrician doesn't like to hold babies?"

The words struck him physically, rendering him speechless. All he could do was return her wide-eyed gaze. Had he really been that transparent?

Harriet backed away from him, her voice a steady confirmation of the decision she must've made in an instant. "I'm going back to England soon enough. In just a few weeks, maybe sooner. No one has to know."

"Harriet, we don't need to make any decisions tonight. Give me time. Time to—"

"Time to want this less than you do right now?" She shook her head in stiff, infinitesimally smaller shakes. If he hadn't felt hyper-aware of her every movement, he might have missed them. "No one has to know. It's not your problem."

His hands clenched and released. Clenched and released. None of this was right. The last thing he wanted was for Harriet to have this moment—the moment she found out she was pregnant—feel like a problem. But he had vowed on his sister's grave never to have children. Had closed his heart to the possibility.

"Is that what you want? What you're happy with?" He could've cracked his head against the wall at the selfishness of his questions.

"It's not as if I've had much time to make sense of this! You just walked in on me."

"I thought someone was breaking into the clinic so I—"

"You thought I was a *criminal*?" She all but recoiled.

"I didn't know who it was. I just saw a figure and…" He stopped himself. Being argumentative with a woman—

*the woman who was pregnant with his child*—when she'd just found out was a bad idea. A very bad idea.

"I think I'd like to go to my room."

"We can talk about this. *Mi amor.*" The words came naturally. The feelings were real. He cared for her and it surprised him to realize just how much.

She shook her head at his words, rejecting his affection. "Harriet," he corrected himself. He'd told her there was nothing between them when she'd barely disembarked from the plane and now he was proving it.

"No. We can't talk about it. I have to decide what I am going to do about my baby. Alone."

It nearly broke his heart to see her skirt round him to get to the door as if fearful that touching him would cause her pain.

He reached out to her, hoping for… Who knew what— a moment of stillness? A moment to absorb the enormity of what was happening?

Harriet pressed herself against the wall, raising her hands as she did so.

"I think it's best if I go to my room now."

Tears were glistening in her eyes. He ached to reach out, soothe them away. Tuck the little stray honey-blonde twists of hair away from her eyeline. Caress away the deep furrow tugging her brows tightly together.

She was right, of course. To back away.

The idea of being a father… He felt his lungs constrict. It was the one thing he had been certain of since his sister had died. He did not want children. He'd said it like a mantra over the years. He did not want children, and yet—

"You don't have to do this alone." As the words came

out he knew they sounded pathetic. He was unconvinced so how on earth was she ever to believe him?

"Don't worry, Matteo." Harriet turned round once she'd reached the safety of the doorway, a bitter-sweet smile tipping up the edges of her lips. "You're right. I won't have to do it alone. I have my sister."

The words were like a knife in his heart. She had a sister.

Harriet couldn't know how cruel her choice of words was. And how perfect a reminder they were of why he'd vowed to never have a family of his own. How could he when he hadn't noticed his own sister's extended absences? Hadn't pinned her down, demanded an explanation, showed her the unconditional love a brother owed a sister? If he had well and truly been there for Ramona, she'd be here today. And Harriet's news could be... It would be good news.

He cursed under his breath. They'd used protection! He should've taken a cue from the monastic lodgings and practiced abstinence. He'd never imagined himself leaving a woman in the lurch, but, more pressingly, he'd vowed to never have a child. He had nothing to offer.

At least Harriet wouldn't be alone. She had family. A loving sister with newborns just a few weeks away. It would be a chaotic household but there was little doubt it would be a loving one. Her family would be there for her, comforting, supportive. There, in every way that he couldn't be. He leant against the closed door and sank to the floor, head bowed in his hands as the numbness of grief began to settle in.

# CHAPTER SEVEN

HARRIET STARED AT the phone in her hand, not knowing whether to feel shell-shocked or elated. Perhaps a bit of both? What she did know was she had about a gazillion questions to ask her sister. And another gazillion she wasn't quite ready to answer.

It was fitting, she thought, that she was up to her elbows in babygrows and stacks of muslin squares when the telephone call came. After a handful of hours when she hadn't even bothered to try to sleep, she'd overheard Matteo telling the casita's matron he was going out for the entire morning on business, so she'd been folding the casita's never-ending stack of laundry in the courtyard, hoping the fresh air would help clear the chaos playing out in her mind. Apart from that, hiding in her room wasn't exactly going to make her *un*-pregnant. Pregnant with Matteo's baby. Right here, right now. And he wanted nothing to do with it. With her.

She'd just closed her eyes to take in a waft of the floral scents exuding from the arbor she'd tucked herself in to avoid the midday sun when her phone rang.

Her sister's news had come in a torrent and the phone call had ended as abruptly, leaving Harriet reeling in her hidden nook of flowers and vines. The arbor shielded her from the rush and buzz of life in the courtyard. Which was exactly what she needed right now. A bit of privacy until she knew how to respond. Which, realistically, she was not going to figure out how to do until she spoke to her sister again.

She punched the long number into the phone and waited for the foreign ringtone to sound in her ear.

"Harri!" Her sister answered before the first ring had finished sounding. "Are you all right?"

"Shouldn't I be asking you that question or jumping on a plane or practicing my double diaper changing skills?" Harriet felt the tension slip from her shoulders at the sound of her sister's laugh. She'd always derived such strength from her. Claudia's passion, drive and overall joie de vivre were unparalleled. The fact she couldn't be with her now was almost physically painful.

"Don't be silly. I told you I was in good hands."

*Oh.*

They'd always been there for each other. Harriet had made sure of it. But this time…did her sister not need her? She shook away the thought and forced on a sunny voice.

"I know, I know. But I think I was in a bit of shock when you told me everything. So…this time I need a blow-by-blow recap." And that was putting it mildly. Harriet was experiencing shock at news of her own pregnancy. Shock at the turn of events in her sister's life. It was a wonder she hadn't lost the plot entirely.

"Where do you want me to begin?"

Before Harriet could respond she heard her sister give a happy exclamation. "Ooh! Beea-*uuu*-tiful!"

"What?" She ached to be in Los Angeles at her sister's side, experiencing the highs and lows of life vicariously, just as she had done throughout her childhood...always a bit too painfully shy to experience her own.

"Sorry, Har! A nurse just came in and faked a faint at my flowers. My big beautiful bouquet of flowers that *he* sent."

"Who?" Harriet all but squealed.

"Dr. Spencer." Her voice softened. "Patrick."

"Patrick?" Harriet's defensive sister radar went on high alert. "Who's Patrick?"

"I told you, he's the obstetrician who was in the elevator. The lift," she corrected herself.

"Where you had the babies."

"Yes! Didn't you listen to anything I said the first time?"

"Of course I..." Harriet faltered. Of course she had—but the news was so huge and with her mind still buzzing with her own pregnancy it was all a bit overwhelming. "I'm an auntie!" Tears sprang to her eyes. A mix of elation and sorrow that her sister had had her babies but that the birth had been so fraught with danger. Six weeks early and trapped in a lift. Things only Claudia could turn into silver linings.

"Harri...is everything all right?" Claudia had always been able to read her mind, even at long distance.

"Of course. I just..." *I'm having a baby and the man I love doesn't want me.* "I can't believe you had to go through so much."

"I must admit I'm actually grateful I wasn't conscious when everything happened with the hysterectomy. I think Patrick went through more trauma than I did—and I will be eternally grateful for what he did for me and my two little baby boys."

"Of course. He sounds—"

"Lovely," Claudia finished for her.

Hmm… Not necessarily the word Harriet would've chosen—but now she knew what her sister thought of her Doctor in Shining Armor. A double birth in a lift chased up by a hysterectomy that had ultimately saved her life. But it meant she would never have any more children. It was hard to believe her sister sounded so…so…vital! Then again, that was Claudia through and through. Vital. Brave. Undeterred. Instinctively, her hand slipped to her own belly, feeling a rush of gratitude for the microscopic life blossoming within her. You really never knew what life was going to throw at you.

This was her sister's moment, though. She would wait to tell Claudia her news another day.

"Well, I definitely owe him a thank-you card for saving my sister!"

"And you're still having the time of your life in Argentina?"

Tears began to trickle down Harriet's cheeks as she nodded. That was one way to put it.

"Harri? Are you sure you're all right?"

"Of course!" Her voice squeaked a bit as she regrouped. "I'm just so happy you're safe and the babies are safe and I just wish I could be there for you."

"Don't worry, little sis. We'll be together in London before you know it. Now!" Her sister's voice turned uncharacteristically schoolmarmy. "I know you and I am officially telling you to quit worrying about me. Go out and enjoy Buenos Aires with that hot doc of yours!"

"I never said he was hot." Harriet bridled.

"You didn't have to." Claudia laughed and then gave a sharp gasp.

"Claudy! Are you okay?" Harriet fretted, instantly forgetting her sister's instruction.

"Yes. Yes—just testing all my new stitches. Harri, everything's fine with me so just go and enjoy yourself for once! No need to worry. I'm in good hands."

Something about the way Claudia's tone shifted indicated to Harriet a certain Dr. Spencer may have just entered the room. She felt comforted and a bit bruised by the realization her sister seemed to have someone else in the role of caregiver. She'd always been the one who was there for her sister when things went topsy-turvy. Hadn't she?

"Love you, sis." Harriet swiped away a fresh whoosh of tears.

"Love you, too, little sis!"

"It was only by a minute!" Harriet wailed by rote.

"Yes. Which makes me older and wiser," Her sister retorted. "Now, go on, have a steak for me! And a dance! Tango under the stars, Harri. Make sure you live a little."

And the line clicked off.

Harriet's fingers instinctively began toying with her locket. For the last ten years it had just been the two of them. Harriet and Claudia against the world! Or, more accurately, Harriet on standby while Claudia took on the world. Now it would be Claudia, her two little boys and maybe….a Patrick?

Was it finally time to stop living life's Big Moments through her sister? Have moments of her own? A child. A family?

Her hands slipped down to her tummy. Planned or not, she had the baby part covered. Just no Mr. Right.

An image of Matteo popped into her mind…all lean, sexy, smiley… He was Mr. Right for All the Wrong Reasons. Like it or not, she knew in her heart she was in love with him and would just have to live with the fact the love wouldn't be returned.

Her fingers traced a circle round her tummy before returning to the laundry, her hands folding on automatic pilot as she processed all the new information.

An auntie! A *mother…* Of all the things she'd never let herself imagine she would be, she was going to be a mother. The news was going to take a while to feel anything close to real, let alone something she would tell people. And by people she meant her sister.

"Someone looks happy!" Matteo called from the courtyard, the usual stream of children following in his wake. She stared at him as if he wasn't real, only to realize he was still speaking. "If I'd known folding made you so smiley, I would have put you on laundry duty from the get-go."

*Play along…just play along for now. There's time.* "Yes, it's the first thing I mastered in Nursing 101." She pushed up from the blanket where she'd been sitting to a kneeling position and considered him.

Was this how they were going to deal with things? Ignore the baby elephant in the courtyard? It would be tough but, then again, they hadn't even had a day to process what was happening. Besides, she was English. Suppressing emotion in the face of adversity was her forté. Time to fly the Union Jack for baby Monticello! Or Torres. Monticello-Torres? No…that sounded pretentious. She shook her head clear and looked up with a smile as he approached.

"I've just had some very good news, actually."

"Ah! Good news! That's something we enjoy here." Matteo's smile hit her straight in the heart and did its usual warm twirly journey around her insides. There was no point in fighting it. He gave her a funny tummy. That's just how things were. But winning his heart as he had won hers? There was no chance of that happening. Zero.

*"Eh, bribónes!* *Vaminos."* He shooed away a gaggle of boys starting up a game of football on the edges of the arbor. "You should all be having lunch now. Make your bodies and brains grow a bit more before we get you back to school, *ai?"*

Harriet smiled. It was nice to see him with the children. He was a complete natural. Funny sometimes, serious when he needed to be. Reliable. She understood perfectly the complexities of working in an orphanage—and it warmed her to see the abundance of affection the children received here. Matteo obviously held the respect of all of them. He wasn't a cuddly presence but he was a loved one. What was it that stopped him from loving babies? Their baby? Suppress, suppress, suppress! *More time to digest...that's what we need.*

"So…" Matteo settled on a bench across from her, grabbing an armful of laundry from her pile as he did so. "What's this news?"

She opened her mouth to tell him and found herself mimicking a goldfish. What took precedence here? The birth of her nephews? The lift? The doctor? The hysterectomy? The fact her sister didn't want her to jump on a plane was the one that hurt most. Harriet the One Woman Support Team her sister always called her. But not this time.

Her sister had *always* wanted her.

Tears popped into her eyes and she knew if she spoke, they'd start cascading down her cheeks.

Uh-oh. Too late. No speaking required.

"Hey." Matteo was kneeling beside her before she had a moment to understand what was happening, the back of his hand wiping away the freshly spilt tears. She batted his hand away. Feeling his touch was too close to affection. Something she didn't want to get used to.

"It's my sister," she managed, surges of emotion tightening her throat.

"What's happened?" He was all alertness now, ready for action. Despite herself, she smiled through her tears, a hiccough working its way to the surface before she managed to speak. She felt about six years old—a first! And her untamable sister was a mother!

She looked at Matteo, knowing that if he was only willing, there were a thousand possibilities lying right there within his arms. But allowing herself to dream would only lead to more heartbreak. She sucked in a breath and refocused. This was about her sister. Not about a romance that was never going to happen.

"She's had her twins."

"*Amor!* That's wonderful. Congratulations to you all." Before she knew what was happening, Matteo's cheek was on hers, kisses being planted on first one side of her face then the other, lips shifting past hers in a happy blur of scent and sensation. She became aware of his hands holding her shoulders first close to him then further back so that he could inspect her.

"So these are happy tears, yes?"

"Of course, yes," she replied, swiping at her wet cheeks, masking her face with her fingers so she could regroup. "It's just…"

She felt him watching her expectantly, looking so *vital* as he waited for information. He wasn't to be her lover.

Or a father to their child. Was she ever going to learn to be near him and not ache for more?

Despite a very early morning email to St. Nick's insisting she already knew Casita Verde fitted the criteria for a new clinic, Dr. Bailey had insisted she stay the agreed duration. Told her it would be good for her. Torture was more like it!

She really needed a friend right now and her choices were startlingly limited. She peeked at Matteo through her fingers. Could she shore up her emotional reserves to face a friendship with him with no promise of love? Maybe if she'd been some sort of elegant film star from the nineteen-thirties…or a rock star….or… Harriet Monticello, Nurse At Large?

Matteo sat next to her, patiently waiting for her to collect herself, pulling one of her hands into his, a thumb idly stroking across the back of her hand. She kept her eyes on his thumb shifting this way and that as she made her decision.

"It wasn't an easy birth," she began. Then the story poured out. The dramatic birth in the elevator, the emergency services, the doctor who had miraculously been in the lift with her at the time, the hysterectomy that had followed.

"It must've been difficult for her, to have had that decision made on her behalf."

"Yes. I can't imagine not having any control over whether or not I had children." The words were out before she'd thought them through.

Matteo placed her hand back in her lap and began to pluck away the petals of a fallen flower, discarding them one by one as if they were thoughts he was no longer interested in. "It sounds as though it's all turned out well, though?"

Harriet dipped her head, swatting at a stray tear. "Yes, that's true. She's got the twins, healthy and sound. So it's not as if she has no children. And she has me," she added, trying to add a bit of chirpiness to her tone. "I told her I'd jump on a plane tonight."

"Oh?"

It was difficult to tell what meaning his tight response held.

"You'd want to be with your sister if she'd just had a baby, wouldn't you?"

It came out defensively. And was meant to have been hypothetical. But she knew in an instant she'd hit on something much closer to home, something deeply, deeply painful.

She started to form an apology but didn't know how. She didn't know what she'd be apologizing for.

"She is very lucky. To have a sister as dedicated as you are." Matteo smoothed past the fractured moment with a cursory pat on her knee. One you'd distractedly give to a child who'd just found out they'd done well on an inconsequential exam.

*What's hurt you so badly? Is it why you want nothing to do with me? With our child?*

"Well, I agree," Harriet shot back, injecting a bit of righteous indignation into her voice. Feeling the need to keep up the facade that something hadn't just happened. "But that's the part…" Her voice caught in her throat again. She couldn't believe how hard it was to say the words.

"Harriet." Matteo's brow furrowed with concern. "What is it?"

"Oh, blimey—it's almost ridiculous! I'm behaving like a child, but…" She all but choked the words out. "She said I shouldn't come."

"What?" Matteo's eyebrows shot up, indignant on her behalf. "Is she not grateful to have a sister so concerned?"

Harriet waved away the shock of his response.

"No, no. I didn't mean it like that. Of course she wants me to meet the babies and things, but she said not to come right away, she's being taken care of. She knows I've only got a few weeks here and she was planning to come to London anyway. You know, once I'm done here. It's just weird not to be helping. It's…um… It's…" She blew a steadying breath between her lips, unsuccessfully stemming the flow of more tears. "It's what I've always done! Been there for her. I've always been the one she could rely on!" The words flew out as a plaintive cry, but were very heartfelt. If she hadn't been feeling so overwhelmed by everything, she'd be feeling like a Class-A idiot. Crying like a child because things weren't going The Way They Always Had.

*C'mon, Harriet! She wants you to live your own life. Not in the shadows of hers.*

"Of course you want to be with her. It's only natural."

Matteo pushed himself up from the ground where he'd been kneeling beside Harriet, sitting well back on the deep bench, elbows dug into his knees, hands holding his chin in support as he thought how to respond. He couldn't bear seeing Harriet cry, but was in no position to make decisions for her. He'd all but denied paternity of their child—and was humbled she was speaking to him at all.

He forced himself to focus on the immediate scenario. If Claudia had been his sister he would've been on a plane in an instant. But that choice was not—and never would be—available to him.

"Your sister is your only family, *sì*?"

Harriet nodded, accepting the handkerchief Matteo tugged out of his pocket, twisting it back and forth in her hands after she'd dabbed at her nose and eyes.

"If you want to go, you must go. Family is paramount." He all but flinched at his own words. He could have a family if he wanted. With Harriet. Yet he'd made it clear it wasn't an option. *Was choosing a life alone really the answer?*

"But she's the one telling me not to come!" Harriet reminded him.

"Is her health in danger?"

"No, no." Harriet gave a tiny shake of her head. "She's in good hands. Receiving excellent medical care. I'm sure of that. It's just—it's not so easy as just hopping on a plane."

"Sure it is. My parents go back and forth to America all the time. They have a company jet. If you need to go, you will go with them. Just say the word."

Matteo tried to keep his expression neutral. He wasn't in the habit of offering rides on his parents' private jet, but this was important. Even they would see that. A stab of guilt accompanied his thoughts. He hadn't rung them in a while. Too long. Perhaps it was time to practice what he preached a bit more proactively. Try to heal the wounds that were smarting like hell right now.

"I didn't mean like that—the logistics." Harriet stuffed his handkerchief into her pocket, making no acknowledgement of what he'd just said about his parents, and began briskly folding the clothes, as if the quick motions would help her thoughts collect and reshape into the best solution.

"Then what do you mean?"

"I mean... Ooh!" She released a cry of exasperation. "Unless you've been a twin to the most amazing sister in the world you just wouldn't understand!"

"Why, Harriet Monticello! I thought you said your sister was the dramatic one." *Risky tactic, but...ah...there's the light in her eyes I love so much.*

"I think she's trying to tell me something by saying I shouldn't come straight away. In fact, I *know* she's trying to tell me something." She gave a short, self-effacing laugh. "Mostly because she said as much. Claudia was never really one to mince words."

"She wouldn't be the older twin by any chance?" Matteo smiled, pleased to be building a more complete picture of who Harriet was. How she ticked.

"Only by one teensy-weensy minute and she never—and I mean *never*—lets me forget it!"

"So why does your older, *wiser*..." he tucked the word into air quotes "...sister think you should hold off coming to see your brand-new nephews?"

He leaned back against the thick wooden beam of the arbor, trying to give her the time, and the space, to think. Regroup. Something he should no doubt be doing himself, but ignoring everything was working pretty well for him so he was going to go with it. He put everything she'd said into order and considered...

Harriet and her twin sounded like chalk and cheese. The portrait she'd painted of Claudia conjured up a woman who never took no for an answer, who ate life up with an insatiable relish. And Harriet? She embodied kindness. Was the definition of gentleness. *Heart.* That was more like it. She was one hundred percent heart. And if he wasn't careful, she could so easily work her way into his.

A smile tugged at his lips as she yanked item after item off the diminishing pile of unfolded laundry and whipped it into shape. Her mind was obviously reeling with putting things in the right order—the emotions she was experiencing playing out on her face as she did. First a smile, collapsing into a frown, chased up by a lifted brow and lips pressed together to shift this way and that as if tasting the air for the hint of a solution.

He was willing to wait all day if that's what it took.

*Que? When did that seismic shift occur?*

Matteo considered Harriet through narrowed eyes— eyebrows rising as he realized how much he had changed since her arrival. He was drawn to her. Kept seeking her out "just to make sure everything was all right." Right now his time would be much better spent filling out grant applications, updating records or looking for future sites, and yet here he was, sitting in a flowery arbor wanting nothing more than to ensure she was all right. Wanting her happiness over his own. And yet he let her believe he wanted nothing to do with her—their child. What kind of man did that?

"It isn't that she doesn't want me there. In Los Angeles," Harriet finally began, a small shake left in her voice, though the tears had now dried. "Like I said, we're all organized to meet up in London at our house, the house our parents raised us in, in a few weeks anyway."

"Then what is it?"

"It's that…it's that she doesn't *need* me." Her face tightened to fight another round of tears. "She said she wants me to be happy—but I *am* happy when she needs me!"

Matteo fought an urge to lift her up from the ground and into his arms, hold her, soothe away the tears. But this was her battle and something told him to stay where he was. Let her work through the emotional turbulence on her own. What she was processing now seemed to be getting to the heart of who Harriet thought she was.

"So, let me get this straight. Your sister doesn't want you to go to Los Angeles so you will be happy—but you won't be happy unless she needs you?"

"It sounds ridiculous when you put it like that but, yes." She tossed him a guilty-as-charged expression.

*Had she said something to her sister indicating she was happy here? With him?*

"Do you think being needed is the same as being loved?"

"Of course not. It's just… I guess it's just always felt like *proof* that I'm worthy of being loved."

"Of course you're worthy of being loved! You're one of the most loveable people I've ever met!" They stared at one another, shell-shocked, his words hanging between them. In that moment he felt that if anyone *needed* Harriet in their lives it was him. If anyone loved Harriet it was him. He loved her, but until he laid the ghosts of the past to rest, he couldn't give her the love she deserved.

He cleared his throat, forcing the clinician in him to step in. The one who took an emotional step back from everything. From everyone.

"Have you told her you're unhappy here?"

"No."

*Nice to know he hadn't been that much of an ogre.*

"And how well does your sister know you?"

"Better than anyone."

"So she would know what was right…for you." He was treading on thin ice now. This was about what was best for Harriet, not about keeping her here. Even though— *¡qué diablos!*—God help him, it was what he wanted.

Harriet tipped her head back and forth, carefully considering his question. "Claudia knows how to live life."

"And you?"

"I know how to care for the living." She shot him a horrified look. "That sounds *awful*! I mean, not the caring part—I love the caring part—but it sounds like… like I'm not living."

Bingo. This, he suspected, was what Harriet's twin wanted for her. To live her own life. Not in the shadows of everyone else's.

"So…what do you want to do?" he asked cautiously.

"To live?"

Matteo couldn't help but laugh. "Are you asking me or telling me?"

"Telling? Telling." She steadied her voice and tried it again. Deeper. "Telling you." Then like a robot, "I. Am. Telling. You. I. Want. To Live."

He watched, delighted as she dissolved into laughter with another rush of tears. Tears, he was relatively sure, that were happier this time. He felt touched. Deeply so. Had he just witnessed an epiphany? Now to just sweep all of the other emotional revelations back under the carpet. He put on his officious voice.

"It sounds to me as if your sister is being well looked after. Are we agreed on that?"

"Yes." Snuffle. Giggle.

He handed over a fresh handkerchief. In his line of work, at least two were needed per day.

"And Claudia loves you very much."

"I like the way you say her name properly." Harriet blew her nose. "No one pronounces it correctly."

He laughed. He loved the way she found pleasure in the little things. Was still in her sister's corner, no matter how minor the infraction.

"Could it be that Claudia finally sees you doing something for yourself and doesn't want to be the one to bring it to an end?"

Harriet looked at him blankly, lifting her hands in an I-don't-know-what-you're-talking-about gesture.

"How often have you been there for your sister?"

"Always," she answered instantly.

"And how often do you put yourself—your needs, your desires—ahead of hers?"

Harriet shrugged uncomfortably. The answer was obviously "Never" and it wasn't sitting well.

"Is being here the first time you've done something for yourself? Stepped outside your role at the hospital: Reliable Harriet?"

"Working at St. Nick's makes me happy." Harriet responded defensively.

"Of course! I'm not saying it doesn't. But there's something in you—isn't there, *amorcita*?—wanting to break free of the role you've cast yourself in. See more. *Be* more."

"I didn't cast myself in the role! My family needed…" She stopped. Reconsidered, eyes widening as she looked at her past from a different perspective. "It was me, wasn't it? I put myself in that role. They loved me no matter what."

"*Exacto*. I would wager anything you were always loved. No matter what." The vision of a family came to

Matteo. Himself, a wife, children—he wasn't sure how many—all of them laughing together as they shared a meal.

He cleared his throat again, giving his chin a rough scrub as he did so.

"Or maybe I am talking complete and utter nonsense." He filled in the growing silence between them.

"Actually…" Harriet drew out the word before conceding with a sheepish smile, "I think you might be right."

Matteo looked at her, his mind temporarily confusing the vision he'd just had with the reality. They were talking about Harriet and her sister, not some fantasy family scenario that could never exist. *Focus. Regroup.*

"My sister does want this for me. She was over the moon when she heard about you." Her eyes popped wide open, cheeks instantly going pink with embarrassment. "I mean, that I was working here."

"And what about you?" Matteo asked, his voice smokier than usual. "Do you want to stay?"

Harriet forced herself to meet the gaze she knew was resting on her, half hoping there would be an answer waiting there. They weren't talking about her sister any longer.

She knew what her heart was saying. *With every pore in my body!* But if staying meant stomping her heart into smithereens every single day…she wasn't sure how much she could take. Decisions she made for herself were now decisions she was making for her baby.

She looked into Matteo's richly hued eyes and saw kindness there. *Friendship.* But no commitment. He'd never promised it and something within her knew he was a man who stuck to his word.

The heart, thumping against her breastbone, was telling her what she already knew. She was in love with him and would have his child.

Her brain shrank to the size of a pea then had its own Big Bang, exploding into countless trains of thought.

Was the whole situation flawed? If that meant Matteo didn't sweep her up, race hand in hand to the judge to make her his wife the moment they'd seen the pregnancy test, sure. But who did that? He was probably still in shock at the news. She knew she was. And a shotgun wedding wasn't what she wanted anyway.

She wanted to marry someone who was in love with her. And in love with babies. All babies. *Their* babies. Matteo, painfully gorgeous and kind as he was, wasn't that man. So. Home it was. Home alone.

She looked away, busying herself with some unnecessary color-coding of the laundry pile. She didn't want her child to think she was a wimp. High-tailing it home to her safe and secure life at the first sign of trouble? Okay... it was a pretty big thing, but it wasn't trouble. It was...a curveball. And there were pluses to staying here. She'd learn more about Matteo. Have more of a fleshed-out portrait to paint for their child one day. Understand what made the idea of having a child so inconceivable to him.

So. She'd focus on the good.

Where would she start? With those lush green eyes she could quite happily ogle until the end of time. And who had hair so beautifully *desirable*? She'd find another way to describe to her baby about the thick black hair she'd thrilled in running—no, *raking*—her fingers through in a moment of unbelievably heated passion. The night of mutual desire they'd shared had been more than she would ever have hoped for even a few weeks ago. And a surprise baby to boot? Life was certainly giving her a triple whammy in the Big Changes department. And she was going to meet them with a smile.

Matteo may not share her feelings but she knew she had it in her heart to admire him for all the things he was. Strong. Impassioned. Driven.

All traits she admired. Ones she would love for the child growing in her belly to possess. So. It was time to choose.

Need. Want. Love.

Letting go of what she'd thought life had in store for her…embracing what she did have?

The words raced around her mind as she worked her gaze round the courtyard. Not even here a fortnight and she was already enjoying the volume of hands-on work her day involved. Being a research nurse was wonderful, but it was watching, observing, noting.

Here, with the absence of resources of St. Nick's, there was little choice but to muck in and she was loving it. From laundry to nursing poorly children to helping pregnant teens give birth. It was like tapping into a side of herself she hadn't seen for a long time—if ever.

Colors seemed brighter. New aromas took her by surprise every day. The lush green and tropical citrusy scent of so many plants bursting to life, despite the fact it was winter. A very balmy version of winter it would be all too easy to get used to, she thought, shivering away the memory of a murky London in winter.

If she stayed for the few weeks she'd scheduled, she could channel her passions towards being the woman she wanted to be for her family. Her growing family.

A smile teased at her lips as she gave the final pile of folded laundry a decisive pat. She heaved up the overloaded wicker basket and shot Matteo a grateful smile.

"Thank you. You've been a great friend."

"I've not done anything." He looked bewildered.

"Of course you have!" *You've helped me to believe in me.*

"Am I missing something? Are we booking you on the next flight to America or…?"

"You're stuck with me for the time being, I'm afraid. If that's all right."

"Of course! You're welcome, for as long as you like." He reached out as if to touch her, then pulled back, stuffing his hands into his pockets. "Are you absolutely sure?"

"Yes. Pretty sure." *No.* "Definitely sure." She twisted back and forth, the laundry basket a buffer between them. "On one condition."

"Which is?"

"You treat me the same as any other staffer here." Her chin jutted out a bit, a visual confirmation that her mind was made up. She would do this thing—and do it with style.

"I will do my best." He nodded his head as he spoke.

"It's all any of us can do." And she meant it.

# CHAPTER EIGHT

"SORRY TO INTERRUPT." Harriet had already tapped on Matteo's door a couple of times, to no avail, but having peeked through the open sliver of doorway she could see he was deep in thought over a pile of paperwork.

*"Si?"* Worry lines creased his forehead.

"Everything all right?"

"Yes, sorry. Just…" He pushed the papers back and stood up from the desk, taking what looked to be a long overdue stretch. "Managing budgets is never much fun.

"No." Harriet gave a sympathetic smile. "That was definitely my least favorite part of the job."

"Was?"

"Is." She laughed nervously. Of course her job back at St. Nick's was still hers. Is. *Is*. "I've obviously taken to fewer responsibilities a bit too easily."

"Are you saying working here is easy?" Matteo gave her the first genuine smile she'd had from him in weeks and… Yes. It still worked. Still made her feel all gooey inside.

She leant against the door frame for a bit of support and smiled back. They'd been flat out for the past fortnight. Births, a couple of emergency Caesareans, infants needing admittance to NICU, not to mention day-to-day care of the older children. And she was getting the impression this was normal. She'd become adept at filling in anywhere there were holes in the staff roster—shifting from art lessons with the little ones who weren't yet in school, to infant care, to cooking breakfast, lunch and dinner, and on to the clinic to for pregnancy checks, scraped knees, blood tests… It had been quite a learning curve and she'd been loving every second of it. Not to mention it gave her a really thorough look at how Casita Verde worked.

The moments with Matteo? Few and far between. She afforded herself a quick scan of the room. Matteo's Inner Sanctum. People either didn't go near it or hovered outside the doorway and waited. A time limit had pressed her to go ahead and knock. It wasn't like he was scary or anything. He was just… Matteo, the casita's Lone Ranger. And his room was… Wow, it was stark. Monklike. She'd hardly imagined him hiding away in a sultan's lair, but she hadn't expected bare walls and a single bed. Hadn't he mentioned parents? Ones who flew around the world in private planes?

"So…what can I do for you?" He was distracted. She was taking up his time.

"Oh! Yes, sorry." She pushed herself back upright and gave her blouse an unnecessary swipe. "Some of the schoolchildren are going to the zoo today and they need chaperones. I was wondering if you minded if I went along."

He stared at her blankly.

"You want to go to the zoo?"

"Well, I wouldn't say it was number one on my tourist destination list, but I haven't seen much of Buenos

Aires and thought it would be a great way to be with the children and see a bit of your beautiful city."

"And you are going to the zoo?"

"Um…" She chewed on her lip for a second. *Did he have something against the zoo?* "If that's all right. They've got *capybaras* and you can feed them!" His eyes widened. *Perhaps that was a bit too enthusiastic.* He was, after all, trying to work.

"The rodents. The large ones," she explained. Another blank look. "You know, I don't have to go. There's plenty to do here." She looked over her shoulder for an invisible to-do list.

"So you don't want to go."

Was he confused or just choosing to be obtuse? Come to think of it, he looked a little…vacant. Had he even heard anything she'd said?

"Matteo." Harriet chose her words cautiously. "You look a bit funny." Okay. Maybe not that carefully.

"What?" He managed to get some ink on his cheek in examining himself for "funniness". She itched to swab it off with her thumb, give his lips a little kiss.

No! No she did not. Being pregnant with his child did not mean she automatically got kissing rights. They'd agreed to be friends. No benefits. It was sensible.

But being sensible didn't seem to have seeped through to Harriet's body, which still ached for him. Honestly? It was difficult to believe she would ever desire someone as much as—

"Sorry, I've just had my head down in the books and all I'm seeing is numbers, numbers, numbers, blurring together in a big mess." Matteo threw his hands up into the air in frustration. "Each of the numbers means a child does or does not get help, receive medicine, have new books to read…" He stopped, gave her a self-effacing look and smiled. "I'm doing it again, aren't I?"

"What?" She'd actually just been watching his beautiful lips move. She'd heard this speech before. Not that he was boring. Not by a long shot.

"Telling you what you already know."

There was that smile again. My goodness, the man had one heck of a bobby dazzler.

"Matteo…"

"Yes, Harriet?" He pronounced her name formally as if they'd suddenly been transported to Edwardian times. It made her laugh. Relax. He was good at that, too.

"Do you fancy coming to the zoo with me?"

"How many buckets of feed do you think we have gone through already?"

"I don't know. Maybe three? I'm sure the children have had loads more!" Harriet squinted up at him, shielding her eyes from the sun.

"The children have had two—I don't think they'll be wanting another now that they're all mesmerized by the bears, the little savages. Quit dodging, Miss Monticello. How many buckets of feed have you gone through?" Matteo didn't really care. It was just fun to quiz her. She had more of her sister in her than she'd thought. Harriet didn't do anything by halves and feeding the free-roaming animals at the zoo was no different. A genuine carer, no matter what the species. Their child would be well loved. He bit down hard on the inside of his cheek, forcing himself to focus on her reply.

"Uh…let me see. The first bucket was when we saw the baby deer…"

Matteo watched avidly as she added a finger to her

bottom lip each time she counted a new bucket. Had he realized how beautiful her mouth was when he'd first seen her in London? Stupid question. Of course he had. Otherwise he wouldn't have... It was meant to be one night! And yet—hadn't he been the one to convince her to stay when her sister had her twins? A twin having twins. His eyes slipped to Harriet's belly. Could she be having...?

"Four?" Her lips parted into an I-don't-know-how-it-happened expression and he couldn't help but laugh. A little bit of panic was in there. Quadruplets? *Hijole!* Then he'd really have to step up.

He swallowed.

Like he was now? At arm's length and promising nothing?

"Four isn't that many buckets of feed, is it?"

Feed. Yes. Of course. They were talking about feed. Plenty of time to confront his demons in the midnight hours.

"There's more kid in you than in some of these kids!" he teased, hoping she'd missed his mini panic attack and had seen instead the hit of genuine gratitude he felt at being invited along. The day had been fun. She was the only person who'd managed to bring out the funster in him. The man he hadn't tapped into since his sister had died. It hadn't seemed right. It hadn't seemed fair.

"Well, it's been ages since I've been to the zoo and you can't feed the animals like this in London. Such lovely, furry, furry little beasts! It's good therapy!"

Matteo rolled his eyes good-naturedly. A few weeks ago he would've rolled his eyes and walked away. Who was he kidding? A few weeks ago you wouldn't have found him wandering round the zoo.

"Is this your covert way of saying I need fixing?"

"Don't worry—I'm the last person who is going to try and fix you!" Her eyes widened, fingers flying to cover her mouth in horror.

Without even thinking, Matteo slung an arm over her shoulder and squeezed her in for a little cuddle. She hadn't meant anything by it. No point in feeling bad.

"*Ai*, you make me laugh, *amorcita*. Not many people are brave enough to speak the truth." He dropped a kiss on her forehead as if he did it all the time. *Wanted to do all the time?*

"It's not normally what I do, either!" She looked up into his eyes, cheeks going pink at the connection. "I guess…you bring out the bravery in me."

He could have pulled her into his arms right there and then, kissed her and kissed her until the rest of the world just faded away. Her soft blonde hair was a fluff of gentle waves, her blue eyes so clear and true. He was already halfway there, holding her tucked under his arm like a delicate, beautiful bird, her chin tilted up towards his face, her eyes asking questions neither of them dared to voice. He felt another deep hit of emotion. *Love?* Had he reached a point where he felt his sister's death had been…been what? Avenged? That didn't sit right. Would sharing his fears with Harriet help her understand? His head bent just a touch closer to hers, his lips parting as he moved. She blinked, but didn't pull away. *Could he give her everything she deserved?*

"There they are!"

Matteo looked swiftly to his right to see a clutch of children on high-speed approach. He and Harriet, it appeared, were the endgame of a pell-mell race to the finish line. They split apart instantly, moved by a gut instinct not to be seen holding one another like lovers, or to be barreled down by racing children.

The littlest of the boys, Tico, emerged from the scramble of children, his face triumphant with near success. They were only a few meters away and against all odds he was pulling ahead of the taller children. Tico was going to win!

*"Oh, no!"*

Harriet saw it coming at the same time Matteo did. One foot tangled with the other and just short of reaching his goal Tico's small body became airborne, crashing into Harriet's—both of them landing on the ground with a *thunk*. When Tico raised his head, blood flowed from his mouth as if he had an endless supply. Matteo didn't know whether to check Tico or Harriet first. The baby. Was the baby all right?

Harriet met his frantic expression, hand on her stomach, and nodded. *Everything was fine.* She and the baby were fine.

*"Me gano?"* Tico asked, adrenaline from the race still pumping through him. Victory was more important than the pain he would soon be feeling.

"Did you win?" asked Harriet, trying not to look aghast at the boy's bloodied face. "What was the finish line?"

"You!"

"In that case…" she smiled, pulling some clean tissues from her shoulder bag "…you are definitely the winner!"

*"¡Gane!"* Tico pushed his hands to the ground to press himself up but instantly yanked his wrist to his chest as if it had been bitten.

"May I see?" Matteo reached out, gently laying out the boy's small wrist across his hand. Swelling had already begun to inflate the area between his hand and his arm. "Looks like you might need a trip to the hospital." He looked up at the other children gathering round to gawp at Tico and his injuries. "We need to get you back to school as well, eh?"

"I'll take him," Harriet volunteered, already making short work of the blood around Tico's mouth in an effort to find the source of the bleeding.

"No! The hospitals here are zoos!" *Ha!* The irony of it all. More pressingly, a pregnant woman in endless queues surrounded by people who had who knew what? It wasn't worth it. Not at this stage in her pregnancy.

If they had their own clinic, they wouldn't be at the mercy of the long wait that would no doubt greet them at A and E. Even having an X-ray machine would make a world of difference. And there it was again—the center point of his conundrum. Being with Harriet, loving her, loving their child would all detract from the undivided attention he needed to have to make the casita a success.

He laid Tico's hand back across the boy's chest, just above his heart, and folded the boy's other arm up to hold it.

"I'll go, Harriet."

"Tico, can you give me a smile?" Harriet continued, her focus on the little boy absolute.

"Why?" he asked before complying. A big, bloody gap was immediately visible. A gap that hadn't been there a minute earlier.

Harriet—in true form—didn't flinch. She just smiled, gave the boy's cheek a stroke with the backs of her fingers. Matteo chided himself. Of course! Her concern was for the boy. His own was for a lofty aspiration that in reality would most likely never be realized.

"You haven't got your big-boy teeth yet, have you?" Harriet asked.

"No. Why?" Tico worked his tongue up to the front of his mouth and quickly realized he was missing his two front teeth. Big brown eyes widened before tears came—fear and pain suddenly overwhelming his joy at winning the race.

"May I have a closer look?"

Matteo pressed himself up to standing as Harriet checked to see whether or not the roots of the teeth had gone. Harriet was doing a good job and obviously didn't need his help. Feeling a bit of a spare part, he called to the other children to once again make more room. As the pain kicked in, there would no doubt be more tears. Tears the little boy would most likely rather shed while being held in the comfort of Harriet's arms.

Matteo's hands balled into fists of pure frustration. He could do with a spell in those arms as well. Had one night with Harriet all but undone ten years of discipline? His entire adult life he'd been able separate physical attraction from his emotions. With Harriet they were becoming so interwoven it was almost impossible to separate them. She wasn't due to stay much longer. The time had raced by. He could do this. He had to do it. For the countless teens and children who needed his help.

"All right, kids. Shall we go and find the rest of your class?"

He ignored the chorus of "No!" and *"Por favor!"* he received at his rhetorical question and began to corral them, away from Tico and Harriet. All children loved gawping at a good injury. Lucky they didn't know what was happening inside his chest right now. He'd have a dozen pairs of eyes on him.

He scribbled out the name and address of the hospital Harriet should go to, promising to call a resident he knew there. "Maybe he'll be able to bump you up the queue."

She shot him a dubious look. Even he knew his hopeful face hadn't looked too positive.

"It's all right. We'll be fine." She helped Tico up to his feet, his eyes still glued to the dirt path in a vain attempt to find his missing teeth. "Perhaps—" she lowered her voice "—the children could have a look for..." She pointed at her own front teeth. "Just in case."

"Of course, *mija*. Anything." Their eyes met again, cinched by the link of so much more than the words they spoke.

She shook her head and looked away. He'd overstepped the mark. Pushing her away, pulling her close again. His intentions were in the right place, but in practice they were verging on cruel.

"Come on, Tico. Let's see what's happening inside that wrist of yours."

She looked over her shoulder as she left, a smile only just visible on her lips. It was for him. To comfort him.

Selfless. Courageous. In a league of her own. He knew who the better of the pair of them was, and yet he was letting her walk away, taking their child with her.

# CHAPTER NINE

"WHAT DID THE orthopedist say?"

Matteo held open Casita Verde's thick wooden door for Harriet and her seven-year-old charge. They'd been gone for hours. Enough time for him to regroup. Be friendly. Professional. Just what they'd agreed their relationship was. Professional.

Then again, meet and greet wasn't usually part of the "professional" service. And "usually" had all but gone out the window since Harriet had arrived. Perhaps a bit more regrouping was in order.

"As you thought…" Harriet ruffled the little boy's head "…it turns out wild races to reach the finish line first sometimes result in a wrist fracture. Not to mention losing your front teeth and gaining a unicorn horn!" The boy gave a gap-toothed grin, a huge lump already coloring the center of his forehead. "You're young—aren't you?" Harriet addressed the lad as if they'd known each other for years. "As soon as your grown-up teeth come along, you'll be as right as rain."

"I didn't mean to trip." The little boy sighed dramatically.

"Of course not, *chiquito*. It was a rather spectacular win. I'm sure the other children were incredibly impressed!" She switched to Spanish to rattle off a list of things he'd have to do to make sure his arm healed quickly. Well, not exactly *rattle*.

Matteo fought a smile as she spoke. In just a few weeks her speech had morphed into an amalgam of her native tongue and his. A lilting Spanglish. It never failed to light up his heart to see the children explaining things to her in Spanish, only to have her reply in English, the children nodding along as if it were the most normal way in the world to communicate. He couldn't quibble. It obviously worked. Who knew a stint of "orphan immersion" could be so effective a language tool? Perhaps he should run courses.

"I'll just take Tico up to his room as it's well past his bedtime and then maybe we can go over some of the children's charts?" Harriet asked, stifling a yawn.

"Absolutely, if it doesn't put you to sleep."

"No!" she protested, embarrassed he'd caught her. "Sorry. I'm sparko every afternoon and I missed out on my siesta today."

"Sparko?"

"British slang for out like a light," she explained.

"Out like a light?" asked Tico, his little face raised to the adults' in consternation.

"*Dormido.* Asleep," Harriet clarified with a grin, another yawn working its way to the surface.

"*Vamonos.* I'll get some *mate* going in the kitchen to help you stay awake!" Matteo thought for a moment. *Yerba mate* flowed in the blood of nearly all Argentinians but it had caffeine in it, something Harriet needed to be careful of in her pregnancy. Maybe mint tea would be better.

He paused, watching her lead the gangly boy away,

her arm protectively wrapped across his thin shoulders. He liked seeing her blonde head tilted towards Tico's jet-black hair, a smile lighting up his face as she whispered something that made the boy giggle.

A natural comforter.

*She'll be an incredible mother.*

The thought came with an unexpected sting of jealousy. If—*when*—she left she would no doubt move on. Could even fall in love with another man. The thought of someone else by Harriet's side, helping to raise his child, having a family of their own didn't sit well. Not at all.

He raked a hand through his hair with a huff of impatience and headed towards the clinic. He was letting himself care too much. Feel too much. Harriet wasn't a permanent fixture. She was here to help secure funding for a proper medical center. Four weeks. That was it.

What they had shared in London?

Best to put all of those thoughts back into the further recesses of his mind and forget about them. Some things were simply not meant to be. Even if his heart kept telling him otherwise.

He pushed open the door to the clinic and was assaulted by a riot of color. Another splash of Harriet.

"You couldn't make do with plain old black and white, could you?"

"Not my choice." Harriet entered the clinic behind him, arms laden with some of the children's files. "It was completely out of my hands. The children chose them."

"I didn't even know we had this many different colors of paper."

"Then you haven't gone down on your hands and knees to investigate the back of the crafts cupboard in a while."

He grunted. Fair enough.

"And do you think your little project is working?" He winced at his own choice of words. He'd already seen the fruits of her labor. He shouldn't have patronized her.

"Yes," she answered solidly, refusing to take the bait. "I do think my 'little project' is working. Staff rotas shouldn't be a secret. You're the people the children count on."

He noted she didn't include herself among the staff. Never mind the fact she was endearing herself left, right and center to every living being at the casita. Didn't it matter to her that she would be leaving them? That she was weaving herself into all their hearts and then would just fly back to England without a second thought? That she was leaving him?

It was precisely why he was the way he was. Pragmatically distant. Nothing was permanent. Nothing lasted forever. Not even family.

"The children have always known there will be *someone* around. Why does seeing who it will be make any difference?"

"Seriously?"

"Yes, seriously." This particular brainchild of hers eluded him. "It's not like we're withholding the information to be all-powerful."

"Then why are you withholding it?" She dropped the files onto his desk, her eyes meeting his for the first time.

"I'm not!" *Okay. That was defensive.*

"Children like to know what's going on around them. They liked to be prepared for things. The same way adults do." She laughed, her blue eyes coming alight. "Except for maybe my sister. And my parents, when they were alive. My mother didn't even like to have a calendar in the house!"

"Is that where you get it from?"

"What?"

"The need to know. The need to plan."

She considered his questions awhile before answering. "I suppose so. To an extent. But my family was exceptionally mad. Musician father. Artist mother. My sister got all the arty genes." She smiled, almost apologetically. "Being the sensible one was what I was good at. 'Oh, thank heavens we have Harriet to keep us tethered to planet earth,' they'd say."

A hint of sadness crept into her eyes. Had she felt it too? The urge to be a free spirit? Only to take on the role of the dependable one because her family had pigeonholed her into it? He knew that feeling from his own childhood. His wild and free sister making the most of her youth while he'd remained fastidiously tethered to his books. A fat lot of good being the responsible son had done him. So intent on proving he was worth something he'd missed what had been happening before his eyes. He should have known his sister had needed him. And now time was punishing him in spades.

"I'll tell you one thing, after seven hours at the hospital, you're definitely right about needing your own medical center."

He smiled, grateful for the change of topic.

"You didn't need to fly over from London to tell me that," Matteo answered drily, instantly wishing he hadn't fallen back on his "safety net" tone. "Sorry." He pulled out a chair for her so she could sit alongside him at the long wooden table he used as a desk. "Did I tell you inspections make me touchy?"

"Really?" Harriet feigned disbelief. "That's been *so* tricky to figure out over the past few weeks. I've never met someone who loves showing a girl his spreadsheets so much."

She smirked at him then used her finger to draw a figure eight on one of the desk's bare spots. 'We were waiting over three hours just for X-rays, even with the call you made to your friend. The resident."

"It's a long time for a child to be in pain."

"It's a long time for anyone to be in pain. A and E was teeming. It made me think of the stories of A and E departments in the UK some of my friends from nursing college have told me. A good reminder how lucky we are at St. Nick's."

"How lucky *you* are." *No need to be narky. You're not cross with her, you're cross with the situation.*

"How lucky the *children* are," she countered. "Which is more to the point."

"Well, we do what we can with what we have." Matteo didn't know if he was apologizing for his country or just being plain old curmudgeonly. Resources were limited. Which was exactly why Harriet was here. To help. He closed his eyes for a moment, took a breath. It was time to stop fighting her so much. Accepting help shouldn't be so...so charged! It was just... For heaven's sake, just look at her! Her pregnancy glow was real, a genuine radiance lighting her up from the inside out. She was one hundred percent beautiful.

"You know what Tico talked about the whole time?" Harriet began to shift the charts into three distinct piles before meeting his gaze. "You."

"*Que?* Whatever for?"

"They love you, these kids. They know how much

you do for them. And they want to give back, but…" She hesitated for a moment. "They aren't sure how to show you how much they care."

"What do you mean?"

"You give. You give so much to them, it's easy enough to see. But I don't think it's as easy for you to receive the only thing they have to offer. Affection," she added, unnecessarily.

"I don't think psychoanalyzing me is going to help us get through these charts," Matteo answered in a way that all but proved her point.

She wasn't the first to have noticed but she was the first brave enough to say anything. But growing up in a house where emotion had been seen as weakness? Where everything had been sheathed in a veneer of false charm? He snapped shut the folder he'd just opened.

"Are you saying I'm not good with the children?"

"No! Not at all." A light flush of pink began to creep along her cheeks. "It's coming out wrong. I'm trying to say they adore you. Absolutely adore you—but they don't seem clear on what it is you want from them."

It could've been a leading question but he could tell it was just Harriet fighting for the children in her own inimitable way.

"I don't want anything from them."

"C'mon. You must have hopes for them. Aspirations. And to get to those, children love to have goals. Have expectations."

"Like your family expected you to keep all the loose ends of their lives together?"

It was a low blow and unkind. She looked away and he didn't blame her. How could she know she was unwittingly hitting all the points he…?

*Oh, Dios.* You had to laugh, didn't you?

Harriet was hitting all the points he'd rather gloss over with a veneer of false charm. Push to the side rather than deal with.

He shoved back from his desk, the chair scraping along the floor as he did so and adding to the air of discord.

"These charts can wait. Come with me. I want to show you something."

"Matteo, I need these figures if we're going to present Casita Verde's case to St. Nick's board properly."

He didn't answer.

"Let me guess. This is another one of your 'show naive little Harriet how life really is' lessons."

Matteo pressed his lips together.

*Yes. In a way.*

"Well, if it pleases his lordship, I'd rather just get on with this work, thanks." She stood to give him a curtsey then looked him directly in the eye. "Just for the record, I think the one here who isn't facing up to how things are is standing right in front of me."

"Very possibly."

He ground his teeth together, eyes linked with hers. She wanted to psychoanalyze him? See why he ticked the way he did? Fine. She'd be leaving in a few days anyway so why keep things hidden any more? "There's an easy enough way to find out why I am the way I am." He opened the door to the courtyard. "Come with me."

"Okay." She nodded. "I will if you do something for me first."

"What's that?"

"Give me a scan."

"Is something wrong?" His chest constricted. To have

a baby he was terrified to acknowledge was one thing. To have and to lose that same child? He'd been through that once as an uncle. He didn't think he could survive it again. Especially as a father.

"I'm fine. I've had a bit of spotting since my run-in with Tico, but I'm sure everything is fine. More to the point, if you want me to learn one of your 'life stinks' lessons, then it's only fair we both see what I'm going through. What makes me think life is *amazing*." Her eyes dared him to deny her request.

Matteo felt like a cornered beast. Logic told him Harriet wasn't questioning his good intentions, but all his sensibilities were being overridden with suffocating waves of frustration and anger.

He faced facts every day. He knew she was pregnant and it had been her decision to deal with it on her own. His teeth pressed together so tightly his jaw ached. But he hadn't really given her much choice, had he? Hadn't opened his heart to all she had to offer. But she was questioning the way he *survived*.

Did he wish he could wake up every morning like so many people did and close their eyes to the world's problems? It would make life so much easier. He wouldn't have to scrimp and divvy out help in the way their limited resources demanded. He wouldn't have to turn away those in need to hospitals already sagging beneath the weight of their own overstretched budgets.

Did he wish he could just glide through life as if all the bad things in the world weren't happening around them? His shoulders lifted as thoughts fought for precedence.

No. Of course he didn't. He wouldn't be doing what he did if he believed that. But something in him knew what he did was still fueled by fury, rage at his sister's unnecessary death. How could he fully open himself up to love—to a future that included Harriet—if what kept him going every day was a ferocious grief at something he could never change?

He took her hand and without a backward glance set off across the courtyard. If she wanted a scan, she could have a scan. And then he'd show her why he had to stay adamantly, *vigilantly* the way he was.

Harriet stood as Matteo flicked on a series of switches. He had a face like thunder but something in her told her they were finally getting somewhere, hitting a breaking point in that cool veneer of his.

She pushed herself up onto the exam table after gulping down a couple of glasses of water, not saying a word as Matteo squirted an excess of lubricant onto the ultrasound wand. She didn't know what had possessed her to make him do this. She could have done it herself, but something in her worried Matteo was denying himself the joy of fatherhood as some form of punishment. She wished she knew what compelled him to live in such a closed-off way when he clearly had a heart of gold. Perhaps the reason was what he was about to show her. And she had to admit she was frightened to know the truth. If he genuinely did not see himself loving someone, having children…

"It'll feel a bit cold."

He was using his doctor voice. The reserved one.

She hitched up her shirt and undid the side zip of her skirt, feeling foolishly embarrassed at having to bare her midriff to him. It wasn't like he hadn't seen everything before! Or touched it. Caressed her luxuriously as if she were a cherished possession. She squelched down the thought and faced the screen as Matteo ran the wand over her womb. She'd be about nine weeks now, by her count. Enough time to see the heartbeat. Her breath caught in her throat and she twisted her fingers into good luck charms. *Please, please, please, let everything be all right.*

She'd seen hundreds, if not thousands of scans herself and yet watching the matrix of gray and black lines comprising her muscles, vessels and internal organs take shape, revealing to her what was happening inside her body was suddenly overwhelming. She kept her hands cemented beneath her thighs, knowing that if she didn't, her fingers would want to weave themselves through Matteo's as they saw, for the first time, the miracle they'd created.

"I'm just looking for the amniotic sac..." Matteo paused as he shifted the wand this way and that before holding it steady, his voice softening. "Here's the heartbeat— Oh! Do you see that?"

She nodded, too overawed to speak.

"Twins." He spoke the word she hadn't been able to. "Just like your sister."

*And I'll be raising them on my own...just like my sister.*

They sat for a moment, each of them absorbing the news, the only sound audible in the small exam room two tiny heartbeats. Harriet watched silently as Matteo gently began pointing out their arms, the two tiny hearts, four little legs and then abruptly he stopped.

"All right!" He made swift work of cleaning up the scanning equipment and officiously tipped his head towards the door. "Ready?"

He was out the door before Harriet had had a chance to wipe the gel off her stomach, register the news she'd just received. Twins!

*I'm having twins.*

Her heart ached at Matteo's response. What should have been an ecstatic moment between parents had been clinical and cursory. And yet there had been *something* there. A slight choke in his voice, a sheen on those beautiful green eyes of his. There had! Hadn't there?

She refused to let herself cry, knowing she was the only one to blame for the scenario. If she hadn't insisted he do the scan... Oh! Who was she kidding? She still would've wondered what his reaction would have been. Would've ached to know how he responded to the first sight of his own child—*children*! Well. Now she did. She tugged down her shirt, secured the fastener on her skirt and yanked open the clinic door, uncaring that it shut with a reverberant slam.

"Where are we going?" Harriet raced alongside Matteo, needing two or three steps to each of his single strides as he bashed out a text on his phone with his free hand. He should slow down. He should be compassionate. Hold her hand, swing an arm around her shoulder, pull her into his arms and kiss her with all of the love he held for her, but if he stopped now everything he'd worked towards would disintegrate.

He needed her to see. Needed her to understand why he couldn't open his heart to those two perfectly formed children they had created. Why he couldn't open his heart to her. There was only one place where she would be able to put together all the places. One place where the door to his heart had learned to stay solidly closed.

"Where are we going?" she repeated.

"My parents'."

"You grew up here?"

Harriet thought of the modest two-up, two-down she

and her sister had inherited from their parents. It was bigger than most nurses in central London could afford but it was no mansion. Three sets of twins would crowd the place out...but here? There was room for ten sets of twins! Maybe more.

If Harriet had thought the exterior of Casita Verde was impressive, she was entirely unprepared for the splendor of Matteo's family home. She had a cloudy memory of him mentioning private jets but had chalked it up to Latin machismo. Oops.

The Torres family home could easily be mistaken for a boutique hotel or the embassy of one of the world's richest countries. The towering edifice was composed of beautifully hewn stone, painted a brilliant white. A whiteness presently taking on the hues of the setting sun. A few steps led up to an impressive portico flanked by two intricately crafted wrought-iron gates. Matteo ascended the steps in seconds as if his body had memorized the fastest route in. Harriet had no doubt he could do it blindfolded.

"Why exactly are we here?"

"For supper." He smiled at her with a charm she suddenly understood only a man who had grown up among so much privilege could perfect. Quite a shift from the stony-faced mute man who she'd given silent speeches to throughout the deathly quiet taxi drive.

How on earth she could have fallen in love with someone so prone to stormy moods was...

The thought shivered through her as she reached his side.

*Love. Yup! That old chestnut was still setting off light displays in her heart!* Annoyingly. This whole scenario would be about a thousand million times easier if she just…didn't…care. Or enjoy staring at his back-side so much.

As she ascended each step she realized it wasn't just the pregnancy that had changed her life. It was her love for Matteo—as frustratingly one-sided as it was. From the moment she'd arrived in Buenos Aires she had really *lived*. And it had changed her. She'd been seeing new things, learning new things, thriving in an environment that wasn't dependent upon her—one she hadn't been obliged to feel needed in. It felt like gaining access to a whole new world she hadn't realized existed before.

She glanced across at Matteo, who was pushing open the broad front door without knocking. She was grateful for the gift, the gift of confidence. The door opened into an impressive foyer—and that confidence all but slithered away. It was like entering a different world, one miles away from the hectic hustle and bustle of the massive city, from the mayhem of the casita. A uniformed housekeeper was rushing to the door as Matteo pushed it open. He smiled broadly, kissed her cheeks and held the gray-haired woman at arm's length, hands on her shoulders as he asked a handful of questions, his voice warm with affection.

He introduced them quickly, efficiently before indicating to Harriet that she should follow him into an intricately tiled inner courtyard. Was this man the real Matteo? A man who looked perfectly at home among expensive antiques, servants, comfort? A life without even a hint of the despair they saw on a daily basis? Or was the Matteo at the casita the real one? The one who didn't mind getting grubby? The one who stayed up all hours to get a much-needed grant for funding?

*"Mama! Como esta?"*

Matteo's arms opened as a beautiful woman, perhaps in her sixties, approached. She was immaculately dressed—heels, sleek trousers, a silk blouse that seemed to have never encountered a wrinkle or the bloom of perspiration that Harriet was experiencing.

Harriet suddenly felt uncomfortable in her "uniform" of A-line skirt and flowery cotton blouse. She nervously ran her fingers through hair she knew could've done with a bit of primping. An untidy contrast to her hostess's jet-black hair pulled smoothly back into an immaculate chignon. Glints of light caught the pair of discreet diamond earrings she wore. A green pashmina, shifting across her shoulder line, brought out the same verdant sea color as Matteo's eyes. At least she knew where he'd got his eyes.

It was difficult to tell if the effusive greeting was a happy ritual or a practiced nicety. Was this what Matteo wanted her to see? A man in control of each microscopic moment?

"Harriet." Matteo beckoned her to join them. "Come, I would like you to meet my mother, Valentina Torres."

As his mother turned to her, Harriet could see her expression shift. Whether it was good or bad eluded her. She felt like shrinking behind one of the enormous pot plants before suddenly remembering...this woman was going to be a grandmother to her twins! She put on a smile and stepped forward.

"So lovely to meet you," Mrs. Torres murmured into her ear as they exchanged air kisses and a variation on an embrace. The greeting was, Harriet realized, terribly... *English*.

The rest of the evening passed in a blur. Matteo's father—Franco Torres—appeared a few moments later, incredibly handsome, terribly charming, straightening his cuff-linked cuffs before offering another series of air kisses. A manservant with a drinks trolley followed in his wake. Harriet was unable to refuse the gin and tonic they insisted all British people wanted but discreetly tipped it into one of the enormous tree planters after a discreet nod of the head from Matteo. It was strange but the move made her feel they were complicit, as though they were finally sharing her pregnancy together. It was a feeling she knew she probably shouldn't get used to, but she liked it. More than was good for her.

She saw Matteo whispering to the servant, who traded out her empty glass for a soda water with lime, complete with a knowing wink. Could he tell? Or had Matteo forewarned him? Unlikely… Her eyes met his, but under the scrutinizing gaze of his parents they were impossible to read.

As the evening got underway, it was a relief to discover Matteo's parents…her babies' only grandparents… were utterly charming. Incredibly well traveled, well read, full of *bon mots*. The evening, conducted mostly in English for Harriet's sake, was nothing less than delightful. And immaculately polite. Harriet was reminded of England's gentry and the slavish obedience to manners above all else. Decorum over honesty? How would they take the news that their son had knocked someone up and wasn't exactly seeing the rosy side of fatherhood?

Then again…what was it exactly Matteo wanted her to see? That his parents were rich and lived by the Miss Manners rulebook? There was something else there. Something deeper, and her heart went out to him. It was clear he and his parents lived very different lives. But there was only so far the apple could fall from the tree. After all, she was who she was because of her family.

Their eyes met as one of the maids began clearing the table and another brought a bowl of fresh fruit along with some delicate pieces of cheese topped with something she'd never seen before. It didn't matter. She wasn't really hungry. Sitting across from the man she loved when loving him would be impossible seemed to blunt her senses. What was he telling her by bringing her here? What were his eyes saying? She sought answers in their green depths, the tug of connection so strong it almost felt physical.

"Harriet? Have you tried *queso y dulce*?" asked Matteo's father. "This is quince jam together with a sharp cheese. I think you have it in Portugal. You must know it, yes?"

She dragged her eyes away from Matteo's, feeling as if a conversation they'd been having had been abruptly interrupted.

"I—I'm sorry?" She shook her head and registered his father's words. "No. I've not traveled much."

"Has Matteo not shown you the hospitality of the Porteños?" His mother scolded her son in advance of his response.

Harriet shook her head, then said, "We've been to the zoo!"

Again, their eyes met. *What was he trying to say?*

"The city has so much more to offer than the zoo." Mrs. Torres trilled a short musical laugh. "Surely, *amorcita*, Matteo has let you out of your…" she looked up towards the lavish chandelier illuminating the dining table as if it would help her find the best word "…place of work to enjoy some of the nicer sides of our country?"

"You mean Casita Verde?"

Was that a shudder? Had his mother just *shuddered*

at a mention of the incredible place her son had built from scratch?

She caught Matteo's eye again. This time his expression was perfectly clear. It said, *See? This is where I come from.*

"You're absolutely right, Mother. I *have* been remiss. Perhaps I should start now," Matteo said brightly, rising from the table and nodding in turn to each of his parents. "Our visit was unexpected and you no doubt have plans for the evening. You wouldn't mind if we missed out on coffee in lieu of a bit of a tour. Would you?" he added, as if they had a choice. He'd already circled the table and was pulling out Harriet's chair so she, too, could rise.

"Of course." His mother silently clapped her hands together, her forehead relaxing a bit as if the evening had, after all, been more taxing than she'd let on.

"It would be a shame for Harriet to miss out on the true delights of Buenos Aires. Why don't you take her to the plaza?"

"Plaza Dorrego?" Matteo's silver-haired father joined in with a glance to his watch. "Splendid idea. There won't be too many tourists this time of year. Yes!" He clapped a hand on his son's shoulder and spoke as if it had been his idea all along. "Take Harriet for a dance in the plaza. A splendid idea. Would you like one of the cars?"

"No, thank you, Papa. We can walk."

Harriet had to press her lips together to suppress a smile at his parents' collective horror at Matteo's suggestion of walking. She jumped in to second his idea.

"Walking would be lovely. Especially after such a delicious meal."

"But you hardly touched a thing!" his mother protested.

"I did! I really enjoyed it!" Harriet insisted, suddenly doubting her own words. The maids had been so deft in shifting away plate after plate she hadn't really noticed if she had nibbled or devoured the four-course meal.

"Shall we?" Matteo reached out a hand to her. Warmth and comfort immediately worked their way through her as they touched. And she was grateful for it. Her mind was spinning from the evening. Maybe now he would explain what this had been all about. So he was rich. Or at least his parents were. And they behaved a bit like characters in a costume drama. Did that make him a bad person? Hardly!

They bade a hasty farewell and as they went out into the cooling evening air Harriet felt as though she was drawing her first true breath of the evening.

"They do that," Matteo said, his eyes straight ahead, his warm hand still enveloping hers as they walked away from the city mansion.

"What?"

"Impose their world over the real one. I sometimes find it hard to breathe in there. You did well."

Harriet nodded, hoping he would continue.

"Did you notice everything they *didn't* talk about?"

"What do you mean?"

"What did they do when you mentioned Casita Verde?" He glanced at her before picking up the pace. It was clearly going to be a brisk walk to the plaza.

"I don't really recall." Saying she'd seen them shudder wasn't really what she thought he wanted to hear.

"That's because they didn't say anything. They never do. Idle chit-chat—it's all they can handle."

"Why?"

"Because if we were talk about us...our lives, what

I do and why I do it…it would be acknowledging their biggest mistake."

Harriet was nearly jogging now, his pace was so fast.

"Sorry. Please, Matteo. My legs aren't as long as yours." She released his hand, needing to steady her pace. Too much was whirling round her mind to make sense of things.

*"Lo siento, amorcita."* Matteo stopped, steepling his hands and pressing his fingertips to his lips. "I always get heated when I see them. I apologize. Here." He took her hand again and turned her towards a small cobbled side street lit with string after string of lights bulbs twinkling over a scattering of outdoor tables and chairs. His hand slipped to the small of her back as they worked their way through couples and groups, all finding just the right place to sit and enjoy the balmy evening.

"Let's get a drink and I will tell you what I should have told you when we first met."

Harriet felt her heart lurch to her throat. So much for breathing more easily!

Matteo laughed softly when he looked at her expression. "Don't be scared. It's nothing to—" He stopped himself, his smile shifted into a tightening of his jaw. Whatever he'd been about to say was no laughing matter. "It will explain a lot."

# CHAPTER TEN

MATTEO GUIDED HARRIET to a quiet table away from the pedestrian traffic but close enough to the edge of the outdoor seating area to see the plaza spreading out before them. He could see the dazzle of lights reflected in Harriet's eyes, her hips and shoulders shifting intuitively to the tango music that almost always played deeper within the plaza's depths. How to begin?

He bought himself a few more precious seconds of thinking time by calling over the waiter and ordering a glass of Malbec from the Patagonia region for himself and a sparkling water for Harriet, knowing she would refuse an offer to join him with wine.

"You're not going to tell me you murdered someone, are you?" Harriet giggled nervously, her paper serviette quickly being reduced to shreds between her fingers.

"No." Matteo looked her in the eye. "But I am going to tell you about the death of my sister."

Harriet's hands flew to her mouth, her eyes wide with horror.

"I didn't know you had a sister! Oh, Matteo..." She instinctively reached out a hand to touch one of his. "I am so sorry."

"You weren't to know." He looked up, thanked the

waiter for their drinks—waiting until he'd set them on the table and left before continuing. This story wasn't just difficult to hear. It was almost impossible to tell.

He drew lines in the condensation forming on the table alongside Harriet's bottle of chilled water as he spoke. "It was a long time ago. Well, when I was nineteen and Ramona was sixteen—so just over fourteen years. Fifteen?"

Harriet gave a small shrug. How would she know? It was his story to tell and it would be easiest if he just got on with it. He sucked in a breath and continued.

"My sister fell pregnant at sixteen and, as you can imagine now that you've met my parents, the news wasn't something they would be thrilled about. The teenage daughter of Franco and Valentina Torres pregnant? The scandal it would've caused." He tutted away the thought. "Rather than risk getting cut out of what you can imagine was a pretty substantial will by telling them, Ramona decided to hide it from us. At least, that's what I am guessing happened—because she left her big brother out of the loop as well." And it still hurt. Until the day he died it would hurt he hadn't been there to help her. If only she had trusted him!

Harriet's eyes remained wide. Free of judgment. Just a clear blue experiencing the pain he was reliving as the words tumbled out.

"I don't know what she was thinking. Maybe she thought she could pay someone to raise it. Maybe she thought she'd find parents to adopt. I don't know. She was too young to go off to Europe without our parents funding it. She never spoke to me or any of her friends. No one." He took a deep draught of his wine before continuing. "Anyway, she was at boarding school, like I had been, so hiding things from our family wasn't too difficult. School holidays? She'd be out with friends. Or so she said. Long story short, she was hiding her changing body from us. All of us. My parents put her prolonged absences down to her going through a wild spell. One she'd grow out of if they just pretended it wasn't happening and I—" He stopped.

This part was on him. He had been at university, doing groundwork courses to become a doctor, for heaven's sake, and hadn't noticed any changes in her. Sure, their paths had rarely crossed but he'd seen her more frequently than their parents had. And he hadn't noticed a thing. She was his kid sister! Maybe a little plump—but what did that matter? She was his kid sister. He loved her. Love handles and all.

"Were you at uni?" Harriet put two and two together without his help.

"Yes."

"It's an incredibly busy time, university. Especially if you are staying on campus."

He cursed under his breath. "You are kind, but you don't have to make excuses for me."

Harriet wanted to console him, but had second thoughts. She could see he needed to get it out. Purge the story that had been holding him hostage all these years.

He took a deep breath, sighing it out before bringing the tale to its painful conclusion. "She became pre-eclampsic. Hadn't bothered getting seen. Hadn't bothered going to a private hospital for check-ups, though, God knows, she had enough 'pocket money'. Even if she'd had no money, the public hospitals are required to see you if you can't afford treatment. But she was obviously trying to protect my parents from being caught in a pregnancy scandal. Social decorum over saving a life! It sickens me to think about it."

Harriet's fingers had crept back up, pressing the color out of her lips, her eyes just visible above her fingertips. A bit of fringe hung across one of her blue eyes. Instinct had him leaning forward to tuck it out the way before he could think better of it. Her fingers dropped away, leaving just a few centimeters between them. Their breaths, just for a moment, wove together before he abruptly pulled back and took another long draught of wine.

"So did you see her?" Harriet asked.

"Before she and the baby died? No." He shook his head slowly, his mood shifting from charged to contemplative. "No. She was taken to a morgue by someone. We never found out who. And my parents paid off the staff at the mortuary to keep it quiet."

"I can't imagine how awful it must have been." For Matteo. For his parents. Just—collectively awful. Harriet could hardly breathe.

"Losing Ramona was hard enough. It was how my parents dealt with it that made grieving worse."

"Which was?"

"To pretend they'd never had a daughter."

Dry-eyed, Matteo took on the polite persona of his parents, speaking as if he'd been explaining how to change a fuse or mentioning there might be some rain later. "Servants cleared her room. I have no idea where any of her things have gone. People had heard she'd died but that my parents weren't receiving condolences. Or if they sent them staff were instructed to burn anything before my parents could see the messages. It was worse than her being dead. It was as if she'd never existed at all."

"And is the reason you set up Casita Verde."

He nodded. "It doesn't solve many pregnant teens' problems, but at least we help some girls. Some children."

"From what I've seen, you've helped hundreds, maybe even thousands over the years! Not to mention the families who get to adopt those beautiful babies who will be loved and cherished."

"I don't know." Matteo finished his wine and signaled for the check. "Sometimes it's hard to see the point when you know there will never be an end to it."

"But surely you know how much better things are for the girls because of you?"

"I don't know about that. Perhaps." His eyes locked with hers. "Sometimes I feel like it is eating me alive to give them their lives back."

Harriet's breathing caught in her throat. This was it. Whatever he was about to say was at the heart of Matteo's grief.

"In order to do this—to keep the casita alive—I have to set limitations on my own life. I keep myself at arm's length from everything…everyone." He avoided her eyes as he continued. "No girlfriends, no family—absolutely no children. I need the perspective. I need not to care, because if I cared…how could I continue?" He choked out the words, his voice ragged with emotion.

"I hate to point out the obvious, but you don't really seem as if you don't care. What's the point in it all if it makes you so miserable?" Harriet looked mystified.

*Because I've met you.*

It's what he should have said but didn't. He couldn't lumber her with such a weight of misery. He gave a wry *humph* and when her expression told him it wasn't enough to justify turning his back on the woman he loved and their unborn children, he continued. "It's ridiculous, isn't it? The unhappy do-gooder. But without my work I can never make it up to my sister. And *with* my work I keep reliving her senseless death again and again. I just keep hoping it will…the happiness of what we do there… I hope it will just happen one day. That one day I will be able to do my work with *joy* in my heart."

Tears leapt to Harriet's eyes as he fought the sting of emotion in his own.

"Do you not see it? All the good you do?"

"The bad statistics will always outweigh the good."

"And that's how you measure your worth? By the statistics?"

"No. It's not that." *I should've been there for her!*

"What is it, then?" she pressed.

"How can I take pleasure in something I wasn't able to fix?"

"You can't," Harriet conceded. "You won't ever be able to. But shouldn't your life be about the future—not about the past? Don't you take any joy from what you do now?"

"Sometimes. Rarely." Matteo shook away both answers, knowing they weren't quite right. He looked her directly in the eye. "When I'm with you."

The silence between them grew as thick as the air. Strangely concentrated for the time of year—as if a tropical storm were brewing. Almost palpable, heated.

*Why couldn't he just say it?*

*Te quiero.* I love you.

Anything else would just be hot air. Useless. But when he had nothing to offer her? No future as a family? What was the point?

He became aware of the music floating from the center of the square. He'd done enough talking for the night and knew what he needed now. What he wanted. To hold Harriet in his arms and just be, letting the story he'd just told her shift away into the ether to settle how it would.

"Care for a dance?"

"Oh…" A nervous laugh underlay her hesitation. "I'm afraid I've got two left feet."

"I doubt that." He rose, holding out a hand to her. This could be the last time he would hold her in his arms. He hardly deserved it, but he wanted it—wanted her—so very much. "Come, *mi cariño*. Will you dance with me?"

Harriet slipped her hand into Matteo's, instantly feeling their connection deepen. She had believed her heart could not have felt more open to Matteo than in those moments when he had laid himself bare, had shown her everything that made him the man he was.

She pressed her fingertips into the back of his hand, hoping he knew she was accepting his invitation to take him as he was—a man struggling with the weight of grief. A man struggling to right a great wrong, unable to believe the good things in life were meant for him as well. A man who would live in her heart until the very end of time.

Her hand felt tiny in his. Protected. And yet, as she looked up to receive his gentle smile and an unexpected kiss on the forehead, she knew what she was feeling was true. She'd be able to tell their children their father was a good man. It didn't make the pain of knowing they couldn't be together any easier to bear…but his grief seemed too deeply entrenched for any external power to change. It would have to come from within and, from what she could see, something utterly earth changing would have to happen to him to change how he lived his life. She smiled back, enjoyed the kaleidoscope of green within his eyes, hoping to memorize every detail she could for their children. Her smile turned bitter-sweet as the idea struck that the twins might get those magical eyes and she could have a glimpse of the man who'd won her heart every day.

People and shops, tables and glasses all took on the blur of a film as Matteo pulled her into his arms, slipping the pair of them among the two dozen or so slow-dancing couples. His every touch brought new life to her body. Life she hadn't let herself believe she'd been aching for since they had been together in London. His fingers spread wide across the small of her back as he gathered her hand up with his other hand, holding it close against his chest.

They swayed in time with the music, its cadence adding an additional layer of sensuality to the dance.

She felt his voice vibrating in his chest before she registered the words.

"I'm so sorry."

"Me too." Her whisper was so soft she wasn't even sure if he'd heard her. It didn't matter. What did matter was the here and now. She pressed her cheek against the soft fabric of his dark blue shirt, willing herself to memorize his scent. As if she would ever forget it. Life had made sure of that. Matteo had made sure of that.

The musicians eventually packed up their instruments. Harriet's chest tightened when Matteo finally released his close hold on her, forcing her to acknowledge the moment was over. Their walk home was lingering and silent, each of them at pains to keep the fragile bubble of intimacy they were sharing intact.

Outside the doors of Casita Verde Matteo pulled Harriet to him and kissed her with the slow, heated sorrow of a farewell. Her entire being ached to be with him. Body, heart and soul. It was almost painful—the ache to understand why they couldn't be together. Why they didn't deserve what so many people enjoyed—a simple family life—knowing, at the same time that things were never that simple. Wrong place. Wrong time. Wrong woman?

She tried to shove the thought down. The pre-Buenos Aires Harriet would've thought that. Would have let insecurity overwhelm her. She couldn't let herself drown in doubt again. Not with two babies to care for.

Matteo held her face between his hands, looking into her eyes as if he were trying to see her soul.

"*Te quiero*, Harriet. I hope knowing that is enough."

"I love you, too." Harriet choked back the tears stinging at her nose, not even sure she'd spoken aloud. She forced herself to withdraw from Matteo's sweet embrace and ran towards the secure confines of her little room.

There was no point in torturing herself. Or him. She could see in his eyes he spoke the truth. He loved her, but she wasn't enough. Not enough to help him battle his demons. Not enough to see the good in what he did. Not enough to want to share the joy of raising a family together. It boiled down to what she had feared all along—she wasn't enough.

Harriet knew it was cowardly but frankly she was going to have to shore up whatever reserves of courage she had to face the next... Blimey, the rest of her life without *him*. Her dark-haired, green-eyed lover was going to have to be consigned to the past.

So!

She snapped her suitcase shut and took a final scan of the room to make sure she'd left no traces behind. No evidence for Matteo to find, reminding him she had ever been there. No need to weigh him down with more memories he didn't want to have.

She tipped her head back and sucked in a deep breath, trying her best to get her nose to wiggle away a new rush of tears.

*What a palaver.*

She gave herself a sharp shake. There wasn't time to feel sorry for herself right now. Thank heavens for time-zone differences and early-morning flights. She hadn't even bothered trying to sleep once she'd reached her room in those pre-dawn hours. Sleep wouldn't have come. There would be plenty of time for that in—oh, maybe about... When was it children headed off to university? She gave herself a *now, now, don't be like that* look at her reflection in the mirror. There'd plenty of time for a nap when she got home. Early. And hid out from everyone for a few days before she put on her brave face and went back to her old life. Her old ways. Routine. Just the way she'd always like things.

Her heart clenched at the thought.

Her little house and regimented life in the UK had all but disappeared from her thoughts in the few magical weeks she'd spent here. She stepped out of her room, giving the courtyard a quick scan, ensuring wouldn't be any awkward Matteo run-Ins. She'd already spoken with the shift nurse. Explained she had to get home. That it was very important. The nurse knew of her sister and the twins so she had let her come to her own conclusions and had accepted the assurances that "Of course you must go" and "Come and see us again soon". She'd nodded, her heart aching with sadness.

She wouldn't be back. This was it. Farewell forever to the place and the people who had changed her for the better. She was different now and would force herself to remember it. She sniffled. Okay, fine. Maybe a bit of pity party could be indulged in first, but by the time she landed back in the UK she was going to be one hundred percent strong. An independent woman. One who may not be enough for Matteo, but one who was going to be more than enough for their babies. So take that, Mr. Latin Perfection on a Stick! You want to see a mama take responsibility? Love and care for her babies?

*This* mama is going to love and care for her twins like a wildcat! A really wild wildcat. With English manners! *So there.* Her internal speech ended with a bit of a whimper, but she had to believe it was true—because she was going to have to test that theory again and again and again over the coming months and years.

Babies of her own!

She'd barely given herself time to think about what it would mean for her. Harriet Monticello…a mother!

She was almost surprised to discover a huge smile was peeling her lips apart before she froze at the sound of Matteo's voice. Her head whipped round. He hadn't seen her, had he? Her shoulders sagged with relief as she pinpointed his voice coming from the clinic. It was still early. From the staccato cadence of his speech and the pauses, he must be on the phone.

She lifted up her suitcase, trying to make as little noise as possible, and in a matter of seconds was out on the street where the people of Buenos Aires were preparing to start a brand-new day.

A brand-new day.

In her case? A brand-life was more like it.

She scanned the busy street, separating the commuters from the taxis on the trawl for customers. Ready to help someone start their life afresh.

The chances of filling the Matteo-sized hole in her heart? Zero to nil. Was there a less than nil?

She raised her arm to the swarm of oncoming traffic, willing a taxi to pull up to the curb sooner rather than later.

If she was going to get on with the rest of her life, she was better off doing so without a backward glance at what never could have been.

He had watched her leave.

He'd seen her crossing the courtyard through the louvered shades on the office door and had actually watched her leave.

A bit of self-flagellation wouldn't have gone amiss, Matteo thought, yanking the cord to the shades up but only succeeding in ripping the ruddy thing from the door entirely. At least a bit of physical pain would take the edge off all the thoughts burning through his mind like corrosive acid.

As the woman he loved had walked out of his life, he'd been on the phone. One of the other homes checking on whether they could send a girl over. She was showing signs of pre-eclampsia and if the symptoms worsened, delivery would be the only option. Another crisis. Another uncertain outcome.

He raked a hand through his hair, enjoying the scrape of his nails against his scalp. It felt raw. Just like he did. More raw than he could ever remember feeling.

"Of course, send her over," he'd said, hardly able to bear the sound of his own voice. It was the well-practiced tone of calm, amicability. The one he'd learned from his parents.

He laughed. Not a happy laugh by any stretch of the imagination—more like one of those bottom-of-the-well numbers. Mirthless. What else could he do? He'd made his own damn bed and it was time to lie in it. It was what he wanted, wasn't it?

To be left alone to stew in the misery of his sister's death for evermore?

*He'd let her walk away.*

He picked up the phone handset, tossing it from one palm to the other as he made up his mind. If he was going to stew here forever, he may as well make it worth it. He'd efficiently ruined the chances of St. Nick's going into a co-operative with Casita Verde. They'd want to protect Harriet and they'd be right.

Harriet. His heart all but punched him in the solar plexus from within. He deserved it. Class-A idiot didn't even begin to cover it. He'd just let the kindest, most beautifully loving woman he'd ever come across—pregnant with his *children* no less—walk straight out of his life so he could mourn something he could never fix. Never in a million years put right.

And there it was. The decision he'd made. Not to fall in love. Not to have children. A wife. A family. This was what it looked like. This was how it felt.

He inhaled deeply, easing the breath out over a long, slow count to ten.

Nope.

Time hadn't changed anything. Ten seconds anyway. Still miserable and only one way to fix it.

He punched the numbers into the telephone handset, his jaw setting tightly as he did. This was one telephone call he had never expected to make.

It was nigh on impossible for Harriet to believe how much had changed in just over a month.

Just four short weeks ago she had taken this exact same taxi journey in the opposite direction. Well, exactly the same plus a few add-ons. The tango music was the same. The really, really bad traffic that would make the journey cost a fortune and probably make her miss the plane was new. Add to that the heartache and the two minuscule babies growing in her belly.

Those things? Those were all brand spanking new. As fresh as a baby's...

Oh... A smile crept onto her lips.

As fresh as a baby's bottom. Times two.

She rolled down the window, getting a much-needed blast of late-morning air.

It hadn't occurred to her for a second not to have them. *The babies.* It almost made her dizzy to think how microscopically small they would be right now, and she felt, in a way that surely must be crazy, as though she already knew them. These teeny babies created with a man she absolutely adored.

Well.

Right now she didn't like him all that much.

No! Even that wasn't true. She loved him. She loved him heart and soul but he'd made it more than clear her love wasn't enough—it would never be enough. Breaking Matteo's protective veneer of grief seemed all but impossible. He'd made up his mind. No children. No Harriet.

Her hand flew to her tummy and gave it a reassuring little rub.

"Don't worry, little ones. I don't know how we're going to do it but I'm going to make sure you know how loved you are. My little good-luck tokens!" She gave her tummy a satisfied pat as the thought of a pot of Argentina's good luck New Year's beans popped into her mind.

*"Mi pequeño haba."*

*"Usted va a tener un bebé? Felicidades!"*

Harriet started at the taxi driver's good wishes. Had she been speaking in Spanish? She gave a little laugh. She'd have to remember everything she could so she could speak to her little ones in Spanish as well.

The smile slipped from her face. For what? So her children could be reminded of the father they would very likely never meet?

The gravity of what was happening suddenly hit her. She sank against the pleather seat of the taxi, willing herself to be strong. All she had to do was get on the plane, go back home and…have twins. Easy. Right?

Matteo looked up from his paperwork with a start. Was that his *father* crossing the courtyard? Franco Torres III in Casita Verde?

This *was* a day of firsts.

He pushed himself away from the desk and in a few long-legged strides was reaching out a hand to his father, pressing cheeks in the customary greeting—something he did by rote. Only this time it felt different. It felt meaningful.

It struck him how much he missed having his father in his life. He was an incredible businessman, a powerful personality and had been his childhood idol. If he had pushed him, really pressed his parents to talk about Ramona's death, would it have made them any closer?

"Shall we?" His father released his hand, indicating they go back into Matteo's office.

Typical. Taking charge of a situation.

"I don't even know why you're here, Papa."

"Come—come inside."

"What? Into my own office?" He felt himself bridling. "You've never even been here before and you're already behaving as if you run the place."

"Now, son—"

"Now, son, nothing!" He reeled round, strangely startled to find they were eye to eye. He was a man facing his father. A grown man. He bit back the insults he could have so easily slung. He was a man now.

It was time to behave like one.

"Please." He gestured to a chair opposite his at the desk. "Have a seat. Mate? Coffee?"

"Coffee, of course." His father had always preferred a rich, dark roast to the traditional tea Argentinians couldn't seem to get enough of.

*"Con leche?"*

It had been a long time since he'd made his father a cup of coffee.

*"Sí.* Some milk would be nice.

Matteo crossed to the far side of his office to a corner reserved for boiling water, making hot drinks for the girls who came to them—needing the length of time it took to drink a cup of tea to begin to process how much their lives would be changing.

It struck him how easily he could deliver news to his father about how each of their lives could be changing if only things were different. Twins—*his twins*—would be coming into the world. His father would be a grandfather, his mother an *abuela*. He wondered how they'd fall into the roles…grandparenting. Making up for mistakes they'd made the first time round? Or more denial?

He picked up the mugs of steaming coffee and placed them on the desk—one in front of his father and the other where he'd cleared away the pile of paperwork he'd have to finish if work on the sorely needed clinic were ever to begin.

"So?" Matteo put on his best idly curious voice. "What brings you to this part of town?"

Just a few minutes later found Matteo staring slack-jawed at his father.

"You want to pay for the entire building?"

*"Sí."*

"With no strings?" That was deeply unlike his father. Something was up.

"It's better than taking out a loan, no?"

Ah. That's what this was about. The phone call he'd made to the bank.

"Papa… Father. I am a grown man. I can handle the loan."

"What are you going to pay it back with?" The question wasn't accusatory. It was just sensible.

Matteo stopped his shoulders from going into automatic pilot and shrug. He didn't know. He didn't have a clue. All he knew was that if he was going to survive life without Harriet he was going to have to work his fingers to the bone to forget—forget everything. The love, the laughter, the tears, the *light*. His children he would never know.

"Would it hurt? To take the money from your father?"

"It's not that, Papa. It's— What has brought this on? How did you even know?"

"Son." His father looked him square in the eye. "Most of our family's money is in that bank. They are not going to take a call from my son without me hearing about it."

Matteo shifted in his chair. This was exactly why he had been hoping to get the funding from England. No family. No strings. No feelings to contend with.

"Your mother and I—"

"Mother is part of this, too?" He was sitting up straight now.

"*Si*. Of course she is." His father looked amazed that it was even up for questioning. "We make all our decisions together."

"So it was both of you who decided to behave as if Ramona had never lived?"

His father blanched. Matteo instantly regretted the harshness of his words, seeing for the first time how much his father had aged in the past ten years. He had been so handsome, so vital when she had died.

Did he really want to relive the hell that had all but rent his family apart? Something in Matteo told him to keep going. He was feeling the need to bring it out in the open now. Feeling it deeply.

"Is that what you think happened? That we just erased her from our minds? Our hearts? Is that what you think of us?"

He didn't need to say yes. He knew his face told his father everything.

His father's shoulders sagged as he accepted the information and the pair of them sat in silence, registering what had just transpired.

"Do you know what your sister said when she came to us?"

Matteo pushed his chair back from the desk. *What?*

"*Que?* She told you?"

"Yes, what did you think? She wouldn't involve us in something so huge? So life changing?"

"I just presumed…" Matteo felt the thunderous weight of a new understanding strike him solidly in the chest.

"What? That she couldn't come to her parents and tell them she was in trouble? That we wouldn't be there for her when she needed us most? Is that what you thought?"

"What else could I think? No one told me anything."

His father's hands scrubbed at his face while he eyed his son. How could people so close have so much hidden away from each other?

"We thought we were doing the right thing."

"By letting me think she died out there because you rejected her?"

"By letting you think it was her choice."

"To die?"

"No, of course not, son. To leave. It was her choice to leave us."

"And that's why you didn't tell me—because you'd been rejected?" Matteo felt his rage dissipating.

"We didn't tell you in part because we didn't have the words. We'd failed. We'd failed as parents. She didn't want us. Or want our help. And you were so angry. At the world, at us. It wasn't like telling you then would've changed anything."

"So why are you telling me now? Offering this money?"

"The money?" He waved it off as if it were nothing.

"We have too much. How could we give it to causes other than the one our son works on, eh?"

"You didn't really seem to think so when I started Casita Verde."

"You didn't want the help. Would've thrown it back in our faces and we were too fragile then. We thought— we thought if we kept our distance then perhaps..." He trailed off, unable to continue for a moment. "We thought if we gave you your space there might come a day when you would be more receptive to us, be able to hear our side of the story."

"What made you think that it was now?"

"Seeing you—the other night—with her."

Matteo didn't have to ask who. He felt the twitch in his jaw as his teeth ground together. If it had taken his father ten years to talk to him about it his sister, he damn well needed more than a couple of minutes to talk about Harriet. About the children he would never know.

"How long have you been in love with her?" His father uncrossed his legs and shifted in his chair, dark eyes gently trained on Matteo.

"It's that obvious?"

"As the hand in front of my face." He held up his palm for good measure.

"And here I was thinking I had it all under control."

"Son, you have never—in your entire life—brought a woman home to us. It meant a lot to your mother and me. And we like her. We'd love for you to bring her by again."

"We're a bit late for that." He all but ground out the words.

"*Que?* She's gone?"

"Back to England." Matteo hated saying the words. Hated the truth in them.

"And you will go for her?"

Matteo smiled, scrubbing at his jaw as he did.

"I think I didn't make a very good impression."

Should he tell him? Tell him he was going to be a grandfather?

"*Mijo*—can I give you a piece of advice?"

"I have a feeling I am going to get it whether or not I want it." He gave his father a wry smile, the warmth of connection turning it into a toothy grin.

"Eh…" His father tipped his head back and forth. "You know your father better than I gave you credit for." He pushed himself forward and locked eyes with his son. The first real moment they had shared in years.

"*Mijo*, when you are in the midst of something so painful you can hardly see straight, you often make bad decisions. We made a bad decision, your mother and I. Hell! We've made lots of them! If there were any advice I could give to you now—which I wish I'd known then, when we agreed to let your sister walk away from us— it is don't be afraid of being wrong. A decision isn't always worth sticking to. Particularly one made in the heat of the moment."

Matteo felt the frenzied wheels of indecision churning in his mind begin to shift gear. Regroup.

What would it mean if he were… He could barely believe he was letting himself think the thoughts. What would it mean if he were to change his stance? God knew, he loved Harriet and when he had found out she was pregnant his first reaction had been a private swell of elation. One he'd hidden from Harriet as they'd each seen, for the first time, two little heartbeats. Chances were high Harriet wouldn't have him now. Not after the way he had treated her.

But…the spark of possibility reignited his heart rate.

"Papa?" He pushed himself up and out of his chair.

His father waved away whatever it was he was going to say.

"Go. We will see you later?"

He gave his father's shoulder a warm squeeze and dropped to kiss his cheek.

"Yes. Come for dinner," his father called out to him, the words following him into the courtyard. "You whet your mother's appetite to see more of her son. And perhaps a daughter-in-law?"

*If there is even the tiniest chance, Papa…even the tiniest of chances…*

# CHAPTER ELEVEN

*"Café con leche, por favor."* Harriet enjoyed hearing the Spanish roll off of her tongue, the waiter accepting her order as if she had lived here all her life and having coffee in the square was perfectly normal. She'd missed the early flight and sitting in traffic for the next one when it was ten hours away? *Bleuch.* The world wouldn't mind if she indulged in just an hour or so in the square where she had last been in Matteo's arms.

She started. Things were different now.

*"Descafeinado!"* she called after the retreating waiter. It would be decaf from now on.

The waiter tipped his chin upwards, acknowledging her change of order. There would be so many changes to come.

She settled back into her chair, trying not to let herself feel too overwhelmed. This was a good idea. *No, it isn't.* Yes. It. Is. She scolded herself. Matteo wasn't evil, he was…he wasn't able to free himself from the past. So she'd let herself indulge in the past for a bit—a past she'd have to let go of if she were to continue with any sort of strength.

Her mind flicked to her sister, busy with newborn

twins. A twist of excitement squirmed through her. She would be telling her sister her news soon enough. Pregnant with twins! She gave a panicked little laugh. Wouldn't it be chaos in their little London house? Two sets of twins, two single mothers… She chided herself for not ringing Claudia sooner. Tell her what was happening. Ask her advice. And how would she begin? *Remember that sexy Latin doctor I told you about?*

"Your coffee, *señorita*."

Harriet froze. She knew that voice and it wasn't that of the young waiter who had taken her order. *Had she just conjured Matteo out of the ether?* She didn't even trust herself to turn around. Her eyes barely moved as the cup of coffee was slipped onto the table by a hand she also knew very well. Her eyes worked their way up along his wrist…a bit farther up, the sleeves of a white linen shirt were bunched once or twice over a well-defined forearm, proof the warmth of the day had increased. She smiled at the thought of just how lovely winter was in Buenos Aires. There would be a tiny bit of summer left in Britain before the days began to close in. Before the cold, dark British winter began.

Her vision began to blur as tears filled her eyes.

"What are you doing here?" She spoke more to her cup of coffee than to Matteo. She didn't dare look at him.

"I've come to tell you what a fool I have been."

Harriet turned at his words, the previously unspilled tears trickling down her cheeks as she did so.

"Come now, *amorcita*." Matteo used the backs of his fingers to brush away her tears, tugging out a fresh handkerchief with his other hand as he did so.

"How did you find me?"

"I—I didn't," he confessed. "Not in the strictest sense."

A streak of disappointment shot through her. Another mistake.

She tugged her hand away from his.

"No, *mija*. Listen. If I was trying to avoid you—would I have brought you your coffee? Be sitting here with you?"

Harriet kneaded her lips in and out of her mouth a couple of times, searching his beautiful green eyes for answers. Could she trust in him?

"Why are you here?"

"I wanted…" He hesitated. "I wanted to come back and think about last night. About telling you I loved you but that I couldn't offer you anything."

The words hung between them, heavy with self-recrimination.

Harriet shook her head. What was the point in this? More *Poor me* before she long-hauled it back across the Atlantic? She had enough baggage, thank you very much.

"So you've come here to make me feel worse than I already do? No, thank you." She picked up her handbag and signaled to the waiter for the check. If the wounds she was already treating were going to be made deeper, she would have been better off sitting in the departure lounge all day. At least there she could think clearly about the future.

"No, not at all. *Por favor*, Harriet. Sit down." Matteo wasn't pleading but there was a depth of emotion in his tone that compelled her to stay put.

She gave him her best *I'm listening* face in a valiant attempt not to crumble to bits all over again.

"I came to try and re-create that moment in my mind, to try and picture how different things would be if I had just stayed open to possibility. *To love.* To love you, to love our children—" His voice broke as he continued. "I don't think I was ever able to see how it would be possible to love a child of my own without feeling I'd betrayed my sister."

"And what makes you think you can now?" Harriet struggled to keep the defensiveness out of her reply.

"You."

Matteo's beautiful green eyes met hers.

"What are you saying?"

"I'm saying you make me better, Harriet Monticello. You helped me see I can be stronger, more courageous and capable of loving. I love you, Harriet. *Te adoro. Eres mi angel!*" He raised his voice as if he were making a joyous proclamation to the square. Which, she realized with a sudden laugh of pure delight, he was.

Her eyes widened, lower lip caught between her teeth. This was a huge about-face. Could she believe him? His expression quickly sobered as the smile dropped from her eyes. "You're my angel, Harriet. The woman who has made me see that life is for living, not regretting. Can you forgive me?"

"What for?" Harriet couldn't even say the words. Her hands did an automatic trip to her midriff, weaving her fingers together across her belly.

"About our babies?"

"Twins can be a handful! Pregnancies don't always go smoothly," Harriet interjected, her eyebrows shooting high above her eyes. "You know what happened to my sister."

"Two babies? Maybe there'll be more after! As many babies as you want." Matteo's eyes glistened with excitement, his own hand reaching out to cover hers so that they lay entwined together on her belly. "There is one thing, though."

"What?" The word shot out of her. She couldn't do this, ride the emotional yo-yo. Not anymore.

"Will you marry me?"

They were words she had never even let herself imagine she would hear from him. She pored over every detail of his face, trying to glean the depth of truth in his intentions.

"Harriet?" Matteo teased her fingers out of the fists she had clenched them into. "Harriet Monticello..." he slipped from his chair and dipped onto one knee "...will you do me the honor of becoming my wife?"

Her nod was so slight at first that Matteo wasn't entirely sure it was a yes. And then it grew, bit by bit until he was certain Harriet had accepted his proposal.

Without a moment's further hesitation Matteo scooped her into his arms to take kiss after long-awaited kiss from her beautiful lips, a handful of nearby coffee drinkers applauding as they did so.

"It was fate, wasn't it," she whispered against his lips as their breathing steadied, forehead pressed to forehead. "Coming to the plaza."

"If fate hadn't lent a hand, *amore*... I can assure you I would have searched and searched the world until we were together again."

"Forever?" she added, knowing in her heart it wasn't necessary.

"Forever a family."

# CHAPTER TWELVE

"I CAN'T BELIEVE it's going to be so big!"

"This is what happens when my father gets involved in anything." Matteo's hands made a shape of something regular sized then ballooned them until it was out-of-control enormous.

"You're not basing that on my ridiculously huge stomach, are you?"

"Of course not, my love. Although…" Matteo eyed Harriet's ever-increasing belly with a studied eye, running a hand across it for good measure. "Are you sure there aren't triplets in there?"

"*Oh, Dios!* I hope not. I think two will be quite enough, thank you."

"You wouldn't have three?" Matteo feigned a hurt expression.

"Of course I would, my love." She went up on tiptoe to give him a peck on the lips, staying just long enough to qualify her answer. "Just preferably not all at once. Besides…" she dropped back onto her feet "…it would be nice for Nicolette and Ramonita to have a little brother to tease one day."

"Ever the practical one." Matteo wrapped a protective arm around his wife's shoulders, dropping a kiss atop her honey-blonde head.

"Practical?" Harriet laughed, thinking how much in her life had changed so quickly. After a whirlwind tour in London to meet up with her sister, the twins and her sister's new husband, they'd come back to Argentina. Now—less than a year after hiding behind a curtain at the first sighting of her Argentine hunk—she was living in a new country, opening up the Ramona Torres Memorial Clinic, married to a man whom she couldn't have dreamed up if she'd tried…and with twins on the way!

"If you call this practical, I'm happy to stay that way." Her eyes widened suddenly, a sharp pain taking hold of her belly. "I think, darling—if we are to be practical—you better hurry up and cut the ribbon for the clinic. I might be needing it very, very soon!"

\* \* \* \* \*

*Look out for the next great story in*
THE MONTICELLO BABY MIRACLES *duet*

*TWIN SURPRISE FOR THE SINGLE DOC*
*by Susanne Hampton*

*And if you enjoyed this story, check out these*
*other great reads from Annie O'Neil*

LONDON'S MOST ELIGIBLE DOCTOR
ONE NIGHT…WITH HER BOSS
DOCTOR…TO DUCHESS?
THE FIREFIGHTER TO HEAL HER HEART

*All available now!*

# TWIN SURPRISE
# FOR THE SINGLE DOC

BY

SUSANNE HAMPTON

Published in Great Britain 2016
By Mills & Boon, an imprint of HarperCollins*Publishers*
1 London Bridge Street, London, SE1 9GF

© 2016 Susanne Panagaris

ISBN: 978-0-263-91492-4

Our policy is to use papers that are natural, renewable and recyclable
products and made from wood grown in sustainable forests.
The logging and manufacturing processes conform to the legal
environmental regulations of the country of origin.

Printed and bound in Spain
by CPI, Barcelona

Dear Reader,

Claudia Monticello has accepted that she's more like her fiery, impulsive Italian father than her sweet and sensible Irish mother. The 'sensible' genes have been lavishly bestowed upon her twin sister Harriet. But she also knows that her impulsive decisions and her desire to take everyone at face value—particularly men—has to stop. Her need to live life to the fullest has led her to the other side of the world on not much more than a whim— and that's the *least* serious of the repercussions!

Claudia has received life-changing news, and she realises she has no choice but to be responsible. And suddenly— and surprisingly—that doesn't seem so hard. Her heart is already consumed with love for her unborn babies, and their needs will for evermore come first. The only men who have a future in her life are her two sons.

That is until she meets Dr Patrick Spencer.

This former obstetrician has left his life in London to start a new life in Los Angeles. But the disappointment that has driven him five thousand miles from home seems to follow him and, despite a new career, he never feels fulfilled.

That is until he meets Claudia Monticello.

They have both left London for very different reasons, but when their worlds collide they are forced to question their decision never to love again.

I hope you enjoy Claudia and Patrick's journey to happily-ever-after. It's a bumpy ride, so you might need to hold on tight…just as tightly as my hero and heroine do from the moment they meet!

Warmest regards,

*Susanne*

To everyone who thought they had closed their hearts to love…
only to be proved wrong by a love
stronger than the heartache they had survived.

And to Alli and Gilda and all of my amazing friends
who constantly provide inspiration for my books.

Married to the man she met at eighteen, **Susanne Hampton**
is the mother of two adult daughters—Orianthi and Tina. She
has enjoyed a varied career path, but has finally found her way
to her favourite role of all: a Mills & Boon Medical Romance
author. Susanne has always read romance novels and says,
'I love a happy-ever-after, so writing for Mills & Boon is a
dream come true.'

### Books by Susanne Hampton

### Mills & Boon Medical Romance

#### *Midwives On-Call*

*Midwife's Baby Bump*

*Unlocking the Doctor's Heart*
*Back in Her Husband's Arms*
*Falling for Dr December*
*A Baby to Bind Them*
*A Mummy to Make Christmas*

Visit the Author Profile page
at millsandboon.co.uk for more titles.

### Praise for
### Susanne Hampton

'A stunning read about new beginnings that is guaranteed to
melt any reader's heart.'

—*Goodreads* on
*Falling for Dr December*

'Probably one of my top ten favourite reads this year. It was
heartbreaking…kept me wanting to read to find out what
happens next.'

—*Goodreads* on
*A Baby to Bind Them*

# CHAPTER ONE

'CONGRATULATIONS, CLAUDIA. You're having twins!'

Claudia Monticello's deep brown eyes, inherited from her Italian father, widened like dollhouse-sized plates against her alabaster skin, a present from her Irish mother. In a rush of panic and disbelief, her gaze darted from the gel-covered bump of her stomach to the grainy black-and-white images on the screen, then to the *pleased as punch* radiologist's face before finally looking up to the ceiling to where she imagined heaven might be. Not that she thought her parents would be smiling down at her after what she had done.

Suddenly the room became very hot and she struggled a little to breathe. The clammy fingers of one hand reached for the sides of the examination table to steady herself. *Two babies*. Her mouth had dropped open slightly, but her lips had not curved to anything close to a smile. In denial, she shook her head from side to side and nervously chewed on the nails of the other hand. There had to be a mistake. The radiologist, still smiling at the screen and apparently unaware of the panic blanketing her patient, gently moved the hand piece over Claudia's stomach to capture additional images.

She must have zoomed in too quickly, Claudia mused.

Double imaged.

Misread the data.

Be new at her job.

But Claudia knew without doubt, as she slowly and purposefully focused on the screen, there was no mistake. There were two tiny babies with two distinct heartbeats. The radiologist was using her finger to point to them. Her excitement was palpable. A reaction juxtaposed to Claudia's. At twenty-nine years of age, Claudia Monticello was anything but excited to be the single mother of twins. For many reasons... The first was her living five thousand miles from home...and the second was the fact her children would never meet their father.

Twenty weeks had passed since Claudia discovered she was to be the mother of two and, as she dropped her chin and looked down at her ample midsection while waiting for the elevator, she was pleased to see they were healthy-sized babies. Her waist was somewhere hidden underneath her forty-five-inch circumference and she hadn't seen her ankles for weeks. Her mood was one of anticipation as she waited for the doors to open on her floor. Her final obstetric visit was imminent and she was thinking about little else than her flight home to London the next day. It couldn't come quickly enough for her. She couldn't wait to farewell Los Angeles.

And turn her back on the disappointment and heartache the city had brought.

Or, more correctly, that she had invited into her life.

The day was warm and she was wearing a sleeveless floral maternity dress, one of three she'd picked up on the sale rack in Macy's when she rapidly outgrew all her other clothes, flat white sandals and her oversized

camel-coloured handbag that she took everywhere. Her
deep chocolate curls were short and framed her pretty
face, but her eyes were filled with sadness. She pictured
her suitcases, packed and waiting just inside the door
of her apartment. She was finally leaving the place she
had called home for almost a year. The fully furnished
apartment was in a prime high-rise gated community
on Wilshire Boulevard and in demand. The home would
have new tenants within days. It had only been temporary, like so much in that town, and she wondered who
would be sleeping in the king-sized bed later that week
and what the future held for them. She hoped for their
sake they hadn't rushed into something they would live
to regret.

The way she had.


Patrick Spencer waited inside the elevator for the doors
to open. It had only managed to travel down one floor
and was already stopping. A sigh escaped from his lips.
He prayed it wouldn't stop on every floor on the way
to street level. His patience was already tested. He was
having another one of those days. A day when he felt
frustrated with life and struggled with a cocktail of re-
sentment mixed with equal parts of doubt and disappointment and a dash of boredom with his new reality.
Not that his reality was devoid of life's luxuries, but it
was missing the passion he'd once felt. It was another
day when he felt cheated out of what he had planned and
wanted for his future, even though he was the one who'd
walked away from everything. A day when he almost
didn't give a damn. And whenever he had those days he
always put on his sunglasses and tried to block out the

world in which he lived. He had been cornered into this new life. That was how he saw it.

If things had not gone so terribly wrong, he would be living in London instead of calling Los Angeles home.

With melancholy colouring her mood, Claudia paid little attention to the tall, darkly dressed figure when she stepped into the elevator. But she noticed the affected way he was wearing wraparound sunglasses with his suit. It was more of the same pretentious LA behaviour.

*Sunglasses inside an elevator?* In Claudia's sadly tainted opinion, all men were hiding something; perhaps this one was nursing a hangover. She rolled her eyes, confident in the fact he couldn't see anything from behind the dark lenses and even more sure he wouldn't be looking in her direction anyway. Probably obsessed with his own thoughts and problems. Just like so many in this town. A town full of actors, many with an inflated sense of self-worth and a complete lack of morals. Perhaps this man filled that same bill, she surmised. She felt sick to her stomach even thinking about the man who had wooed her with lies and then walked out of her life as shamelessly as he had walked into it.

She patted her stomach protectively and, not caring a damn what he thought, she whispered, 'You may have been a surprise, boys, but I love you both to the moon and back already.' Then she silently added, *And I will make sure you don't run away from your responsibilities...or wear sunglasses in a lift!*

'They're very lucky little boys.' Patrick said it matter-of-factly. It surprised even him that he had made a comment but hearing the woman speak so genuinely to her unborn children in an accent once so familiar struck a chord with him. In a town so devoid of anything genuine, Patrick felt compelled to comment.

Claudia thought for a fleeting moment his words had been delivered with genuine sentiment. But her body stiffened as she reminded herself there was little or no sentiment in that town. Maternal hormones, she assumed, had temporarily dressed her vision with rose-coloured glasses. His English accent, for some reason, made her drop her guard just a little. Against her better judgement, she looked over to see the man remove his sunglasses. His lips were curved slightly. Not to a full smile, not even a half smile, but she could see his teeth just a little. They were almost perfect but not veneer flawless.

He was tall, six foot one or two, she guessed, as she was five foot nine in bare feet or the flat shoes she was wearing that day. He was broad-shouldered and, she imagined from the way his shirt fell, buff, but he wasn't overly tanned. His hair was short and light brown in colour and it was matched with a light covering of stubble on his face. His grooming was impeccable but, aside from the stubble, quite conservative. While his looks, she conceded, were worthy of a billboard, his styling was more professional than the usual LA playboy slash actor type. Or, in his case, an English ex-pat playing the LA field.

'I'm sorry?' she finally said after her assessment. She was hoping he would shrug his shoulders, put his sunglasses back on and return to thoughts of himself or his most recent conquest.

But he didn't.

'I said that your babies are very fortunate that you care for them so much even before they enter the world. I hope they make you proud.'

Patrick had not said anything like that in twelve years. They were words he used to say every day as a matter of routine, but never so routine that they were not sincere. But something about this woman and the palpable love he could see in her eyes and hear in her voice made it impossible not to make comment. She appeared different from the women he knew.

And a very long way from the women he bedded. She was cute and beautiful, not unlike a china doll. His women were not fragile like that.

And her love for her unborn children was special. It was something Patrick very much appreciated.

Claudia felt her stance stiffen again and her expression become quite strained. His accent was cultured and, with her own English upbringing and resultant class-consciousness, she suspected he had more than likely experienced a privileged boarding school education. His clothes were high end designer. She knew he must have an ulterior motive. All men did. There were a handful of people she had met in the year since she'd left London to make Hollywood her home who had shown a level of genuine kindness but she doubted this man would join those ranks. In fact, she doubted that any man would ever again join that group. Her desired demeanour was defensive and with little effort she reached it. No man was going to get within a mile of her or, more particularly, her children with any line. She had told herself that she had finished with men and all of their agendas. And she decided to prove it to herself.

Her first step would be keeping this man, albeit a very attractive man, at arm's length. Perhaps even offside.

'You really should refrain from eavesdropping; it's rude,' she said before turning her attention back to the blank gunmetal doors. *There—it was done!* She had stood up for herself and it brought her a sense of empowerment.

It had been a long time coming and she conceded her ire was directed towards the wrong man but she had finally felt strong enough to say something. And it felt good. As if she was claiming her power back.

But the elevator didn't feel good or seem to have any power. It seemed to be slowing and, for want of a better word in her head, since she didn't particularly like confined spaces, it seemed to be *struggling* in its descent. She wished it would pick up speed and get her out of the awkward situation. Deep down inside, she knew her response had been overly dramatic and cutting but she was still proud she had found the strength to do it. There were only another fifteen floors and she hoped the elevator would reach the ground before he handed her a business card and she discovered the reason he'd struck up the conversation. Insurance, investment or even real estate. There had to be something behind the smile. Since she was so heavily pregnant, she felt very confident it was not going to segue into a pick-up line.

With her chin lifted slightly, she felt the colour rising in her cheeks; she played with her small pearl earrings the way she always did when she was nervous.

Patrick considered her in silence for a moment as he watched her fidget with the small pearl studs. He had made an uncharacteristic effort to acknowledge her pregnancy and he was taken back at her disparaging remark. He hadn't expected it as she had appeared at first glance to be very sweet. Her pretty face was framed with dark curls and he thought she had an innocence about her. He hadn't foreseen her reaction and to his mind he definitely did not deserve the harsh retort. He wasn't going to take it on the chin.

Without making eye contact as he stared at the same gunmetal door, he decided to answer her abrupt reply with one equally insensitive. 'I think you're the rude one here. You enter a lift, or should I say elevator, due to our location, with only one other person, that being me, and begin a conversation with your unborn children, for which I did not judge you to be mad, but in fact complimented you, and then you remark that I'm rude for making a comment.'

Claudia was surprised by his formal and acerbic rebuttal. His response had been articulate and he had not raised his voice but she wasn't in the mood to eat humble pie. Men, or rather one man, had just let her down very badly and she wasn't going to break her promise to herself. They were all the same if they were given the opportunity. And she had no intention of ever giving a man such an opportunity with her again.

With her eyes facing straight ahead at their shared focal point, she was about to reply when she was stopped by a twinge in her stomach. Her body stiffened with the pain and she hunched a little, almost protectively.

She knew it couldn't be a contraction. It was too early. One hand instinctively reached for her babies and her stomach suddenly felt hard to her touch. She was grateful the stranger was looking away as she leant a little on the elevator wall. She told herself it must be the Braxton Hicks contractions that her obstetrician had mentioned but it seemed to be quite intense and more than a little painful.

It passed quite quickly and finally, after catching her

breath, she replied, 'I think it was obvious I was having a private conversation. And clearly you *are* judging me, by implying that I'm mad. That's hardly a nice thing to say to someone you don't know.'

'You're right,' he responded and turned to face her. 'I concede it was less than polite but you have to agree that you most definitely left your manners back up on the thirty-fourth floor.' He looked away as he finished his tersely delivered response and checked for mobile phone reception.

By his abrupt tone and the fact he had noticed which floor she lived on, Claudia looked out of the corner of her eyes at him and wondered for a moment if he was a lawyer. Lawyers always paid attention to details that the general public ignored. Of course, she thought, she would have the slowest ride to the ground with an overbearing man with a legal background. She dropped her chin a little but not to admire her middle; instead she looked tentatively across the elevator to where the man stood. He was wearing highly polished shoes. Slightly raising her chin, she noted his perfectly pressed charcoal-grey slacks and finally, with her head turned a little more in his direction as she gave in to her curiosity, she saw his crisp white shirt and jacket. She had thought initially that he was wearing a suit but on closer, but not too obvious, inspection, she could see flecked threads in the weave. And then there was his expensive Swiss watch. Not forgetting the fact he was already in the elevator when she'd entered, which meant he either lived, or had a client, on the only floor above her. The penthouse on the thirty-fifth floor.

Suddenly she felt another twinge. She wanted to get

out of the lift and get to her obstetric appointment immediately. She didn't want to be dragged into a conversation.

'I apologise—I'm sorry,' she returned sharply and
without emotion as she once again faced the elevator
doors. She rubbed the hollow of her back that was beginning to ache. The niggling pain was spreading and
becoming increasingly uncomfortable. She just wanted
the short time in the relatively tiny space to be uneventful, so she took the easy option and hoped the conversation would end there.

But it didn't.

'Frankly, I think I'm a little past caring for your less
than genuine apology.'

'I beg your pardon?' Claudia knew the handsome
stranger had called the situation correctly; she just didn't
want to admit it.

'I think you're just giving me lip service,' he continued. 'Forget I said anything nice at all. To be honest, I'm
sorry I did, so let's just go back to an awkward silence
that comes with sharing an elevator with a stranger and
hope the thing picks up speed for both of our sakes.'

Claudia felt a little tug at her heart. The stranger really
had been trying to make pleasant conversation and compliment her in the process and she had shot him down.

'Gosh, I did sound awfully rude, didn't I?' she asked,
as much to herself as him. Wishing she had not been as
dismissive and had put some meaning behind the words,
she offered a more contrite apology. 'I really am sorry.
I do mean it.'

'Perhaps.'

Her eyes met his and she could see they were not
warm and forgiving but neither were they icy. They were
sad. They were filled with a look close to disappoint-

ment and she felt her heart sink a little further. She had never been quite so rude to a stranger before. Heaven knew what day he had endured and she had behaved abominably.

Circumstance had made her distrust the male population. She had not even thought how her behaviour would affect the handsome stranger sharing the slowest elevator on the west coast of North America, until he'd pointed it out. But she was surprised by his reaction. She assumed most men would have shrugged it off but he seemed genuinely disappointed, almost as if he was directing the disappointment inward for some reason.

With a humble and heartfelt expression she replied, 'I really do apologise. I'm very sorry and there's really no excuse for my behaviour.' Taking a deep breath, she outstretched her hand like an olive branch. 'I'm Claudia Monticello, slightly hormonal mother-to-be and having a very bad day. I could add that I'm perhaps a little stressed right now as I'm flying back to the UK tomorrow and I have so much still to do. I have to see my obstetrician and finish packing. There's so many things I have to remember...' And so much she wanted to forget. But she had no intention of telling the handsome stranger that.

'Well, perhaps you do have a reason to be a little on edge,' he said, looking into her eyes, almost piercing her soul. 'Apology accepted. Patrick Spencer, doctor, not eavesdropper.'

Claudia smiled. She had picked the wrong profession too. As she kept staring into his eyes, she noticed they were a deep blue with flecks of grey. Like storm clouds swirling over the deepest part of the ocean. She felt herself wondering why he hid such stunning eyes behind dark sunglasses. They were too captivating a shade to be hidden. She shook herself. His eye colour was not something she needed to busy her mind with at that time. Nothing about him was her concern, she told herself as she noticed there was only a short trip of eight floors until they reached street level and she would never see the man again.

But it did feel strangely reassuring to be in the elevator with a man with a medical background after the fleeting contraction she'd experienced. She knew they were commonplace nearing the latter part of pregnancy and it appeared to have been a once-off but his nearness made her feel a little safer.

No, *very* safe and she didn't know why.

Out of a sense of awkwardness in the silence that were now sharing, she glanced up again to check how many floors they had travelled. The elevator had not picked up any speed. She was glad they weren't in the Burj Khalifa in Dubai or the boys would be ready for pre-school at the rate they were travelling.

With her mind brought to travel, Claudia was excited to be heading home. Once her obstetrician signed her flight clearance she would be on her way back to London. Her contract with the television studio had finally ended, leaving her free to return home. Instinctively, she patted the recent ultrasound scans tucked safely in her bag. She had no swelling in her legs and her blood pressure had been fine at the last visit. Her pregnancy had been uneventful until the twinge, something which was at complete odds with her disastrous personal life. But she was grateful she had something positive upon which to focus.

As they passed the fourth floor and the elevator seemed to almost pause, suddenly she felt another more intense contraction. Claudia tried to smile through it but suspected it was closer to a grimace. Braxton Hicks contractions were a lot different to what she had expected. She had been told that a woman could experience up to four in an hour but she hadn't thought they would be so close together.

Patrick eyed her with concern but, just as he opened his mouth, the stalling elevator came to a jarring halt. Claudia grabbed the railing to steady herself and they both looked up to see the floor light flickering and waited for the doors to open. But they didn't. Instead the lift dropped what she imagined to be another floor and stopped. Patrick had already taken two purposeful steps towards Claudia and she felt his strong arms wrap around her to prevent her from falling. His touch should have worried her but instead a wave of relief washed over her. She was not alone.

'Let's get you on the floor. It will be safer.' Hastily he pulled off his jacket and dropped it to the elevator floor before gently lowering Claudia onto it.

'Your jacket—it will be ruined.'

'At this moment, a ruined jacket is not my concern. You are,' he said matter-of-factly but with an unmistakable warmth in his voice and one Claudia didn't believe she truly deserved after her behaviour. 'When are the babies due?'

'The twins aren't due for another six and a half weeks and I'm fine, really I am,' she insisted as she tried to sit gently and not move and crease the jacket underneath her. 'I'm flying out tomorrow with the doctor's approval; it's the last possible day that the airline will allow me to travel.'

'You're cutting it fine with the whole long haul at al-

most thirty-four weeks,' he replied with his brows knitted. He added, 'You seemed to be in pain a moment ago.'
It was a question he framed as a statement. He didn't
want to appear overbearing but he was concerned. He
was also doubtful whether she should be travelling at
such a late stage of pregnancy. Even with a clean bill of
health, it seemed risky for her to take a long haul flight
so close to delivering.

'Yes, just one of these Braxton Hicks contractions.'

'You're sure?' His frown had not lifted as he spoke.

This time it was a question and she sensed genuine
concern. It heightened hers.

'Absolutely,' she said, followed by a nod. It wasn't
the truth. The truth was that she had never been quite
so scared in her life but she had to push that reality from
her mind and remain positive. The worst-case scenario
was too overwhelmingly frightening to consider without collapsing into a heap. She had been holding everything together tenuously for so many months her nerves
were threadbare.

'If you say so,' he told her, doubt about her response
evident in his tone. 'Just stay seated till we reach the
ground.' He retrieved his mobile phone from his trouser pocket, but Claudia assumed there was no reception through the heavy elevator walls as he turned and
reached for the emergency telephone.

He didn't take his eyes away from Claudia, even when
the standard response finished and he cut in. 'This is Dr
Patrick Spencer, I'm in Terrace Park Towers, Wilshire
Boulevard, not far from Highland. We're somewhere
between the fourth floor and street level and the elevator's come to a halt. I have a female resident with me.
Approximately thirty-four weeks pregnant.' He paused.

'No, no, there's no immediate medical emergency. I have the resident seated and there's no obvious physical injuries but I want a crew to get us out stat. And after the jolt it would be wise to send an ambulance. The patient may need to head to the hospital for a routine obstetric examination.'

With that he hung up and turned his full attention back to Claudia.

Her resolve to remain calm had deserted her, despite attempts to tell herself she was overreacting. She wasn't overreacting. Her eyes darted to the steel doors, willing them to open, and then back to Patrick, unsure what she was willing him to do.

'We'll be out of here before you know it,' he said and very gently wiped the wisps of hair from her brow, now covered in tiny beads of perspiration. 'They're on their way.'

'Yes, they are… I'm afraid.'

'There's nothing to fear. Just stay calm and the crew will have us out of here very quickly. And there'll be an ambulance on hand if we need one.'

'It's not the crew I'm talking about…it's the babies. I'm afraid my twins are on their way… This isn't Braxton Hicks, Patrick. I'm in labour.'

# CHAPTER TWO

CLAUDIA'S WATER BROKE only moments later, confirming she was very much in labour and going to deliver her babies in an elevator unless a miracle happened. As she wriggled uncomfortably on the hard elevator floor with only Patrick's now soaking wet jacket beneath her, she stared at nowhere in particular and prayed with all of her might that it was a bad dream. One from which she would wake to find herself giving birth in a pretty delivery room in a London hospital surrounded by smiling nurses…nurses just like her sister, Harriet. She always allayed Claudia's medical concerns with sensible and thoughtful answers delivered in a calm manner, just like the way their mother had always spoken to them.

How she wished more than anything that Harriet was with her. She would know what to do. She always did… but, as Claudia looked at her surroundings from her new vantage point on the floor, she knew it was pointless to wish for her sister to be there. Or for a birthing suite. She would have neither. Harriet was in Argentina to do something selfless and wonderful and she was paying for her own irresponsible behaviour by being trapped in a Los Angeles elevator in the first stage of labour.

Giving birth to the babies of a man who didn't give a damn.

With the help of another she didn't know.

The next painful wave of contractions broke through her thoughts. Labour had not come on slowly or gently. And there was no point worrying about dust soiling Patrick's jacket; the piece of clothing was now past being saved.

The jacket was of no concern to Patrick, who was kneeling beside Claudia. At that moment he would give a dozen of his finest jackets to make this woman he barely knew comfortable if only he could. But he had nothing close to a dozen of anything to make what lay ahead easier. The situation was dire. There was no way around that fact but Patrick intended to do everything to ensure Claudia remained calm and focused. All the while he fought his own battle with a past that was rushing back at him. Fine perspiration began lining his brow but he had to push through. He heard Claudia's heavy breathing turn to panting and knew he couldn't give in to his thoughts. Not for even a minute. He had to stay with Claudia.

For the time being at least.

'There's no cell reception but if I can get through on the elevator phone, who can I call? Your husband, boyfriend…your family?'

Claudia shook her head, a little embarrassed by the answer even before she delivered it. Harriet was on and off the communication grid for almost two days while she travelled and even if she could contact her it would be unfair to worry her. And she knew there was no point reaching out to the babies' father. He wouldn't care.

'No, there's no one to call.'

Patrick's eyes met hers in silence. He was surprised and saddened to hear her answer. While she clearly had her defences up initially, Patrick had not suspected for even a moment that a woman like Claudia would be alone in the world.

Unexpectedly, he felt himself being pulled towards her. He was never pulled towards anyone. Not any more. Not for years. He had locked away the need to feel anything. To need anyone…or to be needed. But suddenly a tenuous and unforeseen bond was forming. And he suspected it was not due just to the confines of the elevator.

Claudia wriggled some more and looked down at the jacket. 'I'm so sorry…'

'Claudia—' he cut in as he looked intently into her eyes, not shifting his gaze for even a moment, not allowing himself to betray, to any degree, the very real risks that he knew lay ahead '—you're in labour and you think I'm worried about a jacket.'

'But it's ruined.'

'The only thing I care about now is finding something clean for the babies. Do you have anything in your bag? Anything I can wrap them in?'

Claudia shook her head. While her bag was the fashionably oversized style, it held very little, other than her wallet, apartment keys, her phone, a thin, flimsy scarf, a small cosmetic purse and a bottle of water. And her ultrasound films.

Patrick couldn't wait any longer. There would be two babies arriving and they needed to have something clean to rest upon while he tended to their mother. He was not going to put them on the floor of the elevator. Without hesitating, he began to unbutton his white linen shirt and, slipping it from his very toned and lightly tanned body, he spread it out.

Claudia knew she was staring. She was helpless to pull her gaze away. The man about to deliver her babies had stripped bare to the waist. It was overwhelming and almost too much for her to process. The whole situation was quickly morphing from a bad dream into a nightmare. She was about to give birth to the sons of a man who didn't love her and they would be delivered by a half-naked stranger in a broken elevator. Tears began welling in her eyes as the waves of another contraction came. This one was more powerful than the last and she struggled to hide the level of pain.

Patrick reached for her hand. 'I want you to squeeze my hand when the contractions happen.'

'I'll be fine,' she told him as the contraction passed and she felt uncomfortable getting any closer to the semi-naked stranger than she already was. His arms looked lean but powerful. And she could smell the light tones of his musky cologne.

'I know you'll be fine but if you squeeze my hand each time you have a contraction I'll know how close together they are.'

'I think you will be able to tell without me squeezing your hand.'

Patrick nodded. 'Have it your way, but my hand is here if you need it.'

Still feeling wary, Claudia eyed him suspiciously, wondering who this man was, this man who was so willing to come to her aid. Only a few minutes before, they had exchanged less than friendly words. Now the man she had initially assumed to be a lawyer hiding a hangover behind dark glasses was in fact a doctor literally on bended knees helping her.

'The contractions seem to be evenly spaced at the moment,' he said, breaking through her thoughts.

'But they're awfully close and awfully painful. Does that mean the babies will be here soon?'

'It could but it's impossible to tell.' Patrick hoped that it would be a prolonged labour. Prolonged enough to allow the technical team to open the elevator doors and bring in help.

'Do you think there's any chance they will get us out before my babies arrive?'

'They're doing their best.'

Ten minutes passed with no news from outside and two more contractions. Claudia caught her breath and leant back against the cold walls of the elevator. It was soothing on her now clammy skin. The air was starting to warm up, and she imagined it would be stifling in a short time if the doors were not opened soon. But they would be. She had to hold on to the belief that any minute paramedics would burst through the steel barriers and transport her to hospital.

Patrick stretched his long legs out in front of him and rested against the adjacent cool wall. 'So which London hospital had you planned on having the boys?' he asked as he looked up at the ceiling for no particular reason. All sense of reason had left the elevator when Claudia began labour.

'I thought the Wright Street Women's and Children's Hospital. I checked in online a few months back and it has a lovely birthing centre with floral wallpaper and midwives and everything my babies and I would need. I've booked an appointment with a midwife there next week.'

'Well, you won't be needing that appointment. Not for this delivery anyway, but perhaps you could book in for your next baby.'

'I'm not sure there will be a next,' she replied quickly with raised eyebrows, still not forgetting the pain of the contraction that had barely passed.

'Perhaps you will change your mind and have more but these children will definitely be born in LA. With any luck, the paramedics will have us out soon and they'll be born at the Mercy Hospital.'

Claudia felt her pulse race a little. 'What if that doesn't happen?'

Patrick turned to her and took her hand in his. Suddenly the sensation of her warm skin on his made him feel something more than he had felt in many years. It made him feel close to being alive. He swallowed and pushed away the feeling. That sort of intimacy had no place in his life. For the last decade, whenever he felt a woman's body against his, there was nothing more than mutual pleasure. It didn't mean anything to either of them. They served a purpose to each other and walked away. Feeling anything more was not worth the risk.

He couldn't get attached to a woman he didn't know who was about to give birth to the children of another man. The idea was ridiculous.

'Let's not go there, Claudia. The medical team will be here soon.'

'But they may not…' she argued.

'Then we'll bring two healthy boys into the world on our own.' He said it instinctively but as the words escaped his mouth he prayed it would not come to that.

Claudia took another deep breath. There was a chance they weren't going to be rescued. And she had to prepare herself for the imminent wave of the next contraction and then worse. She closed her eyes.

Patrick studied her. 'Now don't go closing your beautiful eyes on me,' he told her. 'I need you to listen to me and work with me. You will get through this but you have to stay strong. You have your children to think of.'

Slowly she forced her lids open and found herself looking into the warmest eyes she had ever seen. Her stomach did a little somersault and it wasn't a contraction.

'That's better,' he told her with a smile filled with so much warmth she thought her heart would melt. Everything he was making her feel was unexpected. And the feelings seemed so real. Was it just the intense situation they were facing or was there something about the man that was very different from anyone she had ever met?

She wasn't sure.

But his nearness was affecting her. She doubted he was trying to affect—he just was.

'What about you—do you have any children? Did your family move here to LA too?' She rattled off successive questions, trying to deflect the blush she suddenly feared he had brought to her cheeks. She could see there was no wedding band on his hand but, as she knew first-hand, the lack of a ring on a man's finger did not bring any certainty there was no wife. It was out of character for her to be so direct but nothing about the situation was normal.

'No, I'm not married, Claudia, and the rest of my family…well, they're back in the UK…' Patrick's words trailed off. He wasn't about to tell Claudia about his life, his past or his loss. After twelve years it was still raw at times but now focusing on Claudia removed his desire to give any consideration to his own pain. He had to be in the moment for the woman who needed him. He couldn't think about what had happened all those years ago or the price he still paid every day.

He had to let something go.

And that had to be the past—for the time being. But he knew that it would come back to him. It always did.

'Do you want children one day? I guess if you've done this before, bringing them into the world would make you want a brood or run the other way,' she cut in again. As she felt the warmth in her face subside she was slightly relieved on that front but the need for the banter continued. Any distraction would do.

He felt a muscle in his jaw twitch. She was unwittingly making it very hard to stay in the moment. 'No,' he said, not wanting to go into any detail. The answer was not that he didn't like children; in fact it ran far deeper than that. Children meant family and he never planned on being part of a family again. The pain still lingered, twelve years after he had been forced to walk away from his own.

'So am I right—you don't want to take your job home?'

'You're full of questions, aren't you?'

Claudia didn't answer. She felt the next contraction building and as it rolled in she couldn't say anything. She dropped her head to her chest and took in shallow breaths.

Without prompting, Patrick's hands gently massaged her back. Instinctively, he knew what was happening and he kept up the physical therapy until it passed. And then a few moments longer.

She felt his hands linger, then shook herself back to reality. He was a doctor doing his job. Nothing more.

'Why did you move to LA?' she piped up, then bit her lip as she realised it was none of her business and she had no clue what had driven her to ask him such personal questions. She felt as if the pain had taken over her mind. She was acting like a different person, someone who suddenly wanted to know everything about Patrick. Perhaps it was to distract herself. Perhaps not. But she knew the moment the words fell from her mouth that she had overstepped the boundaries of polite conversation. 'Please forget I asked. Blame it on the stress. I really am exhibiting the worst manners today. I've asked the most improper questions and ruined your jacket...'

'Forgiven for both.' Patrick hesitated. 'I guess I'm just a private person, Claudia. I'm happy to answer any medical questions, anything at all, but I'd prefer to leave the rest alone. Suffice to say, my family and I didn't see eye to eye about something that happened and this opportunity came up. So I left London and headed here.'

'Oh, I'm sorry.' Claudia suddenly felt even more embarrassed that she had asked but she also felt a little sad for him. She barely knew the man but, with the way he was taking care of her, she suddenly felt that she wanted to be on *his side* in a situation she knew nothing about.

Patrick knew it sounded as if they had parted ways on something insignificant. He thought it was best to leave it at that. There was no need to mention that he'd made the opportunity to allow him to move to the US. It was something he'd had to do to help everyone with their grief. To not be there, reminding them every day of what had happened.

It was not the time or place to tell a woman he had just met that his sister had died.

And he had taken the blame for her death.

An unspoken agreement not to revisit the conversation about his family was made in the awkward silence by both of them.

'I'll need to examine you in a few minutes and assess whether you have begun to dilate and, if you have, if the first baby is visible,' he told her as he pulled himself from the past back to where he belonged.

Suddenly the elevator lights began to flicker. Claudia bit her lip nervously. She felt her chin begin to quiver but was powerless to stop it. All questions disappeared. She didn't want anything from Patrick other than reassurance that her babies would survive.

Patrick drew a deep breath but managed to keep his body language in check. If they lost the lights, then he could not convince himself there would be a good outcome but he would never let Claudia know that. He even refused to admit it to himself.

'I need to do the exam while we still have some lights to work with; if we lose them it will be challenging as I'll have to work by feel alone. But, whatever happens, I'm here for you and your babies, Claudia, and together we'll all get throughout this,' Patrick told her with a firmness and urgency that did not disguise the seriousness of the situation, but he also managed to make her feel secure in the knowledge that he was with her all the way. He filled his lungs with the warm air that surrounded them, determined he would do his damnedest to make his prayers a reality.

She nodded her consent as the contraction began to subside, along with her uncontrollable need to push.

'Breathe slowly and deeply,' he said while he stroked her arm and waited for the contraction to pass before he began his examination. Twins made the birth so much more complicated, along with his lack of equipment and the risk of losing the lights.

'Have you delivered many babies?'

'Yes, I've delivered many babies, Claudia, but never in an elevator and not for…'

The elevator phone rang and stopped Patrick from explaining how long it had been since his last delivery. Instinctively, he answered the phone. 'Yes?'

'This is the utilities manager. We're working to have you out as soon as possible but it may be another twenty minutes to half an hour. Our only rostered technician is across town. How's the young woman?'

'She's in labour.'

'Hell… Okay, that's gonna be brutal on her.' The man's knee-jerk reaction was loud. 'I'll put the tech to get here ASAP or get an off-duty one over there stat. We've already got an ambulance en route.'

'That would be advisable,' Patrick responded in an even tone, not wanting to add to Claudia's building distress. 'I'm about to assess her progress but you need to ensure there are two ambulances waiting when your technician gets us out. We're dealing with the birth of two premature infants so ensure the paramedics are despatched with humidicribs and you have an obstetrician standing by with a birthing kit including cord clamps and Syntocinon.' Then he lowered his voice and added, 'And instruct them to bring plasma. There's always the slight risk of a postpartum haemorrhage.' With that he hung up the phone to let the team outside do their best to get medical help to them as soon as possible.

He immediately turned his attention back to Claudia, who lay against the elevator wall with small beads of perspiration building on her brow and the very palpable fear of what lay ahead written on her face.

'I don't want my babies to die.'

'Claudia, you need to listen to me,' he began with gentleness in his voice along with a reassuring firmness. 'We *are* going to get through this. Your babies will be fine but you need to help me.'

Claudia couldn't look at him. She couldn't lift her gaze from her stomach and the babies inside of her. Fear surged through her veins. It was real. They weren't getting out of the elevator. No one was coming to rescue them. No one was going to take her to the hospital. The harsh reality hit her. Her babies would be born inside the metal walls that surrounded them.

And they might not survive.

'I am going to have to cut your underwear free. I don't want to try and lift you and remove it.'

Claudia felt her heart race and her mind spin. She was losing control and the fear was not just physical. Deep inside, she knew the odds were stacked against her and her boys but she appreciated that Patrick hadn't voiced that. The man with the sunglasses wasn't anything close to what she'd thought. He was about to bring her sons into the world.

And she suddenly had no choice but to trust him.

Her hand ran across her mouth and tugged at her lips nervously. 'Fine, just do it,' she managed to say as she steeled herself for what was about to happen to her, her boys and Patrick as the urge to push and the pain began to overtake her senses once again.

Patrick ripped off the gloves that had handled the elevator telephone, covered his hands in antibacterial solution and slipped on another pair of gloves. Carefully using sterile scissors, he gently cut her underwear from her and checked the progress of her labour.

'You are fully dilated and your first son's head is visible,' he told her. 'Labour is moving fast and you're doing great. Just keeping breathing slowly…'

His words were cut short by the cry she gave with the next painful contraction. More painful than the previous one.

'I can't do this. I can't.'

'Yes, you can.'

'Should I be as scared to death as I am right now?'

'No,' he said, leaning in towards her. 'Just remember, Claudia, you're not alone. We'll get through this together. You and I will bring your babies into the world.'

He prayed, as every word slipped from his now dry mouth, that he could do what he promised. He had the expertise, he reminded himself. But he also knew that was not always enough. There were some situations that no skills could fight.

Steeling himself, he knew he was prepared to fight for Claudia and her boys.

She closed her eyes and swallowed.

'I need you to try and get onto your hands and knees…'

'Why?' Her eyes opened wide. 'I thought you have babies lying on your back. Is there something wrong?' Panic showed on her face as she stared into Patrick's eyes, searching for reassurance but frightened of what he might tell her.

'It will be easier on you and your babies if you're on all fours,' he told her. 'It opens up the birth canal and, even though it may seem uncomfortable, believe me, it will be far better than being on your back. Just try it. Here, I'll help you.'

He reached for her and she felt the warmth and strength in his hold as his hands guided her into the position he needed to best deliver the babies. He made sure her hands and knees were still resting on the damp jacket, not the bare floor.

'I'd like to put a cool compress on you. It's getting warm in here but I'm running out of clothing to give you.'

Even in pain, Claudia smiled at his remark. It was true. He had given his jacket and his shirt. 'There's a clean scarf in my bag but it's very small. You could wet that.'

Patrick reached for her large tan leather bag and dragged it unceremoniously across the metal flooring. He emptied the contents onto the floor, found the small patterned scarf and then noticed the films.

'Are those films for your obstetrician?'

She turned her head slightly. 'Yes, he was going to check them and then sign the papers to allow me to fly home to London.'

He pushed the envelope to the side and took her bottle of water and sparingly dampened the scarf. Gently lifting the sweat-dampened curls on the nape of her neck, he rested the tiny compress on her hot skin. There was nothing he could do about whatever showed on the films now. They wouldn't change anything in the confines of the elevator. He had no idea what the next few minutes would hold but he would be beside her and do whatever he could to keep Claudia and her babies alive.

Feeling his hand on her skin felt so calming and reassuring and Claudia wondered if it was the touch of his skin against hers as much as the makeshift compress. But neither gave relief when the next powerful contraction came and she cried out with the pain.

Her cries tugged at Patrick's heart. He hated the fact there was nothing he could do. But he needed to focus on delivering both babies or risk losing them all. He wouldn't let that happen.

Suddenly the first baby began to enter the world. A mass of thick black hair curled like a halo around his perfect tiny face.

'Just push slowly and think about your breathing,' he instructed her. 'We need that to control the baby's arrival. We don't want to rush him. You can tear your skin and I want to avoid that.'

The urge to give a giant push was overwhelming but Claudia knew she had to let her breathing slow the pace. She thought of Patrick's handsome face and tried to follow his instructions. There were a few more contractions and finally Claudia's first baby was born into Patrick's waiting hands. He let out a tiny cry as Patrick quickly cleared his mouth of mucous and quickly checked his vital signs.

The baby was small but not so small as to put him in immediate danger by not having access to a humidicrib. Patrick had feared he might have been tinier considering the gestational age and the fact he was a twin. He clamped the cord with a sterile surgical tie before he laid him on the shirt. The baby had endured a harsh entry into the world and the shirt was a far cry from a soft landing but, until his brother was born, there was little Patrick could do for the new arrival. He could not put the child to Claudia's breast as she needed to remain on all fours until the second baby was delivered.

Another contraction began and the second baby was quickly on its way. Patrick hoped that he would not be faced with a foot. That would mean a breech birth and complications he did not want to contemplate.

That next painful contraction came and Claudia cried out loudly but managed with each following breath to push her second baby head first into the world. And once again into Patrick's arms, where the baby took his first breath and cried for the first time. Patrick checked the second baby's vital signs and again was relieved that the delivery had no complications. It had progressed far better than Patrick had imagined.

With beads of perspiration now covering her entire body, Claudia looked over at her two sons and felt a love greater than she'd thought possible.

And a closeness to the man who had delivered them. He was like her knight in shining armour. And she would be indebted to him forever.

Quite apart from being an amazing doctor, Patrick was a wonderful man.

Through the fog of her emotionally drained state, Claudia suddenly suspected her feelings for Patrick ran deeper than simply gratitude for saving them all.

Patrick remained quiet. There were still two afterbirths and Claudia to consider. Despite the peaceful and contented look she wore, he knew they were not out of the woods yet.

Gently he placed the second baby next to his tiny

brother and wrapped the shirt around them both before he carefully helped Claudia from her knees onto her back again. He grabbed her leather bag and made a makeshift pillow for her head. Claudia was past caring about the bag or her own comfort as she watched her tiny sons lying so close to her.

Patrick reached for them. 'I'm going to rest the babies on you while we wait for the afterbirth.'

While the delivery had been relatively straightforward, Patrick was aware that Claudia's double birth put her at increased risk of haemorrhage. Gently he placed the two tiny boys into their mother's arms and he watched as her beautiful face lit up further as she cradled them. Her beauty seemed to be magnified with the boys now securely with her and, with her genes, they would no doubt be very handsome young men.

Within minutes, part of the placenta was delivered but as Patrick examined it he was concerned that it was not intact. Claudia would require a curette in hospital if the remaining placenta wasn't expelled. But, that aside and despite the surroundings, Claudia had delivered two seemingly healthy boys. Patrick took a deep breath and filled his lungs as he looked at Claudia with a sense of pride for the strength shown by a woman he barely knew.

Then he noticed her face had become a little pale.

'I sort of feel a little cold now,' she said softly, as her body began to shiver. 'It feels odd; I was so hot before. There's no pain but...'

Patrick noticed her eyes were becoming glassy and she was losing her grip on the boys. There was something very wrong. Quickly he scooped them from her weakening hold and placed them together beside her, still wrapped in his shirt. He felt for her pulse. It was becoming fainter. He looked down to see blood pouring from Claudia and pooling on the jacket underneath her.

It was his worst nightmare—a postpartum haemorrhage.

Claudia had fifty percent more blood in her body because of the pregnancy, which would help, but, with the amount of blood she had already lost on the floor, it would still only buy them a small amount of time. He needed to encourage her uterus to contract, shutting off the open blood vessels. Immediately he began to massage her belly through to her uterus but after a minute he could see there was no difference. She was barely lucid and he needed to administer a synthetic form of the hormone that would naturally assist, but that was on the other side of the closed elevator doors with the paramedics. It wasn't something he carried in his medical bag. Not now anyway. Once he would have had everything he now needed to save Claudia—but that was a lifetime ago.

'Claudia—' he ceased the massage momentarily and patted her hand '—I need you to try to feed one of the boys. It will help to stimulate a hormone that will lessen the bleeding. Do you understand?'

'Uh-huh,' she muttered while trying to keep her eyes from closing. 'I feel so light-headed.'

'That's the blood loss. I'm going to do everything I can to stop it until help arrives, but again we need to work together. You'll be on your way to hospital very soon.'

He reached down and gently unwrapped the babies and, picking up the larger of the twins, he lifted Claudia's tank top and bra and placed him onto her breast.

Instinctively the baby latched onto his mother and began to suckle while Patrick continued the massaging.

'Do you have any names for the boys?' he asked, trying to keep Claudia focused as he dealt with the medical emergency that was unfolding before his eyes.

She tried to think but the names weren't there. They were special names and they should have spilled out without any effort but she was befuddled, which wasn't her. 'I think…' She paused momentarily as the names she had chosen now seemed strangely out of reach. She blinked to bring herself back on track. 'Thomas…and Luca…after each of their great-grandpas.'

'I think they are strong names for two little fighters. Is this baby Thomas or Luca?'

Claudia smiled down at her son, still attached to her breast but not really sucking successfully. 'Thomas…but I think he's tired already and a bit too small.'

'I think you're right on both counts.'

'I'm feeling quite dizzy again.' She paused as she felt herself wavering and her vision was starting to blur. Fear was mounting again inside her. 'Am I going to die?'

'No, you're going to pull through and raise your two sons until they are grown men.'

Claudia felt weaker by the minute. She knew there was something very serious happening, even though she couldn't see the blood. 'If I don't make it…'

'You will,' he argued as he reached for Thomas, who was unable to suckle, and placed him safely on the floor beside his brother, Luca.

She closed her eyes for a moment. She felt too weak to fight. 'You need to contact my sister, Harriet. Her details are in my phone. She needs to be there for my boys if I can't be.'

'Claudia, listen to me. You're going to make it, but I'm going to have to do something very uncomfortable for you.'

'What?' she asked in a worried whisper.

'I'm going to compress your uterus with my hands. It will further slow the bleeding.'

She nodded but she felt as if she was close to drifting off to sleep. 'If you have to, then do it.'

'Try to stay awake,' he pleaded with her as he attempted to manually compress the uterus with the firm pressure of his hands.

Minutes passed but still the blood was flowing over his hands to the floor beneath her. Claudia needed to be in a hospital and she needed to be there now. This was something more serious than the usual postpartum blood loss.

She was dangerously close to losing consciousness as he gently removed his hands. The manual pressure could not stop the bleeding. Claudia needed surgical intervention if she was to survive. He reached for the films and ripped open the envelope. The films scattered on the floor but, as he grabbed the report, his worst fears were confirmed. Claudia's placenta had invaded the walls of her uterus. Every part of his body shuddered. It was déjà vu. The prognosis was identical to what he had faced all those years ago. There was no way her obstetrician would have allowed her to board a plane with the condition. Claudia would have delivered her sons in America, whether it had been this day or another.

With a heavy heart, he dropped his gloves and the report to the floor and pulled a barely conscious Claudia into his arms, where he held her while he stroked the faces of the little boys lying on the floor beside them. If help didn't arrive within a few minutes he would lose Claudia.

And her two tiny babies would never know their beautiful, brave mother.

# CHAPTER THREE

As CLAUDIA'S BODY suddenly fell limp in Patrick's arms, he heard the doors open behind him and instantly felt a firm grip on his bare shoulder.

'We've got it from here,' the deep voice said.

Patrick turned his head to see a full medical team rushing towards them. He had never been happier in his life than he was at that moment and, with adrenaline surging through his veins, he immediately began firing instructions at lightning speed. The miracle Claudia needed had arrived at the moment he had run out of options.

'We're dealing with a postpartum haemorrhage—she needs Syntocinon immediately and a catheter inserted so that the uterus has a better chance of contracting with an empty bladder. If she doesn't stabilise she'll be looking at a transfusion. Forget cross-matching as there may not be time; just start plasma now and have O negative waiting in OR.'

Patrick moved away as the medical team stepped in to begin the treatment he had ordered. Immediately they inserted an IV line, began a plasma transfusion then administered some pain relief and Syntocinon in an attempt to stop Claudia's bleeding while another two paramedics collected the baby boys and left the elevator with them securely inside portable humidicribs.

'Any idea why she's still bleeding?' the attending doctor asked.

'Placenta accreta,' Patrick said as he reached for the films lying on the floor. He kept his voice low so he would not alarm Claudia. 'I checked the report on the ultrasound films. Only a very small amount of the placenta was delivered and the rest is still firmly entrenched in the uterus wall. If the report is correct, she may be looking at a surgery but a complete hysterectomy should be the surgeon's last option. I doubt she's more than late twenties, if that, so she might like to keep her womb.'

'I'm sure they'll proceed conservatively if they can.'

Patrick nodded. He had no idea what the future would hold for Claudia and he wanted her to have every choice possible. 'The boys appear fine but they'll need a thorough examination with the paediatrician,' Patrick continued, not taking his eyes from Claudia. 'One is a little smaller than the other but let's hope there's no underlying issues with their premature arrival.'

'You did a remarkable job, all things considered,' the paramedics told Patrick as they watched the barely conscious Claudia being lifted onto the gurney and then securely but gently strapped in.

Keeping his attention on Claudia, who was beginning to show signs of being lucid, the doctor added, 'And you, young lady, are very lucky this man was sharing the elevator. It would not have been this outcome without him, that's for certain. You and your boys all owe your lives to him.'

Claudia smiled a meek smile and held out her hand in an effort to show her gratitude. Patrick cupped it gently in his own strong hands and smiled back at her then he turned to the attending doctor. 'I'll be travelling side-saddle to the hospital if there's room.'

'There's definitely room.'

For a little over three hours, Patrick divided his time between pacing the corridors outside Recovery and visiting the Neonatal Intensive Care Unit to check on Luca and Thomas. They had given him a consulting coat to cover his bare chest upon arrival at the hospital. Claudia's dark-haired boys, one with sparkling blue eyes and the other with deep brown like their mother, were doing very well and he felt a deep and very unexpected bond with them. A bond that he hadn't felt towards anyone, let alone tiny people, for more years than he cared to remember.

But these boys were special, perhaps because he'd delivered them in a crisis, or perhaps because their mother was clearly a very special woman. Perhaps it was both but, whatever was driving him to stay, he knew the three of them were bringing out protective feelings in him. A sense that he was needed and almost as if he belonged there. He should have felt unnerved and wanted to run but he didn't. That need to protect himself from being hurt was over-ridden by the need to protect Claudia, Thomas and Luca.

Both boys weighed a little over four pounds, which was a relief. They were still in their humidicribs and being monitored closely but both had passed all the paediatrician's initial tests and were being gavage fed by the neonatal nurses when Patrick left the nursery and headed back to check on their mother. Her surgery had taken far longer than he had anticipated. He had for a moment contemplated scrubbing in to assist when they'd arrived in Emergency and were rushed around to the

OR but he'd immediately thought better of it. A reality check reminded him that his last obstetric surgery had ended his career.

Patrick wanted her to be spared the additional stress and long-term repercussions of the hysterectomy if possible and voiced that again upon arrival. The surgical resident had reassured Patrick that Dr Sally Benton was well respected in the field of gynaecological surgery and that Claudia would be in expert hands. Patrick hoped that the option to give birth again one day in the pretty delivery room with floral wallpaper, midwives and pain relief was not taken away. But, three hours later, he knew the reality of her surgery taking so long meant she had probably undergone a hysterectomy. And she would have to give up on that dream.

'I'm Sally Benton.' She pulled her surgical cap free and outstretched her hand.

'Patrick Spencer,' he responded as he met her handshake. He looked at the woman before him. She was tall and thin, her short black hair with smatterings of grey framed her pretty face and he suspected she was in her early fifties.

'Dr Spencer, I assume.'

'Yes.'

'I wanted to personally thank you for the medical intervention you provided in the elevator. Miss Monticello is in Recovery now and she certainly wouldn't be if you hadn't done such an amazing job delivering her sons and keeping her alive. If you hadn't been with her today, there would most definitely have been a question mark over their survival.'

Patrick drew a deep breath and chose to ignore the compliment. 'Was it conservative surgery?'

'No, unfortunately, Miss Monticello underwent a full hysterectomy to stop the haemorrhaging. She retained her ovaries but her uterus has been removed,' Dr Benton continued as she took a seat in the corridor and indicated Patrick to do the same. 'The attending doctor briefed me on your diagnosis of suspected placenta accreta, but the depth of invasion was not first but second grade. I was faced with placenta increta as the chorionic villi had invaded the muscular layer of the uterine wall so I had no option but to remove her womb. She was lucky that it had not spread through the uterine wall to other organs such as the bladder. Let's just say I'm glad I didn't have to deal with that; as you would know, even in this day and age, there's still a six to seven percent mortality rate for that, due to the complications.'

Patrick knew the statistics for death only too well.

'Thank you, Dr Benton.'

'Don't thank me. As I said before, you did the hard work keeping her alive. And she has two wonderful little boys. Perhaps the loss of her womb will not be a complete tragedy.'

Patrick nodded. He wondered how Claudia would react to the need for a hysterectomy.

'And how are her sons doing?' the surgeon enquired.

'Very well,' Patrick said with a sense of pride that surprised him. 'They're handsome young men and a good weight for their gestational age.'

'Great. Now that's out of the way and we've spoken about our mutual patients, I have a personal question for you,' Dr Benton continued. 'How do you know Miss Monticello?'

'We were just sharing the elevator.'

Her expression revealed her surprise. 'Well, that's serendipity for you. I don't think she could have asked for a better travelling companion. Where do you practice obstetrics?' Then, without waiting for an answer, she added, 'Am I right in assuming, with your accent, and because I haven't heard of you around LA, that your practice is out of state or perhaps abroad?'

Patrick hesitated. He didn't want to talk about himself but he knew the doctor sitting beside him had every right to enquire. 'No, I practice here in LA but I'm not in OBGYN.'

'Really?' Her brow wrinkled as she considered his response. 'What's your field then?'

'I'm a board certified cosmetic surgeon.'

Once again, she didn't hide her surprise. 'I'd never have picked that,' she said with a grin on her somewhat tired face as she stood up and again offered a handshake. 'Well, Dr Spencer, if you ever get tired of your current field, you should consider obstetrics. There's a shortage of experts in the field and you're very skilled. Your intervention was nothing short of amazing in the conditions you were forced to work in. As I said, Miss Monticello owes her life to you. She will be in her room in another two hours or so. She lost a lot of blood, as you know, so we'll be monitoring her in Recovery for a little longer than we normally would. But I'm sure she'd be pleased to see you.'

Patrick met her handshake and she smiled before she left him alone.

Patrick spent the next two hours with Luca and Thomas. He had called his practice and rearranged his schedule. While the boys were being monitored closely he still didn't want to leave. Not yet anyway. Thomas was in a humidicrib and Luca required additional oxygen to be provided through an oxy-hood so he was in an open bed warmer. The neonatologist felt certain that would only be a temporary measure as both appeared to be healthy and a satisfactory weight for their gestational age. Patrick was aware they had some basic milestones to achieve, both in weight and development, before they would be released; he doubted it would be more than three or four weeks before they would be allowed to leave hospital with their mother.

He went downstairs to the florist and picked the largest floral bouquet they had and two brown bears with blue bows. Claudia had told him she had no one she could reach out to and he knew how that felt only too well. He tried not to think of what he had lost when he'd walked away from his family.

Only now at least Claudia did have two little people to call her family. Still, he knew her room would be devoid of anything to brighten her day and lift her spirits and, after the day she had endured, she deserved a room filled with flowers. And something to remind her of the boys when she was resting and not able to be with them in the neonatal nursery. And when she had to face the reality of the hysterectomy she had undergone without her consent.

The nurse at the station arranged for the flowers to be placed near her bed.

Waiting outside the room twenty minutes later, he couldn't contain, nor fully understand, the smile that spread across his face and the warmth that surged through his body when he saw her hospital bed being wheeled down the corridor towards him. She was still pale but not as drained as when he had last seen her, and she hadn't noticed him. In the pit of his stomach he still remembered her limp body collapsing against his and he'd thought the boys had lost their mother.

Patiently he remained outside as she was settled into her room but, as the nurses exited, he tapped on the door that was ajar.

'Are you up to a visitor?'

'Patrick?'

'How did you guess?' he asked as he quietly entered her room. 'Perhaps it's the British accent—there are not a lot of us around these parts so I guess it's a giveaway.'

'In this city, it's a dead giveaway.' It was more than just his accent, but Claudia couldn't tell Patrick that it was also his reassuring tone that told her exactly who was at her door. It was the same strong voice that had kept her going when she'd wanted to give up. It was the voice of the man who had saved her and her sons.

'May I come in?'

'Of course,' she said, ushering him in with the arm that wasn't connected to the IV providing pain relief after her surgery. 'What are you still doing here?'

'Keeping an eye on…your handsome young sons.'

'They are gorgeous, aren't they? The nurses wheeled me on the bed into the nursery to see them a few minutes ago on the way back from Recovery. They were sleeping but they told me they're both doing very well.' She paused and nervously chewed on the inside of her cheek to keep her emotions under control. 'Thanks to you.'

Patrick moved closer to her in the softly lit room. 'Not because of me; you did the hard work, Claudia. I just assisted.'

'Maybe the hard work, but you did the skilled work. Without you,' she began, then her chin quivered as she struggled again to keep her tears at bay, 'they could have…well, they might not have made it if you weren't there with me.'

He reached for her hand. It was instinctive and something he had not been driven to do in a very long time. 'Not a chance. They're as strong as their mother.'

Claudia looked down at his hand covering hers. After the trauma of the preceding hours, it made her feel secure. But she couldn't get used to that feeling of being safe. Not with anyone, no matter how kind. She knew that she and Patrick were bonded by what they had been through and it was a normal reaction to the traumatic experience they'd shared. But now, in the safety of the hospital, she had to accept it was nothing more. Although he had proven her initial assumption of him very wrong, she couldn't afford to get swept away by some romantic notion there was more to it. As if he'd appeared like her white knight, saved her and would steal her away to his castle. That wasn't the real world.

Knowing she needed to create some distance between them, she slipped her hand free and haphazardly ran her fingers through her messy curls that had been swept up in a surgical cap for hours.

The move was not lost on Patrick and he graciously accepted her subtle rebuff. He had overstepped the mark. And he never overstepped the mark with a woman. Perhaps it was because she looked so lost and vulnerable that he wanted to make her feel less alone, but clearly she was not looking to be saved again. And he needed to step away. He was grateful she'd reminded him subtly that he wasn't looking to become attached to anyone.

That time in his life had passed. Being alone was what he did best. *What had he been thinking?*

'So…how are you feeling?' he asked in a doctor-patient tone. 'Your body has been through a lot today, quite apart from bringing Thomas and Luca into the world.'

'You mean the…hysterectomy?'

He nodded then waited in silence to hear Claudia's response to the emergency life-changing surgery. She was a resilient woman but he knew this would certainly test any woman and he would not be surprised if she struggled to come to terms with it.

She dropped her gaze for a moment then, lifting her chin and her eyes almost in defiance at what the universe had dealt her, she nodded. 'I'll be okay. I'm alive and I have my sons. It would be stupid to mourn what I can't change and perhaps it would be selfish to ask for more than what I was given today. My life and the lives of my children is miracle enough.'

Patrick was already in awe of the strength that she had shown in the elevator but her reaction to the news almost brought him to his knees with respect for her courage and acceptance of what she couldn't change. She was a truly remarkable woman.

Her fingers nervously played with the woven blanket for a minute before she looked back at Patrick. 'When I think of how terribly wrong everything could have gone today, losing my womb is a small price to pay.'

While Claudia looked like a porcelain doll, Patrick had learned over the few hours since their lives collided that she was made of far tougher material. Still, it puzzled him that she was alone in the world. Had she pushed people from it? Or had they abandoned her? Had being alone made her that strong? He couldn't imagine anyone walking away from such an amazing woman.

Then he realised none of his questions mattered. She had been his unofficial patient for a few hours. Nothing more.

'That huge arrangement of flowers is stunning. I'm guessing it's from you,' she added as she looked around the room and spied the huge bouquet on a shelf near her. It was getting dark outside and she could see the lights of the Los Angeles skyline. But the flowers were more spectacular than any view.

Patrick nodded and tried to look at her with the doctor-patient filter but it was becoming a struggle with each passing moment. It had been an intense first meeting in the elevator but there was more pulling him to her than the fact he had delivered her babies under such conditions. They were not in the confines of that small space any more and she no longer needed his help but still he wanted to be there for the stunning brunette still dressed in a shapeless white surgical gown.

And he was confused as hell. He had unexpectedly become a passenger on a roller coaster of his own emotions. Before, he had always been the driver. He needed to gain control. Quickly. He needed to make it less personal.

'Have you noticed how drab the walls in these rooms are? I needed to brighten your room somehow. I thought flowers would do the trick.'

'The rooms are not that bad, young man,' a stern voice replied from the doorway. 'My name's Vanda, and it would do you well not to complain. I'll be tending to your wife tonight and, for your interest...'

'Oh...we're not married,' came their reply in unison.

There was a moment's uncomfortable silence as the three of them looked at each other in silence.

'Sorry if I presumed your marital status; it's just habit

at my age,' the nurse, who Patrick imagined to be in her early fifties, with short auburn hair and twinkling blue eyes, said. She crossed the room, manoeuvring around Patrick to get access to her patient. 'I have two grandchildren and their parents aren't married either. *Haven't got time*, they say. Well, as long as they're happy, I'm happy.'

'No, we're not together,' Claudia began before the nurse wrapped the blood pressure monitor around her arm. 'He's my…' She paused, not knowing how to describe Patrick. *What was their relationship?* she wondered. They weren't friends, but nor were they connected as patient and doctor in a formal sense. Their relationship really couldn't be defined…not easily at least…except, perhaps, for *intense* and *sudden*.

'I'm her emergency elevator obstetrician…not the father of her babies.'

As Patrick said the words, he wondered, against his better judgement, who was the father of her children. What sort of man was he? And why wasn't he rushing to Claudia's side? Patrick knew that if he was the father, no matter how forcefully the mother of his children tried to push him away, he would stand fast to the spot.

But he wasn't the father of Claudia's children or anyone's children. And he never would be.

'Oh, of course, you're the young woman who delivered in the elevator this afternoon,' Vanda answered. She confirmed that Claudia's vitals were stable, then unwrapped the arm wrap and packed it away before she turned back to Patrick. 'And you must be the doctor who was in the right place today and brought this young lady's twins into the world.'

Patrick nodded. His mind was still filled with questions about Thomas and Luca's father but he needed to block them out. It wasn't his business. Claudia was alive. And now he could walk away as he should, knowing they were safe.

'Well, I'll compliment you on your skill in the baby-delivering field, which was on the six o'clock news, if you didn't already know. But you'd still do well not to criticise the rooms.' With a tilt of her head that signalled she meant business, then a wink that left them both wondering if she was serious or joking, Vanda left the room and Patrick and Claudia found themselves staring at each other, both confused by her demeanour and a little surprised at her announcement of their prime-time notoriety.

'We were on the six o'clock news?' The inflection at the end turned Claudia's statement into a question.

'Apparently—let's hope they didn't manage to find out your identity so you're not bothered by reporters.'

'I hope not,' she said, slumping back into the pillows and nervously fidgeting with her pearl earrings. Her parents had given them to her for her sixteenth birthday, while Harriet had been given a pearl necklace.

'I'll let the nurses' station and the main admissions know you don't want any interviews or fuss made of you or the boys. I'll head them off at the pass.'

Claudia looked at Patrick and thought once again he was her knight in shining armour... Or, with his modern good looks, perhaps he could be riding in on his stallion, tipping his Stetson and saving her. She hadn't even needed to ask. He just kept rescuing her. But she had to stop him doing it. She needed to save herself and her boys. Patrick wouldn't be there for them going forward. It would only be the three of them until they got back to London and Harriet returned.

'Don't worry,' Claudia replied. 'I'll let Vanda know

to tell them I'm not interested in speaking to anyone. You've already done too much. Honestly, I appreciate more than anything all that you have done but you don't have to do any more. I can take it from here.'

Patrick agreed with her. He had done all that was needed and now she would be taken care of in hospital. She would leave for the UK once she and her children got clearance so there was no point in forging any sort of relationship. Romantic or otherwise.

'Here's my number,' he said, putting his business card on the tray where Claudia's water jug was placed. 'If you need anything, call me. Otherwise, I wish you and Thomas and Luca a safe trip home to London in a few weeks.' He fought the desire to kiss her forehead and stroke the soft curls away from her face. With a deep and unexpected sense of regret that he would never see Claudia again, he turned heavily on his feet and headed to the door, pausing for the briefest moment to look at the beautiful woman who had captured more than his attention that day.

Claudia wasn't sure what was suddenly stirring in the pit of her stomach and surging through her veins, making her heart beat faster, but she knew she was torn about watching him walk away. The day had been so intense but something inside of her wasn't ready to let that happen.

She knew she had to be crazy but she had to call after him.

'Please…wait,' she said then, taking a deep heartfelt breath, she continued, 'I didn't mean to seem rude or ungrateful in any way. I just mean I've put you out and I know you're a doctor and you probably have patients and…'

'Claudia—' he turned back and stopped her speech '—it's fine, really; you're right. I'm sure you can take it from here. I'm glad that you and the boys are well and through the ordeal that was today. I couldn't ask for more and I just want all the very best for the future for all of you.'

Patrick smiled at Claudia before he left but he knew in his heart her first instincts to push him away were right. There was more to the way he felt about this woman than a simple doctor-patient relationship so he had to keep his distance.

The only relationships he had were one-night stands with no strings attached and no feelings involved. And he doubted with Claudia it would be anything like that. She was already stirring feelings he didn't want to have.

It had to be just the intense experience they had shared, he reminded himself. He needed to walk away and let her *take it from here*.

# CHAPTER FOUR

'So what exactly are you saying is the issue with Miss Monticello's international health insurance?' Vanda demanded of the caller on the other end of the telephone. She was frowning and her cheeks were becoming flushed.

Patrick's ears tuned in to the conversation and, against his better judgement, he slowed his steps. Her serious tone caused him some concern, as did her expression as he neared the desk. The exchange of words confirmed it. He couldn't walk away and pretend he hadn't heard there was a problem. Something was driving him to want to protect the woman who he knew he should stay away from. A woman who had given him no information about herself, other than the fact she was returning to London with no explanation of why.

Questions were starting to mount in his tired mind. Was the father of her children in London, waiting for her? Or was he no longer in her life? He felt sure Claudia would have asked to call her husband or boyfriend, if she had one, even if he was away on business or fighting for his country. But she'd told him there was no one. Patrick knew he had no right to ask anything about her life that she had not willingly surrendered. Wanting to know more, let alone feeling the way he did about a woman he had known less than twelve hours, was ridiculous.

It had to stop. He knew he wanted to protect Claudia but he had to be realistic about his feelings. She was alone and he felt sorry for her. That had to be the driving force of his desire to protect her. Perhaps coupled with the desire to see her and her children safely out of hospital. He didn't want to think that there could be setbacks with any of them.

He needed to know they were safe then his job was done.

*How could it be anything more than that?*

'Uh-huh…okay… All right, I'll will let her know in the morning that someone from Finance will have to come and see her and make arrangements. I know she told the nurse in Recovery she was worried about the bills but we don't want her to stress. Perhaps she can extend the policy.'

Patrick looked as Vanda's expression fell further and her brow furrowed at what she was hearing. 'Oh, I see, so the twins can't be covered… Well, that's a bit of a mess but I'm sure the hospital will work something out and she'll have to pay the debt over a period of time. Yes, I appreciate it's an international policy and there are restrictions but in my ward there are no restrictions to her care.' She paused for a moment, drumming her fingers on the desk. 'No, I do hear what you're saying but please listen to my concerns.'

She continued listening with anxiety showing clearly on her face while the other staff bustled around her with the change of shift and handover. Patrick kept his focus on the conversation. She was being very polite but firm with the caller, despite her expression and the colour in her cheeks. He doubted she was the type to lose too many battles, but he couldn't help but notice she was struggling to hold her ground.

'I'd rather not. No, let it wait until the morning. Miss Monticello needs her rest and if she's stressing about hospital bills it won't help her sleep and, after what she has been through today, sleep is what she needs,' she said firmly then paused. 'I will be moving her to a ward tomorrow but tonight she's in a private room that was available. No, she doesn't have any next of kin in California or anywhere in the United States on her admission forms. She has a sister, and she appears to be her only living family, but she resides in the UK.'

With that, Patrick learnt a little more about the mystery that was Claudia's life. She had no one else in the world to call family other than her sister. Then why didn't she call her? he wondered.

'Yes, I do understand the seriousness of the situation but we will handle it in the morning. I'm back on at six,' Vanda said. She was becoming short. 'No, absolutely no. I won't budge on it. My patient comes first so please do not send anyone up now because I won't allow them in to her room.'

Patrick paused for a moment, wanting to offer assistance, but then thought better of taking over the situation. He made a mental note to have his lawyer contact the hospital administration the next day and sort through the insurance issues. After bringing the boys into the world, he wasn't about to stand by and let their mother be stressed after the fact. He tried to tell himself it was his gift to Thomas and Luca. But he knew it was not the boys alone that he was thinking about.

'I'm hanging up now,' Vanda continued sternly. 'We'll

continue this conversation in the morning. There are far more practical problems to solve, like sourcing some fresh pyjamas for my patient. She'll remain in a hospital gown tonight but she has no nightdress or toiletries, not even a toothbrush, poor thing, so I can't sit around chatting to you; I'll have to go and sort out something before I finish my shift or she'll look like Orphan Annie in the morning.'

Patrick continued walking and made his way outside to the cab rank and, as he did, he sent a text to his receptionist. He needed her to run an errand for him.

Claudia woke after an uncomfortable and restless sleep and wanted desperately to see her babies. The uncomfortable part of her night was due to post-operative constraints but the restlessness, she suspected, was a combination of anxiety for her sons and then a strange feeling of emptiness, knowing that she would never see Patrick again. She knew it was absurd to even have any sort of reaction to not seeing Patrick, let alone this feeling in the pit of her stomach. Less than twenty-four hours before, she hadn't known him and now she thought she would miss him. It was as if by meeting him she'd found a piece of the puzzle she hadn't known she had been looking for.

As she lay in bed thinking about the facts she realised how silly she was being. Fact one, she told herself, you are a single mother of twins so your life is already full. Fact two, you are a month away from being an illegal overstay in the US so you need to get back to the UK as soon as possible. Fact three, you don't trust men and never will again. Fact four, you know very little about the handsome man who delivered your babies except that he doesn't seem to want children and you have two of the most adorable children ever born. He was just checking you were all right when he visited last night, as any doctor would, she reminded herself. And he walked away. Said goodbye and good luck. That is as final and impersonal as it gets.

'Besides, it's ridiculous', she mumbled out loud. 'To even think you could miss someone you barely know.'

Her practical side forced her to push any thoughts of Patrick from her mind and blame the funny feeling in her stomach on her internal stitches or her reaction to the general anaesthetic. It had to be one or both making her stomach feel uneasy, she decided, as she pushed the nurse call button. She wanted to see Thomas and Luca as soon as possible. She wanted to hold them in her arms, if she was allowed. If not, she wanted to reach inside their humidicribs and stroke their soft warm skin and tell them that they were safe and she was there for them forever.

That they would never be apart. That she would protect them from life's harms in any way she could.

Just the way Patrick had protected them all the day before.

Her eyes were suddenly drawn across the room to the flowers. The beautiful blooms did just as Patrick wanted in brightening the borderline drab hospital room and she felt her mouth curving a little. The walls of her room were a light beige colour and the blinds a deeper shade of the same with the floor a mottled light grey. The night before she had not paid too much attention to the flowers other than thinking there was a pretty pop of colour in the room. In the morning light she could see cheerful yellow and white gerberas, a white daisy spray and blue chrysanthemums in a lovely white-blue vase, with a checked blue and white ribbon giving a pretty finishing touch. And the two small brown bears with blue bow ties. It was so thoughtful of him to have them in her room when she arrived. But then it seemed that everything he did was so considerate.

But why? she wondered. What was motivating him to be so kind to a stranger? He had already done more than could have been expected of anyone. Blinking furiously, she looked away from the floral arrangement. She had to put Patrick out of her mind. She couldn't allow herself to think of him that way. She had learnt her lesson the hard way not to trust anyone, not even herself.

The nurse, who introduced herself as Alli, arrived and unhooked the IV line. 'I'll leave the cannula in, but I'll tape it down,' Alli told her as she thoroughly flushed the tube and placed strong clear tape across Claudia's wrist where the small cannula had been placed. She was one of the youngest nurses on the ward and, Claudia would quickly come to learn, one of the cheekiest. 'Just in case you want IV pain relief during the day or tonight. Believe me, if they offer drugs, take them.'

Slowly, Alli helped her out of bed and assisted her to take small steps into the bathroom. Keeping the dressings dry, the nurse bathed Claudia while she sat on the shower chair.

'Do you have a clean nightdress?' she asked as she towel-dried her patient.

Claudia shook her head. She had no one to collect anything from her apartment and she only had oversized T-shirts, nothing really suitable for hospital. She had packed a suitcase for her trip home and only left out a pair of comfortable leggings, sweater and coat with flat boots for the flight. The other small boxes of her belong-

ings would have been collected and already be on their
way with the shipping company back to London. She
had planned on shopping for pretty nightdresses for her
hospital stay when she returned to London.

While she had made a few acquaintances in Los
Angeles, after she'd found out the truth about her relationship with Stone and then about her pregnancy, the
obvious questions that would raise had made her keep
everyone at arm's length. She didn't want to make friends
and then have to hide the truth from them, so she'd chosen to be alone.

'Looks like you'll be in a stylish hospital gown again
today,' Alli replied as she left to retrieve another gown.
Moments later, she reappeared and helped Claudia to
dress. 'At least it will be clean.'

'Thank you.'

'Since they have that revealing back opening, I'm
going to give you a second one to wear the other way.
Like a coat to complement your stunning runway en-
semble.'

Claudia smiled. Although normally she did care how
she was dressed and paid particular attention to her
grooming, that morning she wouldn't have cared if the
nurse had dressed her in a giant brown paper bag. She
just wanted to get downstairs to the neonatal nursery.

'Not before you eat, Miss Monticello,' Vanda said,
walking into her room and spying Claudia in the wheelchair, ready to go downstairs. 'You'll be no good to your
sons without both rest and nutrition.'

'But I want to know they're all right,' Claudia argued
as she sat upright. The anticipation was building and
she wanted nothing more than to be with her little boys.

Vanda picked up the breakfast tray and put it on the

bed near her impatient patient, handing Claudia a small plate with some buttered wholemeal toast. Standing directly in front of Claudia and not taking her eyes from her, she said firmly, 'Thomas and Luca are doing very well. I had a call from the resident paediatrician in the neo-natal ICU about an hour ago. They're expecting you but I won't let you visit unless you've had some toast and juice. I'm quite serious, Claudia. Your body suffered a huge shock yesterday and you need to take things slowly and not forget to eat and rest, just as your little boys are doing. I'm Italian and, by the sound of your surname, so are you, so you'll know that Italians take their food very seriously. You will not get away with skipping meals with one of your countrywomen on duty. Food first, before you head anywhere.'

Just then there was a knock at the door and another young nurse brought in a delivery box with the insignia of an exclusive store on Rodeo Drive; it was about a foot long and just as wide and tall. Vanda reached out and took the box.

'Well, what's this then? It's addressed to you. Have you been shopping online overnight, Miss Monticello?'

As Claudia took a bite of her toast, she shook her head. 'Are you sure it's for me? I couldn't afford to shop there in a mad fit.'

'Well, it definitely has your name on it, so someone's been shopping for you. I'll pop it on the bed and you can check it later.'

'P'raps it's a present from a handsome stranger because you were on TV last night,' Alli added before she left the room to continue her rounds.

'Oh, gosh, I hope not,' Claudia said as she put down the toast, as her already fragile appetite completely disappeared. 'I'm hoping no one knows my name or Thomas and Luca's.'

'With the proximity of the apartment complex and the fuss made on the evening news, viewers would probably assume you'd be here but neither your name nor your sons' were released and we've told the main admissions desk to refuse any media requests. It's our usual protocol,' Vanda replied. Then, spying the still uneaten toast on Claudia's plate, she continued, 'Would you like me to help you open the box and put you out of your misery?'

Claudia nodded as she tentatively sipped her orange juice.

'All right, here's the deal. I'll get some scissors from the nurses' station while you finish your breakfast but I won't open the box until you've had both pieces of toast and either your juice or a cup of tea.'

Claudia nodded begrudgingly.

Vanda stayed true to her word and when she returned with the oversized scissors she waited until Claudia had eaten and finished her juice before cutting through the packaging tape on the box. She opened it and handed it to Claudia.

Claudia lifted the tissue carefully. 'Oh, goodness, they're beautiful,' she exclaimed as she pulled the stunning jade-green silk pyjamas from the box.

'Very nice. Whoever arranged for those to be sent has great taste. Hold on a minute; now it makes sense…' Vanda paused for a moment, a strange look on her face.

'What is it? Do you know who sent this to me?'

'No idea, actually, but I had a conversation in handover this morning about a call one of the young nurses took from that store after I finished my shift last night. Apparently they had a phone order and wanted to check if they could deliver to a patient in our ward. They didn't say who and of course we would not have given your details even if they had asked.'

'How curious,' Claudia replied as she reached inside to find there was more. A short nightdress and a long one in varied tones of apricot and a matching floral wrap that picked up the colour palette of all of the other items and added some black trim for dramatic effect. There were also some jade satin slippers wrapped in more tissue at the bottom of the box, along with a toiletries bag. She unzipped the bag and it was filled with everything she would need.

'Was there a card?' Claudia asked, peering inside the box and then closing the lid and carefully checking the packaging. She couldn't see any sender other than the store—it had been a telephone order.

'No, it appears to be anonymous. As you said, very *curious* indeed,' Vanda replied.

Claudia put everything back into the box. 'I can't accept an anonymous gift.'

'I would—they look like silk and they're a whole lot better than your current outfit,' Alli argued as she stepped back into the room to collect the breakfast tray with a huge smile. 'I'll be back in ten minutes to take you to Neonatal Intensive Care so it gives you time to slip into one of those stunning pieces if you like.'

Claudia looked down at the shapeless white gown and came close to agreeing for a split second but then bit her lip and shook her head. 'No. I can't.'

Vanda took the box and put it on the bed again. 'You don't have to accept it; however, you are in need of everything that's in that box, so—' she paused to put her words together '—what if you accept the gift on the condition that you will repay your generous benefactor when you've been discharged from the hospital? I'm sure you can track them down through the store.'

'I don't feel comfortable with the idea and I'm not sure I could afford to anyway.'

'Do you feel comfortable with the idea of staying in your present outfit for a few days? You'll get a fresh one each day, of course, but still the same white number with the lovely back opening! Do you have anyone who could go shopping for you?'

Claudia nodded. 'No, there's no one I can call.'

'I thought as much. You'll be in the nursery a lot over the coming days and the pyjamas and gown would be most helpful. I did manage to find you some toothpaste and a toothbrush and a few other bits and pieces but they are pretty basic and I'm sure whatever has been sent to you would be a whole lot nicer.'

Claudia once again bit her lip as she tried to put everything into perspective. 'I know I need them, particularly the toiletries, but do you really think I will be able to find out who sent the gift and repay them?'

'All I can say is that we'll do our best.'

'I *will* find them and I *will* send them a cheque for the entire amount as soon as I can. I mean it.'

Vanda left the room and Claudia slowly and carefully changed without contorting too much. The softness of the pyjama fabric felt glorious on her skin. Feather-light and cool to wear. Her body felt as if it had done battle the day before and this was a little bit of pampering.

Claudia sat down again to rest. She wanted so much to see her sons. She couldn't wait to hold them and tell them how much she loved them. Alli had not arrived so she decided to call Harriet and give her the good news about Thomas and Luca. Her sister had no idea of what had transpired over the last twenty-four hours or that she was now the aunt of two wonderful little boys. It was eight o'clock in the morning and, knowing that Argentina was five hours ahead of LA, Claudia felt confident she wouldn't wake her sister.

Harriet answered the phone after only two rings.

'Hi, sis, how are you? I miss you so much and I have *soooo* much to tell you.' Her voice then dropped to a loud whisper. 'Oh, I'm so confused. My boring, predictable as mud life has turned completely topsy-turvy. I met this man, as close to Adonis as you would find, well, the Argentinian version of the Greek God anyway... I don't know if there is an Argentinian version, to be honest, but he is so ridiculously handsome as well as intelligent and we, well, sort of had a thing, just one night, actually, back in the UK, and I never thought I'd see him again. But now I'm here in his country. He looks even better under the Buenos Aires sun than he did in London—and he was already an eleven out of ten...'

Claudia was surprised to hear Harriet sound so nervous and clearly smitten by this man but, ecstatic as she was to hear that her sister had a love interest, she was aware that Alli would return to take her to the nursery so she blurted out her news. 'I had the babies, Harriet. You're an aunty!'

'What?'

'I had my babies.'

'So early, Clau? Are you and the babies okay?' She stopped in her tracks.

'Yes, I'm fine and Thomas and Luca are so handsome.'

'Thomas and Luca! You named them after both grand-fathers?'

'I hope you don't mind that I took both names in one fell swoop. I didn't leave you a grandfather for when you have children.'

Harriet laughed. 'Phuh—me? No, I don't think I'll be having children anytime soon. I'm happy you used Nonno's and Papa's names. I still can't believe you had twins! So tell me about my nephews—are they happy and healthy little boys considering they were early?'

'They're doing well, particularly since they were born in a lift.'

'In a lift?'

'Yes, a lift, or maybe I should say an elevator since I'm here in LA.'

'LA? I'm confused. I thought you were heading back to London to have the babies?'

'I was but my water broke in the elevator and Patrick helped me to give birth. Actually, Patrick saved my life because I haemorrhaged and passed out and then para-medics rescued us all and I had an emergency hyster-ectomy.'

'How can you tell me you're okay with all of that going on? I need to get there now.' Harriet began pac-ing nervously.

'No, Harriet.' Claudia's voice was firm. As much as she wanted more than anything to have her sister with her, she refused to pull her away from the first adventure of her life. She was proud that her twin was finally jumping into something with both feet. Maybe they weren't so dif-ferent after all, or maybe they were switching roles. For a while, at least. 'You can't do anything. For once you need to stick with your plans and stop trying to rescue your big sister. I'm fine, the surgery went well and I have two adorable little boys. We'll be heading home to London as soon as they're strong enough and you can meet them.'

'I need to hop on a plane and get to LA now.'

'Harriet, please listen to me. The orphanage needs you more than me. I'm well taken care of. Everything's fine here. I have a place to live until I leave for London.' Claudia had to lie or she would risk her sister doing what she always did—stepping in to save the day. Claudia had no idea where she would live. Her apartment was gone, she assumed her suitcase would have been taken down to the concierge's office, but she had barely any savings to her name and only a changeable ticket back to London. She would have to work things out quickly, but not at Harriet's expense. Her sister had finally found her dream job and perhaps even her dream man and Claudia was not taking either away from her.

'Is the ex keeping his distance? Does he know about the birth?'

'Yes, he's keeping his distance and no, he doesn't know I've had his sons. He wouldn't care. His lawyer told me he didn't want to be updated about the pregnancy. So I thought I would keep the news to myself. It would hardly have had him skipping with joy.' Claudia paused. 'His wife still has no idea that the boys or I even exist. Just as I had no idea she existed when I fell for his lines. It's amazing how he hid his marriage so well. I must be the most stupid woman in the world.'

'You're not stupid in any way,' Harriet countered softly. 'Just way too trusting for your own good. But you're better off without him, Clau.'

'I know,' she said then, thinking back to the tiny little boys waiting for her in the nursery, she smiled. 'But

I have the most wonderful sons so my regrets about my relationship with that man are tempered. He gave me the greatest gifts, Thomas and Luca…and permission to *not* have him in my life. The papers arrived from his lawyer last week. He doesn't want his name on the birth certificates and waived any parental rights.'

'That's so cold!'

'He offered me a trust fund for the boys but I told him to keep his money.'

'Will you be all right without an income?'

'I'll be fine once I get back home in a few weeks. My life will be perfect…'

'I worry about you being alone.'

'I'm won't ever be alone. I have Thomas and Luca, and I'll always have you.'

'That's the truth,' Harriet agreed.

There was also someone else who had momentarily stepped into her life. Claudia was determined that in the future, when he would be just a memory, she would tell her sons as they grew up about the man who'd brought them into the world and also saved their mother's life. Even though they might never meet Patrick, they would always know about him. And how very special he was.

'I'd better say goodbye, though, as the nurse will be back to wheel me down to the nursery any minute.'

'Okay, but you call me if you need me. I can be on a plane and there with you in a few hours. I love you, sis,' Harriet told her.

'Love you too, Harriet,' Claudia replied then hung up before she had a chance to answer her sister's final question.

'Wait, who's Patrick…?'

# CHAPTER FIVE

'Miss Monticello, I'm Dr Wilson, the neonatologist here at Los Angeles Mercy Hospital. I need to speak with you in private for a moment.' The doctor leant down and held out his hand and Claudia tentatively met his handshake. She had only just arrived in Neonatal ICU and had not yet seen her sons. She had no idea why he wanted to speak with her but she felt her heart pick up speed as his tone seemed quite serious. She hadn't considered there could possibly be any bad news after yesterday. The boys both seemed perfect despite what they had all been through.

*What had changed?*

'Please call me Claudia,' she replied as she began to nervously play with her freshly scrubbed hands and continued observing the doctor suspiciously. She tried to contain her emotions and wait for the doctor to speak but questions driven by mounting fear came rushing out. 'Are my babies going to be all right? Is there something wrong? I thought everything was fine yesterday.' She wanted to jump from her wheelchair and find them. Her eyes darted around but she could not see the boys as their humidicribs were blocked by a tall beige partition.

'Claudia, they are both doing very well, all things considered,' he returned, clearly trying to calm her down.

'What do you mean—all things *considered*?'

'I mean their delivery in an elevator and the simple fact they are six weeks early. I was going to come to your room but the charge nurse said you were on your way down here so I thought I'd wait. You can see your boys the moment we've finished speaking. I didn't want you to be anxious in the elevator.' The neonatologist, in his late fifties, had a warm smile; his hair, which was grey around the temples, and his deep brown eyes reminded Claudia of her father. Although the doctor's very contained demeanour was not like her father's passionate, gregarious Italian personality. He was controlled and that was reassuring to Claudia but she was still scared.

'Tell me, is there something wrong?' Her eyes widened as she spoke. While he had said nothing dire nor even hinted at it, Claudia had a sense of foreboding but she was trying very hard not to fall to pieces.

'There's been a small setback with Luca and I would like to talk to you about his treatment.'

Claudia's chin began to quiver with the words coming so calmly from the neonatologist's mouth. She had just been wheeled from the scrub room where Alli had helped her to put on a disposable gown over her pyjamas and suddenly she was being ushered into a small consulting room. She had been so excited to see her boys. She hadn't thought for a moment she would hear bad news. She'd had enough, she felt sure, to last a lifetime.

'I can take Claudia from here if you'd like,' he told Alli and reached for the handles of the wheelchair. 'I'll call the nurses' station when she's ready to go back to her room,'

'Certainly Dr Wilson; I'll come back whenever Claudia's ready,' Alli said gently and reassuringly patted

Claudia's shoulder. 'You'll be fine, honey. Just breathe slowly and stay calm.'

Dr Wilson wheeled Claudia into the small office and sat opposite her. His expression was stern.

'How serious is it? I need to know.' Claudia felt her stomach tie in knots and it was nothing to do with her surgery.

'Luca had a few breathing problems yesterday and that is why he was in the open bed warmer so that we could provide oxygen through an oxy-hood, or head box as we often call it. It's a small perspex box that allows babies to breathe more easily, but Luca didn't improve overnight. In fact he seemed to be struggling so I suspected a condition called PDA. It's short for a longer medical term, and I can give you more information later. I ordered an echocardiogram an hour ago to confirm my diagnosis…'

'What's an echocardiogram? Did it hurt him?' Despite her resolve to remain in control, tears began to well in her eyes but the questions kept coming. 'Where is Luca?'

'Luca is fine at the moment, Claudia,' the doctor continued in a firm but calm tone. 'The echocardiogram didn't hurt because it's much like an X-ray. Luca and Thomas are over there, where they both were yesterday.' He motioned with his hand in the direction her sons. 'The humidicrib with Thomas is beside Luca's open bed warmer and they have one nurse looking after them both. The setback at this time, Miss Monticello… I'm sorry… Claudia,' he corrected himself, 'has been confirmed by the echocardiogram and, while it's not serious and more than likely just due to his premature arrival, we need to keep an eye on Luca and you need to be aware of his condition.'

'Will Thomas develop the condition too?'

'No. There's no sign of PDA with Thomas. We're just monitoring Luca around this issue.'

'And what exactly is the problem, Dr Wilson?'

'He has an opening between two major blood vessels leading from his heart.'

'Oh, my God, no.' Claudia's hands instinctively covered her mouth. She didn't want to cry but the news brought her to the brink.

It was all too much. She'd thought bringing her babies into the world under such harsh conditions was terrifying but this was so much worse. She felt so helpless.

'Claudia, I know you must be very scared by what I'm telling you but that is why I asked you in here to talk,' the doctor continued in a very soothing tone. 'All parents have that initial reaction—it's perfectly normal—but you need to understand a little more about Luca's problem and the treatment options. The opening between the blood vessels I'm discussing is a normal part of a baby's circulatory system *before birth* but it normally closes shortly after birth. While a baby is in the mother's womb, only a small amount of his or her blood needs to go to the lungs. This is because the baby gets oxygen from the mother's bloodstream.'

'So why did Luca's not close?'

'It is probably due purely to his prematurity. You see, after birth, the baby is no longer connected to the mother's bloodstream and the baby's blood needs to go to his or her own lungs to get oxygen. When a baby is born on or around their due date the baby begins to breathe on his or her own and the pulmonary artery opens to allow blood into the lungs, and the other opening closes. But in premature infants it is not uncommon for it to remain open and a small PDA often doesn't cause problems.'

'Does Luca have a small PDA or a big one?'

'We don't know yet but if it's small then he may never need treatment.'

'But if it isn't small, what then?'

'A large PDA left untreated can allow poorly oxygenated blood to travel in the wrong direction, weakening the heart muscle and causing heart problems.'

Claudia's world just became a little darker and her own heart sank. 'Will he need surgery?' She felt increasingly powerless to do anything as she waited on tenterhooks for the answer.

'Not at this stage. His treatment for the time being will involve monitoring and medication.'

Her mind was spinning and her body reeling from the news about her baby boy. She felt so overwhelmed and unsure of where to turn. Then she realised there was nowhere to turn. She only had herself. And her little boys only had their mother. She drew a deep restorative breath and faced the doctor. She had to be strong for the three of them.

'What sort of medication?' she asked, shaking her head.

Before the doctor could respond, there was a knock at the door.

She looked over her shoulder to see Patrick standing in the doorway with the same expression she remembered from the day before. The expression that told her she would get through whatever lay ahead when she had no idea how. Her brow was lined in confusion and a single tear of relief trickled down her cheek. Quickly she wiped it away with the back of her hand.

'Claudia, I came as soon as I could,' he began as he stepped inside the room. And closer to her.

'But I didn't call.'

'No, I asked the hospital to keep me posted about the boys as I was listed as the doctor who delivered them. It was professional courtesy for them to keep me updated. I called late last night and asked to be informed if there were any problems with either Thomas or Luca. I knew, with their premature births, there may be issues and I wanted to be here for them.'

What Patrick wanted to say was he wasn't just there for Thomas and Luca. He wanted to be there for her. But he couldn't bring himself to say it. He felt certain she wouldn't want to hear it and he didn't want to say it and believe it. Having feelings for someone—wanting to be a part of Claudia and the boy's lives—was so foreign to him.

He had collapsed onto his bed after a long hot shower the previous night. After returning from the hospital, he had tried to put Claudia out of his mind. He'd hoped as the steaming water engulfed his body he would come to his senses. But he didn't. Her gorgeous face, her feisty nature and her strength in the face of pain that would have crippled the strongest of men, kept pulling his thoughts back to her. And then there was her instant love for her boys. All of it made it impossible for Patrick to push her image away. He couldn't erase her from his thoughts. He had spent hours trying but failed and gave in to what he knew he wanted to do. Against his better judgement, he wanted to be there for them all if they needed him.

Claudia felt relieved to have Patrick so close but so torn at needing him. She was confused. She said nothing as she looked at him. There was nothing in her head that would have made any sense if she'd tried to speak.

Patrick turned his attention to the doctor. 'Dr Wilson, I'm Patrick Spencer. We spoke on the phone earlier.'

The doctor stood and extended his hand to greet Patrick and, in doing so, broke the tension between Claudia and Patrick.

'Nice to meet you in person. Please call me Geoffrey. And I must commend you in person for your medical intervention in the elevator. You wouldn't want to do all your deliveries that way, I'm sure.'

'No, an elevator delivery is not something I would've willingly opted for,' he responded with a lightness to his voice. He met the other doctor's handshake but gave away nothing more. Patrick's current medical specialty bore no relevance in the neonatal nursery. He had been honest with the obstetric surgeon when asked directly the day before, but offering up information not requested was pointless. His former medical knowledge was still very much intact, even if his career with babies was long gone.

Claudia watched the men's conversational banter with a blank expression on her face. Her emotions were a roller coaster but she still had questions about her boys that were clear-cut. Even if anything to do with her own heart and head was not close to straightforward.

'You mention drugs, Dr Wilson. What drugs are you talking about for Luca? Do they have any side effects?'

The doctor immediately returned his focus to Claudia. 'Ibuprofen will be the drug that will be given to Luca. It's an anti-inflammatory that could help to block the hormone-like chemicals in Luca's body that are keeping the PDA open. Ibuprofen could very simply allow it to close in a very short space of time.'

'Is this condition common?' Her voice was steadier and she felt as if her co-pilot had returned and was standing beside her. Still hugely confused by her own feelings, she was slowly digesting the idea that together they would navigate a problem that only moments ago she'd found overwhelming.

'It occurs in about eight in every thousand premature births but most correct themselves in a very short time frame and some in only a few hours.'

'So Luca will be all right?' she asked with her eyes still searching for reassurance, moving from Patrick to Dr Wilson and back again.

'I am fairly sure that over the next day or so the condition will correct itself,' Dr Wilson offered. 'But you still needed to be informed. I don't like to hide anything.' Claudia felt reassured to hear those words. She didn't want anything to be hidden from her ever again.

'And you agree, Patrick?'

He nodded. 'I do.'

Patrick's eyes met hers. The level of vulnerability in Claudia's eyes made him want to pull her into his arms and comfort her but he couldn't. He was providing medical advice. He had to behave as a medical practitioner and refrain from doing what he wanted to do as a man.

'I don't think we should cross a bridge that hasn't presented itself,' he volunteered from his professional viewpoint. 'Luca has a high chance of avoiding any invasive treatment so let's not overthink the situation.'

'Then I won't worry any more.'

Patrick sensed from the doctor's curious expression that he was trying to read the relationship playing out before him; he opened his mouth to speak but Patrick cut in quickly. 'Have you visited with Thomas and Luca today, Claudia?'

'No.'

'Then, Dr Wilson, now Claudia is fully versed with Luca's condition, may I wheel her over to see her babies?'

'Certainly,' the older doctor replied before he could ask anything else. Together they left the small room, with Dr Wilson showing the way and Patrick pushing Claudia's wheelchair. Patrick glanced down to see Claudia still fidgeting with her fingers and suddenly felt very protective. She lifted her face and smiled at him and a warm feeling rushed through his body.

It was as if he was where he needed to be and where he belonged and he hadn't felt that way in a very long time.

He pulled Claudia's wheelchair between the humidicrib and the open bed and then sat down beside her. The neonatologist tended to some new arrivals to the nursery and left them with the neonatal nurse.

'They both look almost red, and I can see their veins… I didn't notice it yesterday.'

'You didn't notice because you were so happy to see them alive and you were lucky to be alive yourself. I don't think you were up to focusing on the details.'

'But is it normal?'

'Yes, premature babies appear to be red as well as much smaller than you had imagined. You can see all the blood vessels through their skin because there hasn't been sufficient time to develop any fat underneath.'

'There are so many wires attached to them. Will I be able to hold them?' Claudia asked as the desire to have them both in her arms was stronger than any need she had ever felt before.

The nurse approached and shook her head. 'Not yet, but you can certainly stroke them both and that is important. They need to feel their mother's touch. While Thomas and Luca aren't the smallest babies in here, we still need to allow them to remain in temperatures stable enough to keep them both warm without needing to be wrapped up in blankets.'

'It also decreases the risk of an infection,' Patrick added as his eyes panned from one baby to the other. 'The humidity in the crib is controlled to help maintain the baby's hydration and prevent water loss. And Luca on his open bed is wearing a cap to help limit the heat loss.'

Claudia gently stroked Luca's tiny arm and prayed that Patrick was right and the problem with his heart would pass in time.

'Patrick,' she began, 'I know you said not to cross a bridge that isn't in front of me, but I can't put blinkers on and pretend there's no chance of something serious. I need to ask just one question and I want you to be completely honest with me.'

Patrick had a million questions for Claudia but he knew she might not stay in town long enough for all of them to be answered. He accepted the simple reality that whatever time they shared in the next few days might be all they would ever have.

Their lives had collided and they had both shared the most precious and intense experience. But it was not the real world and it would all end soon enough. And one burning question in particular still resonated in the back of his mind. *Where was the man who should be by Claudia's side?*

He pushed that thought away and took a deep breath. 'Certainly—what's your question?'

Claudia looked over at Thomas inside his glass humidicrib and then back to tiny Luca. The question erred on the side of the worst-case scenario, which she didn't want to think about. But she needed to know and, if she had to, she wanted to hear the worst from Patrick. 'Can they guarantee the ibuprofen will work?'

Patrick paused, wishing he could tell her there was a written in stone guarantee but there was no such guarantee. 'No, to be honest, the medications aren't one hundred percent effective and if Luca's condition is severe or causing complications surgery might be needed, but that is not something you have to consider now. Luca's doctor seems very hopeful that the drugs will work.'

'But if they don't?'

'Claudia,' he said, taking her hands in his instinctively and, against his better judgement, he looked at the tears welling in her eyes. She wasn't looking at him any more. She was lovingly watching her tiny son but he noticed she didn't flinch or pull away and left her hands in his. He hated admitting it but there were undeniable sparks as her skin touched his. She was lighting a fire inside him where he'd thought there were only cold embers incapable of feeling any warmth ever again. 'Like I told you before, let's not worry about something over which we have no control. If surgery is needed we'll deal with it then but now is about remaining positive and optimistic about your boys and getting yourself well too.'

Claudia turned her gaze back to Patrick and then to his hands protectively holding hers. Who was this man who kept saving her? she wondered. Should she let him get close to her? He appeared to be so upfront and honest and caring but she still needed to protect her herself from further disappointment. He'd only come into her life twenty-four hours before and she really knew very little about him. There were so many unasked questions. Maybe he wasn't hiding anything but he wasn't overly forthcoming either and that worried her.

She had been promised a life by the boys' father that was just a lie. How could she be sure that Patrick was any different?

She felt herself wanting to believe in him and everything he was saying and she was feeling, but she was scared. Was it just because of what they'd shared the day before that made her feel that she could trust him? Or was it more than that? Perhaps she felt indebted to him for saving her life and her babies. She knew she had never felt about a man the way she did at that moment.

It was as if she had known him for years.

Her head was spinning. Why could she imagine herself wrapped in the comfort of Patrick's strong arms, her body pressed against the warmth of his…and his lips reaching for hers…? She shook herself back to reality. She was in no place to be having those thoughts.

It wasn't right…but it was happening. And, try as she might, she couldn't pretend it wasn't.

She had feelings she didn't understand for a man she really didn't know.

It didn't make any sense, she thought, as she slipped her hands free.

She had to channel thoughts of Harriet: what her sister would do and how she would think. She would certainly be more realistic and practical. That was how she had to behave. It had to be about her sons from now on. There was barely enough of her left emotionally to give both sons the love and undivided attention they deserved. She had to consider them in every decision she made. She needed to keep it simple, despite the way she felt herself drawn to the handsome Englishman. To her knight in shining armour.

Perhaps they could be friends.

She threw away that idea as quickly as it had arrived. The electricity she felt surge through her body when Patrick was near made *friends* untenable. She just had to manage her feelings for the short time he was around and behave as the unofficial patient of a very handsome, charismatic doctor would. However difficult that would be.

'Is there something else on your mind?'

'No, my mind's still reeling from the news about Luca. You'll think I'm absurd if I keep asking questions...'

'Claudia, never apologise for asking questions. These are your babies and you have every right to have each and every question answered honestly and to ask it again and again if need be.'

Claudia drew breath and with a tremble in her voice continued, 'Why is only Luca affected?' As she spoke, she looked at Thomas and wondered if she had been told everything. Or if there was more she should know.

Patrick wanted so much to hold her close and comfort her. She was frightened and there was nothing as a professional he could do other than provide standard advice, albeit in an empathetic manner. For some inexplicable reason, he wanted to offer so much more but he couldn't. He had to veto the feelings that were stirring in him. And before he swept her into his arms and kissed her more passionately than he had ever kissed a woman before.

It wasn't going to be easy but he couldn't allow romantic thoughts to invade his mind and his heart. With his arms folded across his chest, he answered her. 'Dr Wilson isn't worried because Thomas doesn't have the condition now, so he can't ever have it. The opening between two major blood vessels leading from his heart closed naturally after birth. You need to understand that Thomas and Luca are fraternal twins so they are quite different developmentally in a number of ways. While they're twins, they're essentially just like any siblings so not all of their developmental conditions are going to be shared. Fortunately, this is one of them.'

Claudia was relieved to hear everything that Patrick was explaining and his calm bedside manner was alleviating her concerns. 'I have a non-identical twin sister,' she offered, as he watched her appear to relax a little. 'Harriet. She's the complete opposite of me. She's my rock. She's a nurse, quiet and sensible, always thinking about other people. We've been there for each other since our parents died nine years ago.'

'I'm sorry you lost your parents while you were still young.' Patrick had been an adult when he'd found himself alone so he could understand the overwhelming sadness that must have been Claudia's world when she lost her parents.

'It was just before our twentieth birthday, so we weren't that young, but we had been very protected, growing up in what was essentially a close-knit household. We grew up quickly. Harriet more so than me.'

'You're obviously close to her. Was there a reason that you didn't call her from the elevator yesterday?'

'She was on her way to Argentina. I wasn't sure if she was still in transit and I didn't want to worry her. I mean, there wasn't anything else she could have done except worry.'

'I suppose you're right. Have you spoken to her yet?' he asked as he sat back in his chair a little and glanced over at Thomas and Luca, both still sleeping soundly. 'Does she know she's an aunt?'

'Oh, yes, I just called before the nurse brought me down here.'

A smile crossed Claudia's face. It was the first full smile that he had witnessed. And it made her even more beautiful, if that was possible.

'Of course,' she continued, unaware of the effect she was having on Patrick. 'And, in typical Harriet style, she wanted to rush here to be with me. Drop her life to rescue her big sister. I was born first so I'm older by three minutes but she always behaves like the older, far wiser sister.'

Patrick smiled. 'So she's on her way here then?'

'Absolutely not,' she said with an expression that told him she thought he should have known better. 'I wouldn't allow her to. She's working in an orphanage and I'm not going to have her alter her plans. I'll see her at home when she finishes her work over there in a few months.'

'So you lived together back in London?' he asked and then curiosity got the better of him. 'Were you on holiday here or a work exchange of sorts?'

Claudia went a little quiet and Patrick wondered if he had asked too many questions. Perhaps he'd been too intrusive.

'You know what, forget I asked. It's none of my business. I'm here to help answer any questions you have about your boys, not interview you.'

She paused before she spoke although she hadn't intended on opening up about the details of her past. Looking at Patrick, she couldn't help but feel they had known each other for a long time. She had felt that way from the moment he'd taken off his sunglasses in the elevator and she had looked into his grey-blue eyes.

'My sister and I still share our family home. I came over here for work. I won an internship with a weekly drama series on a major network. It was a huge opportunity and I took it. Again, I jumped in with both feet like I always do,' she announced as she gently ran her finger over her tiny son's shoulder.

'I don't think jumping in is a bad idea. You experience all that life has to offer that way.'

'And some,' she muttered under her breath and felt a shiver of regret run down her body. 'Anyway, my contract is over so, as soon as the boys are strong enough, we will all head back to London. That's where I want to raise them,' she added, turning to look Patrick squarely in the eyes. 'And my leaving is something the boys' father does not object to... In fact, he is quite...' She stopped. There was no need for Patrick to know any more. 'Let's just say my leaving is not causing him any grief.'

'Well, then, we need to get them strong enough to travel.'

Patrick stayed with Claudia for another twenty minutes, then excused himself as he needed to get to his practice. He had an afternoon roster of new patients and a few post-operative.

'I'll leave you with your boys, but if you like I can call again over the next few days to check up on all of you.'

'I'd like that,' she said instinctively but the moment the words passed over her lips she knew she shouldn't have given him that answer. It was opening them both up to the inevitable.

She now had a date with a potentially sad farewell looming on the horizon.

Claudia had spent two days sitting beside Thomas and Luca, praying for them to reach the next tiny milestone and, despite the rush of hormones after the birth, she was feeling better emotionally but physically exhausted. She had stroked both boys between their gavage feeds and she chatted with the nurses and doctors. The doctor had reassured her that Luca's condition was already showing improvement and he believed that within days they might be able to stop the ibuprofen.

She had also received a call from Harriet. Her sister wanted an update on her nephews but she seemed distracted. She hadn't been disinterested at all but there seemed to be something on her mind. Claudia put it down to the tireless work she must be undertaking at the orphanage. She had nothing but admiration for her sister and could hardly wait for Thomas and Luca to meet her.

After she hung up, she suddenly felt tired and a little sore as they had ceased the IV pain relief and she was just having four hourly tablets. She decided after dinner to stay in her room and have an early night and get up early to spend the next day down in the nursery. To her surprise and relief, she had been able to stay in her private room.

She had missed seeing Patrick the previous evening and during the day and wondered if she would ever see him again. Perhaps he had done his heroic act and then disappeared into the night, she thought. Her eyes drifted to the night lights of Los Angeles that she could see from her bed and she wondered where he was. Was he thinking about her and the boys?

While he had every right to be enjoying dinner or drinks with another woman, a crazy part of her felt jealous. Was he dining at an elegant Beverley Hills restaurant or somewhere swank in downtown LA? Was his stunning date enjoying his company, laughing at his anecdotes or just mesmerised by his stunning eyes?

Was the thought of the woman who had ruined his jacket and shirt the furthest thing from his mind?

Hesitant to overstretch, she gently moved her body to the edge of the bed so she could put her teacup back on the bedside cabinet. Then she eased back into a comfortable position and plumped up her pillow before she nestled under the covers. Thinking about Patrick and actually spending any time caring what he was doing at that time of the evening was ridiculous, she berated herself. And having flashbacks to the moment he'd removed his shirt in the elevator was borderline torturous since she knew they would never have a future together.

She looked up at the ceiling, wishing suddenly that her parents were alive to meet their grandsons. They would stroke their tiny cheeks and kiss them from morning to night and the boys would have loved their grandparents. If only they'd had the chance to meet them.

And how would her parents have reacted to Patrick? They would most certainly thank him for bringing Thomas and Luca into the world. Her father would shake his hand and then pull him into his strong embrace with a hearty laugh. Her mother would be a little more reserved but still tell him how grateful she was for what he had done in saving their precious grandchildren.

She felt a tear slip from her eye and onto the pillow.

Her heart ached for what she had lost, now more than ever.

# CHAPTER SIX

PATRICK STOOD OUTSIDE the door of Claudia's hospital room, trying to resist the temptation to knock. He wondered why he had returned. He had tried to stay away and had almost succeeded. But something drove him to see the gorgeous brunette.

Was there a man who still owned Claudia's heart? Despite alarm bells ringing, he knocked on the door. Why was he going against every rule he had followed for over a decade? Never get close to someone, never form a bond or risk his heart, never look for more than one night. His decision to become an island had been born of necessity and it had served him well. But that resolve had never been so tested as it was now. The idea of Claudia, Thomas and Luca featuring in his future was a recurring thought that haunted him.

His rejection of family and his family's rejection of him were combined in fighting his thoughts about Claudia and the boys. And Claudia and the boys were winning.

'I hope it's not too late. The nurse said you were still awake.'

It was a voice that the sensible part of Claudia's brain

didn't want to hear but one that made her hopeless heart do a little dance. She wiped her eyes with the back of her hand and tried to pull herself up in the bed as Patrick walked into the room. He was dressed in dark clothing and he cut a ridiculously attractive figure. His trousers were black and he had a charcoal polo top and black leather shoes. His clothing highlighted his sun-kissed brown hair and light tan and the stubble that she imagined would be soft to her touch.

His appearance was intoxicating. He wasn't fighting fair, she thought. How was she supposed to keep her thoughts to doctor-patient when he looked so damn good?

'You shouldn't have come; it's so late and you probably have far more important places to be than here.' Her voice was crisp and it belied how truly happy she was to see him. She didn't want to need him the way she did. She didn't want to repeat the mistake of thinking she knew everything about a man, only to have her heart broken by what he was hiding.

But something about Patrick made her think he wasn't hiding anything.

*Was he an exception to the rule?*

Patrick looked into her eyes in the dim light of the room and searched for something.

He didn't find it immediately but he persisted and moved closer to the bed.

He saw her full lips curve into a smile. And her eyes were smiling too. He found what he was looking for. Despite what she was telling him, there was a welcome on her beautiful face. Part of him didn't want to see any warmth there. He normally chose women who weren't looking for the picket fence and happily ever after because he couldn't provide it.

With one look he was reminded of just how different she was and how he didn't want to walk away without knowing more about her.

'I'm sorry I couldn't be here earlier today or last night. I had patients until late and a surgical roster today that finished about an hour ago.' There was more he wasn't saying. He had forced himself to stay away. Tried to push thoughts of her from his mind and pretend that she hadn't crept under his skin.

He had no choice but to give in to his desire to see her.

'You know there's no obligation to come. You're a busy doctor and I suppose there are lots of women having babies.' She fussed with her bedclothes and averted her gaze as she spoke. She didn't want to fall into the warmth of his eyes.

He looked at her for a moment in silence with a curious expression.

'What is it?' she asked, sensing she had said something silly but not understanding why.

'I'm a doctor, Claudia, but I don't spend my days delivering babies.'

She shot him a puzzled look. 'What do you mean—are you a children's doctor, not an obstetrician?'

While he had not articulated his specialty during labour, with the risk of raising her anxiety level, she had obviously not read his business card.

'Do you still have the card I left you in case you needed to reach me?'

'Yes, it's in the cabinet. Why?'

Patrick crossed to the cabinet with long purposeful steps. 'May I?' he asked as he reached for the drawer.

She nodded. There was nothing personal in there.

'Here it is,' he announced, the small white card in his hand. 'You haven't read it, have you?'

Claudia shook her head. 'I had no reason to. I haven't called you.'

She put her hand out and he passed the card to her. Squinting in the soft lighting, she searched the card for his details and read the words aloud.

'Dr Patrick Spencer…cosmetic surgeon?' She collapsed back into her pillow in horror. Her arms instinctively folded across herself in an attempt to feel less vulnerable. There had to be some mistake. 'You're a plastic surgeon? You're not an obstetrician? Why didn't you tell me?'

Patrick shook his head and drew in a deep breath but, before he could begin to answer Claudia's questions, she asked more.

'Then…how did you know what to do—are you even qualified to deliver my babies?' Her voice was a little raised and equally shaky. She felt physically sick that she'd put her life and the lives of her babies in the hands of a cosmetic surgeon.

'I knew what to do because I'm a doctor.'

Claudia frowned. She felt exposed. 'Why didn't you mention that you were a cosmetic surgeon?' she asked, looking directly at him. She was angry that he hadn't told her. His announcement brought reality home. She really knew very little about Patrick and, except for the few words they'd exchanged, which had come mostly from her, he was like any man she could have passed in the street.

Only something inside had made her want to believe

that he would not wilfully hurt her. *Had she done it again? Had she trusted someone at face value?*

Patrick rubbed his neck slowly and in silence. 'You need to listen to me for a minute.'

'I'm listening. Go ahead—explain why you never shared your real medical specialty with me when you were cutting free my underwear and examining me!'

Not needing to give his reply any thought because it was the truth, he answered her quickly. 'Because telling you might have sent you into a panic. The situation wasn't desirable, you were understandably anxious and the last thing you needed to hear was the man about to deliver your babies hadn't done so in over a decade. I was confident I could do it as well as anyone but you wouldn't have known that.'

'So you have delivered babies then?'

'Yes, I delivered babies many years ago and, to be honest, in the situation we were in two days ago, anyone sharing that elevator with you would have been sufficiently qualified to help. You could not have done it alone.'

With the bedclothes tucked up firmly around her like a shield, she continued. 'So these babies you delivered, were they during your training then?'

Patrick didn't want to go into too much detail but knew Claudia deserved more of an explanation. The boys were safe now but she needed to know that they had been safe the entire time. 'I was an obstetrician in the UK. I worked in the field for a number of years so that's why you and your boys were, all things considered, in safe hands.'

It made sense and it was logical but it still unsettled her. 'Why didn't you just tell me that?'

'Because it had been almost twelve years and I knew that it still would have heightened your fear. You would have worried that I might not have been competent. I knew I could do it but I couldn't spend my energy reassuring you of the fact.'

Claudia accepted his reasoning and even agreed in part but still...

*Was there anything else he hadn't told her? Was there something else she should have known?*

She fixed her eyes on him intently and decided to just ask. 'So why did you change profession? Why did you stop delivering babies?'

Patrick lowered his tall frame onto the chair beside her bed. He had never wanted to tell anyone anything about his past as much as he did Claudia at that moment. He wanted to be honest about what had transpired and the future that had been so unfairly taken from him, but he couldn't. It had been locked inside for too many years to bring it up. He had moved on and so had everyone else. He would have no idea even where to start and he was worried where it might end.

So telling Claudia made no sense, he thought. He shook his head. 'I needed a change of scenery and thought I would change my specialty at the same time.'

'So you just upped and moved countries so you could surgically create perfect noses and big...' She paused and looked down towards her breasts.

'Yes, I perform breast augmentations and facial enhancements,' he admitted. He was proud of the work he performed but it had never been his dream. Bringing children into the world had always been what he had wanted to do until he'd had to walk away.

'You said it was over a decade but when exactly did you deliver the last baby before Thomas and Luca?'

Patrick felt his jaw tense. He had made his mind up not to relive that painful time in his life, so made his answer brief. 'Twelve years ago next month and it was back in the UK…'

'Why did you give up?' Claudia interrupted him as she sought to uncover a little more detail. She sensed Patrick was perhaps not telling her the entire story. His story about leaving obstetrics in England to pick up cosmetic surgery in Los Angeles seemed to be missing a piece. What was his motivation for the change? She was curious about the handsome man beside her, whose subtle woody cologne was suddenly penetrating her senses.

'Like I said, time for a sea-change and a challenge.' He felt cornered. It wasn't a lie but it wasn't the entire story either. 'You need to know that I wanted only what was best for you in that elevator. Maybe I should have told you, maybe I was right in not telling you. We'll never know now.'

'I guess we won't.'

'You're an incredibly brave woman; I hope you know that.'

'I had limited choices.' Her mood was still pensive and his compliment didn't sit well. She had been deceived by the father of her children and, while this situation was different, it felt horribly similar. She didn't like the truth being hidden from her, no matter what it was.

'You're an amazingly resilient woman. You made a conscious choice to face adversity head-on,' he replied. In a perfect world he would open up to Claudia and let her into his past. But his world wasn't perfect. In a perfect world he would still be Dr Patrick Spencer, OBGYN in the Harley Street practice he had dreamt of opening. But if compensation for his years of disappointment came in the chance meeting with Claudia, and even if it only lasted a brief time, he felt at peace with that. She had a positivity and strength that he had never witnessed before and he felt in time he would be a better man just being around her.

Not that he would have much time.

Claudia had been let down once; he didn't want to be the second man to let her down. He wouldn't make any promises other than to enjoy the weeks until she left. To be someone she could depend on during those weeks.

A rock for her.

It all sounded so logical in his head but his body had different ideas and it took every ounce of willpower not to kiss her. Not to press his lips against hers and taste the sweetness he knew her mouth would hold.

Claudia Monticello was testing Patrick in a way he had never expected.

Claudia leant back against the pillows and felt her eyes becoming heavy.

Being close to him and reacting the way she did confused her. Looking at the curves of Patrick's handsome face in the soft lighting of her hospital room, she struggled with what she knew she had to do. What she wanted to do was to find any excuse to have him nearer to her. To feel the warmth of his breath on her face, smell the sweet muskiness of his cologne and wait expectantly for his mouth to claim hers.

But what she had to do was to push him away. She had to have learned something from her last disastrous relationship. She couldn't allow herself to develop feelings for Patrick, only to find herself disappointed again. This time she had her boys to consider. Becoming involved on any level with Patrick would be risky for everyone. Not to mention pointless. She was leaving soon anyway.

Patrick watched as Claudia seemed lost in thought. 'I should go.'

'I am a little tired,' she said, agreeing.

'Would you like me to call in to see you tomorrow?' he asked as he stood.

Claudia hesitated before she replied. She was torn. 'I'm not sure that's a good idea, Patrick,' she replied in a low voice.

'I really am sorry that I didn't tell you everything outright but there was nothing self-serving about what I did, I can assure you of that.'

'It's not that.'

'Then what is it?'

'There's no point to this…to…you and me…' She stumbled over her words, unsure of how to define a relationship she didn't understand. And one that scared her.

'To me visiting you when you have no one else in the country because your only family is the other side of the world?'

'It's not that, it's just that I don't really know you and…'

'We shared a life-changing experience and, quite apart from that, I enjoy your company. It doesn't have to become complicated.' Patrick knew that wasn't entirely true. Just being near her was driving him to want more.

'I'll always be grateful for what you did, saving my boys and myself, but I'll be returning to London soon. And there's no need for you to keep me company when you have your own life.' She paused for a moment to cement the resolve in her mind. To make sure that she was doing the right thing. To remind herself that no good would come from stringing out the inevitable. Nor could she become involved on any level with a man who hid the truth, no matter how seemingly insignificant it might appear or whatever logical reason he could provide. It was a shaky point to hang her argument on, but it was all she had and she would use it.

She had to try to be more sensible like Harriet and less impetuous. And it had to start then and there. There was no time to rethink.

'You should find a nice young woman who lives in Los Angeles. Remember I have two little boys and you don't want children. You told me as much in the lift.'

'Whoa, slow down,' he said. 'You're thinking way too far ahead.'

Claudia smiled at his response. 'I have to, Patrick. I have my sons to consider.'

'And I would always consider your children. I helped bring them into the world and they are special little men. I couldn't forget about them.' It was the truth. Patrick's feelings for Claudia and her sons had grown very real. And his desire for her was equally real. 'Can you just let this play out and see what might happen?'

'No…' She drew a breath. Whilst it was lovely to know how he felt, it didn't change what she had to do. She needed to look after her boys and forget about romance. It wouldn't be in the cards for her now or anytime in the near future and he was making her feel that it could be. And *should* be.

She had to cut him free and remove any risk of her becoming attached.

'I'm sorry, Patrick, but I think it's for the best if we say goodbye tonight…for good.'

# CHAPTER SEVEN

PATRICK WALKED INTO his house, feeling more alone than before he'd met Claudia. He dropped his keys by the door and decided to take a shower and try to forget her. Put everything in perspective and move on.

As he lay in his bed, looking up at the ceiling in a room lit only by the moonlight, he wondered why he cared so much.

He didn't want a future. Or a family. She was being sensible and clearly he wasn't. For the first time in more years than he could remember, he had allowed his heart to lead him.

And his desire to kiss the woman whose face would not leave his mind that night.

He had so many questions he'd wanted to ask Claudia but he hadn't. Perhaps that was where he had gone wrong, he thought as he tossed again, throwing the bedclothes free of his body, dressed only in boxer shorts. If he knew more about Claudia he might better understand her need to push him away. She had obviously been hurt by someone.

He ran his fingers through his still damp hair and looked towards the bay window of his bedroom and the full moon suspended in the clear night sky and knew it had to have been Thomas and Luca's father who had broken her heart. She had put on a brave face when she had spoken of him having no interest in his sons but there had to be more to it. Walking away from the boys' father or watching him walk away surely wouldn't have been easy for a woman like Claudia. Her family values seemed so strong.

In that case, the man who'd fathered her children must have made her fearful of getting close to anyone. But why, he wondered, would any man treat a woman that way? It didn't make sense in the way he saw the world. A man should protect a woman, and particularly the mother of his children. He should lay his life down for her and his sons.

That was what Patrick knew in his heart he would do if he had been Thomas and Luca's father.

After a restless night and the acceptance that Claudia wanted to be alone, Patrick knew he had to keep a distance between them. But there was one last thing he intended to do. He would visit Thomas and Luca one final time to say goodbye. Even though they would never remember him, he would never forget them.

And he would always remember their mother too.

Claudia showered and changed into the silk nightdress and wrap. As the cool softness of the fabric fell against her skin, Claudia wondered who had been so kind yet secretive in gifting them to her. Could it even have been Patrick? She shook the thought from her mind. He couldn't have known she needed a nightdress and he'd had no time to go shopping as he had been spending all of his spare time with her. Running a soft brush through her hair, she looked in the mirror and thought it was definitely the prettiest nightdress she had ever seen, let alone worn.

And, as soon as she could, she would be contacting the store to find a way to repay them.

Claudia was feeling physically stronger by the day but emotionally drained. Insisting a man like Patrick leave her had been a choice she hoped not to regret but one she had an uneasy feeling that she just might. But she wasn't prepared to take the risk that she might be hurt again. Not any more.

The man made her feel butterflies in her stomach whenever he was near. Dropping the brush onto the bedside cabinet, she wondered what on earth had come over her. If she didn't know better, she would think that she had developed a crush on Patrick.

'Thank goodness, he's left your life,' she muttered to herself as she put the brush into her handbag and waited on the bed for her breakfast. She could hear the clanging of the metal plate covers as the trays were being delivered in the adjacent rooms.

'Here's yours, sweetie,' the food service worker said, bringing the tray into her room. He was an older man of African-American heritage, and he'd served her dinner the evening before. He'd been quite chatty then too.

'Thank you very much.'

'You're looking happy this morning. Any reason?' he asked, a curious smile on his time-weathered but cheerful face. 'I hope it's contagious 'cos there's some biddies on this floor that don't smile near enough for me. It's like they drink vinegar not tomato juice!' His smile wrinkled the skin around his warm brown eyes.

Claudia laughed at his words. 'I'm just looking forward to seeing my sons in the nursery as soon as I've had breakfast. The head nurse insists I eat before I'm allowed to travel downstairs so I'll eat quickly and get back down there.'

'They are very lucky little boys to have you as their mother,' he said before he left the room.

Claudia felt a lump form in her throat. That was exactly what Patrick had said when they'd met in the elevator. He had given her the same compliment and she had spat back at him something acerbic. She couldn't remember exactly but she knew it had been rude and uncalled for. She felt ashamed. Had she pushed him away unnecessarily? Had she overreacted yet again?

She also felt terribly confused. How could those few words from a friendly old man bring her emotions back to a level of chaos?

What was happening to her? Was Patrick already inside her heart and that was why the words hit home? She took the first bite of her toast and then dropped it on the plate and slumped back in her bed.

Patrick arrived at the hospital a little after eight. The heaviness in the warm morning air set the tone for the day. He had been gutted by Claudia's hasty and unexpected dismissal and had no choice but to accept he wouldn't see her again. But he would see the boys one last time.

The first patient at his private practice was scheduled for nine-thirty so he had plenty of time to visit Thomas and Luca and then head to his surgery near the corner of Rodeo Drive and Santa Monica Boulevard. He had been practicing in the ultra-modern office building for almost seven years and had no need to advertise as the post-operative faces and bodies willing to admit to having been his patients were testament to his skills. As were those people who wanted further freshening up over the years. However, he did set a limit and directed those who he suspected of addiction to cosmetic procedures to a therapist who was better placed to address their issues with body image.

The waiting list for a consultation and surgical procedures was growing but his passion for his work was not. He was dedicated and skilled but not excited. He missed that sense of excitement. The delivery in the elevator had been everything he missed about his former profession…and more.

Patrick strolled into the nursery and spoke with the attending neonatologist about the boys.

'So Luca has improved? How is the closure of PDA progressing?'

'It's looking good.' The doctor nodded as he continued to read Luca's notes on the computer screen. 'I think we'll be able to cease the medication in a day or so.'

Patrick's mouth curved to a smile as he looked at the tiny infant, dressed only in a nappy and pale blue booties that had been kindly knitted by the Mercy Hospital Women's Auxiliary.

'And Thomas? Is he still progressing?'

The doctor nodded again. 'Yes, no major problems with Thomas. There's a few milestones to reach yet, including weight gain for both of them, before they'll be discharged but they're going from strength to strength.'

'Great to hear.'

'I'll leave you to visit with them,' the doctor said and walked away to attend to another tiny patient.

Patrick stood watching over both boys. It had been three days since their birth. Three days since he had met their wonderful mother. He wondered what their future would hold on the other side of the world and knew if things were different that he would ask if he could visit. Travel over to London and spend some time with them—and with Claudia. But that couldn't happen. He would never visit that city again.

He stayed longer than he had planned; being with them was a joy to him that was unexpected but welcome. Finally he stroked their tiny foreheads and turned to leave.

'What are you doing here?'

Patrick's gaze lifted to see Claudia staring at him. He couldn't read her expression.

'I came to say a final goodbye to the boys. You made it clear that you didn't want to see me again so I thought I'd call in and check up on them for one last time and leave. I didn't mean to stay as long as I did. I won't intrude again.'

Claudia looked closely at the man standing next to her sons. He had been watching them the way a father should look at his children. She knew their father would never do that. She had noticed the gentle way Patrick had stroked their little faces. They would never feel that love from the man who had requested she sign a confidentiality form and not mention his *involvement*.

Claudia wasn't sure if she was doing the logical thing but it suddenly felt right. At least it felt right for the next few weeks.

'Please, Patrick, you can sit a while longer if you like.'

Patrick did just that and then did it again every day for the next four days. Just after breakfast and before his day began, he travelled to the Mercy Hospital to sit with the boys and with Claudia. He still knew little about her past but whatever had happened had made her the woman she was and that was all he needed to know. Just being around her made him feel alive.

*Could he possibly feel more?* Could he take a chance of being a part of their little family? He wasn't convinced he would ever be ready but Claudia had made him want to believe it was possible. He tried to ignore the simple truth that his happiness would be short-lived, with her imminent return passage to London. Instead he enjoyed every moment he spent with her and refused to question the reality of what they shared and for how long it might last.

Claudia needed to stay until Thomas and Luca were discharged and that would give them even more time to get to know each other better. Perhaps if things went well she might extend her stay. He knew he was being hopeful but nothing about their meeting in the first place had been straightforward. Perhaps fate would intervene again.

Patrick smiled as he scrubbed and entered the nursery. Claudia was already with the boys and he couldn't help but let a grin spread wide across his face as he approached the three of them.

'How's my two favourite little men and their mother this morning?'

Claudia looked up at him from where she sat holding Thomas. 'We are all very well, thank you. In fact the doctor said the boys could be released before their due date. They might be ready to go home in four weeks.'

'That's great news,' Patrick said, feeling a little deflated that the three of them would potentially be leaving his life. Although he was thrilled to hear that Thomas and

Luca were progressing so well, it also dashed his hopes
that something might develop between Claudia and himself. All they had now were the next four weeks. He just
had to make the most of every minute.

'I have a small confession,' he said one morning as they
took a walk around the hospital gardens for fresh air after
visiting Thomas and Luca in the nursery. Claudia was to
be released the next day and he doubted they would see
much of each other after that.

'What?' she asked, feeling very relaxed in his company and equally not wanting their time together to end.

'I'm very sorry that you gave birth in the lift and all
that you and the boys have been through, but I'm not
sorry that you shared *my* lift that day.'

Claudia felt her heart flutter but she knew she should
fight her desire to make more of it than it was. Patrick
lived in LA and she was heading back to London. She
had to put their relationship in context. This feeling
would not lead to more. No matter what her heart was
trying to tell her head.

'I'm exceptionally glad I shared *your* lift,' she said
lightly, patting his arm. 'If I'd shared a lift with a pizza
delivery boy none of us might have survived…or at the
very least the pizza boy would have been scarred for life.'

'Pizza boys do have to deliver under pressure, so that
the pizza's still hot. He might have coped.'

'Now you're being silly,' she said.

Claudia turned to see the look in his eyes. His expression was serious. Almost a little brooding.

He took her hand to draw her in. 'I mean it, Claudia.
I'm glad I was there. But not just because I could help
deliver your sons. I'm very glad I met you.'

Claudia couldn't agree more but she couldn't tell him that. She felt her stomach fill with butterflies at the tone in his voice, the intensity in his eyes and the feeling of his hand against her skin. It was soft and warm and it pierced through all of her defences but she didn't want to give in to how she was feeling. She didn't want to get hurt again. She had to make him believe that she saw nothing between them when in fact she thought she was close to falling hopelessly in love with him.

They arrived back at the entry door to the nursery. They both stepped back as a nurse entered and collided softly with each other. Claudia felt the warmth of Patrick's firm body against hers. A tingling sensation overtook her entire body and it took a few seconds to calm herself. She closed her eyes for a moment, not trusting herself to turn and look up into his eyes so close. As she turned tentatively to face him, his lips hovered only inches from hers and she wanted nothing more than to lean in to him a little longer.

But she couldn't. She had to put a stop to any hint of her feelings. She was leaving the hospital. She had leased an apartment the other side of town and, while it had been wonderful with Patrick visiting every day and demystifying everything medical that was happening with the boys and being there when they'd both been transferred to the nursery on day six, she had to face the rest on her own.

She would be happy if Patrick continued visiting her sons but she needed to stop fantasising about what might be between them. Nothing could become of them because she couldn't stay and explore that possibility. She belonged back in London with her only other family—her sister. She didn't want to be on the other side of the world in this city where—apart from with Patrick—she'd experienced little kindness. Her boys deserved a clean start in life and so did she. While Patrick seemed so very perfect, he was also perfectly settled in LA.

She couldn't tell all of that to Patrick. She would rather he didn't know the sordid story about Stone and hoped he would think of her fondly after she left. She had reminded herself of that every night as she lay alone in her hospital bed, wondering how it would feel with his strong arm around her. Or imagining the softness of his lips against hers when she woke in the middle of the night and all she could think of was him.

She waited until they were alone and Patrick had taken a seat beside the bed. 'There's something I need to say.'

'I'm all ears,' he told her as he stretched out his long legs and leant back in the chair.

'It's just that I'm leaving the hospital tomorrow so I guess this is the last morning we'll be spending together.'

He sat up, pulling his legs underneath the chair. 'You're leaving the hospital, not the country, Claudia. There's no need to make it sound so final.'

'It is final,' she replied. 'I've leased a place for a month…'

'You've found a place? I could have helped you out,' he said, cutting in, a little surprised that she had found somewhere to live without mentioning it before then. He'd planned on helping her to secure somewhere or even offering a room in his own home. It was far too big for one person and he would have been happy for her to take the guest room. But it was too late.

'I think you've been too gracious in offering help so I did this alone. I found a realtor and he secured a home for me. It's a little bit further out of town but it will be fine for the next few weeks.'

Patrick could sense her need for independence so he backed off.

'I'll more than likely be visiting the boys during the day and you'll be at your practice or operating so we might not bump into each other. That's all. But I'm happy for you to call in and see the boys if you like. They smile whenever you're around.'

'I don't think they recognise me quite yet; I think it's more likely wind but I'd like to continue to keep an eye on them.'

Claudia laughed. 'That means so much to me.'

'And you mean so much to me.' As soon as he'd said it, he knew it was too soon. But it felt natural and he didn't regret telling her.

'Please, don't. You don't know me. Not really.'

'I'd say, after what we shared, we know each other very well. We survived the most stressful situation. Surely we share a special bond.'

Claudia wished her world was different. But it wasn't.

'You're a good man, Patrick, but we can't be more than friends.'

Patrick reached for her hands and he wasn't deterred when she pulled away this time. He reached further until he had them firmly inside the warmth and protection of his own. 'We can be anything you want us to be while you are here.'

That was just it. It would only be while she was in LA. *Then what?* Claudia felt tears welling in her eyes and she couldn't blame it on hormones. Her heart was breaking just a little.

'I enjoy spending time with you,' he continued.

'There—I said it. I'm not promising anything, any more than you are. We are two expats on the other side of the world who happen to enjoy each other's company. Unless you don't enjoy my company?'

She took a deep breath. 'Of course I enjoy your company. I enjoy your company very much, but...'

'There are no buts from where I'm standing.'

'You're not making this easy.'

'No, I'm not. I think you're amazing and I think that it would be stupid to say goodbye tonight when you will be in the same city as me for the next four weeks, maybe more.'

'It seems a little pointless...'

'I disagree.' He paused over the words. 'I think we should continue to enjoy each other's company until you have to leave.'

Patrick knew that their relationship, whatever it might be, would have to end. He would never set foot back in the UK for reasons that he couldn't bring himself to share. His family were there and he couldn't see them again. Not after what had happened. In his mind it was better for everyone concerned for him to forget he'd once had a family.

'How are you getting to your new home tomorrow?'

'A cab,' she quickly replied.

'How about I take you? Absolutely no strings attached to my offer,' he continued with even greater speed. 'I'm operating in the afternoon. So I have the morning free to pick you up and settle you in. It's your choice, a smelly cab or chauffeur driven by me?'

Claudia felt her lips curving to a smile. He wasn't giving up. 'Not all LA cabs are smelly.'

'Not all...but why take the chance?'

She shook her head a little with frustration. Why did he have to be so handsome, so charming and so persistent? 'Okay…thank you.' There were a hundred things she could have said and each one would have been closer to how she was feeling but she couldn't allow herself that luxury.

'I'll see you back here in the morning,' he told her as he walked away.

Claudia offered him a smile as she wondered what she had let herself in for. And that thought played on her mind all through the night.

# CHAPTER EIGHT

PATRICK ARRIVED MID-MORNING, just as he had promised. He knocked on her door.

'Anyone here needing a smelly cab?'

'Come in,' she replied, still feeling apprehensive about spending time together away from the hospital. It became a little more frightening to be in the real world with Patrick. 'I'm nearly ready. I spent a bit more time in the nursery with Thomas and Luca as I wasn't sure if I would be back again today until late.'

'No need to rush,' he told her. 'The meter's not running.'

She came out of her tiny bathroom with a few toiletries and, as always, her breath was taken away. He looked gorgeous and she felt sure his smile could melt an iceberg. She dropped the things into her oversized handbag and went back in to brush her hair.

'The address is on the bed,' she called out. 'I wrote it down on a scrap of paper.'

Patrick crossed to the end of the bed and picked up the paper. As soon as he read the address he shook his head. It was not a good part of town. In fact, it was straight out unsafe and, despite his resolve to respect her boundaries, he couldn't let her unknowingly put herself at risk. He decided not to say anything until she had seen it first-hand. It might not be as bad as he suspected. Her independence was akin to stubbornness, and he hoped once she had seen the location she would change her mind. He typed the address into his telephone so he could get the directions. He knew the general direction but it wasn't a part of town he frequented so he would need the GPS to find the street. He waited until she emerged in a pretty sky-blue sundress. It skimmed her knees and against her porcelain skin it looked, in his opinion, stunning.

'You look beautiful, as always.'

'Thank you,' she replied with a smile.

'Shall we go?' he asked as he picked up her bag and headed for the door.

'What about the account?' Claudia asked at Administration.

The young assistant flicked through the paperwork and then checked the computer screen. 'It's all been taken care of.'

'Are you sure?'

'Yes, your insurance company has covered you. Your sons' accounts will not be due until they leave the hospital in a few weeks' time, according to the notes.'

Claudia was relieved to hear that and Patrick was relieved she didn't ask any more questions about the insurance. His lawyer had contacted the international carrier and worked out an arrangement so that Claudia had no out of pocket expenses. But, with all the uncertainty between them, he didn't want her knowing he had stepped in to help.

They drove along with the top down on his sports car. The fresh air felt good after so long in the hospital air-conditioning. They talked about the boys and a little about Patrick's surgical roster for the afternoon and the time went quickly. As they drew closer to the street, Claudia began nervously chewing the inside of her cheek. The suburb was not what she had expected.

Finally they pulled up outside a run-down semi-detached house. It was worse than Patrick had thought it would be. He suspected a cab driver would have dropped her off without so much as a second thought so he was glad that he had insisted on taking her there. The two foot high wire fence was rusted and missing a gate and the front yard was devoid of any plants or lawn, save for the weeds that had made their way through the broken concrete. He looked over at Claudia and, while he could see her expression had dropped, she said nothing as she released her seat belt.

'You don't have to go in, you know that,' he told her.

'Don't be silly. I've given the realtor a deposit and I'm moving in today. The shell's a little worn, but I'm sure it's probably lovely inside. Besides, I'm not buying the property, I'm only renting it for a month.'

Patrick remained silent but he felt a chill run through him as they walked up the cracked pavement to the faded teal-blue house that looked as if it had not been loved in many years. Perhaps many decades. The wire screen on the security door was torn and would be useless in providing any level of security.

He watched as Claudia took the key she had been given by the realtor and, pulling back the screen door, unlocked the wooden front door and stepped inside. He followed closely, pausing for a moment to look over his shoulder at the neighbouring properties as he did. It was not a good part of town.

The house was quite dark inside for the time of day. Claudia reached for the light switch but nothing happened. They both looked up in the poor light to see the globe was missing from the hallway. An electrical cord was hanging down from the ceiling but there was no light fitting.

'I can get a new one,' she said as she made her way down to the brightest room at the end of the short corridor, which turned out to be the kitchen and was equally well worn. The floor was covered in pale green linoleum and it was almost bare, torn in more than a few places and lifting by the back door. There was a small table and two chairs but the wicker weaving was unravelling on one of the chairs, rendering it useless. The refrigerator motor was rattling and the back window looked out onto a car-wreckers' yard. There were no curtains or blinds and the hotplates on the stove were coated with years of burnt grime.

'It's only for a few weeks until the boys are ready to travel home. It's not as if I'd be bringing them here. It will just be me.'

Patrick remained silent, but he arched one eyebrow as he followed her into the bathroom. The shower was over a bath stained with rust where the water had been dripping from the tap and running down towards the drain. And the shower curtain was missing. The mirror on the cabinet above the basin was cracked and blackened in places by mildew. There was a small window of smoky glass for privacy but it too was cracked and Patrick suspected that with very little force the window would break completely.

'Let's see the bedroom,' Claudia announced, swallowing hard and trying to sound optimistic as she made her way into the larger of the two bedrooms. There was a double bed but no bedhead and a blue nylon bedspread with a faded floral pattern that couldn't mask the dip in the mattress. A free-standing oak stained wardrobe that had one door slightly ajar stood by the window. The dirty cream-coloured net curtains covering a stained blind sagged where they were missing hooks. Claudia crossed the dark brown shaggy-carpeted floor to close the wardrobe door and discovered that the handle was broken. 'I'll be living out of my suitcase anyway so the door doesn't matter. I'm not about to be picky,' she said.

'Claudia,' Patrick began in a serious tone, 'you can't be considering living here.'

'Of course I am. I backpacked around Europe in my late teens. It'll be an adventure just like that,' she replied as she walked towards the front door, noticing there were holes in the plasterboard that looked as if someone had put their foot through the wall. 'Shall we get my suitcase so I can settle in and you can get back to the hospital? I know you have surgery this afternoon.'

'So you're moving in?'

'Yes.'

'Then I'm moving in too; we'll be house mates. I backpacked around Europe in my late teens too, so I'll share the adventure with you,' he announced. 'Let's go take a peek at my room. I hope it's as nice as yours.'

'You're not living here; that's ridiculous.'

'And you don't think you living here is ridiculous?'

'No, that's different.'

'Not in my opinion. If you move in, then we'll do it together and both risk our lives and general wellbeing!'

Claudia shook her head and narrowed her eyes at him before she walked across the narrow passageway behind Patrick to the darkened room. Reaching for the light switch, Patrick discovered it didn't work so he used the light of his phone to see the room. It was smaller and there was a single bed and what looked like a grey chest of drawers. He walked across to the window and lifted the blind to allow them to see the room properly. It took him three attempts to lift the damaged blind but when he did he could see another short electrical cable hanging down from the ceiling. There was no light fitting and again the globe was missing.

'Looks like we both need light bulbs when we head to the store.' He patted the bed, not daring to think about how many years the faded orange bedspread had gone without washing. It was stained and frayed in places along the hemline. Then he noticed the chest of drawers was actually a filing cabinet and he walked over and pulled open the top drawer. 'Great, I can keep some of my patient files in here to work on in the evenings.'

'Don't be awful. You're teasing me now.'

'Not at all. If it's good enough for you, then it's good enough for me.'

'You're being stupid. You don't need to babysit me.'

'I'm not thinking of babysitting. In this part of town my role would be more bodyguard.'

Claudia put her hands on her hips and shook her head. 'It's not that bad. I used to drive through here on the way to the studio every day. I never saw anything untoward happen.'

'And what time was this exactly?'

'What do you mean?'

'I mean did you drive through this street after dark?'

Claudia thought back. 'Not dark but early evening and early morning.'

'Then you and I will spend one night here together and if everything is fine then we'll discuss it again but I think you'll find that after the sun goes down this isn't a nice place to live. There are gangs in adjacent areas.'

'I have an idea. Why don't I ask a neighbour, or the business out the back? They'll tell me what it's really like.'

Patrick ran his long fingers through his hair in exasperation. Claudia was as stubborn as she was beautiful and intelligent. 'Let's ask, but if you get the answer I expect then I hope you agree we should just leave.'

Claudia didn't agree to anything. She showed no emotion as they walked out of the house and along the sidewalk beside the fence to where they found the owner of the wrecking yard locking up for the day. He was pulling the tall wire fence closed and securing it with a heavy padlock. Claudia picked up speed so he didn't leave before she had a chance to speak with him.

'Excuse me,' she called out. 'I'm wondering if you could tell me a little about the area. I'm thinking about renting the house that backs onto your property.'

Patrick watched as the man's face fell.

'Listen, lady, do you see the two dogs over there?'

'Yes,' Claudia answered, looking at the two heavy-set black guard dogs that were chafing at the bit, waiting for their owner's signal to begin patrolling the yard.

'They're not here for their good looks. There's not enough money in the world to make me live in this neighbourhood.' He tapped his watch with his grubby fingernail. 'Three o'clock every day I'm outta here. I've got some clients that look after the yard, if you know what I mean. I work on their cars and they make sure that my yard and my dogs are still here in the morning.'

'Perhaps the dogs will look after me too. They'll scare away anyone who thought to break into my place.'

'Not a chance unless you want to live in my office. Sorry, miss, but you're on your own if you move into that house. You'd be dead crazy if you did.' He signalled to the dogs before he climbed into his utility and drove away. Immediately the dogs rushed towards the wire fence, gnashing their teeth and making Claudia jump back nervously.

'So do you think you need a second opinion or can we leave now and find you other accommodation? Unless you want to wait and ask a not so friendly gang member his opinion.'

'Okay, I get it. I suppose you may have a point,' she said with a decidedly sheepish look upon her face.

'May have?'

'Fine, the man confirmed your suspicions about the suburb. And I concede the house is not as nice as the realtor described on the phone. I can't believe he lied to me.'

Patrick didn't comment. There was nothing he needed to add except to ask her to get into his car while he locked up the house.

A few minutes later they were on the freeway and heading towards Beverly Hills. 'I'll only stop at your home long enough to make some calls and secure another short-term rental,' she told him. 'I can make a reservation in a hotel tonight if necessary.'

'Whatever you think is best, but my home is big enough for both of us.'

'Thank you, Patrick, but I won't get too comfortable. I'll be leaving in a few hours.'

It was only ten minutes on Freeway 405 and then three miles on Wilshire Boulevard before Patrick turned into a street lined with towering palms. The sweeping grounds of each of the palatial homes was perfectly manicured, and small gardeners' vans were dotted along the street with men in wide-brimmed hats busily planting and trimming the gardens. They drove a little way to a slight bend in the road and then slowed. Heavy black electric gates slowly opened and Patrick drove the car inside and the gates closed behind them.

He drove the car up the driveway to the front door of the double-storey white stucco mansion he had called home for two years. The property also boasted a tennis court, a heated swimming pool, spa and a four-car garage but Patrick didn't mention any of it. Cosmetic surgery had been kind to him, he admitted, but equally he had worked hard in his new field and had been recognised as one of the best by Hollywood's very particular clientele.

He helped Claudia out of the car and then opened the front door. 'Please go in; I'll get your bag.'

'I won't be staying,' she reminded him. 'Perhaps you should leave my things in the trunk.'

He smiled to himself. He wondered again if she had always been that fiercely independent or had circumstance made her that way? But, whatever the case, he understood she had every right to want to make her own decisions. He just hoped they didn't include another dubious choice of realtor.

'I'll get your belongings in case there's anything you need.'

Claudia spun on her heel to take in the magnificent surroundings. The foyer had a large atrium with a stone water feature. The sound of running water echoed in the large open space. Looking past that to outside, she could see more gently moving water. It was, she assumed, an endless pool and a panorama of the Hollywood Hills formed a backdrop.

'I will let you find your way around. The guest bedroom is on the ground floor, third door on the left, if you'd like to have a shower or a lie down. It might do you good to rest for a while. I can take you back to the hospital to visit the boys this evening.'

'You're being too kind. And too generous. It's unnecessary, honestly.'

'Claudia, it's a big house. I live here all alone and you're most welcome to stay here until you leave. I'd rather you were here than making *friends* in that neighbourhood! And, by the way, never recommend that realtor unless you really dislike someone,' he said with a wink before he closed the door and left her alone.

Claudia was more confused than she had ever been in her life.

The most handsome, kind, considerate man wanted her to live with him. She owed her life to him. And she wanted to be with him more than anything, but she couldn't. He had made it obvious he had feelings, not only by opening his home but also the way he kept reaching for her. But she wasn't ready to take that leap of faith and trust again. He was a kind man and as much as she wished he was the father of her sons, he wasn't. And she couldn't risk them all falling in love with Patrick. What if he walked out one day— the way that the boys' father had done? And turned her life upside down.

She had to be sensible and see the world the way Harriet would. Put a practical filter across her decisions and stop being led by her heart.

Certain and confused in equal amounts, she found her way to the guest bedroom and, kicking off her shoes, she sat on the bed. She suddenly felt a little tired and the bed felt very soft and comfortable so she thought she might just lie down for a moment. She told herself that she wouldn't fall asleep but just close her eyes for a moment, then she would call another realtor and find another short-term lease. And that night she would stay in a hotel.

Patrick came home to a darkened house but in the light from the porch he could see Claudia's suitcase still lying against the wall in the hallway. He turned on the lamp in the living room, unsure if she was at home or had caught a cab to the hospital. Quietly, he walked through his home and found her asleep on the bed. While it was still warm outside, the air-conditioning had kept the house cool and she was wearing a thin sundress so he pulled the throw rug up over her and closed the door. She was exhausted and he had no intention of waking her so he put a call through to the hospital to check on the boys. His call was connected to the neonatal resident.

'Dr Spencer, I've just finished reading the boys' notes for today. I did try to call Miss Monticello but had no luck getting through.'

'It was a big day for Claudia and she's taking a nap now so that's why I've called. I will pass any updates on to her.'

'Thomas is still progressing well, as he did from day one, and Luca's PDA appears to be self-correcting. He'll be having another echocardiogram tomorrow but Dr Wilson is confident no further treatment will be required. So please let Miss Monticello continue to rest. She can come in the morning to see them. Both boys are asleep and will have their gavage feed in another two hours.

There's no need for Miss Monticello to be here when the rest would do her more good.'

Patrick thanked the young doctor and hung up the telephone before he ran upstairs to change into shorts and a T-shirt. He would take a dip in the pool later but first he would cook some dinner for the two of them. He knew it was stupid to think there would be anything between them after the next few weeks but she was getting under his skin and he couldn't deny it.

For some inexplicable reason, he didn't want to let the dim future get in the way of a happy few weeks.

Life was short and so he intended to enjoy whatever time he could with her. She challenged him and just being around her made him feel alive. Her accent and her very British mannerisms surprisingly made him think almost fondly of London and even fleetingly of his family. And, in a deep dark corner of his mind, he thought perhaps there was a chance, however slight, that she could change her mind and stay in the US.

Claudia woke to the smell of cooking. Her eyes struggled to focus and for a moment she forgot where she was until suddenly it came back to her. She had lain down for a moment in Patrick's guest room. It was dark but she could feel the light weight of a throw rug over her. She didn't remember pulling it up so assumed Patrick must have returned home and covered her. The curtains were billowing with the cool evening breeze and there was light creeping under the now closed bedroom door.

Suddenly she sat bolt upright. She hadn't called a realtor. She reached for her phone and discovered it was after six, in fact closer to seven.

'Darn, bother, you silly cow,' she said as she rubbed

her forehead and silently continued berating herself for falling asleep. Now she would have to find a hotel as soon as she had visited Thomas and Luca. She swung her legs down and felt around for her shoes before she headed in the direction of the light. She would thank Patrick for his hospitality and get a cab to a hotel, check in with her bags and then head straight to the Mercy.

There was no way she could accept his hospitality. Their relationship had already overstepped the boundaries of common sense.

Moments later, Claudia stood in the doorway to the kitchen, watching Patrick stirring something that smelt delicious on the stovetop. Suddenly her heart felt lighter. But her head felt terribly confused. He turned to see her watching him and she felt very self-conscious. A tingling sensation crept up her neck and onto her face and she felt certain the blush had spread across her cheeks.

'Well, hello sleepy-head. Did you have a nice nap?'

His eyes twinkled as he spoke and she tried to ignore her increased heartbeat.

'I did, thank you, but you should've woken me. I slept for far too long. I need to get to a hotel and then see the boys.'

He lowered the heat underneath the pan and turned around to face her. He was wearing a tight white T-shirt and cargo shorts. His toned physique was cutting through both. His feet were tanned and bare on the large terracotta tiles.

'I've checked on Thomas and Luca and they are both doing very well. They were sleeping when I called but,' he said, glancing at the roman numerals of the large wall clock and then back to Claudia, 'they will have been fed again and should be tucked in again for another four hours or so.'

'I should have been there for that feed.' She was angry and disappointed in herself. She was convinced her boys needed her more than she needed sleep.

As if he sensed her self-reproach, he added firmly, 'You can't do everything, Claudia. The rest you had this afternoon was important. In fact, I told the neonatal unit that you wouldn't be back to visit the boys until tomorrow.'

Claudia was taken aback by his announcement and she felt her body tense. 'Why would you say that to them without asking me? Whether I see my sons or not is not your decision to make.'

'Well, in my capacity as a doctor it is. You need to get your own strength back, as I have said to you more than a few times. You'll be no good to your sons if you run yourself into the ground the first day out of hospital.'

'But I want to be with them.'

He shook his head and turned back to the stove. While he admired her strength, he found her stubbornness in ignoring her own wellbeing frustrating.

'I'm all they have in the world.'

There it was again. Her reference to Thomas and Luca having no one but her.

Patrick nodded his understanding of her need to be with them but he wanted to at least get some food into her so she could keep up her strength. 'Then I'll take you there after dinner.'

'There's no need for you to take me. I can do it after I book into a hotel.' Her arms were crossed across her chest and her eyes were narrowed.

'Claudia, I know you have a need for independence

above all else, but you have to look after yourself. And since you don't seem to understand the importance of taking care of yourself I'm more than happy to step up to do the job.'

'I'm perfectly capable of looking after myself and my boys on my own. I'll be doing that when I return to London in a few weeks.' She felt her neck tense with the thought of depending on any man again.

Her words cut through him like a knife. He wasn't sure if that was her intention but, if it was, she had succeeded.

'Point made,' he replied as he returned to the task at hand. Listening to his heart had been something he'd successfully avoided for many years and it appeared, from Claudia's reaction, it was something he needed to continue avoiding.

Disappointment suddenly coloured his mood. The heat was still under the large pan of boiling water so he dropped in the fresh pasta. 'If you want to share dinner before you grab a cab then you're welcome. If not, then I can help you out with your bag when the cab arrives.'

Claudia looked at him as he turned his attention back to preparing dinner and wished they had met under different circumstances. Before she had been so badly hurt and disillusioned. He appeared to be everything she'd once dreamed of finding in a man…but she was no longer looking and she doubted she ever would again.

He turned back to her for a moment. 'I don't want you to feel pressured, Claudia. That was never my intention.' His reply was truthful, his voice gentle and low—almost a whisper. 'I just wanted to help you…but I would never force you to do anything or stay anywhere you didn't want to be.' His voice trailed off.

Claudia wasn't sure how to respond. He had been

a gentleman up to then and she doubted that would change…unless she invited him to alter his behaviour towards her. She started to wonder if perhaps she had overreacted. Once again since meeting him, she had been rude.

The first time had been due to her aversion to men and now, looking back, she knew he didn't deserve to be punished for another man's mistake. At the time she couldn't seem to help herself. But this time it was something else driving her to push him away. It wasn't his fault she was starting to have feelings for him. She wished she had Harriet on speed dial to give her logical, solid advice but it would be selfish to pull her sister away from something far more important in Argentina to ask her whether she should stay for dinner, stay the night or stay for a month.

No, she had to do this alone. She had to make a decision not based on another man's behaviour or her own doubts and insecurities. She had to make a decision based on Patrick's behaviour. And that had been nothing other than exceptional.

Just as exceptional as his broad-shouldered silhouette looked while stirring the delicious-smelling pasta sauce.

'If the invitation is still open, then perhaps I'll stay for dinner. But only for dinner.'

# CHAPTER NINE

As CLAUDIA HUNG up her clothes in the walk-in wardrobe she prayed she had made the right decision. This was the second time she had rushed into moving in with a man she barely knew. Her life had changed so completely in the time since she'd arrived in Los Angeles and not much of it had been for the better, except for the arrival of her sons. She longed to return home. To where she felt life was a better fit and to where she felt a sense of family. Her internal compass was directing her back to London.

But she had unexpected mixed emotions about Patrick.

Where did he fit into her life? Would he be a part of it once she left Los Angeles or would he become a memory? A sweet memory, but nothing more.

Claudia had tried to think logically about moving in. They had only known each other a short time, but she and Patrick had a bond that she knew she would never share with another man. He had brought her sons into the world, saved their lives and saved hers as well. He was a brilliant obstetrician and while she wondered why he had not continued in that line of work, it was not her place to question him.

Was the fact he too was of English heritage a deciding

factor in her feeling comfortable enough to move in? she wondered. Did he remind her of home? Did that make her feel safe? She prayed it wasn't a false sense of security.

There had been absolutely no pressure from Patrick over dinner; in fact he had even suggested a couple of hotels near the Mercy Hospital for her to stay in that night. His lack of insistence that she stay in his home but his genuine offer made her feel more comfortable to accept his invitation. And to apologise for being rude.

Everything happening in her head, and her fear of accepting Patrick's help, was her problem to deal with and in no way related to him.

'I will pay you exactly what I would be paying at a hotel,' she'd told him as they'd put the dishes into the dishwasher and sat down in the living room.

'The going rate for a hotel around here is just over a dollar a night.'

'Beverly Hills certainly isn't as expensive as it's alluded to be,' she joked. 'In all seriousness, I must insist…'

'Here's my business proposition,' he interrupted as he looked into her eyes, melting her heart a little further. 'Since I arrived in the US I haven't been able to find my favourite English toffee with almonds. It's amazing and nothing comes close. The almonds are toasted and the toffee's covered in dark chocolate. If you manage to find some, we'll call it even. Perhaps even arrange some to be shipped over after you return home. It used to be available at Harrods. There's no deadline, just a promise that one day I'll get my toffee.'

'English toffee in exchange for living in a home this beautiful?' She turned her head and, from her seat on the sofa, she surveyed the beautifully decorated room.

It was elegant but simple. It wasn't stark but nor was it cluttered and the colours were warm earthy tones and the lighting softly added a glow to the room.

'You don't like the terms? Too steep?' he asked, staring into her eyes when they came back to meet his gaze. His lips curved to a smile and softly lined the stubble-covered skin on his jaw.

His voice sounded like the warm dark chocolate he was describing as the words flowed from his lips and Claudia involuntarily bit her own. Her heartbeat picked up unexpectedly and she closed her eyes and tried to blink away thoughts she was having about her landlord. He was far too gallant and handsome for his own good and most definitely for her own.

The French windows onto the balcony were open and the warm July breeze felt wonderful after the hospital air-conditioning so she carefully stood up and made her way to the door. Each day the physical scars were healing, but she just wished the emotional scars inflicted by the city would fade as quickly.

At that moment she needed to move away from Patrick, and the feelings she was having, being so close to him. She needed to step outside and clear her head in the balmy night air. She looked over the balustrade to the moonlight on the gently moving water of the pool. It was a perfect evening. The perfect house. The perfect man.

But, in Claudia's mind, she was so far from perfect.

And life for her had never been perfect.

Patrick watched Claudia from his vantage point on the sofa. Her feet were bare and her short hair was gleaming in the moonlight. She seemed so at peace with the world at times, but at other times almost tortured. And so vulnerable. He had to control the urge to step behind her, pull her into his arms and tell her that everything would be all right. Protect her from whatever had hurt her or could in the future.

But he had no clue what the future held for her or for him. He barely knew anything about Claudia's past, apart from her losing her father and mother. Where had she gone to school? What had made her take the position in Los Angeles? And why didn't the father of her children want anything to do with them…? But, strangely, nothing about where she came from mattered to him any more. It wasn't her past, her family or her career that made him want to be with her. It was her attitude to life. Her strength. Her independence. Her beauty.

And her love of her children.

The next morning Claudia woke early and dressed in the shorter of the two nightdresses before making her way to the kitchen for breakfast. She thought she would make something to eat for them both and then head in to change before Patrick rose. Cooking breakfast would be her way of repaying his kindness.

But he was already up. And he took her breath away. Standing at the bench with a knife in his hand, he was cutting vegetables and fruit and placing them into a large glass bowl. Nearby was a small high-tech food processor. But her eyes were drawn to his bare chest and his low-slung shorts. Swallowing and trying not to stare at the perfection of his body, she looked out onto the patio, where she could see a gym bench and weights.

'Good morning, Claudia. I hope you slept well. If you need more covers or anything just let me know.'

She coughed to clear her throat. She needed to be

polite and meet his gaze but that meant looking at his half-naked body again and worrying about her clothing being a little skimpier than she would normally choose. Ordinarily, that would not be a problem, but Patrick had to remain in the generous landlord category and she had to stay inside those parameters. She couldn't afford to entertain fantasies. She vigorously rubbed her arms as if she was cold. She wasn't. His presence was making her hot and self-conscious.

'Good morning,' she managed, trying to look around the room and avoid the obvious. Gorgeous, jaw-dropping Patrick, with both a body and smile to die for. And, first thing in the morning when most were struggling to open their eyes and look human, he was poster perfect. 'So you've been working out.'

He smiled back. 'Yes, I like to get up early and start the day using the outside gym. There are deck lounges out there so be my guest today and enjoy the stunning weather.'

'Stunning…weather.' She found it difficult to look at him and not have her eyes wander over his body in appreciation.

'I'm making a health blend with kale, carrots and a bunch of fruit. I didn't want to turn it on until you woke up since it sounds like a small lawnmower,' he said with a smile. 'Would you like one—I've prepared enough for both of us.'

'I'd planned on getting up early and cooking for you. You're already done so much for me.'

He shook his head as he crossed to the sink and washed the stickiness of the fruit from his hands then he slipped on a T-shirt that was hanging over the back of the high-backed kitchen chair. 'I'm always up at the crack of dawn in summer and I like a liquid breakfast after a workout. It gives me energy to face the day and I've got a full day of surgery scheduled so this will keep me going. Will you join me?'

Claudia was relieved that he was partly covered and her breathing had slowed accordingly. 'I'd love to, thank you.' She sat on a chair near to the bench where he was working and thought she would steer the conversation towards his work. 'So what surgical procedures are on today? Which starlet is going double D?'

He was dropping the chopped fruit in to be blended but paused to answer her question. Both of his lean hands rested over the top of the machine as he looked at her. 'I have two post-mastectomy reconstructions. A young mother in her early thirties and a slightly older patient who just celebrated her sixtieth birthday.'

Claudia felt so stupid. 'I'm sorry.'

'Don't worry; everyone does it…'

Shaking her head in frustration at herself, she continued. 'Just because everyone thinks the same way doesn't make it right. I was condescending and I made a sweeping generalisation. I'm so stupid for saying that. I should have known there would be more to your practice.'

'Thank you. Most people just shrug and don't apologise so please don't feel bad.' He paused for a moment. 'And, to be honest, I do my fair share of purely cosmetic augmentations. The holy grail of boob jobs, the double Ds and a few Es. Those surgeries allow me to perform the worthwhile ones at a much lower cost.'

'That's wonderful.'

'Well, I have a lovely home. Don't go putting me up on a pedestal.'

Despite what he said, in Claudia's mind he was a true

gentleman and already up on a pedestal and she doubted he would fall off anytime soon.

One morning after Patrick had left for work, Claudia thought she would sort out the matter of the generous benefactor before she left for the hospital. She found the delivery docket in her purse and called the Rodeo Drive store. She was determined to repay the stranger's kindness and at the same time ensure she was not in their debt.

'I'm sorry, madam, but I can't divulge the sender's details. As with all of our account holders, they're a highly valued customer. This is an awkward situation and I would truly like to help but store policy won't allow me to do so. However, you are very welcome to exchange anything that you don't like or need in another size.'

'No, I don't need to change anything. It's all perfect.'

'We do pride ourselves on the styling and quality of all of our garments.'

The young woman's delivery was very eloquent and her tone leaning towards pretentious but Claudia knew that came with the location of the store. She bit the inside of her cheek. She wasn't going to accept the gift. She had to repay the sender but she needed to think of a way quickly before the young woman ended the conversation, no doubt politely, but, however it ended, her chance to repay her benefactor would be over.

'I have an idea,' she began in an equally polite tone, hoping to sway the sales assistant to agree to the thought that had popped into her head. 'Could I buy a gift certificate to the same value as the gift sent to me and you could mail that to them? If they have an account then you would have their mailing address. You are not breaking confidentiality because their details have not been given to me and you have just doubled your sales because they will have to visit your store to spend the certificate.'

There was no answer for a moment and Claudia assumed the sales assistant was considering her proposal. 'But they may want to know who sent it.'

Claudia wondered at the slight double standard when it came to account holders and mere mortals.

'That's fine. I don't have any problem if you let the sender know it was from me. In fact, I would be happy for them to know I had repaid the gift.'

The deal was done. Claudia gave her credit card details over the phone but the amount was even more than she had imagined. But, since she wasn't paying rent, she could afford it. There was nothing more she needed to buy for herself. She drew a deep breath at how extravagant the anonymous benefactor had been and would be hand-washing everything, hoping that it lasted for a few years, knowing what it had cost.

Claudia watched her little boys grow day by day, week by week. She was able to hold them and bottle-feed them and on the twentieth day they moved from the neonatal nursery into the general nursery. The warmth and serenity that she experienced every time Claudia held them made her happier than she thought possible and she didn't want them to be out of her arms. As she touched their soft warm skin and looked into their big trusting eyes she knew her life was complete. There was nothing she wouldn't do or give to Thomas and Luca for as long as she lived. Each milestone they reached in weight or developmental markers made her heart sing. She could imagine decorating Christmas trees with them and watching the joy on their faces as they unwrapped their birthday presents.

The boys' little faces filled out a little more every day and she could see subtle differences. Thomas was a little bigger and his mouth a little fuller and his mop of hair was thick and straight, while Luca's hair was curly and he was a leaner baby. Whether that had anything to do with his initial heart problem, she was unsure.

Claudia would arrive first thing in the morning at the Mercy Hospital and leave just after the sun set as the boys had settled into a routine and were ready for sleep. They had two feeds during the night, one at eleven and another at three in the morning, but the nursing staff insisted she get rest and come in the morning. The first time she was allowed to bathe them one at a time she had tears of joy in her eyes that fell from her cheeks into the tepid water. She was so nervous as she supported their tiny bodies in the water and then gently let the water splash over them before she wrapped them in a soft white towel and held them for the longest time.

When the weather cooled just a little so it wasn't too extreme, Patrick suggested a picnic outside for the four of them. At first Claudia was uncertain but when he walked her downstairs she caught sight of the checked blanket on the ground, complete with picnic basket, she nodded her approval. Together they collected the boys after their feed and took them down to the shady place beside the small pond. The sound of the water trickling over the rocks and running into the pond filled with over-sized goldfish was relaxing.

'I think they'll enjoy fishing.'

'And what makes you think that?'

'It's just a feeling I have.'

Patrick didn't want to say that if they were his sons he would teach them about fishing, the way his father had, and they would learn to love it as he did.

Claudia watched him fussing over her sons and she had the feeling that, despite what he said, he would be a wonderful father.

The basket was brimming with wonderful picnic food; there were assorted sandwiches. It truly was a family outing. Whatever family meant, moving forward.

Claudia took photos of the boys with her phone camera every day as they grew. It would be a reminder of how far they had come and a keepsake for them when they were older. She decided to have a photo of each of them framed for Patrick. He had been so wonderful and she wanted him to have a memory of the little boys he had brought into the world. It saddened her that soon they would be worlds apart but it was a fact she had to accept.

She stopped at the drugstore on the way home one day and had two of the cutest photos printed and bought two silver-plated frames. And as she walked into his bedroom that afternoon to place them on the dresser as a surprise, she felt strangely at home. The room had a masculine feel to it but it was also warm…and inviting. It was decorated in muted warm tones of grey. Heavy deep grey drapes framed the window and the softest pale grey carpet covered the floor. The bed and bedside cabinets and the dresser were black and there were three large charcoal drawings on the wall behind the bed, also framed in black. The bed cover was the same tone as the drapes. It was a simply decorated room but stunning. The longer she stayed, the more she felt at home. She would have preferred that she felt like an intruder but she didn't.

Placing the frames on his bedside table, she left the

room, her eyes surveying one final time where he slept every night. She wondered if his bed was as soft as hers and if he slept on his back or on his side. Did he toss the covers off or did he sleep peacefully...?

Every few days Patrick would stop at the hospital to check up on the three of them. And each time he did, Claudia felt her heart flutter as she watched him tenderly hold one of her sons. She couldn't help but notice that he was completely and utterly consumed by whichever baby he was given. He didn't take his eyes away for even a minute and he spoke to them in great detail as if they understood every word. Claudia had to remind herself that he was not their father. He gave such attention and love to them, it was often difficult for her to remember that simple fact.

Patrick gave her the use of his silver imported SUV to travel to Mercy Hospital. He knew it would help her to feel independent by not asking to be dropped off or catching cabs at all hours. He wanted her to feel the freedom she needed but still feel a sense of belonging. And it worked. She was extremely grateful to him but he did not exploit that gratitude in any way. She initially refused, as he expected she would, but when he pointed out the safety of late night trips back from the hospital she reluctantly agreed. But she insisted on putting in the gas and having it washed each week.

She cooked dinner for him two or three nights a week. And he continued to rise early and make smoothies in the morning. Occasionally Claudia would eat at the hospital so she could stay a little later with Thomas and Luca. And Patrick made Friday night their night together at the hospital. He brought fish and chips from a store owned by an expat from North Yorkshire who had relocated to LA and opened a café on Melrose. The shop was always busy and he would line up for thirty minutes just to place his order. Then Claudia would meet Patrick downstairs in the visitor gardens to eat their fish and chips together. It felt so good for both of them to step outside. They had enjoyed four Friday date nights and they were planning the fifth, the date they both knew would be the last. Claudia would be heading back to London in less than a week and, while she was looking forward to returning home, she realised leaving Patrick would be one of the hardest goodbyes she would ever have to say.

But she had no choice.

As they sat together on the patio at home one evening, Claudia sipped on her iced tea and looked up towards the stars, wondering if her parents approved of the man sitting beside her. She felt certain they would and it made her want to be honest with him about something they had never discussed. She curled her bare feet up under herself and turned to him.

'Is there anything you want to know about me? I mean, I've been living here and you've never pressed me about anything.'

'You have a sister, whom you adore. And she's over working in South America. And you worked in television.'

'What about the big elephant in the room? The one we've walked around since we met.'

'And that would be?'

'The fact you've never asked me anything about Thomas and Luca's father.'

He studied her for a moment. 'It's not my place, Claudia. I've just thought all along, if you want to tell me you will but if you don't then I respect you. You must have your reasons for wanting to keep it private,' Patrick told her honestly. He knew he had no right to ask. After all, he'd kept his past to himself.

Claudia smiled at his reply. It was so refreshing in a town where everyone wanted to know everyone else's business and it somehow made her want to tell him. Many times over the weeks they had spent together she had wanted to open up but hesitated, a little scared that his opinion of her might change if he knew the truth. Then she questioned why it mattered so much what he thought of her.

'I assume it's over between you.'

'Over as soon as he discovered I was having a child.'

'Don't you mean children?'

'No, he never stayed long enough to find out I was having twins. His lawyer informed me early on that he didn't want to have his name on the birth certificate and relinquished all parental rights. He's actually...' She paused as she stumbled over her words.

'There's no need to go there,' he cut in angrily. He was furious any man would behave so poorly and sensed she was feeling torn about discussing the boys' father. 'Unless you're in witness protection and hiding from a mobster, I have no interest in knowing about a man for whom I have no respect.'

Claudia smiled. 'I'm not in witness protection.'

'That's good news then...nothing else matters.'

Claudia nodded in silence. Up until now, she had given too much thought to telling anyone, let alone Patrick, that her sons' father was a married man. *Don't do it now*, said a voice inside her head. She felt confused by her desire for him to know everything about her. 'I thought he was a good man when I met him...'

'Claudia, any man who would leave you alone and pregnant with his children is a low-life bastard. I never want to lay eyes on him. If I did I wouldn't hold back so maybe it's best I don't.' His voice was loud and filled with anger.

Claudia was taken aback. She had not seen that side of Patrick. His emotions had always seemed so moderate but hearing that reminded her of her father. She knew he would have said the same if he was still alive. Suddenly she felt more protected than she had since her parents died.

'I didn't expect that response from you.'

'I don't sit on the fence, Claudia,' he responded. 'I don't tolerate cowards or fools and the man was both.'

Claudia was compelled to confess her part in the ugly situation. She was shaking inside because she was so aware that his opinion about her might change but all of a sudden she knew she wanted to tell him anyway.

'It's more complicated than that,' she began and then paused for a moment. 'The boys' father...he was married.' The words just came tumbling out. Her heart began racing as she saw his jaw tense and his eyes become more intense.

'Married! The guy is a bigger low-life than I thought. How dare he hide that from you and disrespect his wife at the same time?'

'You're assuming I didn't know he had a wife without me saying anything?'

'Claudia, I know that you would never have become involved with a married man if you'd known he had a wife. It's not who you are. It's obvious he kept it from you.'

'He did,' she said with her head bowed a little. Patrick was visibly distraught but Claudia realised with relief that he wasn't disappointed in her. His anger was towards the man who had betrayed her. But she wanted him to know the full story. She had to take the blame for her part.

'I should have asked more questions. I was naive…'

'He was probably a seasoned cheat and wouldn't have told you the truth anyway.'

'Perhaps,' she agreed.

'This town is full of predators. I've *freshened* up a few of them. Actors, producers, agents.'

'He's a producer, quite well known in the soap opera industry. I was working on his show and, as I said, I had absolutely no idea that he was married. He managed to hide it because his wife was away overseas, working on a remote set. She's an actress, much younger than him but not well known, not yet at least. She was apparently heading back to LA about the same time I discovered I was pregnant. He left the apartment we were sharing the day I announced we were to have a baby and I haven't heard from him since. Only his lawyer.'

Patrick ached inside to reach for her but he didn't. He didn't look at her; he stared straight ahead, scared that if he did look into her eyes he would sweep her into his arms and never let her go. It had only been nearly six weeks since they had met on the day the boys had been born but it seemed longer to Patrick. All along he'd suspected she had been hurt and now he knew by whom. The father of her children had been the one who'd inflicted the heartache.

He wanted her more than any woman he had ever met but he needed to wait until she was ready. If that never happened then so be it. But if she did open up and let him know she wanted him then he would make love to her with every fibre of his being and he would hold her in his arms all night long for as many nights as she would give him. He would try to heal every hurt she had every experienced. He would make her whole again, if she would let him.

'He'll pay the price for the rest of his life by not knowing his sons.'

Claudia opened her mouth to respond but couldn't think what to say. He had not questioned her or doubted her for a moment and she wondered how and why such a wonderful man had come into her life. Without thinking too much, she leant in to kiss his cheek but he turned his face at that moment and the softness of his lips met hers. It was an unexpected kiss but neither wanted it to end. She willingly pressed herself against his hard body. She wanted him as much as he wanted her. A welcome vulnerability washed over her as she realised how much she trusted the man she was kissing.

She trusted him more than she'd ever thought possible. And she was falling a little more in love with him by the day.

His hands trailed down the curve of her spine and she could feel his heart racing through the cool fabric of his shirt. Her heart synchronised with the beating of his and their kiss deepened as he explored her mouth. Without warning, he slowly and purposefully stood and reach for her hand to pull her up from the sofa. Once she was on her feet, he swept her up off the ground and into his arms, his mouth possessing hers again. Claudia's hands wrapped around his neck as he carried her into his bedroom, where he slowly removed every piece of her clothing. And then his own.

That night they both opened their lives, their hearts and their bodies to each other.

# CHAPTER TEN

THE EARLY-MORNING SUN slipped through the gaps in the drapes and filtered onto the bed where they lay entwined in each other's arms. Claudia opened her eyes to see Patrick's handsome face only inches from hers. He was still asleep and she could feel his warm breath on her skin. Gently, she eased herself from his arms and moved to the edge of the bed in search of her clothing. It was his room, not hers, and there was no clothing in reach. Her eyes roamed the room, to find her things scattered all over the floor in a trail that led to the bed.

'Looking for something?'

She turned to see him propped up on his elbow watching her.

'My underwear.'

'I don't think you'll need that today,' he said, a spark in his eye as he pulled her back into his arms.

An hour later, Claudia woke to the smell of freshly percolated coffee. They had made love again and she had drifted into a deep and wonderful sleep. Patrick appeared in the doorway in denim jeans but no shirt. His face was freshly shaven. His hair was wet and slicked back.

'Why didn't you wake me?'

'Because, my darling, you needed your sleep.' He crossed to the bed and kissed her tenderly. 'You can have a shower and, when you're ready, there's breakfast on the patio.'

'You are spoiling me terribly.'

'I hope so,' he said as he kissed her again and she melted into his arms.

'I should get ready now,' she finally said as she pulled herself away. 'I want to be at the hospital for the boys' feed and bath.'

'Not a problem. We can eat and head over there together—it's still early.'

With that he disappeared and left her alone in the still warm bed with even warmer thoughts of him.


'There's one thing I really want to know,' she said as she traced circles with the tip of her finger on his warm bare chest and looked up lovingly at the man who had captured her heart as they sat together on the patio sofa enjoying the morning sun as they shared breakfast. She had showered quickly and they planned on being at the hospital by ten. 'Why did you really change career?'

'I found something else I enjoy—something that's rewarding and important.'

'I know, and I appreciate that you're not just fixing starlets' noses and breasts. I understand the other wonderful work you do, but you're very good at delivering babies too.'

'You only have your delivery to go on so I think your opinion may be somewhat biased.'

'There's no bias; I'm serious. You stepped in and saved us all. We owe our lives to you, Patrick.'

'You were the perfect patient...'

'Perfect patient?' She laughed and she lay back on the soft oversized outside pillow, staring at the cloudless sky as her thoughts rushed back to the day she'd given birth. It was overwhelmingly frightening sometimes when she thought about that fateful day and other times she felt so blessed and fortunate, as if the stars had aligned to place them both in the elevator. That morning, as she snuggled next to Patrick, she felt as if it must have been serendipity and she was so very lucky. 'I was perfectly horrible to you.'

'Initially, perhaps, but when labour started I think you handled yourself incredibly well. You were braver than any woman I know.'

'I don't know about the brave bit, but I do know that I was flat-out rude and chose the most inconvenient place for you to deliver the boys.'

'You didn't have much say in choosing the venue.'

'That's true…' she began but her words were cut short when his warm, soft lips pressed hard against hers and he didn't let another word escape until he had tasted her sweet mouth for the longest time.

Finally he released her. Her head was spinning, her heart was racing and it took her a moment to catch the breath he had stolen. Her thoughts about everything except the man beside her were muddled. Those thoughts were crystal-clear. She was unashamedly falling in love with him. She knew they had no certain future and they had no past, having known each other for not long over a month, but they had the present. She was falling for Patrick the way she had never fallen for a man in her life and knew she never would again.

'Let's get to the hospital and see your strapping young

sons—they may have gained weight overnight and be ready to come home.'

It wouldn't be *come home*—it would be *go home*—to somewhere far away, she thought with a pang of sadness in her heart.

Claudia smiled as Patrick helped her to her feet but his words had cut like a hot blade, piercing her heart and reminding her that home for the boys and her would be London. And Patrick's home was in Los Angeles. Their brief romantic affair would be that.

Just a short, sweet affair.

As they drove to the hospital, Claudia glanced over at Patrick. His slender masculine hands that now held the steering wheel had only a few hours before been stroking her naked skin and bringing her such pleasure that she'd never wanted it to end. His profile in the morning sun was the same handsome face that had woken next to her that morning. And she hoped they would wake together every morning until she left.

But, no matter what the future held for either of them, she wanted to know more about her devilishly good-looking obstetrician. And that meant understanding the decision he had made over a decade before. She wanted to be able to answer any questions her sons might have over the years. And even if they never asked a single question, she still wanted to know all there was to know about Patrick. He was such a wonderful man, but she sensed there was something he was hiding behind the sunglasses resting on his high cheekbones, gently shaded by morning stubble. It still seemed unusual to move to the other side of the world and begin all over again. To study another medical specialty and leave behind his family and friends. To never return home when there were clearly no financial barriers was all very puzzling. And, for an inexplicable reason, she had to know what had driven him away from the country she loved.

'Patrick,' she began softly as they pulled up at traffic lights only two blocks from the Mercy Hospital. 'Can I ask you a question?'

He turned to her with a smile that melted her heart. 'It depends.'

'Depends on what?'

'Will you let me plead the Fifth Amendment if I don't like the question?'

'The Fifth Amendment? But you're not an American citizen!'

'No, I'm British—we both know that,' he replied as he changed gear and took off as the traffic lights turned green. 'But I've been here long enough to feel comfortable using their constitutional loopholes.'

Claudia watched him smile. He was obviously trying to find a way to make light of something about his past he didn't want to discuss and his expression showed her he thought he had won.

'You know what, let's talk tonight.'

'Sounds fine to me,' he said as they drove along in the traffic heading towards the hospital.

Later, as they sat together on the patio in their swimsuits after a late-night swim, Claudia broached the subject again.

'I think you know everything there is to know about me,' she began as she ran her fingers through her wet curls to push them away from her still damp face.

'Where exactly is this going?' he asked as he began

to kiss her neck where the water was trickling down from her hair. 'Because I would like to take it back to the bedroom.'

'Me too…in a minute, but first I want to take it back to the question I wanted to ask this morning.'

He stopped kissing her. 'Do we have to go there?'

'But you don't even know the question.'

'Do I really want to know? Let's leave the past where it belongs… I'm doing very nicely without it.'

Claudia sat up and turned to face Patrick. She doubted what he said was accurate. He had left everything behind. The reason had to be enormous. 'What is the deal with your family? Did you fall out?'

'I'm definitely pleading the Fifth Amendment. I told you I would this morning. Nothing's changed.'

His smile seemed forced. There was more behind it. She intended to find out exactly what. A man had once hidden a secret from her that not only changed the course of her life but that of her children. She would not and could not accept a man at face value, no matter how handsome that face.

'Patrick, I need to know a little more about you. It's important to me.' She drew a deep and slightly nervous breath. 'My cards are on the table. You know everything, good and bad, and you still want me in your bed, so please give me the same credit.'

Looking into Claudia's deep brown eyes, Patrick felt her searching his face for answers and realised that she wasn't going to let it go. Perhaps she had a right to know. She had opened up to him about her life. Perhaps it was his turn. Maybe if she understood his reasons then she would consider staying in Los Angeles and they could be together. He suddenly had to face the truth that he had more to lose by not opening up.

He could lose Claudia.

'Fine. We are…estranged. There's been no contact with anyone from my past for close to twelve years.'

'That's sad; I couldn't imagine life with Harriet.'

'Well, I suppose that's where you and I differ then,' he said flatly. 'I can live quite nicely without my family.'

Claudia suddenly felt as if the man beside her was not the same person. How could he not want to be with his family? Family meant everything to her. Losing her parents had been a crushing blow and to think he'd just walked away from his confused her.

'Have you tried to sort out your differences?'

'This is a little deeper than simple differences. I've rebuilt my life and don't want to look back or go back. My past and my family are not relevant to me.'

As he said it he knew it wasn't the truth. Every day he thought about his family. Where his mother was, what she might be doing. His nephew would be twelve now and he had not seen him grow up and it saddened him. But there had been no other option but to walk away and let them live their lives without him.

'It's relevant to me… I mean it was significant enough to make you pack up and leave,' she replied softly. 'I don't want to open old wounds but I do want to understand you better, understand why you won't return to the place you were born.'

He stood and reached for Claudia's hand and helped her to her feet 'Then let's go inside and forget about this conversation. Just accept my past is something I don't want to relive. It will do no good. My family and I have all moved on from each other. End of story.'

* * *

Claudia lay in Patrick's arms that night but they didn't make love. Nor did she sleep well. She couldn't. It worried her that there were things in his past he wouldn't share but they were significant enough to make him leave the country he had called home, leave behind his family and never make contact again and even change his profession.

It was all so confusing.

Who was the man lying beside her? Had she made a mammoth mistake in letting him have a piece of her heart?

She climbed from bed early the next morning and had a shower before he woke. She didn't want to pry any further. Clearly he had shut down her attempts and she was not going to push him for answers. But she knew she couldn't continue to see anything between them. Honesty and openness could not be a one-way street. And while he had not promised he would open up to her, in fact he had made no promises at all, she couldn't plan a future with a man who didn't have the same values as her.

What if she and the boys did stay in LA to be a family with him and he walked away from them all and never looked back if it became too difficult? Family was everything to her and she and Harriet had already lost those they loved most. How could he not value family the way she did? To not reach out in so many years, to patch up differences and make amends—it was all incomprehensible to her. Even if she had planned on staying in LA, it wouldn't work between them if he could place such little value on the importance of family and not explain why.

She gathered up her belongings, set them by the front door and sat on the patio and waited for him to wake.

'I'm guessing you can't leave this alone?' he said as he appeared in the doorway, dressed in shorts and a T-shirt. His expression was serious.

'No, I *can* leave it alone; in fact it's what I'm planning to do, but if I do then I have to leave us alone too. I rushed into this,' she said, shaking her head as she looked around the lovely home they had shared for over a month. 'I didn't really know you when I moved in. And I shouldn't have shared your bed for the past two nights. We're too different.'

'We're not different...'

'We're so different,' she argued. 'I would give anything to have my mother in my life. And you haven't spoken to yours in years for a reason you won't explain so I can't begin to understand. I think in time we will find more differences and I can't bring the boys into something that maybe won't last. What if you up and walk away one day and don't look back at the boys and me? My life back in London will last. My family is there. My sister. It's where I belong.'

'You don't think we have any future?'

'Not when you won't share a past that has fundamentally changed everything about who you were.'

Patrick sat down on the chair opposite her and took in a breath that filled his lungs. His long fingers ran through his hair as he looked at the ground. He realised he had no choice but to share his past or risk losing Claudia completely.

'It was almost twelve years ago,' he began without prompting. 'August seventh, to be precise.'

She remained silent but the fact that the date of his story came so easily to mind showed her just how traumatic the memory was for Patrick.

'It was a Thursday night and I took a call to assist with a high risk delivery in the county hospital where I worked in Durham,' he volunteered but the strain in his voice was obvious. 'I was an OBGYN resident and I loved what I did.'

She waited in silence for him to continue, which he did without any prompting.

'It was late, about ten o'clock, when a young woman was rushed into Emergency, presenting at the hospital in the early stages of premature labour.'

'You said you were called in; you weren't on duty then?'

'No, I had the night off. I was at the local pub with some friends from med school. It was a warm summer night; one of them had secured a placement at a hospital in New Zealand and we were giving him a send-off. Anyway, I got the call to head back. The senior obstetric consultant had left for London to speak at an OBGYN conference and couldn't get back until the next morning.'

'But if you were at the local pub you would've been drinking,' she cut in, her frown not masking her concern at the direction of his story.

He shook his head. 'Normally the answer would be yes, and by ten o'clock I would ordinarily have had a pint or two. But that night I'd finished my shift at the hospital with a bit of a headache coming on and, since I had an early start the next morning with a surgical schedule, I thought if I had even one glass of alcohol that I wouldn't pull up well. I stayed on ginger beer all night. I was perfectly fine to take the call—to be honest, I wish I had been drinking and had to refuse but I accepted and headed in to what would essentially be the end of my career in obstetrics.'

Claudia began nibbling on her lower lip. 'I still don't understand. You did nothing wrong; you hadn't been drinking…'

'I hadn't…but, with the tragedy that unfolded, some thought otherwise. That was the only conclusion they could find for what happened in the operating theatre. They couldn't accept that a high risk pregnancy extends to a high risk delivery. Anyway, I scrubbed in and began the Caesarean, but very cautiously as there was a complication, as I mentioned. The placenta was growing outside of the uterus wall and, despite me doing everything textbook and taking precautions along the way, the patient began to haemorrhage. I lifted the baby boy clear of the womb but as there was so much blood I couldn't see where to begin the repair. The blood loss was too great and, despite the whole team doing everything we could, we lost her on the table. There was nothing I, or anyone, could do. The theatre staff knew I had done everything right and told me as much but the jury were sitting outside in the waiting room and, to be honest, the worst juror was myself. I took the blame before I saw them—they just reinforced my feelings.'

'Why would you do that? You knew it wasn't your fault and the medical team knew it wasn't…'

'For me, overwhelming guilt that I had not been able to save her and, for them, their own grief turned to anger when they were told I had been seen having *drinks* at the local only an hour before. It cemented it in the minds of the family that I had to have been drinking and that was why their little girl died giving birth.'

'Why didn't you fight? Surely there must have been something you could have done? It's so unfair that you did the right thing in returning to the hospital and you tried to save the woman and you had the family blame you on circumstantial evidence.'

'It shattered my world. I was grieving too, and they needed someone to blame for the loss of her life. I decided it was my duty to take that blame.' Patrick paused and stared at Claudia thoughtfully and in silence for a moment. He didn't want to tell her any more. He had omitted the most important fact in the entire tragedy. The one that had changed his life completely. But he had to be honest. She deserved to know the truth.

With a heavy heart, he closed his eyes. 'The young woman who died…was my sister.'

# CHAPTER ELEVEN

'YOUR SISTER DIED having her baby?'

He nodded, unable to bring himself to say the words again.

'So it was your own family that blamed you? It's so sad that she died, but why would they do that? I don't understand—families don't do that to each other.'

'It's not their fault. It was complicated,' he said, trying to validate their behaviour. 'No one knew Francine, or Franny, as we always called her growing up, was a high risk so to them her death had to be due to negligence.'

'Surely your brother-in-law knew there were complications?'

'No, he had no idea.' Patrick shook his head. 'I assume she kept her medical condition from us because she didn't want anyone to worry. We had just endured another tragedy a few months before, so she was trying to protect everyone.'

'What sort of tragedy?

'My younger brother, Matthew, died six months before.'

Claudia covered her mouth with her hands as she gasped, 'Oh, no.'

'My father and mother had divorced a long time before; I was young when it happened. My mother raised us. One Saturday my mother went up to Matthew's room to wake him as he had friends waiting downstairs to head to Brighton for the day. She found him in bed, which was unusual since he was an early riser. She patted his legs to wake him, but my brother was unresponsive so she pulled the covers down and found he was bleeding from the nose and mouth. My mother called out for help from his friends and dialled for an ambulance, hoping the paramedics would somehow revive him. They couldn't and he was pronounced dead on arrival at the hospital.' Patrick's jaw was clenched and Claudia could see he was struggling to make eye contact.

Claudia's brow was knitted in confusion. She wondered if it might have been a drug overdose but she said nothing. Asking such a question seemed cruel and unnecessary. The details made no difference. Patrick had tragically lost his younger brother.

'The autopsy report from the coroner's office came back with suspected lung aneurism,' Patrick offered without prompting. 'In simple terms, it's a ruptured artery in the lungs, which meant he drowned in his own blood. It's extremely rare and nothing that could have been predicted. Matthew had been a medical time bomb for a very long time.'

'I'm so sorry.' Claudia couldn't find any other words. Nothing she thought to say seemed to be adequate for the tragedy she had heard. His family had been dealt an overwhelmingly sad time.

'It was the worst time in my mother's life, in all of our lives. My father attended the funeral but after that he kept his distance again. My maternal grandmother was alive, but only barely, as she was living in assisted care; the shock of the broken marriage was difficult but hearing that her grandson had died was what I believe sent her into a depression that she never really recovered from.

'Then Franny discovered she was pregnant. It brought some joy back to our mother and to our family. She was focusing on the new baby on the way and I don't think that Franny wanted to bring her down with worry. She wanted her to hold on to something. The thought of a baby arriving gave us all a light at the end of the tunnel. We knew she was having a boy, that part she shared, and in some way I think the fact another boy would join the family made losing Matthew *almost* bearable for our mother. I'm assuming Franny didn't want our mother to be anxious and, while I understand her wanting to protect her, she should have confided in me. I could have ensured the best antenatal care and would have been prepared, going into surgery.'

'So she never took her husband to any of her obstetric visits?'

'No, Will never attended any of them.'

'Still, whether they knew or not, I can't believe they would blame you.'

'They didn't understand, even when I explained that her medical condition translated into a high risk delivery.'

'But, without any medical knowledge, it still doesn't make sense to throw the blame your way; it all seems unfair and so wrong.'

'Don't forget I'd been seen in the pub; they forgot everything about her condition and focused purely on my supposed drinking.'

'But you hadn't been drinking. Couldn't you have a blood test and prove it?'

'I didn't think to have the test the night she died as,

since I hadn't been drinking, it didn't cross my mind to cover myself and the allegations came out the next day from my brother-in-law's family. One of his cousins had seen me at the pub and, despite me telling them otherwise, they didn't believe that I had been completely sober.'

'But couldn't your friends corroborate your story?'

Patrick nodded. 'They tried, but his family was convinced it was just my medico mates covering for me. The whole medical fraternity banding together to protect each other conspiracy theory.'

'And your brother-in-law believed them?'

'He was upset, he was half out of his mind and he got swept up in the witch hunt. There was even footage taken on a mobile phone of another celebration in which I featured in the background. It was all over. You have to remember I lost my sister that day. I couldn't argue in my frame of mind. I was grieving too.'

'What about the rest of your family? Your mother and father?' Claudia frowned in perplexity. It all seemed so wrong.

'My mother was barely functioning and she believed what she was told. My negligence had taken away her beloved daughter.'

'But you had tried to save your sister, with no knowledge of her medical condition…and I know it couldn't bring her daughter back, but she had a grandchild. The grandchild that you had brought into the world.'

Patrick ran his hands through his hair in frustration. 'I was hung, drawn and quartered by the town. There was no coming back from that so I left. It was best for everyone.'

'Are you sure about that?'

'The grief blanketed both families and I guess I just couldn't face the arguing. I made the decision to leave. If either family wanted to look into it further I left the name of her obstetrician, but they never called. They didn't want to look further than me for the cause. It was their choice to direct the blame at me and it was my choice to walk away.'

'It's all so terribly unfair.'

'Yes, but it's done.'

'And your brother-in-law and his son…?'

'Will named the little boy Todd after his father. Todd turned twelve this August. He's a tall boy like his father and doing well at school.'

'So you speak with your brother-in-law then?'

'No, I haven't heard a word from him since I left. A friend from university lives not far from him; their boys go to the same school. He keeps an eye out for them and keeps me up to date. I set up a trust fund to cover his college education. Will gave up work for a period to raise Todd and then found it hard to get back into the workforce so had to start again at entry level. I feel I owed him to take care of Todd.

'So now you can understand why I choose to live over here. It's simpler for everyone.'

Claudia saw everything so differently. 'While I understand your need to leave, and I think what happened to you is almost unforgivable, it's still your family. You can't turn your back on family. Your mother lost her daughter and both sons within months of each other.'

'I'm still here. I didn't die.'

'No, but you left her life. For a mother it would be the same level of grief.'

Patrick leaned back against the chair. 'No, it's not

the same. I'm here but she chose not to contact me. Nor did Will.'

'Perhaps your absence cemented their doubts about what happened. You could have gone back anytime over the last twelve years and cleared it up.'

'I'm not about to stir up all that again. I have built a new life here and reconstructive surgery has been good to me.'

'So you gave up obstetrics because you couldn't save your sister.'

'Yes,' he said solemnly and without hesitation. 'I had nightmares about her lying lifeless on the table at my hands… I lost the will and drive to practice.'

'But it wasn't because of anything you did.'

Patrick felt his body tense. 'I couldn't face that sense of helplessness again. Being unable to save Franny was something I could not relive.'

'But you did…with me. And you saved me. You didn't know I had a serious condition and you saved me from dying.'

'No, the paramedics came in time to save you.'

Her face became even more serious. 'They took over but you had kept me alive.'

Patrick knew the best thing he had done was to walk away from obstetrics and his family. And he knew that Claudia was testing that resolve. 'Fine, I kept you alive but I can't go back to that. I'm content with my work. I live here now and I'll never set foot back in the UK.'

'But your work here, now, it's not your first love.'

'No, but you can't always have everything you want, Claudia, including your first love.'

She couldn't ignore the resolve in Patrick's voice.

'Have you never thought about returning to Durham and facing your accusers and telling the truth?'

Patrick rolled his eyes and did not hide his exasperation. 'There was no evidence. Nothing to support me and everything to support their accusations.'

She shrugged. 'But you walked away from your career…and your life…because of lies.'

Patrick's body went rigid and his voice became harsh. 'I didn't walk away from anything. I left to make it easier for everyone.'

'Why can't you face the past now then? Rebuild your life in London? It was twelve years ago and I'm sure your mother would give anything to hold you in her arms again. You're her only living child.'

'No. I can't and I won't go back. My life there is over. It ended the day I left.'

Gaping at him, Claudia exclaimed, 'That's so dramatic!'

'My sister died, Claudia. They all think I caused her death. *That* is dramatic.'

Claudia frowned at him while she scrutinised his face. His expression was severe. His jaw appeared more pronounced. 'I'm just saying perhaps you could explain it properly. Have your peers explain it again. Franny's obstetrician could sit down with your mother and tell her the truth. It would have been near on impossible for your mother to pick up the telephone and speak with him. But you could facilitate that conversation. Make her see reason. Would that be so hard for you to do?'

'It's too late. They've moved on with their lives.'

'It's never too late. No mother moves on from a child.'

'I'm not so sure.'

'I am. I couldn't imagine a day without Thomas and

Luca in my life. I would travel to the end of the earth to be with them and you should do the same for your nephew. You've chosen to give up without a fight.'

'Fighting is overrated.'

'Not in my books. I need a man who will fight for family.'

Patrick stood up and crossed back to the doorway. His face was taut as he knew at that moment exactly how Claudia felt.

Claudia sat staring ahead. Her heart was aching with the reality that had just been spelt out to her. 'It's been a long time and your mother would probably be stronger now. Don't you think you owe it to her to let her know what really happened? I would want to know.'

'Claudia, let it go.'

'You mean let us go?'

He rubbed his clenched jaw. Claudia noticed his eyes suddenly looked tired, almost battle-worn as he spoke. 'The choice is yours.'

# CHAPTER TWELVE

PATRICK STIRRED FROM a tortured sleep the next morning, knowing that his every reason for waking up was gone. Claudia had left. She had grabbed her belongings and caught a cab. She'd told him where she would be staying if he changed his mind and wanted to talk but he left the slip of paper by the bed. He had no intention of calling. She was right—she deserved to be with Harriet. Family was important to her. He had learned to get along on his own for a long time. He missed his mother and his brother-in-law and wished with all of his heart some days that he could be there to watch his nephew grow up. But he couldn't. The wounds had healed on the outside and he didn't want to rip them open by travelling home.

It was better to let her rebuild her life back in the UK. She would settle in quickly and no doubt move on.

She would forget about what they'd shared in time and someone else would take his place.

But he wasn't sure he would ever move on.

Claudia had brought more joy and happiness into his life than he had dreamt possible. She was everything he could wish for in a woman and more. And he had let her walk away.

He had never felt so empty and it filled him with regret to walk away from Claudia but there was no other choice. What she expected from him was impossible. How could he face his family again? Where would he start? Would the blame still be there? The desolation in his mother's eyes—so empty, so blank, so lost and hurt by him that he could never go back. He just couldn't. It was better to leave the past behind.

When he'd discovered she had left that morning he had tried to push what they had shared from his mind but, waking on the second day, it became a reality. And he could no longer ignore the way he felt. A cloud had moved over his world and it was suddenly a much darker place, devoid of everything he had come to love.

Glancing around the room, his eyes came to rest on the bedside table, where the framed photos of Thomas and Luca were resting. It was the first time she had reached out to him and let him into her world. He now knew how difficult that had been for her but she had fought her doubts and insecurities, and waded through the hurt, to let him know that he meant something to her and the boys.

Next to the photographs was the note she had left— and her pearl earrings.

A rush of memories assailed his mind.

The day they'd met in the elevator. How beautiful he'd thought Claudia was and how he'd quickly discovered her looks were matched with her feisty spirit. She was a strong woman on the outside but inside she was filled with love. That day he had witnessed the level of that love for her sons and, weeks later, experienced first-hand her capacity for love when she'd shared his bed.

And he had let her leave.

Perhaps she was right. He had taken the easier option.

But that suited him. He had adjusted to the values in the city. At least that was what he would have to tell himself. He climbed from bed and headed for the shower. He had the day off and no idea how to spend it. Claudia was gone and he couldn't visit Thomas and Luca. He had to become accustomed to life without them and that wouldn't happen if he tried to reach out to them even one last time.

After a quick shower, he dressed in a polo shirt and jeans and, looking for something to occupy his mind, he decided to head to his practice. His hair was still wet and he was unshaven but he knew he wouldn't be seeing anyone at that hour. There had to be some paperwork to finish, reports to finalise and mail to check. Anything to stop him rethinking the decision he had made.

As he entered the garage he looked at the SUV that Claudia had been driving and made a mental note to call a dealership and trade it in. He didn't want to be reminded of what he had lost every time he saw the car that he now considered to be hers.

There was little traffic that early in the morning and he was at work in less than ten minutes. The cleaner was leaving as he pulled into the undercover car park; they acknowledged each other with a wave before the young man climbed into his van and left. Patrick took the stairwell to his first floor office. It was empty and quiet. So quiet that his own thoughts were almost deafening. He wished the cleaner had stayed so the sound of the vacuum could drown out the doubts that were pounding inside his head.

He rifled through the papers on his desk and then noticed the pile of mail that his receptionist had sorted and put aside as not urgent. He hadn't looked at it for a few weeks but he trusted Anita would have brought anything important to his attention.

He read them one by one but nothing brought even a hint of enthusiasm to him. There was an invitation to attend a benefit for the Screen Actors Guild at the Beverly Wilshire; an invitation to drive a new luxury sedan that had arrived at a dealership in Santa Monica; a bi-monthly magazine from the Cosmetic Surgeons of America and numerous professional association offers and advertisements. It was all as he'd expected.

Then he spied a gift certificate from an expensive women's store on Rodeo Drive; it was only three doors down from his practice. He picked up the beautifully presented certificate and noticed it was for a sizeable amount. He wondered if they had made a mistake sending it to him, then he froze. This was the same store where his receptionist had ordered some pyjamas and toiletries for Claudia all those weeks ago. But why would they be sending him a gift certificate? It was far too generous to be a thank you in return for his business. He turned it over and found a note on the back.

*Dear Dr Spencer*
*Miss Monticello insisted that she repay the kind-*
*ness of the 'anonymous' customer. We did not re-*
*veal your details; however, she insisted that she*
*provide a certificate of equal value to you. We hope*
*a lovely lady in your life can enjoy shopping in our*
*store in the near future.*
*Warmest regards*
*Camille and staff*

He closed his eyes and dropped his head back to look up at the ceiling. He knew he had to be the most stupid man in the world. She still had no idea that he had sent the parcel. She'd just wanted to repay a stranger. She could have just walked away but she had so much pride and honesty she had found a way to return what she didn't feel in her heart was hers. In a city of people who were only too willing to take, Claudia wanted only to give. And he knew she would have struggled to have covered the cost. She had so little money but she still did the right thing. She never let her values slip or chose the easy way out.

She'd fought so hard to bring her boys into the world. She never gave up on who or what she loved, no matter what obstacles she faced.

Claudia was an amazing, wonderful woman and he had just let her go.

She had dropped her walls, despite all the disappointment she had endured; she had let him into her life and her heart, and how had he repaid her? He had been as cruel as the father of her children. Perhaps even worse, he berated himself, because he knew what Claudia had been through. And she had allowed him to become a part of her babies' lives.

His head was upright as he stared at the door. His jaw flicked with mounting fury. At himself and the lies that had changed his life. He drew breath and filled his lungs, and suddenly felt adrenaline rush through his body.

He wouldn't let it happen again. Walking away from a life with Claudia, Thomas and Luca was not what he wanted to do. Not now, not ever. He wasn't sure he deserved them but he knew he wanted to fight to have them in his life. The thought of the boys' birth certificates having no father listed made him want even more to be the father figure in their lives. To guide them and to love them. If Claudia would let him, he would willingly take on that role. Forever.

He knew that meant reconciling with his family, no matter how difficult that might be. Perhaps time had healed some wounds, perhaps not. But Patrick wasn't about to base his future on assumptions. He would visit and see first-hand. And if they didn't want him back, then he would accept it but he wouldn't run away. He wanted a life back in London with Claudia…if she would have him.

He threw down the certificate and raced from the office. He had to prove to Claudia that he would fight for her and her boys and their future. He would do whatever it took. It was time to take a stand.

There was just one thing he had to do before he left to find her—he had a flight to book to London.

Claudia had packed her suitcase and left it by the door for the concierge to collect as she made her way to the hotel lobby to check out. Her tears had finally dried. She told herself firmly that Patrick Spencer would be the last man she would waste precious tears on. She would concentrate on raising her sons and forget about any other love. Her boys would be enough to fill her life and she knew they would never let her down. And, more importantly, she would never let them down. She would be there for them and give them everything they needed, growing up. And she hoped one day as grown men each would find their true love and she would be happy for them.

With a sigh for what might have been, she approached the reception desk.

'Good morning, Miss Monticello, are you checking out today?'

The young woman was dressed in a corporate char-coal suit, tortoiseshell glasses and a pleasant but predictable smile. Her hair was pulled back in a sleek chignon.

'Yes, I am. Can you please add a bottle of lemonade I took from the minibar to my credit card along with the room charges? I was staying in Room 303.'

The receptionist checked the computer screen and handed over the account.

Claudia passed over her credit card then tucked her hair behind her ear as she stood waiting for the card to be processed. She felt for her pearl earring, the way she always did when she was nervous. But it wasn't there. Her hand switched to the other ear. That one was missing too. She hadn't even thought about them for two days. Her head had been filled with thoughts so much more demanding of her time than her jewellery. She suddenly remembered she had left them on the bedside table. Patrick's bedside table.

'Are you looking for these?'

Claudia spun around to find a dishevelled Patrick standing behind her, her earrings in his outstretched hand.

'I would like to speak with Miss Monticello in private,' Patrick told the young woman at the desk, now looking at both of them. 'Do you have a room available?'

'The business centre has some private meeting rooms,' the receptionist told them, adjusting her glasses. 'You're more than welcome to use one of those.'

'Thank you,' Patrick replied, glancing around the lobby and spying the business centre.

'There's no need to thank her; we won't be using the room,' Claudia retorted, shaking her head in defiance.

'There's nothing I need or want to say to you, Patrick. I'm leaving today. We're over.'

'There's so much I want to say to you and I'd like to say it in private.'

With a look of discomfort Claudia felt certain was due to the potential for a situation to play out in her lobby, the receptionist interrupted. 'As I said, you're both more than welcome to use any of the meeting rooms and at this hour they're all free.'

Patrick led the way and crossed the lobby foyer with long purposeful strides and waited by the door of the business centre for Claudia's response. In silence she begrudgingly walked up to him. With each step across the large Mexican-inspired tiled floor of the lobby, the ache in her heart made her more resolute in her decision to end this meeting as soon as possible and never see Patrick again. She was angry and hurt in equal proportions that he had made her so vulnerable. She would hear him out then leave before she weakened and let her heart tell her what to do. She couldn't live her life with a man who had such different values to her own.

He softly closed the door behind them. 'I've got so much to say to you, Claudia, and it begins with an apology.'

'There's no point. I don't want an apology.'

'But you deserve one. I should never have let you walk out of my life and I apologise for that. I've been the biggest fool and you were right. I need to fight for what's important. That's you *and* my family. Claudia, I don't want to lose you and I'll do whatever it takes for us to be together, if you'll let me.'

'What do you mean *if I'll let you*?' she demanded. 'What are you telling me?'

'I want a life with you and your sons.'

'I can't stay here in LA; I told you that.'

'I know that and I wouldn't want you to stay here,' he said, taking her hands in his. 'I want to come home with you. I want to go back to London and do what you made me realise I should have done years ago. I want to set things right with my family. At least try to anyway.'

Claudia didn't pull her hands free as her expression turned from confusion to something closer to joy. 'Are you really serious about that?'

'I've never been more serious.'

'But why now? What's changed in two days?'

'I had time to think. Time to miss you and realise it's something I should have done a long time ago. Because I don't want to lose you or the boys.'

'And when are you planning on doing this?' Her voice did not betray the happiness she felt building inside. She did not dare to allow herself to believe he wanted a life with her, only to be disappointed again.

'As soon as I can sell the practice, I will move home to the UK permanently. You're right, my first love has always been obstetrics. And I can do it. I can honour my sister's life and her bravery by bringing more children into the world, not trying to forget what happened.'

'You really want to go back to what you had before?'

'It won't be exactly what I had before. So much has changed, but I will deal with everything if I have you in my life.'

'This is a huge commitment to change everything about the life you lead. It's a big adjustment.'

'And it's one I need to make.'

'Then I will see you when you arrive,' she said, hoping with all of her heart that it wasn't an empty promise.

She had become a realist and knew it might take time to sell the practice. In that time he might change his mind.

'You will see me sooner than that. I'll be travelling with you in about four hours' time,' he told her as he looked at his watch. 'You'll need help with the boys on the long haul flight…and to settle into your home.'

'You're travelling from LAX to Heathrow with me tonight?'

He pulled the airline ticket from his back trouser pocket. 'If you'll let me.'

Claudia smiled in return and immediately felt herself being pulled into Patrick's strong embrace and his lips pressed tenderly against hers. He pulled back for a moment to look lovingly into her eyes.

'I love you, Claudia Monticello, more than I ever have or ever will love anyone and more than I thought possible. You've given me the reason and strength to fight for what I want. Don't doubt, even for a moment, that you're my reason for waking up every day because that is what you've become. I don't want to live without you and if you'll marry me you will make me the happiest man in the world.'

Tears of happiness welled in her eyes as she nodded. 'Of course I'll marry you, Dr Spencer.'

'DADDY!' CRIED THOMAS and Luca in unison as they ran to greet Patrick.

Thomas was a little taller than Luca but they both had mops of thick black hair and smiles as wide as their chubby, and slightly ruddy, little faces.

'How was your first day at school?' he asked as he scooped both of the boys into his strong grip, resting one child on each hip as they wrapped their little arms around him. 'Did you enjoy it?'

'I like it home with Mummy and you better,' said Luca and he nestled his head onto Patrick's broad shoulder.

'Me too, Daddy,' Thomas agreed. 'But there's a turtle in the classroom so it'th not too bad.'

'Yeth, I like the turtle very much.' Luca lifted his head from Patrick's shoulder and chimed in. 'I think I might ask Father Christmas for one.'

'And Mummy got some of your favourite toffee from the lolly shop today too,' Thomas exclaimed. 'The special one with the yummy chocolate all over it.'

Just then, Claudia walked down the hallway of the beautiful Knightsbridge townhouse they had called home for almost five years and a smile spread over Patrick's face. She looked as stunning as she had the day they married and he loved the thoughtful things she did, like buying his favourite chocolate-covered almond toffee and kissing him every day, the same way she had done the very first time. He placed the boys both down on their feet again and ruffled their hair with his hands before they ran off to play outside.

'And how was your day, darling?' she asked as she threw her arms around Patrick's neck and kissed him.

'Not too bad, but it just became much, much better,' he told her as he kissed her tenderly and pulled her closer to him.

Claudia held her body against his, relishing the warmth of his embrace. Every morning she woke in his arms and fell a little more in love with the man who had made her believe in love again.

'Did you deliver any gorgeous babies today?'

'Two, actually,' he replied with a proud grin. 'And I'm inducing one of my IVF patients tomorrow morning. She's overdue, so she's been admitted to hospital this afternoon. The whole family is on standby and very excited.'

'Well, my day was wonderful too. Harriet and Matteo have finished renovations on their kitchen and want us over for an early dinner on Saturday. Matteo built a sandpit for the twins so the four of them can get messy together.'

'Sounds great. Matteo's quite the handyman. Perhaps he can help me to build one for the boys.'

'Oh, and Will called and he's coming over on Sunday with Todd and your mother for a roast. Todd's looking at universities for the year after next and wants your advice. His heart's set on studying medicine like his uncle. Thinks he wants to specialise in OBGYN.'

'Well, I'll do my best to talk him out of that.'

'You'll do no such thing. Where would I be today if you hadn't studied obstetrics?' she argued playfully. 'Just tell him to always have his medical bag handy when travelling in elevators and be prepared for anything if there's a pregnant woman in there with him.'

'Even falling in love.'

'Yes, even falling in love,' Claudia replied as she looked lovingly at her husband.

He pulled her close to him and kissed her again. 'Did I ever tell you that I am the luckiest man in the world and that I couldn't possibly love you any more than I do now?'

'You haven't told me today, Dr Spencer,' she said, running her fingers lightly down his chest. 'But you have mentioned it once or twice over the years.'

'Once or twice?' He laughed as his hands slipped down her spine and rested on the curve of her bottom. 'Well, just so you know how much, I will show you, Mrs Spencer. Once the sun has set and our boys are in bed, of course.'

She kissed him again and, hand in hand, they walked down the hall, both hoping the sun would set early that night.

And every night for the rest of their lives.

\* \* \* \* \*

*If you missed the first story in*
THE MONTICELLO BABY MIRACLES *duet*
*check out*
*ONE NIGHT, TWIN CONSEQUENCES*
*by Annie O'Neil*

*And if you enjoyed this story, check out*
*these other great reads from*
*Susanne Hampton*

*A MUMMY TO MAKE CHRISTMAS*
*A BABY TO BIND THEM*
*FALLING FOR DR DECEMBER*
*BACK IN HER HUSBAND'S ARMS*

*All available now!*

# MILLS & BOON®

## MEDICAL ROMANCE™

**THE ULTIMATE IN ROMANTIC MEDICAL DRAMA**

---

## A sneak peek at next month's titles...

### In stores from 16th June 2016:

- **Taming Hollywood's Ultimate Playboy** – Amalie Berlin
  *and* **Winning Back His Doctor Bride** – Tina Beckett

- **White Wedding for a Southern Belle** – Susan Carlisle
  *and* **Wedding Date with the Army Doc** – Lynne Marshall

- **Capturing the Single Dad's Heart** – Kate Hardy
- **Doctor, Mummy...Wife?** – Dianne Drake

---

Available at WHSmith, Tesco, Asda, Eason, Amazon and Apple

*Just can't wait?*
Buy our books online a month before they hit the shops!
**visit www.millsandboon.co.uk**

**These books are also available in eBook format!**

0616/03

# *Lynne Graham has sold 35 million books!*

## To settle a debt, she'll have to become his mistress...

Nikolai Drakos is determined to have his revenge against the man who destroyed his sister. So stealing his enemy's intended fiancé seems like the perfect solution! Until Nikolai discovers that woman is Ella Davies...

*Read on for a tantalising excerpt from Lynne Graham's 100th book,*

### BOUGHT FOR THE GREEK'S REVENGE

'Mistress,' Nikolai slotted in cool as ice.

Shock had welded Ella's tongue to the roof of her mouth because he was sexually propositioning her and nothing could have prepared her for that. She wasn't drop-dead gorgeous... *he* was! Male heads didn't swivel when Ella walked down the street because she had neither the length of leg nor the curves usually deemed necessary to attract such attention. Why on earth could he be making *her* such an offer?

'But we don't even know each other,' she framed dazedly. 'You're a stranger...'

'If you live with me I won't be a stranger for long,' Nikolai pointed out with monumental calm. And the very sound of that inhuman calm and cool forced her to flip round and settle distraught eyes on his lean darkly handsome face.

'You can't be serious about this!'

'I assure you that I am deadly serious. Move in and I'll forget your family's debts.'

'But it's a *crazy* idea!' she gasped.

'It's not crazy to me,' Nikolai asserted. 'When I want anything, I go after it hard and fast.'

Her lashes dipped. Did he want her like that? Enough to track her down, buy up her father's debts, and try and buy rights to her and her body along with those debts? The very idea of that made her dizzy and plunged her brain into even greater turmoil. 'It's immoral… it's blackmail.'

'It's definitely *not* blackmail. I'm giving you the benefit of a choice you didn't have before I came through that door,' Nikolai Drakos fielded with a glittering cool. 'That choice is yours to make.'

'Like hell it is!' Ella fired back. 'It's a complete cheat of a supposed offer!'

Nikolai sent her a gleaming sideways glance. 'No the real cheat was you kissing me the way you did last year and then saying no and acting as if I had grossly insulted you,' he murmured with lethal quietness.

'You *did* insult me!' Ella flung back, her cheeks hot as fire while she wondered if her refusal that night had started off his whole chain reaction. What else could possibly be driving him?

Nikolai straightened lazily as he opened the door. 'If you take offence that easily, maybe it's just as well that the answer is no.'

Visit **www.millsandboon.co.uk/lynnegraham**
to order yours!

# MILLS & BOON®

# MILLS & BOON®

## The One Summer Collection!

Join these heroines on a relaxing
holiday escape, where a summer fling
could turn in to so much more!

Order yours at **www.millsandboon.co.uk/onesummer**

# MILLS & BOON®

Mills & Boon have been at the heart of romance since 1908... and while the fashions may have changed, one thing remains the same: from pulse-pounding passion to the gentlest caress, we're always known how to bring romance alive.

Now, we're delighted to present you with these irresistible illustrations, inspired by the vintage glamour of our covers. So indulge your wildest dreams and unleash your imagination as we present the most iconic Mills & Boon moments of the last century.

Visit **www.millsandboon.co.uk/ArtofRomance** to order yours!